SACRED MOUNDS

Sacred Mounds

A novel

by

JIM METZNER

Adelaide Books
New York / Lisbon
2020

SACRED MOUNDS
A novel
By Jim Metzner

Copyright © by Jim Metzner
Cover design © 2020 Adelaide Books
Cover Art and Design: Tilman Reitzle

Images & sources: Serpent Mound (Sylvan Thorncraft); monarch
butterfly silhouettes (ksana-gribakina/iStock); head (Jolygon/iStock);
1888 Railroad Map of Mississippi (Library of Congress)

Published by Adelaide Books, New York / Lisbon
adelaidebooks.org

Editor-in-Chief
Stevan V. Nikolic

For any information, please address Adelaide Books
at info@adelaidebooks.org

or write to:
Adelaide Books
244 Fifth Ave. Suite D27
New York, NY, 10001

ISBN: 978-1-951896-99-7

Printed in the United States of America

Sacred Mounds is available as an audio book, published by Skyboat
Media and Blackstone Press, available on Audible Books and
Amazon.com.

For Eileen

Advance Praise
for Sacred Mounds

"Jim Metzner's *Sacred Mounds* draws you right into the action with high energy prose, strands of mystery floating in the wind, and lively characters. A great read, with Metzner's usual deep insights into the amazing workings of the natural world seeping into you while you are caught up in the flow. Enjoy!" *Robert Thurman, President, Tibet House, US, Je Tsongkhapa Professor Emeritus of Indo-Tibetan Buddhist Studies at Columbia University*

"Metzner's time-bending style is interwoven in a well-researched novel about the great Natchez Nation and the mysterious mounds across the midlands of America. This is a witty and inventive historical fantasy that seduces with twists and turns accompanied by lively street-wise contemporary dialogue. It will keep you magnetically amused right up to the surprise ending." *Jaune Quick-to-See Smith, Member, Confederated Salish and Kootenai Nation, MT*

"Sometimes it takes a whirlwind to pull us into the center of ourselves. Jim Metzner has created two such tornados in different timeframes and two protagonists who must lose their identities in order to find them. A Natchez Indian from the distant past and a modern New Yorker are compelled to switch more than their bodies, in this novel that is a striking metaphor for humanity's ongoing schism with itself…This immensely entertaining book will take you to new heights of inner madness and well as delight. Sacred Mounds explores the human psyche in ways reminiscent of Huxley and sparkles with satire that brings Vonnegut to mind. I highly recommend taking the ride." *Joyce Yarrow, author, "Ask the Dead"*

Foreword

The Natchez have significantly impacted what America is today. We have been, both in pre-history and the times of written documents, great keepers of tradition and native medicine. This continues today. Natchez medicine people were and are known for their abilities in healing, for their songs, for their dignity and love of this earth.

Jim Metzner can really spin a yarn. This story is filled with historical reality as well as spectacular descriptions of what could be. Some of his imagination is not-too-far from actuality. Once one is certain of the characters' personalities, one can step into our ancient world and follow Lewis through the great forest onto our Emerald Mound. There is literally no doubt that you will enjoy the action and adventure within these pages. It deserves your attention and perhaps that of producers of motion pictures.

Yes, we have people here in Oklahoma just like Metzner describes. In fact, he met some of our youth at an event held at the Grand Village of the Natchez Indians in Mississippi. Our kids appear to be characters in this novel! Like their characters, they are respectful of their elders and just feisty enough to be challenging to those elders, "scrappy!" and emerging to be leaders.

There are many challenges that our Natchez people still face. Lots of us continue to be busy confronting poverty. Retention of our language and quality employment in our communities are of high priority. The basis of this novel is in reality. Things do happen and we must join together to resolve issues or prevent disaster. The key is to unite like Jim Metzner's Society of Light and do our best to work toward positive results.

Jump into this book. Feel the challenges of the characters. Join with the Shining Ones. The adventure is yours!

K.T. "Hutke" Fields

Tsokup Kvhvp

Principal Chief – Uvcenv Cunv Uvsel

Natchez Nation, Oklahoma

Chapter One

2012

He didn't believe in demons and other realms. Or homeopathy. Even so, there was a vision that refused to go away, a cat that kept sneaking back into his dream house. No words for it, only ghosts of feelings. Invariably, someone would attempt to poke around under the hood.

"Give me something, a smell, a color, a sound.."

"There was a sound coming from behind."

"What did you see?"

"Nothing, it was behind me! Look, I really don't want to talk about this any more."

"You're the one with the hole in your memory."

He'd never seen a psychiatrist. Shrinks were for broken people, and most of his life things hadn't needed fixing. True, there was stuff that modern medicine couldn't quite get a handle on. Like Lyme Disease. The homeopath had helped cure him of that scourge of suburban life. Hard to imagine taking an infinitesimal amount of Sulfur could accomplish anything at all. Miraculously, it had worked, but now that he was in the maintenance mode, taking those tiny white pellets wasn't enough. His homeopathic practitioner insisted on getting into his head, awakening the ghosts. Time for the cat to get kicked off the premises.

"Maybe next time."

He paid for the visit, gave the ritual farewell hug and walked out the front door of the homeopath's house, a caramel Swiss chalet, oversized and out of place in the foothills of the Catskills, farmland rubbing shoulders with suburbia. It didn't quite belong.

He could relate to that, not quite belonging. Born in New York City, raised in the suburbs, he'd lived in Boston, Vermont, Colorado, San Francisco, London. They were all just places, disconnected dots on a map and none felt like home. Where the heart is. He wondered where his heart was.

A crisp autumn day; the leaves beginning to turn, reds and yellows showing, some green stubbornly hanging on to Indian summer. Reminded him of the fall scene in *The Exorcist*. Spooks, Halloween, the borderlands between sense and scary stuff. Everybody liked to be scared, so long as when the thrill ride ended you could walk away.

Going on twilight, the time when all things seem possible, including the prospect of getting home. He drove north, following the Shawanagunk Ridge past Mohonk and the one-way tunnel whose safe passage was an act of faith. The Rondout Valley, shrouded in mist, lay before him; beyond it the Hudson River and Kingston.

He figured homeopathy for an act of faith. The likelihood of an atom-sized particle being able to cure you was surely the territory of disbelief. He had hoped the white poppyseed-sized pills would keep the memory of his own spooks buried. His thrill ride had been real enough to get under the skin, infecting his neurons deeper than Lyme Disease spirochetes. In fact, as big a pain in the ass as it was to get LD, it had served as a sadistic distraction from whatever kind of horror show he had gone through and mercifully forgotten. About a year ago, he'd fallen asleep at a campsite in Mississippi and awakened three months later miles away, with no idea how he or the tattoo on his right palm got there. Spectral images invaded his dreams. Memories or hallucinations were slowly beginning to burble inside his waking life like a fumarole. In college, an LSD trip had thrown him into an other-worldly hole so deep and terrifying, he would never speak about it, let alone remember. He'd just as soon it all stayed buried, but like the first glimmerings of nausea, the inevitable loomed. Sooner or later he was heading towards a mighty psychotic hurl.

He turned on the radio, left side of the dial, the territory of public stations and the wolf pack of religious broadcasters trolling for any heathen they might convert. There was the familiar nasal intonation of Adrian Frye, the omnipresent voice of public station WBND, preparing listeners for the upcoming fund drive, like lambs for slaughter. The theme was Teamwork. They were launching the drive with an intrepid group of volunteers person-ing the oars of a flotilla of boats on the Hudson river. The idea was that listeners would contribute to different teams of rowers as they passed milestones on the river, the way you'd sponsor a marathon runner. Frye warned, "We need a thousand dollars by the time the first team reaches Saugerties lighthouse!" Or what, they'd torpedo the boat? He didn't catch all the details, but it sounded like a Bad Idea. They were always looking for some angle with these drives, but the basic principle was to hijack regular programming. You want it back? Pledge.

He wondered if aliens were monitoring our radio broadcasts, would they contribute to a fund drive? When the message arrived in Alpha Centauri a thousand years from now would radio even exist? Would his life be a memory, a footnote in some forgotten microchip?

Fast approaching the Golden Mean of his probable existence, he was part of the massive post-war generation that had shown so much promise and attracted so much flack. A respectable bump on the population graph, they seemed destined to be marginalised every quarter-inch of their parabolic curve, starting with the name *Baby Boomers*. Doomed to carry that infantile baggage all their life. In the Fifties, an Eisenhowerish vision of prosperity lingered inside them silently doing its work, like the polio vaccine. In the Sixties, a glowing moment of collective conscience, they were hippies, consciousness pioneers, lifestyle experimenters, not to mention freeloaders, gadflies and socialists. In the Seventies and Eighties, they'd segued into Yuppies, becoming everything they'd been programmed to be in the Fifties. Doctors, lawyers, actuaries. Having been through their vision quest and tasted the fruits of their labors, they'd seen themselves ridiculed as self-centered airheads bent on sanitizing neighborhoods at the expense of anything gritty and authentic. Hippies became puerile caricatures lost in the nostalgia of bell-bottom long-haired Halloween costumes. As if affirming this notion, he drove past the Eggs Nest Café, whose clientele included farmers and therapists amidst a décor of flotsam and ephemera, an ever-evolving psychedelicatessen collage. Seated by the windows, he noticed plenty of representatives of post Yuppiedom within, all on the cusp of seniorhood in a state of disbelief, hungry for a more authentic moniker, one that would characterise their vision of artful ageing, mellowing like ripe cheese, approaching grandparenthood with a cautious grace. *Seniors*, conjuring up a loose aggregation of geezers and dweebs, didn't cut it. They needed an emblem, a badge to wear proudly, like a favorite sweater. A non-threatening cuddly word which basically said, we mean no harm and jeez, there sure are a lot of us.

Hippies, yippies, dippies, puppies, guppies…

Guppies.

Why not? He savored its nose of innocence like a fine wine, picturing his Eureka Moment going viral from the synapses of his imagination to the blog-du-jour, to the cover of Time Magazine, to late night television. "It came to me while I was driving past the Eggs Nest." A legend is born; *Guppy Pride* T-shirts and ball caps, bumper stickers. Win One for the Gupper. Back off, I'm a Guppy!

As he basked in the glow of appreciative applause from the studio audience, the car radio caught his attention, something about the volunteer boats. He turned up the volume.

".. puts them somewhere south of Saugerties. The Coast Guard has been notified. If any listeners have a boat and can lend a hand.."

A hurried, muffled exchange, then the voice of the station manager.

"Hi, this is Adrian. You know our theme for this drive is *Pull Together*. Here's your chance. Don't let the station go adrift. Please support us and our brave volunteers. Here's the number to call."

As he listened with astonishment to what was likely a new low in the history of public radio fundraising, he realised he was close to the Hudson, if there really was a crisis. Throwing caution to the wind - a crummy swimmer, eminently unqualified, he increased the pressure on the accelerator. Guppy Power to the rescue.

He drove north on 9W, through Esopus, past the Headless Horseman Hayrides, gearing up for Halloween and the hordes of people who yearned to be scared. When the road morphed to route 32, he rubbernecked the river looking for any signs of activity, the view blocked by former monasteries, defrocked and devolved into conference centers. A revolving blue light manifested in his rear view mirror like the hand of the Almighty.

He pulled to the side of the road. A State Trooper stepped out of a patrol car, wearing the requisite reflector sunglasses. Close-cropped hair, tall, his grey uniform immaculate.

"Where's the fire?" the trooper asked.

"Boat emergency on the Hudson."

"License and registration."

He reached for the same in his wallet and said, "Officer, you're going to do the whole check-the-license-over-the-radio thing and it's going to take twenty minutes. But there *really is* an emergency on the water. I'm a responder."

Gazing at the license, the trooper read, "Salvador Samuels?"

"That's me."

"A-huh. Mister Samuels. Do you realise you were doing," glancing at his radar tape, "57 miles an hour in a 40 mile zone?"

"I'm a really safe driver. I was just thinking about the people on the river. It's on the radio."

"If you're a responder, where's your emergency light?"

"You got my license, my reg. Maybe you can call it in later? I'll bet they could use your help, too. On the river. Every minute counts. People could be drowning."

The trooper looked at the tape, the license, the attempting-to-appear-earnest face of Salvador Samuels, then back to the picture on the license. "This better be on the level," he said.

"It is."

"Alright. You got a police escort. In an emergency I can bend the rules. And if you're messing with me.."

"You can kick my ass all the way to Albany."

"Where are you headed?"

"Saugerties lighthouse."

The trooper pulled ahead, lights flashing, bending the rules speeding north.

Salvador. The only Jew on the planet answering to this name. His father had been a major Dali fan. Small comfort to a kid saddled with Salvador. After the age of eighteen, he'd made sure that everyone called him Lewis, a name he liked for no good reason.

Nine months ago he had found himself in a hospital room in Mississippi, awaking from a coma that had surgically removed a whole chunk of memory. Not his name, though. And that eye tattooed on his right palm. The episode might come in handy if the whole river thing turned out to be a scam.

I suffer these lapses.

How seriously lame would that sound? If Dan White could beat the rap with the Twinkie Defence, could Lewis Salvador Samuels claim being under the influence of a public radio fund drive?

He glanced at himself in the rear view mirror. The schnoz of his people, a goatee. His foliage was changing color, the polar region beginning to thin. The face somewhere between the current incarnations of Bob Dylan, Richard Dreyfus and the Dos Equis guy. On the street he felt invisible, especially to younger women. His own looks were homogenising, becoming part of the collective greyness of Guppydom. In the mirror, a Laurel and Hardy look at another fine mess he'd gotten into.

Lewis followed the whirling blue light watching cars pull over to let them pass. With a shock, he recalled you can't drive to the Saugerties lighthouse. There's a trail there, but it would make more sense to head to the marina and see if the coast guard had responded. He flashed his lights at the turnoff. The trooper, talking on his two-way, missed the entrance, but executed a nice 180 and followed in a swirl of gravel. In the parking lot, he emerged from his patrol car, walking quickly towards the office, Lewis barely keeping up.

"Sounds like the Coast Guard is up river at some kind of celebration," the trooper said. "Where's your emergency?"

"Somewhere between here and Kingston. That's all I know. Nothing on the police scanner?"

"Couple of 911 calls."

Lewis had a better look at the trooper now. Wiry. Name on his tag read Gleason. They strode up to the marina's office, a corner of a large garage. Inside, a cabin cruiser was being worked on with its engine lying on the floor, various parts scattered around. Coiled air hoses and electrical lines hung from the ceiling. At the office counter, a man in a brown jumpsuit was overhauling a pump. On the wall behind him, a vintage Rigid Tool Company calendar, and a bumper sticker on which someone with a Magic Marker had crossed out whatever it was that Mariners Do It With and added *Fish*. The man in the jumpsuit was stocky, Mediterranean, fortyish, with a Freda Kahlo eyebrow.

"Hey," he said.

"Anybody in the marina?" asked the trooper.

"What's going on?" The jumpsuit guy put down the pump.

"Got reports of a distress call down river. You heard anything?"

"Radio's not working good."

"I need a boat, preferably with a captain," Trooper Gleason said.

The manager scratched his eyebrow. "Guy and his wife are getting ready to head out. Futzing around for hours. 'Second Chance', pier .. three."

Gleason, in mission control mode, sprinted ahead and Lewis followed, reminding himself of the level of his swimming prowess, regretting ever having turned on the goddam radio. No way to wriggle out of this now. A hurried conversation between the trooper and the owner of Second Chance. A bald guy in his fifties. Abe Timmerman reminded Lewis of a goateed Mister Clean. His wife, a blond beauty, stayed behind. Lewis, casting a longing look at the dock, clambered aboard after Gleason. Timmerman cranked the engine, backed the boat out of its mooring and slowly headed out the channel towards the Hudson. The wind picked up a bit. Lewis entered the cabin.

"Have a pretzel," Timmerman said, handing him a cellophane bag. "It's flat here in the channel. Things are getting rough on the river. Where are we headed, by the way?"

"South," Lewis said. "Got any life jackets?"

Timmerman was an ex-Israeli soldier, special forces. Lewis had been a publicist doing outreach for the DEC and local environmental groups, at least until the accident where he'd lost his memory.

"How do you mean?" Timmerman asked.

"Last I remember, I was camping out somewhere in Mississippi. The next three months were just gone like the 18 minutes on Nixon's tape."

"Weird," Timmerman said and Lewis agreed. The weirdest part was he didn't want to remember. He borrowed a windbreaker from the cabin and walked over to whatever the hell they called the back of the boat and stood next to the trooper, who gazed fixedly downstream. Hard to imagine Gleason as anything else but a trooper, as if he had first appeared in the world fully armed like Athena, sprung from Zeus's head.

We live our own mythology, Lewis thought, gripping the side rail of the boat as it turned south towards Kingston, against a rising wind. The channel had been calm, but the waves on the river were close to a foot high, whacking the boat with surprising force, the bow rising and surging into each wave as they revved up to speed. Lewis zipped the windbreaker. Not much boat traffic heading north as they passed Tivoli. Still holding on to the rail, he edged his way back to the cabin gamely trying to maintain his balance on the moving deck.

As he stepped into the cabin, Timmerman asked, "what are we looking for, exactly?"

"Not sure," Lewis said, "rowboats maybe. They got into some kind of trouble."

Timmerman nodded. "Beats sitting around the marina waiting for my in-laws." He reached for the radio microphone. "This is Second Chance heading south from Tivoli. Looking for some boats adrift north of Kingston. Anybody seeing a rowboat in trouble?"

No sooner had he broadcast this message when Gleason, striding towards the cabin, shouted to them, "Field glasses?"

"Maybe," Timmerman said and he asked Lewis to check the bulkhead in front of the cabin, which lay under the foredeck of boat. Lewis ducked inside, rummaged through a duffel, found the glasses and went sprawling as the boat was bucked by a wave.

"Careful!" Timmerman shouted. Lewis crawled through the hatch and handed the glasses to Gleason, who edged his way around the cabin to the prow of the boat. It was starting to drizzle; the wind whipping drops of water into their faces.

Gleason wiped the eyepieces of the binoculars with a trooper issue handkerchief. Leaning against the rain, he trained the glasses downriver, searching for the dot he'd eyeballed a moment ago, not an easy task on a rocking boat.

"Got 'em," he said.

Two craft, one of which looked like a Chinese junk. It was hard to tell with the constant pitching of *Second Chance*. Timmerman steered in that direction. As they approached, what had appeared to be a junk turned out to be a raft with a banner strung between two upright poles. Rudderless, it was heeling in the wind, hammered by the waves. A number of people onboard, some standing, waving their arms. About a hundred yards upstream was a large rowboat filled with passengers. It too was floundering, turning in erratic circles, getting broadsided by waves.

"Head for the raft!" the trooper shouted. "How many life jackets you got?" he asked Abe.

"Six, maybe seven, a few of those for kids."

The banner above the raft read, *Pull Together for WBND*, but the rope which had been towing the raft had snapped and the banner, billowing between the posts, was acting like a sail. Buffeted by the strong gusts of wind, the raft was leaning and threatening to keel over. Three women and two men were aboard. They wore no life vests. Two of the women were attempting to pull down the banner. On the downstream side of the raft, a man wearing a bright orange rain jacket was yelling at them. The other man was paddling the water, attempting to steer. The third woman was waving her arms frantically at *Second Chance*.

The trooper asked, "Can you get us upwind of them?" Timmerman nodded and *Second Chance* pulled away to make a turn. To Lewis, the next few seconds were frozen in slow-motion animation. His heart pounded with the dread of really cold water *way* over his head with a biting wind, high waves and a pelting rain. How strange they were the only boat on the scene. How unjust to see himself cast into this role in his movie, a coward to boot.

As *Second Chance* made its turn, the paddler moved to the upstream side of the raft next to the waving woman. At the same moment, the guy in the orange jacket dove into the water towards *Second Chance.* The impulse of his dive impelled the edge of the raft to dip and then spring up, just as a gust of wind and a wave hit the raft, tipping it over, tossing everyone aboard into the river. The bottom of the raft was now upright, like a wooden sail. A woman frantically grabbed on to the former paddler to stay afloat, pushing him under. The other two women were both holding on to the support posts and the banner as it lay in the water. The man who dived was doing a slow Australian crawl towards the boat.

Gleason shouted orders, "Abe, throw a lifeline to the asshole who jumped. I got the other guy. Samuels, take an extra life jacket and go for the crazy woman. Get your shoes off. You can swim, right?"

Four heartbeats.

"Sort of."

Gleason shouted, "Yes or no?!"

Lewis said, "Yes, I can."

"Go for it."

Gleason having already divested himself of his shoes, weapons, Kevlar vest and miscellaneous trooper gear, dove into the water. Lewis kicked off his shoes, grabbed a life vest and jumped into the Hudson, descending lower than he would have liked. Must have been the weight of the clothes. Like a wetsuit. The water was icy, but he felt the cold mostly on his hands and face.

It was hard to swim dragging the extra vest. The raft seemed further away in the water. Not seeing anyone in the water, Lewis headed for the raft, each stroke taking him further from the safety of the boat. He'd forgotten to remove his wallet from his back pocket and instinctively felt to see if it was still there.

No cries for help, just his breathing, the wind, rain and waves, and something else tugging at the frontier of his memory like a peripheral vision. Closer to the raft, he saw one of the women who'd been holding on to the banner, rise from the water, pull her hair away from her eyes and start to swim towards Lewis in long, smooth strokes. When she reached him, he sputtered "Take this," handing her the life vest. She shook her head. "Go for Martha! She's not a swimmer."

Not wanting to argue the point, Lewis kept the vest and began to swim around the raft, passing alongside its bottom, two rows of barrels now perpendicular to the surface of the water. He reached for one of them as he swam by, a momentary safe harbor. A wave tipped the raft enough for the WBND banner to catch the wind and peel out of the water. Lewis, trying to get a better grip on the life vest, looked up in time to see the rows of orange barrels slamming down on top of him, like the lid of a giant waffle iron.

Chapter Two

One Year Earlier

Built by the Civilian Conservation Corps during the depression, the Natchez Trace runs from Nashville to Natchez, following an ancient path walked by Native Americans and the likes of Daniel Boone. A true Blue Highway, it was a rite of passage for anyone perfectly content to stay in the perpetual slow lane for a long stretch, where not much happened of any consequence. No billboards, no Denny's, First Baptist Churches, Corn Palaces, Mystery Houses, bingo games or giant balls of string. No trace of distraction, just a plethora of pines trees and a maximum speed of 50 miles an hour. You could be reasonably certain no truck was going to attempt to have a meaningful relationship with your tailpipe, but you had to come to terms with the concept that the journey was the thing.

Lewis, recently divorced and needing to mend, was heading south in the springtime, thumbing his nose at the patterns of migrating birds and his forebears. He was, if not happy to be here, at least satisfied with the knowledge that he wouldn't have to deal with attorneys, accountants, cell phone calls, anyone who wanted something from him. He wasn't sure what he wanted from himself. Maybe a little time to recharge. The South knew how to relax, and below the Mason Dixon politeness was a way of life bordering on spiritual practice. That was his fantasy at any rate and it had fueled this journey. He could always head back to New York when he felt the need to be insulted. This was Mississippi, where people sipped mint juleps on porches and smelled the roses.

One of the rare signs on the Trace indicated a mound site was nearby, igniting a memory of a postcard bought in an antique shop, which showed a colorised aerial photograph of the Serpent Mound in Ohio. From on high, it resembled a huge, curving snake with a coiled tail. The serpent either had a large oval head or else its open jaws were about to consume an oversized egg; you could imagine it either way. Lewis had treated the card as an oddity, akin to pictures of fur-bearing trout and antlered rabbits. Except the mound was real, begging the question of whether the first settlers know it was a serpent without the benefit of a polar view. Like the blind men with the elephant. Why had the Indians, or whoever had made it, constructed something that could only be fully appreciated by birds in flight?

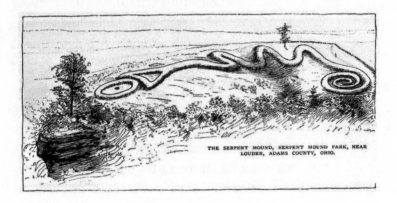

THE SERPENT MOUND, SERPENT MOUND PARK, NEAR LOUDEN, ADAMS COUNTY, OHIO.

He had kept the card as a bookmark reserved for such tomes as "In Search of the Miraculous" and "A Separate Reality", relegating mounds to phenomena which are tangible yet inexplicable, like the sphinx, the game of cricket and women.

The mounds would have stayed in his inner bin of ephemera had he not decided on impulse to check them out, a cleansing of the visual palate after miles of pine trees. He pulled off the Trace at an "Ancient Mound 7 Miles" sign. The road turned from macadam to dirt and after what seemed like 15 miles, Lewis saw it in the distance, a gentle hill breast.

As he anthropomorphised the earth, Lewis wondered whether the planet earthopomorphised him. Hadn't mankind been fashioned from clay, begetting countless sons and daughters who'd forgotten we were all related? The ones who sent Mother Nature birthday cards every Earth Day, the ones who periodically rallied to save the planet we'd screwed up so royally. Lewis doubted the planet really needed saving. The species which had turned Eden into a convenience store had doomed itself. We'd met the enemy and it was us.

A rusted metal sign confessed that archeologists didn't know who had constructed the mound or why. It might be a burial site.

Lewis regarded the knoll with a critical eye. It was about the size of a couple of school busses, end to end. No evidence of it being manmade, just a low hummock with a nearly flat top covered with brush and trees. A lump, a lymph node, an earthen birthmark. An insect without a head or legs. The Beetle Mound. No obvious pathways. Climbing it slowly, looking for fossils, arrowheads, shards of pottery, he picked up a blue Blackjack gum wrapper, an artifact of sorts.

Perhaps this was a burial mound, a communal cemetery with no headstones. Lewis's grandfather had famously mailed the Greenpoint Lodge a burial plot fee every month of his long tenure as a senior citizen, singlehandedly paying for the plots of half the Jews from Odessa. At the age of 94, he died on a weekend, when the Lodge was closed. The cultural imperative to get him underground as quickly as possible forced the family to purchase another gravesite. Maybe a mass interment in a mound wasn't such a bad idea.

He surveyed the surroundings from the summit, roughly 20 feet from the ground. The parking lot was empty except for his car, a hand-me-down orange Chevy Nova, which so far lived up to its name, *no va*, in spanish. The transmission had imploded and the engine was acting like it was next in line. He descended to it, removed his tent and sleeping bag, calculating how far a credit card and cash on hand might carry him, the goal being California and this being Mississippi. Figured he'd save a little money and camp on the mound for the night, as good a place as any to set up a tent. He hated most campgrounds. Inevitably some moron with a boom box would show up, inflicting his playlist on the world at large. No facilities here, but there was bound to be a diner nearby where he could wash up in the morning.

Time enough to pitch a tent before nightfall. He locked the car and carried his gear, working his way up the mound through the scrub and fallen branches, stopping once to turn over a large limb in the latter stages of decay, looking for salamanders. Way past their season, but he performed the act out of habit, an offering to the memory of his father. The old man had never thrown a football, baseball, basketball or anything else at him, except for a plate of pot roast that had been aimed at his brother. Sports wasn't his father's thing. A card-carrying biologist, he went on nature walks. Lewis had tagged or was dragged along on these forays into the world of science, where finding critters under logs was an unspoken ritual. Something magical about rolling over a log and discovering a spotted salamander. No such luck today. Just a reminder of the old man at his best. If only he could forget the rest.

Lewis reached the top and found a relatively clear patch of ground. His tent had a curved, elliptical shape, supported by aluminum poles, gently bent like ribs. It seemed somewhat in tune with the geometry of the mound, a green cocoon waiting for his larval form to enter. So he did, removing his shoes and bringing in a sleeping bag. He zipped up the screen to keep out any bugs, leaving a fly flap open for fresh air. His jacket became a pillow and he lay on the tent floor, listening. A few crickets and a distant bird call.

Lewis closed his eyes, trying to forget what a crummy sleeper he was. He'd read books on insomnia, listened to tapes, even gone to a clinic. They all more or less preached the same practice to no avail. The prospect of another sleepless night was a self-fulfilling prophecy. Bottom line - he was afraid to let go. Whenever that sinking feeling appeared, he invariably struggled against it, refusing to go under; coming up for air, for wakefulness, for life.

Tonight, sleep came in through a side door. Memories of his father yelling at him for leaving a handprint on the living room wall, a handprint with an eye that sparkled in its center and beckoned him outdoors. He ran out of the house, late for school, unable to find his locker, wandering lost through corridors, down an escalator into a bus station, crowds of people going purposefully somewhere. He couldn't catch a bus. No ticket, no shoes. The urban landscape dissolving into what it once had been, a wilder place. An odor of something dank and moldy. Odd to actually smell anything in a dream.

Time to bail, except he could not ascend. A rumble of panic, scrabbling for air. The only way out seemed to be to go deeper into the dream, where everything had grown darker.

Scared now, Lewis walked faster, barefoot on an earthen pathway. He could see nothing, but sensed he had entered a cavernous space, cool and damp. Holding the panic down, breathing heavily, he slowed his pace as the path sloped upward. A sliding, scraping sound close behind him, a shallow breathing, perhaps a hiss. He ran, feeling the path in the dark by some kind of dream instinct. It curved to the right, becoming steeper, until he collided into a post with cross-pieces. A ladder. Lewis grabbed a rung and began to climb, splintering his finger, missing a foothold and nearly falling off. He reached the last rung, pulling himself through a narrow opening of what seemed to be an earthen roof, scrambling out dirty, shaking with fear. Whatever had been behind him had apparently not climbed in pursuit. He felt the warmth of the sun on him, but it was dark. Dark as night.

Chapter Three

Another Time

Glowing tendrils, the sort of colors you'd see when you stared at the sun and then shut your eyes. Except his eyes were open. Dull colored fireworks blossomed, sparkled like the handprint in his dream, then vanished.

An aroma, unfamiliar and enticing. The ground was textured, his pulse rhythmic, the inflow and exhalations of breath short and quick, all earmarks of reality. He had to be awake.

Which was crazy. An attack of some kind. Schizophrenia, an acid flashback. Something like that. Someone inside was seeing all this, an incredulous witness. It had to be a dream, a lucid dream.

A slight breeze gave him goose bumps. He began to shake. A chorus of inner voices screamed, *do something*! Anything besides being scared shitless. He ran his hands over what was clearly not *his* body. Muscular and naked, but for a cloth tied at the waist. His hair was straight, cut to just above his ears, as if someone had put a bowl over his head and shaved off everything beneath it. A monks cut. A finger-width patch of longer hair hung from the top of his head to one side, intertwined with - a feather!

Sounded like there was a forest nearby. He moved towards it tentatively at first, following a savory whiff which promised food. Dream or not, he was hungry.

Moving carefully through trees and brush, Lewis descended a hill, not seeing where he was going, just slashes of color, like flares. Sounds, human sounds ahead. He headed towards them, the shrill edge of his panic dropping lower on the horizon, encouraging him to yield to something inside him which seemed to know intuitively how to navigate. A branch brushed against his chest. His legs side-stepped, another branch whisked past his face. His body began to negotiate the way down on its own accord. He ducked and weaved. Like being a passenger in the back seat with someone at the wheel suggesting sit back, enjoy the E-Ticket ride, and while you're at it, lighten up.

Smack! A branch whacked his face. His legs, instead of slowing down, picked up the pace and after a few more whacks, Lewis wailed in protest, struggling to grab the reins of his runaway body, slamming full bore into a tree.

Someone found him dazed and bleeding, lying on the ground; a woman, from her touch and speech.

"Kos peneguse?"

His mind reeling in confusion, Lewis heard the concern in the woman's voice. She grabbed him by the shoulders and shook him, as if shaking the dust off a pillow. Taking him by the arm, she led him down a slope past what sounded and smelled like a cooking fire, ducking into an enclosure of some kind. She set him down on a bench covered with furs or blankets, wiped his face with a wet cloth, dried it with another, and stroked his back and arms gently while speaking.

31

"Tamahl nesoo!"

Her words were coaxing, rhythmic, soothing, somewhere between speech and song. Lewis pantomimed eating. She left off stroking his arm, came back in a few minutes with a warm, pungent broth in a wooden bowl. He sipped eagerly. She waved a morsel of food under his nose, gently placing it in his mouth. Chewy, not particularly flavorful. Jerky or pemmican. He attempted to speak, but his mouth did not comply.

Chapter Four

A good thing Tell Me A Story was the one who found him. Not the first time Skyfisher had spent the night at the Sacred Place, but nothing like this. Bruised and delirious, he was a stranger to himself.

She had heard stories of young warriors on a dare who went to the mound at night, passing through the ring of posts circling the sacred space, each post with a skull mounted on the top. The young men returned shaking, with tales of ghosts. That was enough to keep most of the village away. Skyfisher had been obsessed with the place his entire life. Some say it was where he had lost his sight. Truth was, he saw more than most others did. Skyfisher could run through the woods as if a spirit were guiding him, dodging any trees in his path. He could look into your heart and tell whether you were speaking the truth. It was one of the reasons she had fallen in love with him.

Strong-willed, wild and beautiful, Tell Me A Story had been courted by a score of young men in Flour Village. She was Panther clan, nobly born and expected to marry someone of a lower standing, a *mitche mitche kupe*. What the white ones called a *stinkard*. It was a rule her people took for granted and left other tribes shaking their heads. In any case, she had rejected all of her suitors regardless of their standing, wounding the pride of the village's best warriors. Most of them shrugged the dismissal off, but some wounds are not easily healed.

One spring afternoon when Tell Me A Story was gathering sphagnum moss on a trail some distance from the village, someone came up from behind, threw a blanket over her head, and looped a rope noose around her neck.

"Cry out and I'll tighten it," a man's voice whispered. He gave the noose a quick tug and let it stay like that for a few moments, long enough for her to get the message. He released the pressure slightly as she gasped for breath. Lifting the edge of the blanket, he tied her hands behind her back. When she struggled he simply tightened the noose. As if preparing a deer for gutting, he pounded two stakes into the ground, hitched up her buckskin jersey above her waist and laid her on her back, looping a cord around one foot, tying it to one of the stakes. Spreading her legs apart, he tied the other leg to the second stake, with a few tugs on the noose to keep her compliant. She rocked her head from side to side, struggling to breathe, to scream, pulling at the restraints as his rough hands explored her body and then fumbled with his garments.

"No!" she gasped, only to be rewarded by another jerk of the noose. Breathing heavily, he slipped off his breeches and leaned close. Rancid warmth. Her body twitched as a drop of sweat touched her skin. Wrapping one arm tightly around her waist, he reached between her legs with his other arm.

A loud crack and her assailant's body collapsed on top of her. Someone dragged him off, untied her hands and legs and loosened the noose. She pulled the blanket off her head, breathed the fresh air as though it were spirit water and stared into the sightless eyes of a man she barely knew.

"Are you here?" Skyfisher asked. She nodded and looked past him at the body of a man lying face down, the back of his

head matted with blood. A wooden club lay on the ground next to him. She tried to speak, coughed and tried again.

"Dead?"

"I don't think so," Skyfisher said.

"Who?"

"I don't know."

She sprang for the club and Skyfisher caught her by the arm.

"Leave it," he said, leading her away from the assailant, lying unconscious and bleeding.

That evening, as High Eagle lay recuperating from a head wound, someone crept into his hut and rammed a sharpened stick between his legs, pinioning his thigh to the ground. He never found out who had done the deed. Not long after, Tell Me A Story and Skyfisher began to appear together publicly.

She was tall, with an erect bearing and an athletic build. True to her clan, Tell Me A Story could run like a panther. Some might think her face a bit long, with straight black hair, usually braided. Her brown eyes had a fierceness that fairly set off sparks when she was excited, enough to intimidate both men and women. Her cheeks were naturally rosy, an effect that most of the village women tried to achieve by rubbing red ochre on their faces. Tell Me A Story blackened her teeth on special occasions, as did many of the village women, with a mixture of tobacco and wood ash. A good listener, she didn't gossip or chatter, but when she spoke, her voice was soothing, easy to listen to.

Skyfisher had no facial tattoos, but an image of an open eye graced his right palm. No longer a youth, he could still sprint as fast as most of the men in the village, and his uncanny ability to run blind through the woods was legendary. He was not particularly handsome. A wide face, plus the fact that his eyes were closed most of the time, gave him a sleepy, owlish look. Whatever his face may have lacked was more than compensated by the expressiveness of his movements, which had a natural grace and flow, like a dancer. His body spoke in a language you could feel, his hands forming pictures, like the sign-talk Tell Me A Story had seen used by the traders who frequented the village from time to time.

Their courtship had been slow. After the assault, Skyfisher avoided her. Tell Me A Story found excuses to visit, bringing him small gifts - herbs or food, a necklace of shells, a sheet of mica cut into the shape of a hand.

It was a new experience to spend time with a man who was indifferent to her appearance, but deeply interested in *her*. What gave her pleasure? What was she afraid of? What animal did she identify with? She famously loved stories and after a bit of coaxing, he began to recount some of the tales he knew.

Like many stinkards, Skyfisher was Raccoon, the singers' clan. He possessed a fine voice, worthy of a song carrier. The songs of their people were given, like family heirlooms, from father to son, mother to daughter, one song carrier to another. There were songs of victories, songs to soothe crying babies, confound an enemy, lighten a heart and bring rain storms. There were songs to call in game for hunters and songs to let the dead know they were not forgotten. Skyfisher could make up a song as easily as a spider spins a web.

"I listen and it sings itself," he confided.

He leaned his head back and let out a long low note, as if the voice behind the wind was his voice too, giving breath to a song that was being sung all the time. Tell Me A Story became a child again, woven into the fabric of words and sounds.

You are soft
Inside, a secret

You are Panther
With claws!

He growled and purred, morphing the purr into a yawn.

"So tired!" he said, mimicking Tell Me A Story's voice, stretching and scratching himself like a she-cat. He licked his shoulder, nuzzling Tell Me A Story until she scratched the back of his neck. Then he rolled away, stood up, rubbed his eyes and stood squinting.

"Now, where did I put those leaves?" a low, raspy voice. Skyfisher hunched over, assuming the posture of Deep Thunder, one of their healers, as he poked on the ground, looking for something.

"Ah! Here they are," miming the old man smelling and chewing the leaves, bending over and blasting out a prodigious fart, worthy of his name, keeping his dignity intact while sniffing as if someone else was responsible for the noxious odor.

Tell Me A Story laughed so hard she cried, then just kept on crying, her body shaking with sobs. The near-rape had shamed and enraged her, a knot inside she couldn't unravel. With the help of this gentle man, she gradually became herself again. Over the coming weeks and months, she felt the growing tendrils of attachment.

Skyfisher rarely spoke of his own past. Tell Me A Story knew he was obsessed with the Sacred Place, visiting it covertly at night. He kept that part of his life a secret, even after their marriage, an event which had been tolerated by her parents. Skyfisher was *mitche mitche kupe,* the caste she was obliged to marry into. Although, as a blind song carrier, he was not considered a prime catch by her family. Still, they did not object, considering that Tell Me A Story had always shown so little interest in marriage.

Most mornings, whenever Skyfisher spent the night on the hill, he would return home silent and saddened. If she asked him about it, all he would say was that he could not say anything at all. Even so, she could sense his disappointment, but Skyfisher refused to let her in to his own forbidden ground.

Seeing him stumble down the hill in such a strange, pathetic state, Tell Me A Story regretted the secrecy. Something had transpired on the mound and she had no idea what to do about it.

She took her husband by the hand, treating him for the first time as though he were truly blind. Leading him through the woods, avoiding the well-traveled paths, they came to a secluded spot on the river which snaked around the western side of the village. A cold water bath was in order, a blanket wrap and then back home.

Outside the hut, a fire was burning, surrounded by a circle of stones. She sat him on one of the stones and rubbed his shoulder through the blanket. He was like a child in a trance. On impulse she began to sing, as he would done have for her.

Can the sky spirits see the sparks from this fire
Leaping into the air like wishes?

One day I will carry our baby
People will see what a beautiful child we have made

They will be jealous of our love
Brighter than the fire, higher than the sparks

Tears welled in her eyes. She brought Skyfisher's hand up to touch them as they coursed down her cheeks.

"Where are you?" she asked. He shook his head in a song of silence.

Chapter Five

A council fire was to be held that evening. As Panther clan, Tell Me A Story was expected to attend with her husband. If she didn't show up, there would be questions. She dressed Skyfisher in his finest deerskin shirt, leggings and moccasins, his breech cloth made of nettle fibers she had woven herself.

Tell Me A Story donned a shift, a ceremonial dress woven from nettle fiber and mulberry bark, a gift from her mother. Four eagle claws dangled from her belt and they clinked together when she moved. Her necklace was a blend of shell, bone beads and feathers. In lieu of a tattoo, she sometimes asked a friend to paint a simple design on her face. Today she filled a wooden bowl with water, watching her reflection on the water's surface. Using a feather tip as a brush, she carefully painted a symbol on her cheek - the outline of a hand with an eye in its center - just like the eye tattooed on Skyfisher's palm, an image connected in some way with her husband's secret life.

She stared into his sightless eyes. *"If you had told me anything, I could help you now. Can you hear me?"* She clapped her hands near his ear and he flinched slightly.

Tell Me A Story blackened her teeth, out of respect for a villager being honored at the council fire. She began to rub Skyfisher's teeth with the ash and tobacco, saying, "teeth!", which

Lewis, the tenant in Skyfisher's body, heard as "*een-tah*[1]". She tapped his incisors for emphasis. When he did not respond, she rapped harder.

"*Entv!*" She stroked his lips gently, tapped the teeth again and slapped his face for good measure.

"*Entv!!*"

He opened his mouth and the ghost of a whisper emerged. She tilted her head to one side and brought her lips to his larynx.

"Mmmmm," she sounded, letting the vibration of her mouth tingle and pass through to him, willing him to speak.

"*Why don't you speak to me?!*"

As she moved to slap him again, his hand shot up, catching her wrist mid-swing.

"*Entv,*" he whispered, and added, "*Tookul Hadshina-agi.*" Falling Star. A brief, almost painful squeeze and his grip relaxed. He seemed lost again, lost and afraid. Yet for a moment he had appeared, speaking a name she knew all too well.

Falling Star was an elder, like Skyfisher, a *mitche mitche kupe*, a stinkard who had married above his rank. His wife had passed away, but he still came to council meetings. Tell Me A Story had never warmed to him. Formal and aloof, he rarely spoke and certainly not to her. On several occasions she had observed Skyfisher and Falling Star deep in conversation, talking about the Sacred Place, she guessed.

Tell Me A Story waited to see if Skyfisher would surface again, but he remained silent. Nothing else to do except head for the council fire and make the best of it. Taking him by the arm, she walked him around the inside of the hut, a few paces at a time, like walking a grown up child. He ducked to avoid a dangling fish net. At least he could still "see".

---

[1] In Natchez: "entv"

"*Good,*" she said.

Discretely holding his elbow, she steered Skyfisher out of the hut towards the place where the council was to be held. Falling Star would likely be at the gathering.

There were two ceremonial lodges in Flour Village, similar to Skyfisher and Tell Me A Story's own dwelling, but on a larger scale. She had never been in the smaller temple lodge, where the sacred fire was kept burning day and night, maintained by four guardians. It was said that if any of the guardians let the fire burn out, they would be beheaded, along with their wives and children. So far as Tell Me A Story knew, this had never occurred. No one was permitted entry to the temple lodge except for the Lesser Sun, the guardians and of course, the Great Sun, a descendant of the Supreme Fire. Although he resided in Acorn Village, a day's journey from where Tell Me A Story lived, the Great Sun rarely visited Flour Village. Some of the elders remembered how when the Great Sun had come to dedicate the temple, he had been carried from place to place in a litter, his feet never allowed to touch the ground. His ancestor's bones were supposed to be interred inside the temple, next to the sacred fire.

The lodge adjacent to the temple had a fire, too. Tell Me A Story had been inside many times with other members of her clan. One door, no windows. Circles of benches surrounded an altar platform where the fire burned. It was a smoky place where more was heard than seen, something she would be particularly grateful for today.

Skyfisher stumbled over a tree root. Tell Me A Story held him firmly by the elbow, checking the fall and glancing around to see if anyone might have noticed. It was turning dusk; the sky dark grey. They walked from a wooded area where their own hut and a handful of other dwellings were, to an open field. Beyond was a long slope which led to the ceremonial huts.

A group of older boys were in the field, absorbed in a game of *Tchung-key*. A pair ran together, one holding a disk-shaped stone and the other brandishing a spear. The first boy threw the stone far, accompanied by a burst of cheers from his teammates. The other boy, running alongside him, waited until the instant before the disk hit the ground and loosed his spear. Both boys, trailed by their teams, ran to see how close the spear had landed near the disk.

At that moment, one of the players noticed Skyfisher and called to him. Though blind, Skyfisher had the reputation of throwing a *Tchung-key* spear with deadly accuracy. The village boys never tired of coaxing him to demonstrate his talent, re-affirming to any doubter that there were things which cannot be so easily explained.

Tell Me A Story waved them off.

"Going to council. Another time!"

The ceremonial lodge stood on the summit of the slope, not far from the temple. The other side of the hill dropped more steeply to the banks of a stream. From the outside, the buildings appeared to be nearly identical – corner posts made of cypress trees sunk deep into the earth, side walls of thick wood covered with mud; one door, and a roof thatched with reed mats and mud.

A fire was burning in the center of the lodge; billowing smoke filled a room which could hold more than a hundred people. No way of knowing how many were already here. Not far from the door, seated on a bench reserved for non-clan men, sat Little Walnut, an elder. He had become his name, brown and wrinkled, nearly invisible in the shadows. With a polite greeting, Tell Me A Story positioned Skyfisher next to Little Walnut, whispering to him that her husband wasn't entirely himself today. Little Walnut nodded. After a moment's hesitation, Tell Me A Story moved through the smoke to the other side of the room, making a tobacco offering to the central fire, circling it three times. She sat on a bench with other clan members, greeted a few women, glanced around for Falling Star, but did not see him.

She was still angry at Skyfisher for keeping her in the dark, and at men in general with their high and mighty secrets. One of her husband's favorite expressions was "every stick has two ends." What end of the stick had he left her? If anyone caught sight of the symbol painted on her cheek, she might still learn something.

Fearless by temperament, Tell Me A Story couldn't help but feel uneasy about Skyfisher. There were those who envied him. If they learned how vulnerable he was, what tricks might they play? What had he encountered at the Sacred Place? Perhaps the same spirits the younger warriors had seen there. Sitting on the bench amidst the swirling, choking smoke, she imagined being surrounded by spirits, too. Grey, ghostly figures entered the lodge, silhouetted against the fire, vaporous, insubstantial.

Stories told of the time when otherworldly beings lived amongst her people, disguised as humans. Perhaps they were in this room. The door was open; they were free to enter to play tricks on people like Skyfisher who stuck their noses where they didn't belong. Maybe they were playing a trick on him now. She just wanted him back.

Perhaps everyone in the room held a spirit inside them, waiting for twilight and an unguarded moment to emerge. She caught a glimpse of High Eagle walking past, no doubt carrying a twisted spirit.

The lodge filled with many people, the muffled sounds of their movements, the clink of women's ornaments as they walked, their murmured prayers, the crackling of the fire, the coughs of those who had not perfected the art of sipping smoky air in small doses.

All these villagers, each with their own stories, dispersed during the day like so many ants swarming about, gathered together in the closeness of the lodge. It didn't matter who they were anymore. In the shadows they became a hive.

A voice wailed high and thin. One of the guardians entered the lodge singing, followed by a principal guest, an elder, singing his song. Another elder and two warriors, each making offerings and chanting their respective songs. Clay pipes were passed. The guardian spoke on behalf of the Lesser Sun, not present at this gathering. Each of the four principal guests spoke in turn, honoring a deceased villager, repeating their chants of praise as if in a trance.

It was the sort of ceremony Tell Me A Story had heard many times before, with little variation. Her mind wandered, thinking of her mother, who was the first person to take her, wide-eyed and scared, to the ceremonial lodge. Before walking in to the lodge, Tell Me A Story's mother had, with a conspiratorial smile, told her there was no need to be afraid.

"When you grow up, you will know these people," she said. *"They will want to tell you their stories. You must listen, or you will never become your name. Each story has a secret wrapped up inside of it. They do not know what their secret is. If you help them find it, you will become their sister."*

Her father taught her the stories of animals and plants, their names and secrets, among them *hahiahop kvheluse,* the yellow flower that brings sleep and *hakshoo,* whose leaves bring the smoke of peace. The greatest secret of all was *e lekshe neshil, Master of Breath,* and she guessed that it was his story Skyfisher had been trying to learn on the sacred mound.

She wondered if she would ever get to hear Skyfisher sing his true story. He had already given her the greatest gift of all, what it felt like to be loved. Now that love was being tested. She would be strong. If the spirits were here, they would not see her waver.

The speeches in the lodge were shifting away from the proscribed formalities to the talk of other villages, tribes and outsiders like the Fran-zay.

"Traders and thieves", she thought, though they did bring wonderful things, some useful, some frivolous. Well-made axes, tools, weapons, jewelry, furs. The Fran-zay had stolen *hakshoo*, the smoke plant they called tobacco, and started their own plantations with slaves captured from other tribes. Flour Village had plenty of its own tobacco plants, but Fran-zay goods were highly valued. Their fire-sticks could kill an enemy at a distance, faster and deadlier than a spear. Up till now, only a few of them had been traded for, but that would change soon enough. With weapons such as these, many wondered if the Fran-zay should be trusted. The Lesser Sun had instructed the guardians to ask those who had contact with the outsiders.

"Skyfisher," a voice called out, *"have you spoken with the traders?"*

Tell Me A Story's heart sank. The guardian spoke once more.

"You know the sound of lies. What do you hear in the Fran-zay talk? The Lesser Sun wishes to know this."

A long silence. Then a voice, Little Walnut's.

"Skyfisher cannot speak now," he said.

"Why not?" the guardian wanted to know. Tell Me A Story held her breath.

"He has taken a vow of silence," Little Walnut said.

"A vow?" asked the guardian, somewhat petulantly. Then he seemed to change his mind.

"So, the Blind One is mute!" he said. A few dutiful chuckles wafted through the lodge.

"The Lesser Sun will want to hear from him when he has finished his vow." Tell Me A Story slowly exhaled and made her own vow to sew a pair of moccasins for Little Walnut.

Chapter Six

Having a woman bath him, moreover a woman he could not see, was something new, to say the least. If it was a dream, than this would qualify as a good one. The water was cold, though not numbingly so. His body shook in spasms. He reached for her, and she let his hands explore her face and arms, even as she carefully washed every inch of him. He felt his sex stiffen and was grateful that at least this part of his new body was functioning, if not his eyes. As the woman dried him, Lewis breathed her in. The scent of someone who had been working with herbs, a gardener perhaps, a cook. He registered the texture, the pressure and intention of her touch. Not the touch of a mother or a sister.

Her face was smooth, her hair long and braided. She rubbed and oiled his hair, re-braiding a feather into the longer strands. She gently pried open his mouth with her fingers. Was she brushing his teeth?

He felt the powdery paste with his tongue. She rapped his teeth hard, attempting to teach him the word for teeth, apparently. Although he could produce sounds, his mouth and tongue did not obey any attempt at coherent speech. He felt like a child trying to learn to talk, earning a few slaps to his face.

Then for a moment, everything shifted. He witnessed himself speak a few words in another language, felt the presence of the man whose body he was inhabiting. The driver had re-entered, briefly taken the controls. Then he was gone. Lewis was left speechless, wondering if the woman was going to start slapping him again.

He let her dress him, his body revelling in the cool sensation of his garments – deerskin, he guessed. An improbable idea appeared, fueled by the intonation of the woman's voice, the odors, the feel of the hut and its surroundings. The shoes he had been dressed in were moccasins, the floor earthen. The woman held his hand and they circled the room together. He could hear the sounds of her breathing and of an encampment outside. What he did not hear was anything automated or electrical. No hint of a refrigerator, a car, or any airplanes. Very few places on the planet were devoid of aircraft noise, most of them uninhabited. Where were the planes? Where was he? *When* was he?

A surge of panic. He grabbed her arm and took long deep breaths to steady himself.

I am alive. This is real.

And yet with every breath, it all seemed phenomenally unreal.

I'm sick or crazy.

Maybe it was all some weird, cruel stunt.

She walked him up a long incline. He could hear the voices of boys playing, shouting nearby. The woman called out to them. Something familiar about the intonation of their language. An indigenous group, perhaps Central or South American. That would, of course, be impossible. This whole experience was impossible. He could be in China or Oz, for that matter. At the same time, he could not deny he was hearing and sensing his surroundings with a new clarity, perhaps because of his blindness. Why be blind in a dream? He bit his lip hard and it hurt. There was no denying he was somewhere, in a blind man's body, walking up a hill. No dream could be so physically palpable. The hill was real. He was on it. The woman beside him was flesh and blood.

It was near sundown; he could tell from the air tempera-ture and from something else, something indefinable. She led him through a doorway to a large enclosure. He sensed the size of it from the sounds within, its acoustic signature. Yet something else about the room was being conveyed, as if he was being informed by a subtle sixth sense. The smoke was anything but subtle. A fire was burning within and the air was barely breathable. He coughed and was rewarded by a firm pinch on his arm.

For some reason he flashed on a memory of the World Trade Center on the infamous day it was bombed. Videos of people emerging from the building. They had just descended countless flights of smoke-filled stairways, their faces covered with soot, effluence streaming like black glaciers from their noses and mouths. Yet the first thing many of them did as soon as they reached the open air was to light a cigarette and take a deep drag. Lewis, a semi-militant non-smoker, had been as-tonished by this sight. Here he was in the bowels of a smoking den, worthy of three packs of cigarettes, easy.

What if he was asleep in the real world and there was a fire? That would account for it. With all the desperate energy he could summon, he attempted once more to pull himself out of the dream, to emerge from this room into a place where he could see and breathe again.

As he stood tense and frozen, the woman gently pulled him down to sit on a bench, speaking quietly to someone seated next to him. A final warning-squeeze to his lips and she was gone.

It was less smoky and more breathable sitting on the bench.

The room filled with other people. A meeting of some kind was going on. Songs and speeches. One sounded like a sermon or a political stump speech. An indian reservation, a pueblo?

There was a long, uncomfortable silence, broken by the man sitting next to him, his voice as dry as reeds. Lewis suspected the remark related to himself somehow. Another song, accompanied by a rhythmic shake of a rattle and the affirmation that this was indeed a tribal gathering.

People began to move out of the enclosure and he was back in the care of the woman. They walked arm in arm slowly down the gentle slope. A cool evening. She pulled closer to him. A man's voice came from behind, impetuous, hostile. They kept walking and the man hovered nearby. He sniffed the air and kept repeating the same word in a mocking tone.

Chapter Seven

"Puant!" High Eagle spat it out like poison.

The Fran-zay had coined the name, thinking that the sauvages who tanned hides were members of some lower, smellier caste - *puants*, "stinkards". However, *puant* had been taken on by clan members as a badge of honor, following the ancient advice of turning your alleged shortcomings to your advantage. Oblivious of this, High Eagle sounded the name as a weapon. Something was up with Skyfisher. He was determined to find out what it was.

"So now breeding stock is taking vows of silence!"

Ignoring him, Tell Me A Story continued to walk down the hill, holding tightly to Skyfisher's arm.

High Eagle stepped close to her, the smell of his breath bringing back the memory of the assault. It was all she could do to keep walking and not scratch his eyes out.

"We'll be waiting to hear what the puant has to say."

They continued on to their hut without further incident. Inside, someone was waiting for them in the darkness. Tell Me A Story froze.

"Forgive me for not asking to enter," Falling Star said.

Holding her surprise in check, Tell Me A Story said, *"Wait here."*

She fetched a burning stick from the communal fire and brought it in to light the fire pit in their hut. The flames caught a waiting pile of dry wood, igniting sparks and shadows.

Falling Star was taller and older than Skyfisher. He walked with a slight limp, an injury from warrior days. Strands of grey streaked his hair, which grew long on one side of his head. The other side was shaved. His brows were thick and seemed perpetually furrowed, giving him the look of someone trying to solve an interminable puzzle. He dressed differently from most men in the village. Instead of a breech cloth, Falling Star wore a long shirt tied at the waist like a tunic. Like Skyfisher, he was *puant*. High Eagle might regard them as drones, but many stinkards were healers and hunters, albeit lower in standing to the Great Sun and his nobles. The laws of their people required those of noble birth to marry stinkards, and since most marriages were arranged, it was a recipe for mismatched pairings. And yet, Tell Me A Story and Skyfisher had managed to find happiness regardless of the machinations of tribal customs.

The Lesser Sun and his clan ruled Flour Village. Each of the surrounding villages had their own Lesser Sun as a leader. The Great Sun, who traced his lineage to the sun itself, ruled over them all from Acorn Village. His authority was being challenged by a faction of Lesser Suns. "Unfit to lead", they said. As a consequence, the Great Sun had been systematically dispatching anyone who openly opposed him, strangling being the preferred mode of execution. His power held sway, but some whispered his days were numbered. Tell Me A Story mused on what other whispers she would be hearing this night.

Falling Star's right palm was graced with the tattoo of an open eye. He gently placed it on the forehead of the man he knew as Skyfisher. His other hand rested on Skyfisher's neck, feeling a slight tremble.

Turning to Tell Me A Story, Falling Star asked, *"May I stay a little while?"* She nodded and poured several cups of twig tea. They sat on log benches, piled with blankets and furs. From the center of the room, the fire sputtered and sent sparks swirling towards the upper reaches of the hut, where fishing nets draped to the side wall. Falling Star's gaze scanned the room. On a side table, a half-carved flute lay next to a pile of wood shavings and a knife. Nearby were bowls of herbs, with others hanging in bunches from the ceiling.

"Your husband did not take a vow of silence."

"No," she agreed.

"Have you tried to speak with him?" Falling Star asked.

"He hears but does not understand." Then she added, *"For a moment, he spoke your name."*

"Is that why you painted the hand-sign on your face?"

"I was angry with him - and you! What has happened to him?" Her voice rose with her anger and he gestured for her to speak more quietly.

"Tell me," she implored.

"Wait a moment," Falling Star said, and he whispered something in Skyfisher's ear and waited.

"You're certain he can hear?" he asked.

"Yes."

"Can you get him to speak again?"

"I've tried."

"Teach him a word."

Tell Me A Story took Skyfisher's hand and held it, stroking his palm.

"Ispeshe."

No response. She repeated the word, touching his lips as if to encourage them to move. How could he have forgotten to speak? He was there, sitting before her, yet he was in another place. Maybe one of those spirits got hold of him. She would pull him back, as he had once saved her.

"*Ispeshe,*" she said, rubbing the eye tattooed on his hand, willing it to see and speak for him.

Skyfisher coughed, cleared his throat and whispered "*Eez–pesh,*" the word for palm. Tell Me A Story nuzzled her forehead against the side of her husband's face and then turned to Falling Star.

"*I thought I had lost him,*" she said.

"*You have lost him. For now. What do you know about that symbol on your cheek?*"

She shrugged.

"*He told me the eye tattoo was nothing I should worry about.*"

"*And the small hill on the north side of the village?*"

"*The Sacred Place?*" she asked.

"*Did Skyfisher ever speak to you about it?*"

"*I know what everyone knows,*" she said. "*Our ancestors made it a long time ago. It's old.*" A sharp crack sounded from the fire and Tell Me A Story flinched. "*Why did you say he is lost?*"

Falling Star watched the flames leaping higher, sending sparks arching through the air, wondering if any of them might set the hut's thatched roof ablaze.

"*You know the story of the sacred fire?*" he asked.

"*Everyone does,*" she said, growing impatient.

"*Become your name,*" he said.

She disliked being treated like a child and shook her head in frustration.

"*Two keepers of the Sacred Fire,*" she began. "*One went away, the other fell asleep. While the keeper slept the fire went out. He was frightened. If anyone found out, his head would be taken. Before the other keeper returned, the one who fell asleep re-lit the sacred fire. He did it with embers from his pipe. Ordinary fire. Bad things began to happen. A Lesser Sun died, then another and yet another. Our people begin to die, too. There was a famine that lasted for years. The keeper who re-lit the fire got sick. He knew he was going to die and went to tell the Great Sun what he had done. First he asked the Great Sun to swear that he wouldn't be fed to the dogs! The Great Sun promised, and the keeper confessed he had let the fire go out. The deaths and the famine were his fault. So they put out the fire, made sure that it was re-kindled from a sacred flame. Whenever this story is told, they say that if the fire had not been re-lit, our people would have died out.*

"*Yes,*" said Falling Star, who seemed suddenly old and tired. He glanced around the hut as if searching for something. "*Very few know what I am about to tell you. Those who know would not approve of my telling you. I don't think they would they would throw me to the dogs, though.*" He took a sip of tea and continued, "*Long ago, a small number of our people were entrusted with a great responsibility. A special duty, like the fire-keepers in the story. For many generations they did what they had to do quietly and well. In the early days, this group of men — only men,*" he added pointedly, "*was known to the Great Sun and a few of the elders. None of the Lesser Suns knew.*"

"*What is this duty?*" asked Tell Me A Story.

"*If I told you that, they would truly feed me to the dogs!*" Falling Star said, with a laugh somewhere between a cough and a bark. "*Like tending a fire, it requires great vigilance.*"

"*You're telling me —*" Tell Me A Story began, "*you're speaking about something real, yes, not a story? Why can't you say what it was they were doing?*"

"*It's tempting. I wouldn't have to listen to your questions anymore and the dogs would find you much tastier than me. I can tell you this. What they were doing was important, for everyone. As important as the air we breathe.*"

"*Then why keep it a secret?*" she asked, earning a bark grunt.

Falling Star didn't like having to explain himself to anyone, especially a woman. He needed this one's cooperation and time was running short.

"Who is the better hunter," he asked, *"Stalking Panther or the Lesser Sun?"*

"Stalking Panther, of course."

"So if your life depended on it, you would rather have Stalking Panther hunt for meat than the Lesser Sun? Even though the Lesser Sun is an exalted person and Stalking Panther is –"

"— a puant, like you," she said.

"Just as a hunter needs to learn to hunt, a long preparation is needed for our sacred duty. It must be performed by those who were trained, for the same reason that the sacred fire had to be tended only by its keepers."

"Alright," Tell Me A Story said, *"I hear your words,"* a polite way of saying she didn't understand. *"What happened?"*

"A series of calamities," Falling Star admitted. *"The last of the truly Great Suns was killed during a raid, along with many warriors. None of the Great Suns since that time have been trusted to reveal the secret to."* He paused, took another sip of tea. In the distance a dog barked.

"Somehow," Falling Star continued, *"our Great Sun learned of the existence of this group - kuash, the Shining Ones, the Society of Light. Without anyone to advise him who knew better, the Great Sun became like a spoiled child, a child with a great deal of power. A few of the Shining Ones were discovered. When they refused to talk, the Great Sun had them strangled."*

"When was this?" she asked.

"Two winters."

"What does this have to do with the Sacred Place?"

"I am kuash. Your husband as well. He is one our hopes have been riding on." He sipped his tea and regarded Tell Me A Story

with a sad smile. *"He is carrying a visitor. I don't know how else to put it. Another man is within his body. You don't believe me. I can see it in your eyes. I don't blame you. But think - a woman carries another life inside her, yes? This is not so different. A man is inside Skyfisher."*

"Who is this man?"

"From another time."

She shook her ahead, not willing to pick up the thread of this story.

"What am I supposed to do?" She finally asked.

"Treat him as an honored guest, just as we hope Skyfisher will be treated, wherever he is. They are both like babies. Only the guest arrived too soon. Too soon! Skyfisher thought he had trained enough. So he went to the mound to become his name, cast his net and caught someone. Even babies come when parents are not ready. The Society of Light and Skyfisher were not ready. He and his visitor are in danger. You too, if you help us. We need your help, although it must be freely given. You're no longer safe here."

She glanced at Skyfisher and noticed that he seemed more animated. He was moving his hands, holding his palms towards Falling Star and then towards her. He was smiling, rare for him even in the best of times.

Tell Me A Story, feeling helpless and confused, went to a bowl of water, dipped in a cloth, and wiped off the design she had painted on her cheek. Falling Star watched her closely.

"Is there any more tea?" he asked. As she poured the tea, Tell Me A Story's hand trembled slightly.

"For your husband, all we can do is keep his body safe for when he returns. We must aid his visitor."

Here was the most unlikely story Tell Me A Story had ever heard, spoken in deadly earnest. She'd sooner believe a talking rabbit.

"How do we help this man?" she asked.

Falling Star took a deep breath.

"The Sacred Place," he began, *"for years, it has been only for kuash. That will change. Everything will soon change. Our people's days are numbered. There are other places. You and the one Skyfisher is carrying must travel to one of these. Go there and learn. Leave here as soon as possible without arousing suspicion. Teach him our language, as many words as you can every day."*

Tell Me A Story began to protest. Falling Star cut her off. *"He will learn quickly."*

She hesitated, then asked, *"Will my husband return?"*

"If we help the one he is carrying."

"Then I will stand with him," she said.

Chapter Eight

As they walked away from the angry man, Lewis could still feel his ill will, like the lingering exhaust fumes from a car. No sooner had he left when another appeared on the scene inside their hut. Where the first man had been forbidding, this was an entirely different persona. Something familiar about him, the sound of his voice, his smell, the way his demeanor translated to Lewis's new realm of receptivity. A tip-of-the-tongue feeling, like tasting a flavor he knew but could not name. The man gently pressed his palms on Lewis's forehead and at the base of his skull.

Lewis sensed a slight jolt pulse from the crown of his head down the spine, spreading a warm wave through his body. Something was released, an elixir of recognition. His senses felt sharpened and deeper, as though they had been lying dormant in a lower sedimentary layer, waiting for the crust covering them to be dissolved. What he had experienced before as peripheral seeing came to the fore now as luminescence. The man appeared as an orb, like one of those New Age aura photographs. The image didn't come from his eyes, but seemed to generate from his body and oddly enough, his hands. As unprecedented as the experience was, his mind was already explaining it.

The Kirlian glow thing. Sure.

He reminded himself that seeing actually takes place inside our heads. Here was simply a new echelon of sensory awareness. However there was nothing simple about this. Nuanced and multi-layered, it was like parsing a language of emanations and vibrations, not words.

Somehow he *knew* this man and the sound of his name, whispered in Lewis's ear. *Falling Star.* He spoke it in a language that Lewis did not grasp, although it shared the same odd sense of familiarity. Lewis turned his newly minted attention, like a searchlight, to the woman, now a glowing orb as well. The contours of her face morphed to a spray of colors, an impressionist's palette of a spring bouquet. The colors of concern. She was the wife of the man whose body he inhabited - an intuitive certainty. He had heard what he guessed was her name, spoke it aloud and sensed her relief as he did.

Lewis bathed in a flood of impressions, reminiscent of a mescaline voyage in the sixties, when so many members of his generation had embarked on hallucinogenic journeys, searching for something they yearned for but could not articulate. Maybe there were special ingredients in the tea he was sipping. Maybe this whole experience was a world-class mirage.

Nonetheless, there was a sense of discovery in simply taking stock of where he was. A flame of fear still burned, yet it kindled a tingling of sensitivity as he came in touch with the shape of his surroundings, the hut and the aura of life it contained. The whole room was vibrating, singing. He followed the rhythm and tonality in the voices of Falling Star and Tell Me A Story, hovering at the edge of understanding.

He would try to connect with them. Pointing to himself, he said, "Lewis".

Falling Star again cupped his hands around Lewis's head.

"Here, you are Skyfisher."

Tell Me A Story laid him down on a platform covered with furs. Lewis heard the murmur of voices in muted conversation, punctuated by the crackle of the fire. The weight of unconsciousness descended as he wondered whose body he would wake up in.

A rain of liquid golden fire, the deepest yellow imaginable, exploding into space as free-falling molten streams, golden droplets drifting through a void, each tiny globule reflecting the azure sphere it was hurtling towards, a blue planet. Surrounding the planet, a spider web network of filaments woven into an enormous cocoon. The golden droplets were caught on strands of filament, like cloud vapor on a fog net. The instant they touched the web, they were absorbed into the spider-silk fiber, whisked around the blue world at breathtaking speed, coalescing in a lightning flash showering ghostly sparks, emanating echoes of the golden drops that shimmered to the planetary surface. Some of the droplets were caught in an air current, like bubbles in a stream pulled towards a waterfall, drawn to a hill that, like the planet, had its own filament network of glowing fibers surrounding it. The pale gold bubbles clung to the web and were sucked into the depths of the hill to a cavern within. Inside the cave, a circle of men sat around a fire pit, with their hands up, and from each of their right palms shone a golden eye suffused with filaments of light.

Lewis awoke from the dream inside a body that was not his, lying next to the luminous outline of a woman.

She was beautiful in a way he had never experienced beauty before, *seeing* her grace and lightness of spirit through an inner portal. He gently stroked her face and neck, letting his hand wander creatively as it descended down her body. She spoke, naming each part and touching the corresponding place on his body, mirroring his own spirit of discovery. In a moment, she had straddled him. He was inside her in both ethereal and corporeal realms, making love slowly and luxuriantly. For Tell Me A Story, a guilty pleasure. Skyfisher had pledged himself to celibacy six months ago. Surely this circumstance skirted any rules of behavior that she - or any other woman - had ever encountered. Falling Star's explanation was unbelievable. Here was her husband in the flesh if not the spirit. Hard not to take advantage of a situation she had long yearned for - a naïve Skyfisher, playful as an otter in spring time. They rolled and wrestled, reveling in the pleasures of love-making.

Afterwards she cooked some corn fritters. Lewis, feeling the pangs of his host's hunger, dove into the first real meal he had eaten in two days.

Tell Me A Story taught him new words and was surprised that he remembered virtually all of them later. By midday, she had exhausted every object in the hut, not to mention every body part, and was at a loss for how to give him the word for something he could not touch or sense. Her husband's way of *seeing* seemed to be returning. He could now walk around the hut freely, avoiding obstacles. When she threw an acorn at him, he caught it mid-air with one hand, smiling.

In the late afternoon, she needed to begin to gather supplies for their journey, and left with, *"I go,"* accompanied by a finger-walk. Then *"stay,"* clear enough to both dogs and men, with the appropriate gesture. To prove that he understood, Lewis repeated the words and panted like a dog, with a somewhat lame attempt at a tail-wag.

"No talk!" !" she added sternly, lest anyone hear he had broken his supposed vow. He held a hand over his mouth, the speak-no-evil monkey incarnate. Satisfied, she left the hut.

Alone, Lewis attempted to make sense of the last 48 hours. Ride the wave. What else was there to do? Nothing in his fifty-some years had prepared him for living inside another man's skin in a strange world and making love to a phantasm. He missed the world of sight. Barely two days distant and already it had the tinge of nostalgia, a colorized home movie. His new way of seeing made him feel like a kid hardwired to a video game with no instruction manual.

The way he thought and felt affected what he saw. The reverse was true, too. The line between thinking, seeing and "taking something in" was blurring. He opened the door to the hut and tuned his senses outside. Focusing his attention, he perceived shimmering, radiating pulses of color extending beyond the physical boundaries of what seemed to be a tree, as though its substance was dissolving and reforming from its own atmosphere.

Shifting his awareness to the hut, he tuned in the wavelengths of objects around him, as if he was the central node of a 360 degree three-dimensional radar system. A clay cup glowed pale blue, a woven basket glimmered in a warmer color he had no name for. Lewis found that if he didn't actually name the phenomena that came into his field of perception, the more dynamic and colorful they remained. Perceiving became an experiment in balance, taking in the impression, absorbing the life of something without pinning it down with a word, like a dead butterfly.

A lifelong habit was not so easily dropped. Lewis spent the afternoon exploring depth perception, distance, size, shape and scale, re-learning to see, not wanting to lose the magic.

He noticed a woven web-like cloth, focused on it, tuned it in, verified his perceptions with his hands, brailing the cloth, fixing the living image of it as deeply as he could. Inevitably, the word came. Fishnet. It shimmered, daring him to see if it was possible to own both the name and the living image.

Lewis began to grasp the subtleties of his newfound ability. If everything in the universe was in motion, here was proof. He was *seeing* the sounds of distant voices as a cluster of colors. One of them was deepening in hue as its vibration came closer. Someone was calling from outside the hut.

"Skyfisher!"

He opened the door and braille-viewed a young man wearing only moccasins and a breechcloth, exuding the colors of boisterous good cheer. He held a long shaft - a spear, in one hand and a disc shaped stone in another. Lewis signed that he could not speak. The youth seemed to understand, yet he motioned for Skyfisher to join him, unmistakably an invitation to come and play.

So long as he didn't say anything, what harm could it do?

Lewis followed the neon silhouette of the young man, avoiding rocks and other obstacles in his path, which appeared like bogies on a Nintendo screen. They came to the same field he had passed through with Tell Me A Story the day before. A gaggle of boys were playing with spears and stone discs. One would toss or roll a disc and another throw a spear, trying to hit the stone before it stopped rolling.

Skyfisher's escort sported an earplug and wore his hair monk-fashion, cut just above his ears. He wanted to pair with Skyfisher in a game of *Tchung-key* and offered him the spear. Lewis hefted it, hoping that his new body could throw well. He took a practice toss, letting his companion retrieve it. Not too shabby. Readying to sling the disc, the youth began to jog. Lewis followed. The boy, whooping with delight, threw the disc a good fifty feet. A beautiful low-arching toss. Before the stone touched the ground, Lewis had loosed his spear, tripping over a branch as he did so. As he fell, Skyfisher's body responded, curling as his head tucked and rolled into a somersault, pushing off the ground with his hands, coming into a crouch and slowly standing up. The boy who had thrown the disc was so intent on following its trajectory that he had missed this feat. Others had seen it and they shook their heads in wonder. The disc landed at the top of a gully and rolled a few feet down its slope. The spear struck about five yards from where the disc had landed, on the rim of the gully. Not up to Skyfisher's usual standards. Fortunately, the throw had been overshadowed by the somersault, and a group of boys approached and crowded round him, tapping his back with the flats of their spears, making low, appreciative hoots. With a wave that he hoped signified thanks, Lewis walked slowly back to his hut, quitting while he was ahead.

That evening, Tell Me A Story cooked a delicious venison stew, which Lewis attacked with vigor. She had heard about his exploits on the *Tchung-key* field.

"Your head is this!" she said, shaking a wooden spoon.

Joining them later that evening, Falling Star dismissed the transgression. What was done was done.

"We plan," he said.

No one in the village suspected Skyfisher was hosting an invisible visitor. Best to keep to the hut with his mouth shut. Falling Star asked Tell Me A Story how preparations were going. Had anyone asked any questions?

"No."

Falling Star advised changing the subject, if they did ask.

"There is bad blood between you and High Eagle. He's no fool. Which reminds me, I've asked the Bald One, Grey Turtle, to join you and Skyfisher."

"You could have asked me first," Tell Me A Story bristled.

Falling Star snorted. *"Grey Turtle can help you."*

Tell Me A Story decided not to fight this battle.

"There must be some way I can reach my husband and speak to him like he used to be. He said your name the other day.."

Falling Star stood up, walked to the entryway and looked outside, as if to make sure no one was listening. He came back to warm his hands by the fire, and began to speak.

"Even before he lost his sight, we knew Skyfisher was special," Falling Star said. *"He was chosen to be kuash, as I am. We cannot speak of it."*

"But.."

"Even if I had words to describe it, you would not understand."

"How can you expect me to help you?"

"I need a moment with this man. Will you trust me? That's what Skyfisher would want."

"You're asking me to leave my home with a man who looks like my husband, but you don't know who he is! You're willing to talk to a complete stranger but not to me. No, I don't trust you and I won't leave. If you want my help, you have to trust me."

Falling Star sighed. As a commoner, a stinkard, he was obliged to follow the wishes of a high noble clan woman, even though he was acting on behalf of something outside of tribal custom. He managed a smile and said, *"You're strong. A good thing. You'll need to be strong for whatever awaits you."*

He turned to Lewis, putting his hands on his shoulders and pressing the nape of his neck and a bit below it, he began to sing.

"Master of Breath
We who serve..."

He stopped as four warriors burst into the hut without warning. Among them, High Eagle, who surveyed the hut and addressed Falling Star.

"*The Lesser Sun condescends to see you. Besides,*" he added with a laugh, "*this man cannot speak to you. He has taken a vow of silence.*"

Falling Star stepped close to Tell Me A Story, whispered something in her ear, and left with the warriors.

Tell Me A Story sat for a moment, stunned, regarding the man next to her, the shell of her husband.

"*We leave tonight,*" she said, knowing that whoever was inside the shell would not understand.

Chapter Nine

His first night at the Sacred Place still haunted Skyfisher's dreams. After two days of fasting, seeking a vision, he ascended the hill on a warm spring afternoon. Shadows lengthened at sunset, crickets hummed their music and a wolf howled in the distance. He waited. As the moon rose, his spirits sank. No vision would come to a young buck fumbling his way to manhood.

Just when he was ready to leave, a gust of wind blew across the hill. Strangely, none of the tree branches moved. Then, in an instant, with no time for commentary or understanding, something akin to an intake of breath. A funnel of wind whipped through and around him, churning, opening the roof of his head, cascading down his spine, branching into his legs out through his feet into the ground.

Roots germinated from his toes, reaching into the earth, drawing forth a flow of firewater that burned its way back through his body, emanating from his eyes and hands with a cascading yellow-gold light that radiated in spasms of ecstasy. For an instant, he blazed like a beacon fire as incandescent as the sun. Then he was alone on the hill, with an afterglow that never left his sight.

The vision had blinded him. At least that was what others thought. In truth, the Sacred Place had given him another way of opening to the world of appearances, seeing the fire-light in all things. It had taken years to learn precisely how.

That night, Skyfisher had found his way to Falling Star's hut and asked if he was being punished.

"No," Falling Star said. *"A true gift from the One Breath. But you must never speak to anyone else about this."*

He was invited to join *kuash,* the Shining Ones, the Society of Light. They tattooed an eye on the palm of his hand. He began training the next day, expecting to experience another ecstatic vision. Which didn't happen.

"You're not ready," the elders said.

One day, they said, he would join with the blazing light and kindle a flame that would change the world. Until then, stay away from the Sacred Place.

For years, Skyfisher followed their guidance, fasting, taking long silent walks, listening for the wordless instructions of the One Breath, dancing with the movements of the clouds, parsing the subtleties of light, color and shadow that permeated all things, until he was convinced he'd learned everything that Falling Star, Marsh Fox, Grey Turtle and the Nameless had to teach him. He dreamed of the Sacred Place, reliving the golden moment, tormented by a longing to feel the fire course once more through his veins. In secret, he began to visit the mound again late in the evening, hungering for another vision.

Last night he'd gone again, falling asleep on the mound's top, surrounded by a grove of young trees.

He awakened with a powerful ache in his head. Tentatively, he opened his eyes, breaking the crust of sleep-sand. An

overwhelming flood of light, accompanied by a thudding inside his skull.

Seeing, truly seeing, through his eyes! Was it always as
painful as this? The morning light was such an assault on his
senses, he had to retreat back into the safe haven of blindness.
With eyes closed, his senses tried to make sense of the shape of an
enclosure he was in, blurred as if in a fog. He was lying encased in
a warm blanket, like a seed in a pod, underneath a cloth structure.

Could he have done it, jumped in time, something the
elders had only hinted at? He might yet become worthy of
his name, a fisherman of the heavens. What had he caught, or
what had caught him?

An older man's naked body, not particularly muscular.
Old and slow. The physical evidence of his gender intact and
apparently operational. The urge to relieve himself.

Skyfisher pulled himself out of the pod. Clothing and
other assorted items lay strewn about him. An undergarment,
a white cloth tube with thin straps. He tried it on, putting each
foot through one of the strap-loops, pulling the garment up,
leaving his manhood dangling between the straps.

Upside down. If Tell Me A Story were here, she'd say,
"How like a man to mistake his private parts for his head."

A pang of remorse. It had been the hardest thing not to
honor her name and tell her the whole story, that he might
leave and perhaps never return. In this strange place he could
be of service in a way that few men had ever been. A story
yet to be told. He was a tiny part of it, a seed in the husk of
another body, many revolutions of this world around the sun,
many lifetimes away from his home. For the Master of Breath,
a few exhalations.

If the prophecies were correct, his people were nearly all
gone now. A new race, like locusts, had taken over his village

and the rest of the world. What would they think of the Society of Light? In Skyfisher's own time, his fellow villagers would have called it heresy if anyone tried to explain *kuash* to them. Could he do any better in an unknown world?

The throbbing in his head made it difficult to think clearly. Falling Star and Marsh Fox had been right. He wasn't ready.

There was a flap on the side of the cloth hut. With some fiddling he was able to open it and poke his head outside. The light was intense, painful. He retreated back inside and examined his surroundings the way he usually would, impregnating himself with life-emanations, color flows, the subtle rhythms of everything that moved and breathed around him.

He searched through the hut. Several small rectangular flat loaves smelled like they might be food, enclosed in thin skins like peeling birch bark, with images and inscriptions on them. An offering of some kind?

On the floor lay a pair of heavy moccasins tied with thongs, each containing a cloth foot-sack. Tucked in the corner of the hut, a knife which folded its blade into a protective case. A container of water. You could see the water inside as if the container was made of ice, yet it was not frozen. Skyfisher puzzled out how to remove the top of the jar, drink the water and reseal it. There were objects whose purpose he could not divine, toothed flat metal strips on a metal ring. He placed them and a few other items that looked handy inside a cloth sack with carrying straps, then dressed himself in breeches, a light weight hooded garment and the heavy moccasins.

Skyfisher opened the flap of the cloth hut, sensing the surroundings outside. Same physical location as before the time-shift. The sacred hill.

He would listen to the sounds, the movements, the life of his inner world, the blood pulsing through the channels of his newfound body. He would face the four directions, join with the Sun Breath and invite it to penetrate every part of him.

Turning towards the solar disc, Skyfisher was overwhelmed by its intensity. He'd never felt the Sun Breath so powerfully, like trying to stand still in the current of a raging river. The drum beating inside his head was unbearable. Still, he would do something. If the thread of a connection was still there, he would send a message. Visualizing two words in the shape of a spear, he intoned and hurled them towards his own time. *Falling Star.* An ally who could help the man in Skyfisher's body.

That done, he pulled the hood of his upper garment over his head to block the sun. The ache behind his eyes diminished slightly, competing with the urge to relieve himself. He would not do that in the sacred place. Carrying the cloth sack with some of the belongings he'd collected, Skyfisher descended the hill.

He missed his own body. His host's back slouched, the stomach protruded. The arm muscles were slim; the knees protested all the way down the slope.

He headed towards an open space where the ground was flat, hard and black, perhaps a ceremonial or playing field of some kind. In one corner stood a metal wagon with thick, black wheels. The upper sides of the wagon's carriage were made of sheets of the same ice-like material as the water jar. You could see inside. There were seats. In front of one of them, a wheel. He could smell that an animal had recently pissed on one of the wagon's four outer black wheels. Why would a wolf or a dog choose this place to mark its presence?

Perhaps the wagon was designated for such activity. Fumbling with his breeches, he anointed his body fluids on the same wheel, noting the particularities of their passage through an older body. The little wagon house was designed to be moved. Clever idea. If you were in a large village, you could sit inside the carriage, do your business, then roll it into the woods later to bury the waste.

His upper garment wasn't blocking the sun well enough. Turning the garment around protected his eyes better, leaving only the back of his head exposed to the light.

With the grey hood covering his face, Skyfisher hoisted his sack and sense-walked along the black ground until it narrowed to a pathway just wide enough for a wagon. The hard surface of the pathway changed to dirt. After a while, he removed the heavy moccasins to feel the earth more properly, placing the footwear in his sack. The soles of his host's feet were soft, not used to walking barefoot, so he kept the cloth footsacks on them. A crisp spring morning. Skyfisher recognised a number of bird calls and a few that were new to him.

In the distance, a strange sound. A swarm of bees, a flash flood? Something moving at an incredible speed heading right towards him. He ducked behind a clump of bushes in time to see a metal wagon with the same kind of see-through walls whizzing by, faster than a horse could gallop. No horse was pulling it! Someone must have been in a great hurry to relieve himself. If another shit cart came by, he would not run.

Soon enough, a second wagon came zooming along the pathway, passing him and coming to a screeching stop. This one had an open cart in the back and a smaller carriage-hut in front. It slowly backed up and the transparent wall slid down to reveal someone sitting behind a wheel in the little hut.

"What you up to, Bo?"

A large, sweaty pale-skinned man, dressed in a top garment - the same kind that Skywalker had mistakenly put his legs through, wearing a hat with a stiff flap in front, like a bird with a long bill. His words sounded like the language of the Anglay traders. Skyfisher, not wanting to be rude, stepped closer to the wagon, pulled the hood off his face, grimacing as flashes of pain knifed through this head.

"You in trouble? Speak English? Habla Anglo?" After a pause, he said, "Better get in the truck. C'mon, get in," opening the portal to the little metal hut, beckoning Skyfisher to enter.

It smelled bad inside, not exactly like a urinal, but close. Old rancid odors that might have once come from food. The man was drinking what the traders called Water of Fire. Skyfisher did not trust it. His instinct was to back off. He was on uncertain ground, not knowing the customs here. The man seemed to be offering help. Perhaps he was the caretaker for the traveling relief-cart.

The darker interior of the little wagon hut offered some respite from the harsh sunlight. Skyfisher climbed in, holding his sack with one hand and covering his eyes with the other.

"Shut the door," the man said. When Skyfisher did nothing, he added "Super dumb. Well…" He pressed down on something with his foot and spun the wheel in front of him first to the left and then to the right. The wagon lurched forward like a spurred horse, swerving until the portal slammed shut.

"Dukes of Hazard!" the man exclaimed, then ripping off a loud fart, added, "Taco Bell!" The smell was truly noxious. Skyfisher tensed, hoping that this was not the prelude to some communal purification rite. Astounded by the wagon's speed, he dared to glance outside the transparent sheet at the landscape rushing by, wincing in pain when a shaft of sunlight hit him full-face.

The big man glanced at him and said, "Your eyes hurt; anybody can see that. 'Cept you!" Big laugh. "Try these," he said, handing Skyfisher what appeared to be two black circles joined together, with thin arm-wings on either side of them.

When Skyfisher did nothing, the big man, keeping one hand on the wheel opened the arm-wings with his other hand and placed the circles in front of his own eyes, balancing their joining-place on his nose, resting the arm-wings on his ears. Then he handed the circles to Skyfisher and beckoned him to do the same. Following the lead of the big man, Skyfisher rested the circles on his nose and gingerly opened his eyes to glimpse a darker world. The sun hammered, but the dark circles dampened the blows. He was grateful to the fat man and put his hand to his heart in a gesture of thanks, bowing his head slightly.

"You is something else, Bo."

Unable to bear the throbbing pain, Skyfisher again pulled the hood up over his face and sat motionless, as if asleep. After about ten minutes of seeing his passenger immobile, the driver leaned over and grabbed Skyfisher's sack with his right hand. Keeping one eye on the road, he rummaged inside the sack, found a leather folding pouch and glanced inside at a card with a picture on it.

"Sal-va-dor." He read further, "Kingston, New York. Long way from home, Bo. We gonna run you into town. This oughtta cover the gas," he said, pulling out a crisp green paper from the leather pouch. Before he could pocket it, the passenger, his face still hooded, shot his hand out with surprising speed and grabbed the paper. The carriage swerved and the wallet went flying. Skyfisher's other hand caught it mid-air and calmly put it and the green paper back in the sack.

"Sweet Jesus," said the big man, looking at the hood for the hint of a peep hole, "how the fuck did you do that?" He reached into his jacket pocket, comforted by the touch of something metallic.

"What the hell am I gonna do with you?"

Chapter Ten

"*White Apple Village,*" Falling Star whispered the name to Tell Me A Story just before they'd taken him.

She'd gathered what supplies she could - dried meat, skins, knife, a bow, a few arrows; the forest would provide the rest. No time to find Grey Turtle, the Bald One. They needed to leave Flour Village quickly and reach the creek which ran west, emptying into the big river.

They left the hut in the middle of the night when a quarter moon hung low in the sky. Tell Me A Story took the lead, skirting the open field, avoiding a few smouldering campfires.

They passed the sacred mound and Lewis had the impulse to climb it again, as though he could find something he lost there, some clue as to why he was here. A dog barked. They stopped in their tracks, waited ten heartbeats, slowly resumed walking. Every few steps, Tell Me A Story would pick up a twig lying in their path, lest Lewis step on it. So far, so good.

Lewis's new way of sight-sensing had given him something akin to night vision. Sticks, logs, dead leaves - life forms in some phase of decay, appeared on his radar as brown shapes with a low-intensity glow, organic Colorform stickers pasted flat on a landscape. Anything alive - trees, plants, insects, animals, had a 3D vibrancy which at first overwhelmed him until he began to become familiar with their shifting patterns. Animals seemed to change colors with their level of anxiety. Birds just going about their business were mostly shades of blue, morphing to orange-reds when they became excited. Easy to mistake a cardinal for a bluejay.

For the moment, the woods were calm. Pulsing crickets, the calls of a pair of owls. They reached the boundary of the village, and helped by the light of a rising moon, continued on through the night, pausing to rest briefly, but not sleep.

To Lewis, the woods seemed formidable and dense, a virgin forest. He didn't understand why they were leaving the village so quickly or where they were headed. Some kind of danger; that was clear enough.

Tell Me A Story kept up a blistering pace. Although the body Lewis inhabited was in better shape than the one he'd left behind, he had to stay vigilant to avoid walking into branches or tripping over rocks and fallen limbs, like being the central character in a relentless video game. After two hours, he was exhausted from the mental and physical exertion. He called out to Tell Me A Story, who slowed a bit, but refused to stop.

The creek trail was a foolproof route to the big river, well known to travellers, which would include anyone from Flour Village sent in pursuit. Tell Me A Story did not doubt they would be pursued, having left without permission. The Lesser Sun had asked Skyfisher's advice, an honor and an insult to be so flagrantly disobeyed.

Lewis heard the creek well before reaching it, as the first signs of dawn flecked the horizon. They followed its course west as the light brought hints of color to the forest, revealing a palette that Lewis had never experienced before. Day-Glo oranges blended with turquoise and purple hues. He was spirit-walking in an impressionist painting which pulsed and transfigured. An oak tree was greenish blue, the leaves of a nearby birch blood-red, as if in the throes of autumn. Hard to tell if the color changes were random, or if he was tuning into some kind of life force orchestrated by the sun.

His stomach growling, Lewis kept up, trusting this woman who had appeared like a spirit guide in his waking dream. They walked silently, witnessing the forest coming to life. Morning birds fluttered and called in the canopy. Squirrels scampered up trees. At mid-morning, Tell Me A Story lost an arrow in a thicket, trying to bring down a hare.

They stopped at the foot of a large oak. Laying a deerskin on the ground, they covered themselves with a second skin and lay close to each other for warmth, not daring to light a fire in case they were being pursued.

"Nanole."

Tell Me A Story spoke the word for sleep and Lewis embraced it.

A group of men were sitting around a council fire. Indians, dressed in ceremonial garb, passing pipes. Falling Star was among them, wearing a leather helmet and bands on both wrists.

"I have opened you," he said. Each of the men spoke their names in turn, their faces imprinting on Lewis's memory: Falling Star, Marsh Fox, Grey Turtle, Lightning, Black Hawk, Wind on Water, Rattle Spirit, Rough One, Twisted Foot. Lewis tried to speak to Falling Star, but he was gone.

Chapter Eleven

Having fallen down the rabbit hole into Frontier Land, Lewis expected to wake up raving in a psyche ward with a needle in his arm and a bandage on his head. No time to feel sorry for himself or think rationally about his situation. Best he could come up with was the ridiculous assumption he had travelled back in time. However implausible, it fit the facts. True, this could be some extremely well-financed version of Fantasy Island; these folks all consummate actors. That would not explain his blindness and newly-honed senses, or the subtle odors, the hand-hewn lodges, the worn out buckskin jerkins, the smoked fish hanging to dry on nets, the thousand gritty, organic details that could only come from life, not scenic design. No sound of electricity, no motors, cars, airplanes, no english. A lunar landing could have been simulated at a warehouse in Roswell, but not this.

He recalled hearing someone in the smoke-filled room saying "Franzay", which sounded like Francais - the French. But that was not the language these folks were speaking. He would have to learn it and find out why and how this had happened to him. He would follow this woman who knew him somehow. Their love making had been real enough.

Why had they left the village? Falling Star had been able to speak to him without words, conveying an intuitive trust.

Lewis had never encountered anyone like him and lord knows, he'd never met anyone remotely like Tell Me A Story. Waking up next to her might just be worth falling down the rabbit hole.

Images from last night's dream washed over him. A circle of men speaking their names, dissolving into the sounds of a creek and the calls of birds and insects. Can you fall asleep and dream inside a dream? He was surely awake now. This was all palpable, real. He could smell the moist soil and touch it. In his sensory array, Tell Me A Story gleamed like a translucent icon.

"Utchimok." Hungry.

She spoke the words for deer, bear, wolf, bird, rabbit and fish, each animal accompanied by a graphic mime. Her imitation of a lumbering, sniffing bear had Lewis demanding an encore.

He said, "You, me, run?" Dumbfounded look, with fingers jogging down her leg.

"Warrior come," she responded in her language,

Fierce look, fist punching hand, finger-walk up his leg. Again she spoke in her own tongue.

"You and me."

Pointing, look of despair, one hand grabbing her walking fingers. *"Captured!"*

Finger sliding across her neck with a throat-slit sound that needed no translation. He wanted to ask why, but no amount of finger walking could do justice to that. Her anxiety and the impulse to get moving was self-evident. More hand gestures.

"Talk later."

The forest would protect and provide, as it always does to those who know its stories.

She began to make an arrow to replace the one lost, carving the point from a shaft of cane. A gesture for Lewis to pick up his spear and practice his aim. Skyfisher had been deadly accurate with a spear. Perhaps Lewis could pick up the skill with a little prompting. Tell Me A Story pointed towards the creek, enjoining him to be worthy of her husband's name. He waded in barefoot, and after failing several times to spear a fish the way *he* would have done it, Lewis stopped and felt a shiver descend his spine, the same frisson Falling Star had tapped into when he'd touched Lewis's head. Then something new, a visceral memory, his host body reminding him what it could do.

The cold stream numbed his legs. Spear in hand, moving slowly against the current of the creek, he found rather than trying to sense-glimpse a fish, he needed to listen. Unidentified arpeggios noodled across the surface. Insects? A deeper vibration blossomed, disappeared, and subtly hummed. A fish? He was quite still now. Silent, vigilant, tuning into the vibrancy of another life form, avoiding the distractions of shadows and light reflecting off the the water.

Lewis's attention reached beneath the water's surface and found a heartbeat, a rhythmic cycle of breath, and several twangs of muscle flicks which impelled the fish against the current. He and a brother creature were alive, sharing the One Breath. To survive, Lewis must take its life force. On his second throw, he speared a good size bass and brought it to Tell Me A Story with a feeling of triumph.

"*Thank fish?*" she asked, sounding to Lewis like a mother asking a child if he'd washed his hands.

They ate in silence, Lewis watching Tell Me A Story eat each morsel with reverence, while he felt a bit guilty about being at the top of the food chain. Wasn't the bass itself a merciless forager of smaller fish and insects? What made us any different from wolves, eagles or any predator that fed on whatever it wanted to with impunity? Somehow, we humans weren't satisfied with just sustenance. Lewis's whole generation had been famously dissatisfied, hungry for more than its daily bread. A way of life that made sense. He too had been searching, not knowing what he was looking for. Maybe it had finally found him.

Certainly the mosquitos had. At dawn and sunset a relentless onslaught of skeeters, chiggers, black flies and other stinging delights pursued Lewis with a vengeance. To make matters worse, they didn't appear to bother Tell Me A Story.

Something else seemed on the verge of finding them as well, a noise in the distance, a voice, barely audible above the hiss of the creek. He gestured to Tell Me A Story. She had heard it too, was already strapping her bow to the basket she carried on her back and handing Lewis his pack. She spread loose tree litter over where they had lain, and quick as a cat was scampering up a tree, pointing to a nearby tree for Lewis to do the same.

Chapter Twelve

Lewis managed to ascend about fifteen feet, high enough to be out of the perception of someone focusing on the trail. Dogs were another matter. A wiry mutt scouting ahead of its master was sniffing excitedly, tail wagging, circling first Tell Me A Story's tree, then Lewis's. Three barks, loud and clear. Tell Me A Story climbed into the upper branches of her tree, an old hickory. Lewis's oak didn't offer as much leaf cover, but he managed to edge a few feet higher.

From her perch, Tell Me A Story could just make out a party of three men coming down the trail from the direction she and Lewis had been heading. Laughing, talking in the easy manner of old friends. A young warrior in breech cloth and moccasins, with a hedge of hair down the middle of his scalp, was accompanied by two older men wearing leather jerkins and leggings. Between them they dragged a narrow sled piled with goods and supplies. They stopped to congratulate the dog, thinking it had treed a squirrel. One of the older men looked up and noticed Lewis. He alerted his companions while prudently backing away behind a tree for cover. The dog barked with renewed vigor. After a few moments, the man attempted to quiet the dog and called out to Lewis in a friendly tone. One of his companions cautiously circled around Lewis's tree to see if he was carrying weapons or had any accomplices. He did not see Tell Me A Story.

She figured them for a trading party from a neighboring village, perhaps bringing goods from the Fran-zay. They seemed harmless enough. What would they make of a blind, speechless man in a tree?

Tell Me A Story still had no real idea what Skyfisher and Falling Star were up to. The Society of Light and its secret mission made little sense. This man wore her husband's body like a robe. Why should she risk her life for some ghost? If they took him, she could head back to the village, claiming Skyfisher forced her to leave against her will. Few would believe that story, and there would still be the likes of High Eagle to contend with, not to mention her conscience. The ghost man might be the only means she would ever have of seeing her husband again. Sitting in this unlikely perch at the top of a tree, Tell Me A Story had to admit she responded eagerly to his lovemaking, something Skyfisher had abstained from for the sake of his mission. The visitor had a lightness and a sense of humor that was like a ray of sunshine after months of austerity. He seemed to accept blindness without complaint, not that he was able to express it in words, but attitude needed no translation. It was his readiness to adapt with grace and a touch of something child-like that she found attractive. She would not abandon him, but neither would she come down from the tree.

The dog was excited to see his prey descending. Leaving his sack in the upper branches, Lewis reached the ground and raised his hands. His palms faced a squat, sturdily built man who was catching his breath from pulling the sled. He had the odor of someone who had not washed for a week or two. The man asked a question in a voice without malice. Lewis pointed to his mouth, shaking his head, hoping the man would understand this gesture. The trader laughed. Two men came up from behind Lewis, one with a vibrancy and scent like the first, but a bit more wiry. The other was taller and seemed to have more vitality. Younger. They addressed Lewis with the same result. One of them tried a few words in what sounded vaguely like French.

Lewis exaggerated his blindness, stumbling over a tree limb. Maybe they'd think he'd wandered and lost his way. The trio talked amongst themselves animatedly. From her perch, Tell Me A Story saw the young warrior head off to scout further down the creek trail, probably checking to see if there were other members of the blind man's party. So far, neither men nor dog had noticed her. Lewis took pains not to turn his head upwards, just in case.

The two older men again tried to communicate with him, and when he did not respond, one of them checked Lewis for weapons, then placed a hand on his shoulder and led him to a clearing nearby, coaxing him into a sitting position up against a tree. In short order they had a fire going and the smell of cooked meat was in the air, sorely tempting Tell Me A Story to come down and join the feast. The traders placed some food in Lewis' hand, encouraging him to eat. It tasted like rabbit, somewhat chewy, but he welcomed the flavor of cooked meat and ate with gusto. The two men shook their heads, laughing loudly. One of them held up his hand, holding the meat. Lewis, in an unguarded moment, *saw* the offering as a glowing morsel and took it. He realized his mistake too late, suddenly sensing the tension and wariness in the man who had offered the meat to a blind person. The banter dissolved into an atmosphere of suspicion.

The traders whispered to each other and one of them stood up and forced Lewis to put his hands behind his back, tying them together with a leather strap. The other man spoke sharply, reached for a burning stick and waved it near Lewis's face. Sensing it coming, Lewis managed not to flinch. The stocky trader took a knife from his sheath and brought it to Lewis's face. He spoke in a low, gravely voice, moving the knife point across Lewis's cheek, leaving a line of blood. Then the trader lifted the knife point in front of Lewis's left eye. Lewis could sense the blade clearly on the video screen inside his head, wondering if he would be completely blind if the man, with a flick of his knife, removed the eyeball from its socket. The man pulled the knife back slowly and then with a rapid thrust, brought it forward, stopping a hair's breath in front of the eye. Miraculously, Lewis did not budge. The man grunted and pulled the knife back for another parry.

"Go ahead," Lewis blurted. "This is a dream. You're not real!"

"Ah!" exclaimed the trader. "Anglais!" He nodded, slowly twisting the blade in front of Lewis's face.

A whooshing sound, a thunk, and a spear point protruded from the trader's neck. He gagged, spewing blood from his mouth, drops splashing on Lewis's cheek. The man leaned forward, still grasping his knife. A few crows raised an alarm and flew from the branches they'd been roosting on.

Lewis was stunned, his head whiplashed back, reeling. One more freakish moment in this hallucination. The smell and feel of the blood was real enough. The astonishment of the others hit him like a shock wave. The trader was keeling over, a spear pinioned to the back of his neck, gouts of neon blood pooling where he lay. Amazing that Tell Me A Story had the chutzpah to take on two men. What a throw from a treetop!

He was mistaken. Heading up the trail as casually as if strolling along a country lane, was the shimmering outline of a giant. Unless Lewis' radar vision was playing tricks, the man appeared to be at least seven feet tall and built like a halfback. He carried a wooden shaft curved at the end like a hook. In the curve of the hook rested what was either a thin spear or a long arrow. Without breaking his stride, the big man hefted the weapon to his shoulder. He took aim at the second trader who was staring at his partner, impaled by the same sort of projectile. As the trader turned to run, the giant whipped the hooked shaft in a downward arc, slinging the projectile with tremendous force. It entered the small of the man's back and emerged at this belly. While the trader screamed in agony, Lewis, hands still tied behind his back, rolled to his knees, stood up and began running down the trail as fast as he could, the giant striding after him like a juggernaut. The dog barked furiously, snarling and baring his teeth at the big man, attempting to bite his leg. He dealt it a savage kick that sent the dog flying.

Skyfisher's body was lighter and faster than his pursuer. Lewis figured he could outrun him, as long as he could stay out of the flight path of that monster sling-thrower. He fairly flew down a long slope, jumped a fallen tree like a rabbit, sprinting flat out when he hit the bottom of the hill, rounded the trunk of a large tree, and slammed full force into another man, sending them both sprawling to the ground.

High Eagle, momentarily stunned, twisted as he fell backward, breaking the fall with his arms. Lewis, hands still tied behind his back, careened over High Eagle, sliding onto his face and stomach. Staggering, he tried to get to his feet. High Eagle grabbed him by the ankle. The giant lumbered down the trail and hovered over them.

"*We have caught a big fish,*" High Eagle said.

The big man nodded. They tied Lewis to a tree, hand and foot, and walked out of earshot.

"*His woman will not be far off,*" said High Eagle.

"*Ask him,*" said the other.

"*If we drop coals on his body, he would not talk,*" High Eagle said. "*But he will break his vow of silence when he comes before the Lesser Sun.*"

They walked back to where Lewis stood, tied to the tree.

"*This one is running in the woods,*" High Eagle said speculatively. "*He slips and falls.*"

The big man stepped closer and delivered a quick punch to the left side of Lewis' chest. There was a cracking noise and he doubled over in pain.

"*Enough,*" High Eagle said.

Chapter Thirteen

Tell Me A Story descended from her tree and approached the bodies. She had seen men die before, but not like this, pierced by atlatl darts. One of the traders stirred and moaned on the ground, clutching his stomach. It would be an act of mercy to kill him, but a slice across his throat would draw attention to her presence. No sign of the third man, the young warrior.

Following the slope in the direction the big man had gone, she could hear a conversation in the distance. Moving a bit closer, she recognised the voice of High Eagle. His companion got to his feet and from her vantage point, she could make out the outline of his head and shoulders. Judging by his size, it could only be the one they called Little Rock.

His history was widely known. As a boy Little Rock had killed a man in the rough and tumble game of stick ball, ultimately became something of a legend as a relentless warrior. He hated his name, a joke given his size, tolerating it only from those he was close to. Everybody else had to call him Buffalo, a creature whose size and strength matched his self image. Whatever the name, he was unstoppable, yet she had to live a story that would stop both him and the man who had nearly raped her. The thought of High Eagle filled her with disgust. There had to be a way to clip his wings.

Skyfisher was tied to a tree. Nothing to be done for him at the moment, not against those two. They would take him as a trophy back to the village to face the Lesser Sun. First, they would try to find her.

She would become her name, remembering walks in the woods with her brother and father, who gave them gifts wrapped in stories. The squirrel that escaped its enemies by scampering up trees, the leaf insect that was a master of disguise. It looked exactly like the bush or tree on which it rested and could stay motionless for hours. Her brother had always complained the stories were about running and hiding. He wanted to hear about standing and fighting.

"There is a time to stand and fight," her father had said, *"and a time to run and hide."*

Now she must be the leaf insect, which meant getting utterly filthy, the first requirement for being disguised in the woods. Moist dirt smeared on face and limbs, handfuls of dead leaves kneaded into hair. She rolled in a puddle, rubbing her back in the mud, like a wild boar taking a bath.

Spreading debris to cover her tracks, Tell Me A Story ran light-footed, searching for a tree whose trunk most closely matched the color of the drying mud on her body. She found one with branches low enough to climb, high enough to hide in, and placed two fist-sized stones next to its base. A plan was forming in her mind, but it was dangerous.

Shouldering her sack, Tell Me A Story began to climb, thankful she was still strong and agile, not soft like some of the village girls. More than halfway up the tree she found a limb that could support her weight, tied her sack to the tree, covered her entire body with leafy branches, and made her herself as comfortable as possible.

She waited. The limb was hard and she couldn't help shifting her weight whenever the pain in her back and legs became unbearable. Birds settled in the tree. A good thing, it would offset suspicious eyes. One landed right next to her, flying away as soon as she stirred, something she must not do if anyone came near.

She heard the snap of a twig being stepped on, followed by footfalls and leaf rustling. The footsteps came closer. Tell Me A Story held her breath. A movement on the ground below. A glimpse of a man's face looking right at her.

It was not Little Rock, High Eagle, nor anyone she recognised from her village. After a moment, he moved on. Either he had not seen her or was choosing to behave as if he hadn't. Perhaps this was the young warrior who had left to scout when the trading party had first spotted Skyfisher. It complicated things, but there was nothing to be done.

Tell Me A Story forced herself to take her mind off the pain in her back and go over all the possibilities as carefully as when her father planned a raid. He considered every option and its consequences, every detail, as though he were drawing a picture in his mind. The terrain, the time of day or night. The light, the wind, the season, the foliage, everything. She followed the story path, coming up with several possibilities, rejecting every one of them as too risky. Yet there was no way out of this without taking risks.

She had never killed anyone. As foul as High Eagle was, Tell Me A Story did not want his maggoty spirit invading her dreams, nor the stigma that would come with murdering a member of her clan. The prospect of killing Little Rock was so incongruous she smiled in derision at the thought.

Her course of action would depend upon how they positioned themselves in their campsite tonight. Would they both be asleep, standing watch, in the open? Tell Me A Story considered what could go wrong and what would need to be done when things *did* go wrong. After reviewing all her options, she looped a leather thong under her arms and around her chest, tied the other end to an upper branch, closed her eyes and tried to rest. Exhausted and filthy, she was stiff with cold and pain. The limb was as hard as stone.

How much worse it must be for Skyfisher, lashed to a tree. Perhaps the ghost man inside did not share the pain of his body, but that seemed unlikely. He knew pleasure, so he must also know pain.

Tell Me A Story had seen Little Rock approach Skyfisher and heard the crack of his body blow. A whirlpool of anger and fear enveloped her, along with a voice that counselled, *sleep while you can.*

In a dream, she was a hummingbird hovering over the Sacred Hill. An open grave. Surrounding it was a group of men, Falling Star and the Bald One among them. They were lowering Skyfisher into the ground, wrapped in ceremonial robes, covered head to foot with powdered red ochre. Skyfisher's skin split open like the shell of a locust, parting from the top of his head right down the middle of his face and chest. The body of another man was nested within, covered with a milky sap. He opened his eyes and called to her in a language she did not understand.

With a start, Tell Me A Story awoke, leaning precariously to one side of the limb, the thong tied around her body checking her fall. It was dark, her muscles cramped and stiff, her skin itchy and swollen. The sounds of crickets filtered through the woods. Untying the leather strap, she stowed her sack, rubbed her arms and legs and slowly descended the tree. The sky was clear, the foliage so thick the moon and stars were not visible. As her eyes grew more accustomed to the dark, she felt around the base of the tree for the two rocks positioned there earlier, pointing in the direction of the place where they had tied Skyfisher. Hopefully they had not moved their camp.

Tell Me A Story slung her bow and took several arrows. A knife was secured in a sheath tied to her waist. She removed a medicine bag and a length of rope from her sack, leaving the sack at the foot of the tree.

With the medicine bag tied to her waist belt and the rope looped over her shoulder, she set off, testing the ground with each foot before committing her weight to a step. The warrior mouse.

She tried to keep her body oriented in the same direction even when skirting bushes and trees, not obeying the impulse to move quickly when the terrain opened a bit, trusting she was still headed towards the camp. Off to the right and further down a slope, a glow in the distance.

Tell Me A Story approached warily, stopping and listening every few steps, feeling a pulse beat pounding in her ears. Crouching low, she moved from tree to tree towards the crackle of fire and the tips of flames rising above the surrounding brush. Just a bit closer.

A stick hidden under a bed of leaves yielded to her weight, its snap sounding like a rifle shot. She froze; no one in the camp stirred. Either they were asleep or the crack had been masked by the sputtering campfire.

After a while, Little Rock rose to his feet, prodded the fire with a stick, added a log, then sat down again, leaning against a stump. On the other side of the fire, Skyfisher stood tied to a tree, his head bowed. On the ground next to him slept High Eagle. Tell Me A Story memorized their positions and slowly backed away.

It had to be done quickly. She went over the escape route, looking for the best locations to set a few surprises, far enough from their fire to avoid anyone hearing her preparation.

A short distance from the campsite was the ideal sapling; tall, bendable, but thick enough to spring back with force. There was time to strip the upper branches, but not enough time to craft a trigger from a notched stick pounded into the ground. Too noisy.

Something rooted in the ground would have to do, but nothing was within the reach of the young tree. Further away, she found another sapling with a sturdy root nearby, and quietly carved a v-notch in the root, facing away from the tree.

She tied a small fixed loop near one end of the rope, adding a large slip-knot loop a few feet away at the end. The other end of the rope was tied to the top of the sapling. Bending it over, she attaching the small loop to the tip of the v-notch. The larger noose-loop was laid on the ground, with one end of the noose resting hands-length above the ground on a forked stick. In the dark, anyone who stepped, or better still, ran into the noose, would tug the small loop out of the notch. The straightening tree would tighten the noose and whiplash the runner off his feet. Probably hold for only a few moments. All the time she would need. Her medicine bag now hung on a branch next to where the trap was laid.

With the rest of the rope, Tell Me A Story set to work on a second snare further down the trail, noting a nearby boulder that marked the spot. No room for mistakes. If she lived, this would be a story worth telling.

She paced through the escape route like a dance, hoping to remember where to side-step the first snare and jump over the second.

A deep breath, a prayer for strength and back to the campsite.

The moon was peeking through the tree tops. Nearing the glow of the fire, she forced herself to slow down. Tremors of excitement and fear.

Tell Me A Story slid into a position behind a bush where she could see the camp more clearly. High Eagle was now sitting watch while Little Rock slept.

She moved closer to check on the line of sight between the two men. If she was seen before reaching Little Rock, things would go badly.

Skyfisher was still tied standing, his back against the tree. Stifling an impulse to run away, Tell Me A Story focused on the ground, checking for the best entry and exit points, looking for anything, a branch, a rock, that might stall her flight. She circled towards her exit point, leaving her bow and arrow, then returned to the entry point, lying down and crawling forward towards the fire, making slow progress. The mud camouflage helped mask her in the firelight. Moving forward bit by bit until she dared go no further, she heard Little Rock's heavy breathing and soft moans, as if dreaming. He began to snore, quietly at first, then with vigor. Tell Me A Story timed her movements to the rhythm of his snoring, inching closer to where the big man lay. She could see his feet now clearly in front of her, the bulk of his body blocking her from High Eagle's sight. At least she hoped it did.

Suddenly, Little Rock stirred, turned over on his stomach, belched loudly and then drifted back into sleep. Tell Me A Story, rigid with tension and ready to bolt, forced herself to stay calm, then realised her good fortune. Turning over, Little Rock the Buffalo had exposed the fleshy sinew of his leg. Now or never.

Tell Me A Story curled into a ball on her side, rolled to her knees, and rose swiftly. Crouching above Little Rock, she pulled her knife from its sheath and sliced it deeply across the back of his leg just above the knee. He roared in anger. Tell Me A Story sprang back as he slapped his leg as if swatting an insect. She bolted, but High Eagle had seen her and leapt in pursuit.

Exultant and terrified, she grabbed the bow and arrows at the edge of the camp, the deer running for its life, looking for the medicine bag. Where was it? Had she taken a different path? There was the boulder. Tell Me A Story stopped, trembling, notched an arrow, and waited. For High Eagle to choose the right path he had to see her. She lingered longer than a deer would have. High Eagle was coming on fast, crashing through the brush. Tell Me A Story dropped to the ground. As soon as he came into view, she sprang to her feet and began to run again. High Eagle picked up the pace, ran past the boulder, stepped into the noose and was swept off his feet.

She turned and moved towards him with her bow drawn. High Eagle's right foot was dangling in the air, his body and arms flailing wildly. He was furious, cursing himself and Tell Me A Story.

"Drop your knife on the ground or I will shoot you," she said, confident that she could not miss him from a body length's distance. He reached for the knife cradled in the sheath at his waist.

"Toss it to the side," she said. High Eagle grasped the knife and made as if to toss it, then quickly bent his arm for a throw. Tell Me A Story loosed the arrow, piercing High Eagle's thigh. The knife throw went wild.

She groped for it in the bushes; couldn't find the blade in the dark. Notching another arrow, she walked around High Eagle to see if he had any other weapons, careful to stay out of his reach. He was clenching his leg in pain.

At that moment a roar came from the direction of the campsite, followed by a series of thrashing noises. With a gleam of triumph in her eyes, she ran back to find a wounded Buffalo, lying on his back, his good leg hanging several feet in the air, caught in the first noose, the blood on his other leg glinting in the light of a rising moon. His body, much heavier than High Eagle's, had bent the sapling to the ground, his arms scrabbling, looking for hand holds, branches, something to throw. He was pulling at the noose, madly whipping his body from side to side. With his tremendous strength, the noose would not hold for long. She approached with the second arrow notched, but her shot went wide of its mark by a hand's length as he thrashed his body from side to side.

Tell Me A Story cursed herself, notched her last arrow, stepping closer. Too close. Little Rock flung a handful of dirt and small stones at her face, momentarily blinding her. He reached for his staff, lying next to him on the ground, threw it hard at her bow, snapping its string and sending it flying.

Little Rock began to sing in a high, keening voice, as a warrior does when preparing for battle.

This was not her battleground, not against a wounded monster.

She regretted the bow, but would keep to her story. Stumbling, rubbing her eyes, she circled around Little Rock and headed back to their camp, knowing there was precious little time.

The campfire was glowing. Her husband was still tied to the tree but his head was up and alert. Tell Me A Story ran to him, removed her knife from its sheath and began to cut the bonds at his neck, hands and feet. He crumpled to the ground, his arms and legs cramped and useless, his chest on fire where Little Rock had hit him.

She kissed him between the eyes. He knew the word for *run* and she spoke it now and began rubbing his legs to help restore circulation. Lewis could barely walk. Tell Me A Story spoke High Eagle's name and mimed his being caught in her snare. Lewis shook his head, not comprehending.

"*High Eagle!*" Grabbing Lewis's ankle, she wrapped an end of the rawhide he had been tied with and handed him the rawhide and mimed tying his hands behind his back, again saying High Eagle's name and pointing in the direction she had come from. Lewis nodded. She tried to help him to his feet.

"*Run!*"

Lewis's legs simply would not carry him. Coaxing her husband to his knees and shouldering him to his feet, Tell Me A Story pushed him towards the bushes, slapping his behind like a horse's rump. There was something almost comical about the sight of him trying to move in short, stumbling bursts. She would have laughed had their lives not been in such danger. In the meantime, she kicked at him. Anything to get him moving.

"*Run!*"

Buffalo had freed himself from the snare and was coming closer, singing. Lewis reached a clump of bushes and turned back to her. She grabbed a stick and threw it at him.

"*Run!!*"

He limped into the bushes out of sight. Tell Me A Story hoped he would get to High Eagle, binding him before he too freed himself from the snare. Wounded with an arrow, he was likely to still be upended. She strode towards the campfire and waited. Little Rock's voice rang out in song.

"*Tell Me A Story!*"

He came on, lumbering through the brush, bursting into the clearing of the campsite, leaning on his atlatl staff, eyes blazing like demons dancing in the campfire light. His leg wound pulsed blood at every step. She took hold of the end of a stick on the edge of the fire and waved its burning end as if to ward him off. He came on.

"*That's good!*"

Little Rock took a burning stick from the fire as well, waving it until the flame turned to a red glow. He brought it to his wounded leg, heard its flesh sizzle. His head arched back screaming, the howl transmuting to a wild, manic laughter.

She threw her stick at him. He swatted it away with his staff and lunged for her.

She turned and ran. Not too quickly. He had to be stopped now, while he was wounded and battle-crazed. At the very least, she'd lure him away from her husband.

The moon had risen and by its light she could see and been seen.

Tell Me A Story reached the meadow. Feigning exhaustion, she stopped, breathing hard, giving him time to catch up. Leaning on his staff and singing, Little Rock came on like a slow rolling ocean wave. She headed across the open meadow, looking for the edge of the woods, searching for the story that would save her and Skyfisher.

She fell, scrabbled on the ground as if looking for something she had dropped, frantic, confused. Easy prey. Behind her, Buffalo's high-pitched voice singing a litany of all the things he would do to her. A lunatic tantrum from Little Rock in the body of a man.

She stood up, and in her effort to put on a good show of fright, tripped over a thorn vine, a snare from the Great Mother, pitching forward to the ground. Wrong story.

As she rose to her feet again, Tell Me A Story heard a *whoop!* and caught sight of figure running across the meadow full bore, heading right towards Buffalo. The young warrior who had seen her hiding in the tree.

Shouting a battle cry and raising his hatchet in the air, he charged like a war chief. A beautiful sight, fierce and glistening, a moonlit falcon descending on its prey. But falcons don't take on buffalo.

"Throw the axe!" she shouted.

Caught up in the frenzy of his charge, he did not hear. Little Rock saw him coming, kept singing, slowing his pace slightly, now that Tell Me A Story had stopped to watch. She willed the warrior to throw his weapon. He did not. Running hard, yellow hatchet held high, he meant to bring it down on the big man's skull.

As his assailant neared, Little Rock dropped his staff, stepped to his left and reached up with his right hand, stopping the hatchet handle mid-swing, as if the warrior had tried to chop a tree limb and had been grabbed by the tree. The young warrior lost his footing as well as his weapon, and slammed to the ground on his back. Little Rock tossed the hatchet aside and shouted.

"You should have thrown it!"

Looking at Tell Me A Story, Buffalo took hold of the warrior's wrist and upper arm, twisted it. Kneeling, he brought the young man's arm down on his thigh, snapping the arm in two as if it were a twig.

"For you," Buffalo shouted to her.

The warrior screamed. Buffalo took hold of him with one hand at his neck, the other at his crotch, lifted him high above his head facing the sky and jerked the body down on his massive shoulders in one swift, savage gesture. Then he tossed him aside like a broken doll and came for Tell Me A Story, singing.

Chapter Fourteen

"Why are you here?"

The gentleman posing this question sported a black suit, grey shirt, bolo tie with a small turquoise clasp and dark glasses. Tall, lean, with angular features and long straight black hair pulled back in a ponytail. A relaxed voice that carried the barest hint of a threat. A voice used to command.

Behind him, a map of greater Natchez, Mississippi, with multi-colored flags pinning various locations. Surrounding the map, an entire wall of butterflies and moths, each labeled. Blue Morphos from Brazil, Canadian Buckeyes flecked with orange and purple, a pale green Luna Moth from Ohio, hundreds of others, festooned like shards of a rainbow. The gentleman's name was a mystery to Jean-Baptiste, who only knew him as The Man. Under his scrutiny, JB was already doubting the wisdom of bringing the weird hitchhiker to be inspected like a new kind of butterfly.

"This is something special boss. You got to see this guy."

"You brought someone. Here?" The Man interrupted, each word an accusation. He was sitting behind a glass top desk. Two of his bodyguards stood by, dressed formally in suits and ties, muscular versions of their employer.

The room was light enough to keep several large potted palms growing. A liquor cabinet, three desks with Apple computers, phones and desktop debris. A row of shelves held a collection of binders. In front of the shelves was a comfortable looking couch of a reddish color Jean-Baptiste could not name. His wife was the artist; she knew the names of colors. He'd done some auto body work for The Man, patched up a few dings with no questions asked, but these days he was pretty much an errand boy. Did what he was told to do. One of the things he had been told *not* to do was bring someone here unannounced.

"You got to see this Bo'. He is something."

"No, I don't have to see him," The Man replied with the ghost of a smile. "Because you've been useful up to now I'm going to overlook this transgression." He paused, then asked, "You know what 'transgression' means?" One of the bodyguards sniggered.

"It means," the Man continued, "that you made a mistake. You fucked up, Jean-Baptiste. You understand *that*."

"Yes, but.."

"No buts. You show your Special 'Bo to Davey. He'll report to me. That's it."

Jean-Baptiste shook his head like a bobble head doll and turned to leave. The Man was not finished.

"One more thing," he said. "Another mistake and you're through. Got that?"

"Yes," Jean-Baptiste said miserably, escorted to an adjacent office by one of the bodyguards. Davey stayed behind.

"Check them for wires?"

"I did," Davey said.

The Man whispered something and Davey left the room.

It had been warm outdoors; inside the building was unnaturally cold. A bad medicine place. You could feel it in the air, like someone had died. The fat man in the fast moving wag-on-house brought Skyfisher here, left the room and returned in the company of another man, thinner, wary, emanating impatience and disdain. The fat one was sweating, even in this cold place. He laughed nervously, coughed and patted Skyfisher on the shoulder, the way you'd be to a dog you wanted to perform a trick. A trick for the angry man.

"Davey. You will not believe this," the fat man said. Skyfisher had the dark circles covering his eyes, his hooded garment was still on backwards. With a flourish, the fat man pulled the hood up over Skyfisher's face. Then he made as if to hit him with his fist, stopping just before impact, but the man under the hood did not budge.

"Uh-huh," said the one called Davey.

Telegraphing his next move, Jean-Baptiste slapped Skyfisher hard on the side of the face, knocking aside the hood. The dark circles clattered to the floor. Skyfisher squinted in the light, bent down and groped on the ground for them.

"Impressive, JB," Davey said. "Your man can take a punch. Anything else?"

Jean-Baptiste felt the room closing in on him. A drink, even water, was what he needed. He flashed on a cartoon he'd seen as a kid. Construction worker discovers a frog inside a block of concrete. Takes the frog out of the block and it begins tap-dancing like Fred Astaire, singing its brains out. The guy's amazed, dollar signs floating in front of his eyes. Gets the frog a tiny top hat, puts him on a doll-sized stage and invites friends, family, neighbors, newspaper reporters. Big day arrives and he proudly opens the curtain. *Ta-daah!* The frog sits there, let's out a single croak, nothing more. After everyone has jeered at him and left, the guy is alone with the frog, who starts singing and tap-dancing again, better than before.

Jean-Baptiste couldn't recall what the construction worker did next, let alone what *he* could do now. What would it take to get this guy to do his thing? He pulled the hitch-hiker's hood up again, reached for his sack, made a show of fishing for his wallet. Opening it, he took out a twenty, pulled its wings a couple of times , and slowly pocketed the bill. No reaction.

"That's great, JB. You're learning how to steal from - what is he, blind or something? Give me the money."

Davey took the twenty, put it back in the wallet and re-turned it to the sack along with the sunglasses. He regarded Jean-Baptiste and shook his head.

"You're gonna take your friend here, leave the premises and consider yourself lucky."

Jean-Baptiste let out a long breath.

"I don't know what you're trying to pull," Davey said, "and I don't want to know. I just hope The Man don't ask me, 'cause I haven't the slightest idea what the fuck I'm supposed to say to him. Just get your sorry ass out of here and be glad you are going in one piece. Take this joker with you."

Jean-Baptiste headed out the door into a bright sunny day, Skyfisher trailing behind, taking in the sudden melange of buildings, crowds, wagons, hard ground, unrelenting noise and undercurrent of fear. You could hear it in people's voices.

"Jesus, what a dumbass move," muttered Jean-Baptiste to no one in particular.

Skyfisher stopped, reached into his bag, took out the crumpled green paper from his leather folder and handed it to the fat man, pointing to the thing with the dark circles.

"Keep the sunglasses and your money," Jean-Baptiste said. "You frogged me, didn't you? Frogged me good, you little shit. I am not sorry I hit you."

Then he recalled what the construction worker had done. Sealed the frog back up in a concrete block.

"I should take you back where I found you, bury you in that big 'ol mound they got there. That's what I should do." A waste of gas and time.

"You got some major weird juju floating with you 'Bo and I'm done with it. Done."

Couldn't just leave him there on the sidewalk in front of The Man's HQ.

"This is what happens when you do somebody a favor. I oughtta get my head examined. Hah! That's what we gonna do. Get yo' head examined."

Jean-Baptiste led him across the street into a brick building. Smelled like the floors had just been waxed. He searched the directory and led Skyfisher up the stairway to an office on the second floor. The name on the door read *Dr. Eugenie Summers*. His wife's shrink, who she called a therapist. Waste of money. Whenever he brought this up, she'd say any woman crazy enough to marry him needed therapy.

They walked into the waiting room. A good looking dark haired, dark-eyed woman in her thirties sat behind a counter in the adjacent office. She glanced up from her paperwork .

"If isn't the Ragin' Cajun. What's up, Baptiste?"

"Hey Inez, how's your flag flyin'?"

"Just fine, Baptiste. You know, your wife's not due here until..." she leafed ahead in her appointment book, "two weeks from now."

"Yeah, but I was just bringing this 'Bo up to see the doc."

"Has he got an appointment?"

"Yeah, I guess. Ain't he in your book there?"

"What's his –. What's your name, sir?"

"He - uh," interjected Jean-Baptiste, "he don't talk much. Look, I - me gotta' fly. Busy. So, bye!"

He ducked out the door, leaving Inez shaking her head and gazing at the fiftyish oddly dressed man standing in her waiting room.

"Your name, date of birth? Habla espanol? Parlez francais?"

Skyfisher, glad the fat man had left, regarded this woman with curiosity. She seemed to be dressed in the same kind of clothing that men wore here. Something familiar about her.

There was music in this place, but no singers or instruments in sight. An older woman walked into the room, perhaps one of the musicians.

Skyfisher did not know the local language, but he was a song carrier. Quietly, he began to chant *Going to Water*, a good song to get rid of bad things. Strange to hear it in a voice that was not his.

Hone ah wae
Hone hone ah wae
Hone ah wae

"Is this my 4:30?"

Dr. Summers stood in the doorway, half-smiling. In her late forties, she had refused on principle to get a dye-job. Strands of grey threaded her wavy, reddish-brown hair. Reading glasses hung from a chain around her neck. She fiddled with them as the man in the waiting room continued his chanting.

"I've had patients laugh, cry, scream, throw-up, but I don't think anybody's ever sung to me before. A first. Inez honey, you alright?"

Inez was staring opened-mouthed at the patient.

"Jean-Baptiste just dropped him off, I…"

"Is he my 4:30?"

"No," Inez said, recovering. "Mrs. Montgomery is late, as usual. She hasn't called."

Dr. Summers eyed the patient. Middle aged, slightly bald, in need of a shave. Might be handsome behind those shades. Decent corduroys, running shoes. Didn't exactly fit the homeless profile, except for that backwards hoodie, which could be some sort of fashion statement. Looked like he'd recently been hit.

"Did you get his name? Does he have insurance?"

"Hasn't said a word except - sing."

"Well," sighed Dr. Summers, "we really can't have him singing here, can we, although I wouldn't mind him scaring off Mrs. Montgomery." She tapped her glasses chain. "It's the end of the day. What's protocol?"

"I'm not sure he understands English," Inez said.

"JB brought him in? I'll have a word with his wife. We could call the hospital. They'll get him in the system, send him over to the psyche ward in Whitfield, courtesy of the state of Mississippi. Seems harmless enough. I suppose he could just be escorted outside. Would you mind? If he does anything weird, we'll call emergency."

Inez nodded to the doctor, straightened her desk papers, slowly got to her feet and wavered. She'd recognized the song the patient was singing.

There was something unaffected about this man, his manner as relaxed and natural as if he were singing a lullaby, no hint of a performance. Not trying to impress. She was about to say something to Dr. Summers, but thought better of it.

"Alright," Inez said, "if you'll watch the phones, I'll take him down." Throughout this exchange, the man in the waiting room wearing the sunglasses had continued to chant softly, like some minstrel.

"Are you sure?" asked Dr. Summers. "We could call the police, but that seems a bit extreme, since he hasn't really done anything. Singing isn't against the law in Mississippi."

Except for protest songs in the sixties, Inez thought. She re-garded this character with curiosity. Looked like a rumpled professor after a weekend bender, yet he was singing one of the songs her grandmother used to sing to her in the language of her people, a language all but forgotten except for a few isolated Natchez. Completely incongruous, yet there he was. Some kind of prank? She went from behind her desk into the waiting room. He stopped singing as she approached.

"That's a nice song. Where did you learn it?"

He touched his fingers to his mouth, mimed speaking, and shook his head. She touched him lightly on the shoulder, ges-turing towards the door and accompanied him there, with a nod to Dr. Summers signifying everything was under control. As they headed down the stairway, Inez debated what to do next.

The office would close in twenty minutes. Send him on his way or take him to meet someone from her tribe? An elder, for sure. They'd know what to make of him. She took him across the street to the Natchez Coffee Company, paid for a cup and a muffin and spoke softly to the counter waitress who sported dreads, overalls and a somewhat pouty expression.

"Relative of mine. Doesn't speak English. Could you keep him tanked until I get off of work?"

No problem. Inez left a tip, sat the stranger down at a rear table, poured milk in his coffee and beckoned him to drink. He sipped, wrinkled his nose, took a bite of muffin.

"OK," Inez said. "I'm going to leave you here," pointing to the clock and showing five fingers. "I'll be back at five. Stay here," she said, touching the chair. He nodded as if he understood.

"Good!" she said, and with a flicker of a smile, he responded. "Good."

Chapter Fifteen

Davey was a detail man. Not one of those steroid football refugees. Malone, Jimmy, Nelson, the Man's other bodyguards, were all borderline goons. Davey had finesse, dressed well without calling attention to himself, and he was thorough. You wanted something capital d - Done, no loose ends, he was your man. The secret was following the maxim of the New York Yankees, *Assume Nothing*. Might take a little while, but he would get to the root of a problem like a goddam ferret. Guy he knew in Jersey had set him up working for The Man in the wasteland of Mississippi as a kind of internship.

"Get some experience. We bring you back up." Not, he hoped, as some greenhorn shit kicker from the south. He was biding his time, paying his dues.

The Man had him frisk JB and the guy with the glasses, asking Davey to keep an eye on this oddball, just to make sure he wasn't some kind of law. Didn't smell like a cop, but weirder things had happened. This was weird enough. Not every guy shows up in town and he's taken to meet The Man, boom, just like that.

Davey had glanced at the stranger's drivers license when he'd commandeered his wallet. Something didn't add up about Salvador Samuels from Kingston, NY. From a discreet distance, he'd observed JB take the stranger inside a professional building. Doctors, lawyers, accountants, that sort of thing. Shortly after, Baptiste departed the building alone, followed in a few minutes by Samuels, still wearing that sweatshirt backwards with the hood hanging in front like some kind of gecko. The kicker was his chaperone, that cute receptionist from the doctor's office. She dropped him off in a cafe across the street, and returned in short order to pick him again, walking arm in arm. Not exactly undercover cop procedure.

Davey recalled some rumors floating around about the receptionist, rumors he had discounted. There was a balance between perseverance and discretion. This may have crossed the line into a need-to-know situation.

"Mister Samuels, you are now officially on my radar." Davey whispered.

Chapter Sixteen

Inez Delos. She liked the name. Simple enough, though people rarely seemed to get it right it the first time. She'd been Iris Peelos and Alice Deals, among others. Didn't know what the real family name was. Her father had changed it to Samson as an homage to the Sam brothers - Archie, Wat and Creek, the last fluent speakers of Natchez. Though not related to the Sams, her father claimed they were family. His way of keeping a finger in the pie, should by some miracle the tribe ever be officially recognised. She had chosen Delos in honor of one of the sacred sites in ancient Greece, and also because it carried a hint of the Samson antidote. Delilah.

With olive skin and jet black hair, people often asked if she was Greek. One of her Anthro professors said she reminded him of Irene Pappas. Her expression was thoughtful, even brooding, and more often than not, she was.

Trained as an archaeologist, Inez was top of her class at the University of New Mexico, studying the Natchez and other tribes of the lower Mississippi valley. Now, having abandoned the shrunken fruits of academia, she was a therapist's administrator. Anything was better than asking her father for money. He supposedly had connections with Natchez elders, but Inez hadn't spoken to him for years. This was partly in response to the way he had treated her mother. There were other, darker reasons. They were on different paths, different worlds. The less she had to do with his world, the better.

The man walking beside her reminded Inez of Kaspar Hauser, an archetypical Mysterious Stranger who showed up one day in the early 1800s on the streets of Nuremberg, like a found object, with no history or memory. His mystery had never quite been unraveled.

They walked down Main Street through the business district, turning onto Pearl Street, where they passed the stately pillars of Magnolia Hall, home of the Natchez Garden Club. Inez stopped beside a stand of trees and cleared her throat. When that brought no reaction, she gently lowered the hood from the stranger's face. He winced, even with his sunglasses on.

"We'll stay on the shady side of the street," she said.

Weird walking next to someone with a hood covering his face. Thankfully, no one she knew passed by. God knows what story she would have told them. He could be some kind of nut job, but there was no hint of violence in him.

The song had been unmistakable. How could he possibly know it? One thing at a time, that's what Grandma would have said. A Cherokee-Natchez mixed blood, she had passed away when Inez was still a child. A few years later, Inez's mother had followed Grandma into the spirit world, poisoned with liquor and anger. She'd lost touch with the family after that.

There were actually very few "Notchie" – that was the way her grandmother pronounced the name - in the city of Natchez. The tribe had once been a powerful and pervasive force in what was now Louisiana and Mississippi. No one knew exactly how many were left. Might be possible to consult with an anthropologist, but Inez figured she knew as much as any ethnologist did about her people. She was also not willing to risk exposing herself to an academic as the victim of a fraud. Who else was there to ask? Maybe it was best to let this man go his own way, song and all.

For better or for worse, his appearance had awakened a longing for a connection with her roots. It's not every day that a living puzzle literally walks through your door. There must be someone who could help her solve it. In the meantime, she was not without her own resources.

Home was a pleasant, two family wood frame residence that Inez shared with a nurse who worked the night shift at the hospital. There was a small garden in the back, Inez's "sweet respite." Inside the house, recalling the stranger's sensitivity to light, Inez lit a candle rather than turn on the overhead lighting. She gestured to a couch.

"Sit".

Skyfisher removed his sunglasses in the darkened room, descended to the couch and gravely intoned, "Sit".

A simple, unaffected gesture, but it struck Inez as comical. She laughed, the first genuine laughter Skyfisher had heard in this place.

Where to begin, Inez wondered. She needed an ally.

It would have to be Hilton, an old, resourceful friend, albeit a challenging one. He'd find out sooner or later anyway. Might as well be sooner. They'd never been lovers, but at several crucial moments in their adult lives, they'd been there for each other to throw a lifeline or a crying towel, the dispenser of brotherly or sisterly advice. They were also capable of driving each other crazy. Hilton in small doses was fine. Beyond that, visions of death by strangulation were not uncommon. She phoned him and left a message to come by asap.

"Hungry?" she asked her guest, miming eating.

"Hungry!" he nodded enthusiastically. Inez whipped up some Mexican scrambled eggs and toast and watched him considering the cutlery, as if seeing silverware for the first time.

She picked up a fork and went through the motions of using it to taste the eggs. He nodded, intoned what sounded like a prayer in Natchez, placing bits of food from his serving on the table until there were four spoonfuls surrounding his plate. Grasping the fork a bit tentatively at first, he soon got the hang of it, his appreciation of the eggs obvious.

"Good," he said, spearing the toast with his fork, Inez demonstrating that hands were alright for eating bread.

"Hands, see?" she said.

"Hand see," he replied.

By the end of the meal, he had absorbed the words for every item he had eaten or touched.

Patting her chest, she said, "Inez." She pointed to him. *"Nasookta Shudef."*

"Oh my gosh," she said.

"O - my - gosh," the response.

How could he possibly know Natchez? The last fluent speaker, Archie Sam, died in 1986. Which gave Inez an idea.

At that moment, her guest stood up and mimed a man taking a piss, complete with sound effects. Inez showed him to the bathroom, lit dimly by a wall-socket night light. Nasookta Shudef was clearly nonplussed about the room and its fixtures.

Wishing Hilton would show up and half-suspecting this could be some stupid, elaborate practical joke, Inez scanned the room for any evidence of a hidden camera, then proceeded to dispassionately demonstrate the workings of the toilet and its accessories. Her guest's eyes widened when she turned on the hot and cold running water. An expression of delight when the toilet flushed for him, too.

He glanced in the mirror with a look of unabashed wonder, touching his face, running his fingers over every feature. His astonishment was so genuine, that Nasookta Shudef was either a consummate actor or he was in fact seeing his face in a mirror and witnessing the marvels of a bathroom for the first time. She closed the door and left him, hoping he'd put it all together. Several flushes and running water ensued.

A knock at the front door.

More than anything else, Hilton reminded her of a pilgrim, neck length straight hair parted in the middle, clean shaven, slightly overweight, medium height. You could easily miss him in a crowd or underestimate him in a conversation, until after a moment of silence he would proceed to point out in graphic detail every weak point of your argument along with a better solution. Like a depth charge. Although Hilton tried not to be smug about his mental acuity, it tended to narrow his list of amigos. Inez grudgingly admitted that most of the time he was right, damn his eyes.

"Look at you," Hilton said, standing in the doorway.

"What?" Inez responded.

"You actually seem happy to see me!"

"Indeed I am. Come in. You're not going to believe this."

"I am willing to suspend…Holy Shit!" The bathroom door flew open and a middle-aged man wearing sunglasses and a hoodie turned the wrong way round emerged, carrying a candle. It was satisfying to see Hilton taken aback, although he quickly recovered.

"You doing a séance in here or something?"

"I'd introduce you to Nasookta Shudef, but he apparently only speaks — well, I think it may be Natchez."

"Natchez? You're serious?!" Hilton eyed Skyfisher suspiciously, then gave him a weak smile.

"Jean Baptiste - you know him, don't you? Works in one of the car repair places? Dropped him off at the office. No explanation, just left him there. He doesn't speak or respond to English and he's ultra-sensitive to light. That's why the candle.." She trailed off, looking at Hilton for signs of complicity in the hoax scenario. "I was going to escort him out of the office when he started to sing." She paused, waiting to deliver her whopper.

"Hotel California?"

"A song my grandmother used to sing to me. In Natchez. No one knows that song. You can't buy it or hear it online. I doubt even Cherokee know it. Only a song carrier would, someone like my grandmother."

"Whew! Well, clearly he learned it somewhere. Sure it's the same song?"

"Positive."

Hilton chewed on that and she watched the wheels turn. He turned to Skyfisher and said, "Boy, am I rude. Hilton," he said, pointing to himself, then turning his finger towards Skyfisher, he muttered, "Help me with the pronunciation here, "Na, nas.."

"*Nasootka Shudef,*" Skyfisher repeated his name, then gestured back at the pale faced man, "Hilton."

"No Shit-Ka Shoot-Off," Hilton managed with a straight face, extending his right hand. Skyfisher looked at it, then at Hilton's face, and brought his own right hand up slowly, mirroring Hilton's gesture. Hilton grasped the hand awkwardly and gave it a slight shake.

"We'll work on that later," he added. "So," he turned to Inez, "what do you want me to do?"

"Wash him. See that he gets cleaned up."

"You're serious? He's a big boy. Surely he knows how to dress himself." Glancing at the reversed hood, he added, "Sort of."

"When I showed him the bathroom," Inez said, "it was like he was seeing it for the first time."

"Doesn't make sense. How can anybody just show up out of the blue looking kind of normal and not know what a bathroom is? He's obviously washed himself," Hilton sniffed, "more or less recently. OK, he's getting a little ripe, but, I mean, maybe he's escaped from one of those institutions or something. Have you checked him for any ID?"

"I will, I will," she said. "Please do this. It'll be a growing experience for you."

"A growing experience. You think I'm going to get turned on?"

"Just do it, Hilton," Inez said with a touch of exasperation, "for me. It would help if he smelled halfway decent. He's got a knapsack over there, maybe there's some clothes in it. I might have an old shirt that'll fit him."

"Guy shows up, sings you a song and you're giving him your clothes! Helluva song. You been drinking too much Mu Tea lately? I don't get it. This like a merit badge project for the Girls Scouts or something?"

"You'd rather *I* washed him?' she asked.

"I'll be *he* would."

"Look, Hilton. I know this is off the charts of everyday behavior, but since when have you become Mister Normal? For once, could you just do this for me without trying to figure out all the angles? Can you do it because one of the few people on the planet who can put up with you is asking nicely?"

Hilton looked at her, then at the improbable visitor, sighed deeply and said, "Alright, but if Mister Natchez decides to get too friendly, I'm pulling the rip chord."

Knapsack in hand, Hilton led the visitor into the bathroom and closed the door behind him. His voice rang out, "Will you get me the candle? I'm not going to shower in the dark with this guy. I don't care if he starts singing the national anthem in Swedish."

Inez handed Hilton the candle, along with a loose-fitting shirt and painter's pants, with the request that he also go over the use of toilet paper. Hilton muttered something unintelligible.

Inez descended to her basement to search for a particular box that had survived several moves - a time capsule containing mementos, old letters and a gift from her grandmother, several cassettes of Archie Sam speaking Natchez words and their English equivalent. An aural dictionary. To her delight, she found it hidden behind a carton of Christmas tree ornaments, along with a reprint of a brief English-Natchez dictionary compiled by the Oklahoma Historical Society in the seventies. A further excavation through the contents of several other boxes yielded an old portable cassette recorder. The rest of what she needed was upstairs.

Inez called outside the bathroom door, "Wait a few minutes before you come out, OK? I want to set up a few things."

"Fine," Hilton shouted, "we're just prettying ourselves up for the Pilgrimage Pageant," referring to one Natchez's rites of spring, where high schoolers in period dress portrayed episodes from the city's history in dramatic tableaux. "Petticoat Junction", Inez called the Pageant. Another opportunity to fleece tourists with the mythology of the South.

"If you come out in a hoop skirt, it's going on Facebook," Inez said. She cleared the dining room table and set out a few artifacts from mound excavations, some genuine, a few replicas, plus a few aardvarks.

"Whenever you're ready," she shouted.

Hilton came out of the bathroom shortly thereafter, closing the door behind him.

"Our boy is checking himself out in the mirror," Hilton said. "Underwear seems to be a new concept for him and either he's studying Stanislavsky or this was his first shower. He did seem to be familiar with soap."

"Yeah, I showed him that," Inez said. "Who's Stanis -"

"- lavsky. Method acting. Marlon Brando."

"Funny, I had the same thought, this being some elaborate prank that you were in on. He seems quite natural though."

"Bet you he's a Jewish boy from the Borscht Belt."

"Very funny."

"Checked out his sack while he was in the shower. There's a wallet with a driver's license. His name is Samuels. Salvador Samuels from Kingston, New York. The Catskills. Maybe he does standup comedy. 'Funny thing happened on the way to Natchez...'"

"Huh. But it still doesn't explain.."

"'Salvador' doesn't sound very Jewish. Could be the Lost Tribe. Probably call him Sal, for short."

"Are you done?"

"I'm just getting rolling."

"Put a lid on it. I want to try an experiment. Find out who he really is."

Chapter Seventeen

Skyfisher wiped the water vapor from the sleek, flat surface. Like the face of a pond, only much better. He studied the reflection and even though he could see and verify its shape and texture with his hands, it wasn't *his* face. A mask, a costume body he was deep inside of. In a strange way, he felt protected, as if he could do anything and it would happen to the body he was encased in, not him.

The dim flame of the candle was only slightly painful to his eyes. *Eyes!* He'd forgotten what real seeing was like, not a ghost outline or glowing phantom hues. Things had clearly defined edges. Colors were softer. He wondered if this way of seeing showed only the outer skin of things, their husks, their masks.

Skyfisher closed his eyes and tried to sense his *real* face. Its contours gleamed and subtly vibrated as he breathed. The particles of mist and air commingled, absorbed into his body, beginning to be transformed, reminding him why he was here and what needed to be set into motion.

Salvador Samuels, aka Nasootka Shudef, emerged from the bathroom clean and glowing.

"Let's see what he knows," Inez said, leading them into the dining room, gesturing to the table. Skyfisher regarded the objects closely. He ran his fingers over a Tibetan hand bell and a Gnaawan cymbal from Morocco. Smiling, he picked up a stone pipe fashioned in the shape of a frog and said, *"i dsaksht hakhesk,"* making the sound of a croaking frog.

"Hilton," Inez said, "would you grab a pen and paper from my desk?"

"Your majesty," he replied.

Pen in hand, Inez prompted her guest to repeat the pronunciation and she wrote it down phonetically. Holding her breath, she paged through the printout of the dictionary. Astonished, she whispered, "he just said 'frog-pipe', ee dsaksht hakhesk." Skyfisher nodded and corrected Inez's pronunciation, putting the accent on the first syllable. In a daze, Inez repeated the words, then handed him a replica of a stone disc. Skyfisher named the object, hefted it, and mimed throwing it and a spear in the same direction, prompting Hilton to duck out of the way of its imaginary trajectory. Inez pointed to a clay burial urn on the table and Skyfisher mimed someone asleep or dead. He picked up a bowl containing red ochre with a significant look at Inez, as if he longed to say something and then changed his mind. He mimed a woman applying the ochre to her cheeks like makeup, and Inez laughed.

"Spot on," she said. "Every object. He knows what they are. He knows their names in Natchez. How do you explain that?" Hilton raised his eyebrows and shoulders.

Inez handed Skyfisher the pen and paper and demonstrated how it worked. Another look of surprise and wonder, akin to a seven year old opening a birthday present. The last time she had seen an adult face with such an expression was an Alzheimer's patient recovering a scrap of memory. She gestured for him to draw something. He sat in the chair, another seemingly novel experience, took up the pen and attempted to draw, cautiously. After a few false starts and ejaculations of "Ah!", he continued in earnest. Inez turned to Hilton and entreated him for another favor.

"I think the corner store is still open. Can you pick up a pack of double A batteries?"

"How about we throw in some Chinese food? I'm starved," he said.

"You're on."

Skyfisher drew a circle with an outer ring of rattlesnakes, and inside the ring, the palm of a hand with an eye in its center. Inez recognised the design and shook her head in disbelief. There was no sane way to account for this. Her training as an anthropologist kept demanding logical explanations.

Hilton returned with batteries and Lo Mein. A few lighter moments ensued as their guest attempted to negotiate noodles with chopsticks. With a lesson from Inez, in five minutes he was manipulating the sticks "as well as anyone in Natchez", which Hilton noted, tempered the achievement somewhat. Inez showed Hilton Skyfisher's drawing, explaining that it was a motif found etched in stone at a Mississippian-era mound site in Alabama. "It has been published, though" she added.

"How many mound sites are there?" Hilton asked.

"In the states? Lots of them. They've been plowed over, bulldozed, ignored, desecrated without anyone having a clue. It's estimated there were once thousands, probably tens of thousands of them throughout the south and southeast, straight up the Mississippi valley to the Midwest. Big-time through the Ohio River valley. They're found as far south as Florida, as far north as North Dakota in the west, all through the Great Lakes over to New York and the St. Lawrence. I've got a map somewhere. There are mound sites all over the world - South America, England, Australia, China."

"You said they were destroyed without knowing what they were made for. We still don't know?" Hilton asked.

"Not really. For years, they were thought of as burial mounds and people were certainly buried in some, but not all of them. As a rule of thumb, round-top mounds were mostly burial sites, and the flat-topped ones - platform mounds, were ceremonial sites. Temples were built on them, along with chief's houses. We think rituals were performed on the platform mounds. They and the burial mounds were hallowed ground. You've been to the Grand Village here in Natchez haven't you?"

Hilton shook his head no. "I'm the guy who lives next to the Empire State Building and never goes in."

"Well," Inez continued, "the Grand Village mounds and the Emerald Mound – that's like, ten miles away, they were thought to be ceremonial sites. My people, the Natchez, were the last group known to have lived and worshipped on them. There are records of the Desoto expedition encountering what was probably the Natchez, and then later the French came along. Most of what we know about the Natchez was from the diaries of French missionaries. The stories they tell –," she gazed at the objects on the table, "Well, the Natchez were remarkable people in many ways. These artifacts are just eye-blinks."

"Desoto. They named a car after him," Hilton said.

"The beginning of the end for all Native Americans. Certainly for the Natchez."

"So what happened? There's like, five of you left, right?

"Sometimes it feels like that. But no, there's more. Hundreds at least, maybe thousands. We're scattered. Most of my mother's family is in Oklahoma, I think. The tribe was absorbed into other tribes after 1730, when the French nearly finished us off in retaliation for the so-called 'Natchez Massacre'. All it took was a few Indians to do something reckless and the rest of the tribe had to pay the price."

Inez rubbed her elbows for a moment, realising she was giving Hilton the Cliff's Notes version of her people, but not wanting to linger on the painful facts of history.

"It was complicated. Long simmering resentments, greed and anger, egged on by the English, who had their own agenda. The Natchez killed several hundred French settlers and in response the French systematically wiped us out. Many were taken as slaves, including The Great Sun, the tribal leader. Some escaped and were adopted by other tribes - the Cherokee, the Choctaw."

She squeezed her forehead, as if she could pull the memory out of her thoughts.

"You know, we never invited the French here. Or the Spanish or the English. They just showed up and began to divide and conquer."

"Anybody still speak Natchez?" Hilton asked.

"Present company excluded, I have no idea," Inez said. "Supposedly, the last fluent speaker passed away in '86. That's why this whole business is so crazy. Let me see that ID card."

Hilton retrieved the knapsack and the wallet. He pulled out the driver's license and showed it to their visitor, pointing at the photo.

"This you?" Hilton asked, turning his finger from the image to Skyfisher. Again, Inez had the sense of a man-child experiencing a new phenomenon for the first time. Skyfisher took the card, touched his face and then headed to the bathroom, his hosts in tow. He looked intently into the mirror and back at the image on the card. Inez held the ID up to the mirror so that he could see both images at the same time. The photograph had been taken a few years ago, but the resemblance was unmistakable. She read the name on the license and pointed at him saying, "Sal-va-dor Sam-yoolz". He turned to face Inez and Hilton, patted his chest and said *"Nasootka Shudef."* Pointing to the card he said, "Shal-fart-er Shah-Mule," as if naming a species.

Hilton laughed. Inez crossed her arms.

"OK, Nasootka, lets see what you make of this."

She took the batteries Hilton had purchased, inserted them into the cassette player and popped in the Natchez audio dictionary tape.

The first words were a brief introduction in English. Skyfisher looked around for where the person who was speaking might be. He lifted up the recorder, checked underneath it, and then remembered the disembodied voices he had heard in the place where he'd first met Inez. The same magic.

He nodded and when the first Natchez words were spoken on the tape, *ho-kakis*, to abandon, *tapituha*, to be about, he stood up and began speaking to the recorder. Inez stopped the tape and then showed Skyfisher how to work the recorder, pressing play to hear the next words: above, ablaze, abridge, accept, followed by their Natchez equivalents.

"Who made these choices?" Inez wondered.

She showed him how to rewind the tape and play it again. More marvelling. Inez let the tape play until she heard something at least demonstrable. Repeating "Adam's Apple", she pointed to hers, paused the tape and waited for Skyfisher to say *hanaksh*, which was validated by the recording in short order. She played "All" and gestured expansively with her arms spread wide, repeating the English word and joining with Skyfisher to repeat the Natchez, *latashi*. Skyfisher annotated this a bit; apparently there were several words for "all".

"Entirely appropriate," Hilton said.

Inez took the recorder into her bedroom, played past the English for "ant", re-entered the room, and hit the play button.

"Wele," at which point her visitor mimed something tiny crawling across the table.

"Ant," Inez said, and Skyfisher repeated the word.

"Rosetta Stone." said Hilton, "He's a fast learner."

And so he was. Skyfisher immediately recognised the value of this strange speaking device that knew his language and theirs. He figured English was the Anglay the Fran-zay traders spoke of with such disdain. He would learn it, and over the next few weeks he mastered every word on the tape, from abandon to young, a feat which impressed even Hilton.

He preferred being addressed as Nasootka Shudef, which - with a bit of mimicry, translated to Sky-hunter or Sky-fisher. The Rosetta Stone had no word for fisherman. In the tradition of nick-names not being chosen, he became Salvo, as dubbed by Hilton.

For the time being, Salvo would stay in Hilton's apartment as a roommate-in-training, sleeping on the couch, doing chores like dishwashing and house cleaning, until he learned enough english to explain himself.

Hilton's first impulse was to expose his new roommate to the time-honored friend of parents and babysitters.

"Sit here on the couch. I'll turn on the Tube. You'll learn the lingo and the way of the world, such as it is."

After fifteen minutes of daytime television, Skyfisher walked to the window and observed a crimson throated hummingbird hovering at a honeysuckle, drawing nectar from a flower. To him, the ghosts on the television screen were doing the same thing, sucking mind-juice right out of his head.

"Hilton," he called. "Eat, speak."

Hilton had no brothers, sisters, nieces or nephews. He'd tried his hand at being a substitute teacher once and had bailed after a day in Middle School, feeling like he'd been fed to the lions. These days, he worked at the library. Outside of his parents, Inez was really the only person he had a close relationship with, somewhere between a sister and friend. He'd promised her he'd mentor this homeless Jew from another dimension, who might just be a genuine candidate for a sanatorium. The candidate had switched off the TV and was calling him. A promise being a promise, breakfast was as good a place as any to learn.

"Eggs," Hilton said, pulling a carton out of the fridge, "butter, bowl, fork." He placed these objects on the kitchen table, Skyfisher dutifully repeating their names. Hilton broke an egg into the bowl and invited Skyfisher to do the same.

"Mess," Hilton said.

Hilton went in search of a paper towel to clean up the remains of the egg that had exploded in Skyfisher's hand. When he returned, half a dozen eggs had been broken into the bowl and Skyfisher was attempting to extract bits of shell.

"If you want to make an omelet —" Hilton began. He had Skyfisher chop up some scallions and mushrooms and fried them. Next came grating a piece of cheddar, scrambling the eggs, pouring half of the mixture onto the hot pan, multi-tasking the bread into a toaster, and at the right moment adding the ingredients to the omelet, folding and flipping it. Hilton was tempted to do his Julia Child imitation, but considering his guest's reaction to television, he demurred.

They sat at the kitchen table and Skyfisher placed bitefuls of food at the four corners of his plate. Hilton did the same and had his guest repeat the name of every ingredient. They devoured the omelet and Hilton, still hungry, offered an invitation to Skyfisher.

"Now you make. Use anything - *all.*"

Skyfisher went to the fridge, found a jar of peanut butter, commandeering the leftover cheese and some hot peppers. It produced an omelet Hilton would never have dreamed of, but which rallied his taste buds nonetheless.

Over the coming weeks, Hilton did his best to help Salvo-Skyfisher with his grammar, impressed by his ability to quickly learn a language, and bit by bit, absorb a culture. Objects were easy. Anything in sight or pictured in a book was fair game. Candle, glass, toilet, water. Concepts were another matter.

"Hilton, I need word."

The Oklahoma Historical Society's dictionary only worked one way, from English to Natchez. There was a word for defecation but not destination, for ghost but not goal.

"What word this?" Skyfisher asked.

"Map."

"We on map?"

"We *are* on *the* map. Here." Hilton pointed.

"What this?"

"The Mississippi river."

"This?"

"The Grand Village."

"Aah."

It took over an hour, but eventually Skyfisher conveyed the concept of wanting to go somewhere, and together, they found *destination*.

"You say, 'Salvo, give water me! Salvo, do dish!' What word this is?"

The words in Natchez were *hallish* and *pihao shi shish*, which boiled down to "task" and "duty". Hilton suggested "mission".

"I are mission."

"OK," Hilton said warily. "Tell me."

"Soon."

More hours sifting through images of artifacts, mound sites, pyramids, menhirs, dolmens, navigating through "religious, spiritual and magical", brought another word for Skyfisher's growing vocabulary. Sacred.

Chapter Eighteen

Sporting Steampunk sunglasses, Skyfisher gradually became more acclimatised to bright daylight. Hilton took him on walking tours of Natchez. They'd head to a cliff that overlooked the Mississippi, watched the steamboat churn its way upstream, or strolled along Main Street, gazing at the influx of tourists. Walkways were crowded alongside cafes, antique and furniture stores. Nandinas and crepe myrtles lined the sidewalks. The question of whether the moving wagons were mobile latrines was laid to rest.

"Although," cautioned Hilton, "many of those cars are pieces of shit." Each day, Skyfisher would add a cache of new words to his lexicon, a random selection limited only by his curiosity and Hilton's patience: bicycles, bagels, nachos, smoothies, ice cream, backpacks, strollers, smart phones, cameras. Not to draw attention, they devised a system where Skyfisher would notice something, nod, and Hilton would name it, discreetly.

"Tourist. Nice wheels. Jail bait. Cigar. Wino."

Encountering a similar entity again later on, Skyfisher would ID it, demonstrating his prodigious memory or simply showing off, as Hilton claimed. Skyfisher had yet to learn discretion.

"Old Dog. Righteous Babe. Yuppie Scum. Nice wheels! Piece of Shit.."

Passers-by were not amused.

He was leery of cameras and people who took photographs. For Skyfisher, eye-seeing was a miracle. He revelled in colors, savoring the deep yellow of ripe banana skin, the creamy pink of strawberry ice cream veined with bits of red fruit, the cobalt hue of a SUV, the many shades and subtle variations of skin on the visitors to Natchez. He was particularly delighted to see tattoos on both men and women, and every once in a while, pink or green hair. In spite of an endless variety of passersby, Skyfisher rarely saw anyone who looked like one of his own people. He was surrounded by the descendants of invaders, encased in the body of one of them!

The invaders were still trading for things. More things than he could imagine. The number and variety of their possessions was astounding, from cars to clothes. An entire village could live for a long time off the contents of one supermarket. Some of the items had images of what they contained. One box pictured a black gentleman, smiling graciously.

"Hilton, what this?"

"You mean, 'what *is* this?'"

"What *is* this?"

"Uncle Ben's Rice."

"Uncle Ben?"

"Later." Hilton said, not wanting to explain branding, advertising, or capitalism, let alone justify them, to a visitor from another planet.

Back on the street, they passed a window displaying images of colorful designs imprinted on human flesh. Hearts with arrows through them, lightning bolts, coiled snakes, eagles.

Good idea, thought Skyfisher and beckoned Hilton to accompany him inside.

Both Hilton and Inez were withholding judgment on their guest while he learned their language. One day soon he would shed light some light on his cryptic *mission*. In the meantime, it was like living with Rip Van Winkle as he slowly becoming acculturated. Hilton and Salvo began to have actual conversations, with the star pupil absorbing words and expressions like a prodigy.

Sipping his morning brew, Skyfisher said, "Coffee strong. No. Coffee *is* strong."

"Yeah, it is," Hilton rejoined. "You like?"

"No. I like tea, and but or coffee *is* strong. Strong is good."

"We'll go with that," Hilton said.

"Where we go?"

"We stay here."

"Good."

"You like tea," Hilton said.

"Yes."

Long pause.

"Inez, she *is* woman you with?"

"You mean, is she *my* woman? No. Inez, is my friend. Like you. You and me - friends. Inez and me - friends."

"She *is* strong, coffee is strong. Inez is - coffee?"

"She is like coffee."

"Ah. She like coffee."

"We've got to find you a tutor."

They couldn't afford one, nor did Hilton or Inez feel comfortable having to explain Salvo as a pupil. The next best option was a free online ESL course. Skyfisher disliked computers, but he recognised their usefulness, like the tape recorder. So every morning, he spent time conjugating verbs and other eccentric delights of the English language, moving away from what Hilton called "Tonto Speak".

They spent most evenings at Inez's house, where Skyfisher proudly displayed a newly tattooed eye on Salvo's right palm, prompting new efforts to tease out his story. He had many questions for them as well.

Wielding the recorder like a talisman, Skyfisher had found a word which intrigued him.

"You have tem-pell?"

"We're a bit short on those," Hilton said, figuring a temple as the sort of place Salvador Samuels might have frequented. But this wasn't Samuels anymore and Hilton hadn't the foggiest idea of how to behave inside of a synagogue.

"Short?" Skyfisher asked.

"We got churches. They're like temples. We got churches up the wazoo," Hilton said, quickly bringing up his hand in the stop gesture.

"Many churches," he said.

"We go?"

"We can do that."

Although not a churchgoer, Hilton was intrigued to see how Mister Notchie would respond to a dose of religion. They attended a Sunday Mass, Skyfisher nodding as he saw people go to one knee and mark the four directions on their breast. He breathed in the incense, the singing, the ritual, the interminable homily. Things were not so different in the temples of his people.

When he saw parishioners making donations, Skyfisher reached into Salvador's wallet and dropped a twenty into the collection basket, prompting a raise of the eyebrow from a watchful sexton.

"Who *is* this one?" Skyfisher asked *sotto voce*, glancing at a mural of a man nailed to a cross.

"Jesus, son of God," Hilton said.

"God!" Skyfisher exclaimed, remembering the English word for *Master of Breath, life-giving.* There was no single word in Natchez for an all-pervasive ongoing mystery.

"He wounded?" Skyfisher asked.

"Dying. He died on the cross."

"They no bury him?"

"*Not* bury," Hilton corrected. "Anyway, they did bury him. He came back."

"Ah. Where he is now?'

"This was long ago."

"He is dead?"

"Well, yes. No!" Hilton said, reaching the frontier of his knowledge of scripture. "He - is in heaven now," gesturing towards a ceiling populated by images of children with wings and golden circles around their heads.

"At least, he's supposed to be. But he was a real guy. It's not just a story," Hilton added.

"He is like Great Sun," Skyfisher said.

"Maybe."

When the service ended, they were met at the doorway by the sexton, a bald, heavy set man wearing horn-rimmed glasses and a brown robe of office.

"Thank you for coming! Haven't seen you at church before."

"No, first time," Hilton said, hoping for a quick exit. The sexton, cheerful but determined, pressed on.

"Where you boys from?"

"I'm local," Hilton said, "my friend is - from out of town. He's had some, ah, medical problems. Doesn't speak very well. You know how it is." The sexton nodded sympathetically. Speaking very slowly, emphasizing each word, he looked at Skyfisher.

"How..do..you..find..our..city?"

"I have mission –, Skyfisher began. Hilton interjected.

"My friend is interested in the missionary work of the church, as we all are. Wonderful job you're doing. Inspiring," shouldering Skyfisher out into the street. "We really have to be going. Nice to have met you. Great service!"

It was only after they had walked a block and gone around the corner that he turned to his friend.

"Salvo, yikes, you gotta be careful!"

"Careful?"

"Yeah. Danger, not safe. You start talking about your mission in church, they will nail you up, like the guy in the painting!"

Out in the street, they saw other church folk in their Sunday best. Heading towards them on the sidewalk, a mother and daughter licking ice cream cones, the girl trying not to get any chocolate drips on her white gloves. Across the street, a group of young men laughing loudly, flirting with every coed they passed. Each of them carried a bag on their shoulder.

"Men have metal sticks. Weapons?" Skyfisher asked.

"Clubs, golf clubs."

A discussion of golf followed, along with the admission that, in a pinch, the metal club could indeed be used as a weapon.

They walked back to Inez's house and settled in to a Sunday brunch of scrambled eggs, bacon and buttered grits. When Inez heard of their adventure in church, she agreed they had to keep their star pupil on a shorter leash.

"People won't understand," Inez said. "I surely don't. Starting with, where in the world are you from?"

The word *world* initiated a post-brunch foray into the realm of maps and the awe-inspiring globe. Skyfisher wanted to know the word for *planet* and whether it meant the same thing as *world*. He knew about the sun, stars and other planets.

"You hear stars and planets?" he asked.

"No", Inez said, "we see them through telescopes." She showed him photographs of Saturn's rings and Jupiter's Great

Spot, which he stared at in wonder. Questions about time, calendars and local maps of the Mississippi valley.

"Look at this," Inez said, unrolling a large map on the dining room table, showing the known mound sites in the eastern United States as constellations of black dots throughout the river valleys and coastal areas. Skyfisher ran his fingers lightly over the dots as if he was reading braille. When he started to draw a copy, Inez brought home a smaller xerox of the map, which Skyfisher regarded as sacred iconography.

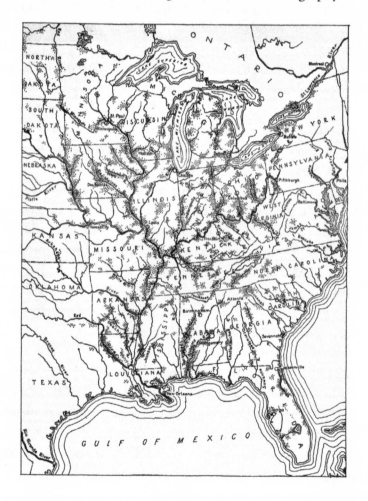

"Thank-you deep much," Skyfisher said. "I bring Almighty Greenbacks to house. Hilton say."

"I appreciate that," Inez said. "Your English is getting better, too. Soon you can tell us where you're from. Why you're here. In the meantime, we'll get you some work so you can help with expenses."

The next day, with the aim of making Skyfisher presentable for prospective employment, the odd couple went clothes shopping at the local Walmart, with money borrowed from Inez. Skyfisher picked out a pair of green pants.

"This is the Women's section," Hilton said. "Men's are over there."

Skyfisher found the men's clothing selection drab and gravitated to the other side of the aisle where a bright yellow shirt beckoned.

"Salvo, something you're not telling me?"

"Not telling?"

"You like women, right?"

"Yes."

"OK. 'Skyfisher'- he's married, right? He, you I mean, have a wife?"

"My wife is *Tell Me A Story.*"

"You like her?"

"Yes."

"Alright. We buy clothes in the men's section. Trust me."

They were an odd pair, to be sure, Salvo and Hilton. S & H, like the trading stamps Inez's mother had collected whenever she went grocery shopping. Inez began to call the two of them the Green Stamps.

Hilton's brand of humor was a pastiche of double entendres, word play, trivia laced with cynicism. He distrusted anything folksy, deeming it the provenance of granola-eating, navel-gazing, well meaning, witless New Agers. Hilton's version of Purgatory was being forced to watch Deepak Chopra videos.

Salvo was the ultimate straight man, oblivious to any snappy repartee. His apparent discoveries of the conveniences of western civilization were a continual delight to behold. Here was a quasi-Indian with the nose of an east coast Jew and the name of a surrealist painter, plowing his spoon into a grapefruit, managing with uncanny accuracy to zap Hilton in the eye with a salvo of juice, all the while maintaining a demeanor of deadpan seriousness and an aura of innocence.

"I know who you are." Hilton commented, with a hint of malice. "The bastard son of Buster Keaton."

Yet whenever the conversation veered to who he was and from whence he came, the bastard son demurred.

"Soon!"

Every morning, Hilton would head to work as a part time "reference librarian without portfolio". In the afternoon, he tutored kids in science and English. He professed being the only person in the state of Mississippi who actually knew how to spell. A fast learner himself, Hilton felt admiration laced with a tinge of jealousy for how quickly and effortlessly Salvo was able to pick up anglo-speak. Unless it was all some weird fraud. Hell, people were still sending him emails offering to deposit half the treasury of Nigeria into his savings account.

After spending a few weeks with the man of mystery, Hilton had come to doubt any duplicity. Memory loss, some weird brain malfunction maybe, but there was no trace of deceit in his roommate. Hilton's own efforts at learning Natchez were hamstrung by his inability to pronounce them. Somehow, in a matter of weeks Salvo had memorized several hundred words on the tape, and made a major dent in level one of the online ESL course.

He needed allies. This evening, armed with the limited language he'd acquired and the tools he could requisition, Skyfisher was going to tell them why he was here and enlist their support.

On the way to Inez's house in the afternoon, there was a noticeable increase in traffic.

"Spring Pilgrimage week," Hilton said.

Tourists came in busloads to tour the mansions interspersed throughout the city of Natchez. The Green Stamps walked past the visitor center, which had a series of billboards outside, each marked with a color representing a group of different mansions that were open for tours that day.

Hilton stopped outside the center to tie his shoe. Glancing up, he caught sight of a man in a raincoat on the other side of the street, someone he'd noticed before but not paid attention to. Something about the way the man quickly looked away and busied himself as soon as Hilton eyeballed him. "Assuming an air of indifference", was how he put it to Inez later that evening.

"I realize I'm being paranoid here," Hilton confessed, "but it really felt like the guy was following us."

"You might be right, though I doubt it," Inez said. "An old professor of mine once said to me, 'If you hear hoof-beats outside your window, it could be a herd of zebras, but most likely it's horses.' Did you ask Skyfisher if he recognized the man?"

"Maybe I've been watching too many cop shows on television, but I didn't want to call attention to the fact that I noticed the guy. Let's face it, Salvo isn't exactly subtle."

Inez nodded and they left it at that, Hilton's description of the stalker having been patently nondescript.

"Our genius has something he wants to tell us," Inez said. "I've been waiting for weeks to hear this."

They headed into the dining room where Skyfisher was standing beside the table.

They would not believe him. They'd not been prepared to fulfill the role that human beings had been created for, a role they had forgotten. He wondered how Salvador Samuels was doing in the past, living in Skyfisher's body. He had not been prepared either, like a child abducted from another tribe. The Shining Ones had the best of intentions, but would Samuels cooperate?

It was the same dilemma Skyfisher faced now. How could he help anyone see beyond their world? They knew the stars and planets were not theirs to command. There were things they didn't know.

Skyfisher had once asked Marsh Fox how it was possible to influence a world, a planet, a sun.

"We're like insects crawling on a buffalo!"

The elder had responded, "Have you never seen a bee sting a bear?"

"Yes," Skyfisher said. "They get swatted!"

"But a *swarm* of bees must be reckoned with," Marsh Fox said. "They have the power to overcome a bear if they're threatened."

So he would begin to make a hive, gathering what he needed. A few artifacts from Inez's collection, the map of mound locations, a pencil and drawing pad, a copy of one of her books that had pictures of ancient earthworks.

Books were magic. Skyfisher enjoyed hearing Hilton read aloud from a book. All those thoughts in one place! One day he would ask to hear the story of his people, knowing it would be bad news. If only there was a book that explained his mission in a language they would understand. It could not be passed on by words alone.

A knock on the door startled them all.

"Must be a Jehovah's Witness," Inez said, opening the door. Standing in the doorway, was the one Jean-Baptiste had called The Man, dressed in an immaculate black suit and sunglasses, which he now removed. Inez took a step back.

"Dad?!"

Alex Samson, age 42, had an MBA from Pepperdine. The original family name was lost, along with his birth certificate. He'd opted for Samson, keeping both a vestige of his roots and a respectful distance. Figured he was at least half-blood Natchez, but that was on a need-to-know basis and most folks didn't need to know. Alex was one of largest landowners in the county, and he had done it discreetly. Any one of consequence in the city of Natchez had heard of him, partly from his generous donations to local charities. He had few friends; however it was known in certain quarters that if you had a problem that Natchez's Finest were unable to tackle, The Man's crew could take care of it quietly, efficiently and affordably. Jobs were often taken on as favors plus expenses. Over the years he had collected enough favors to ensure that certain building permits and acquisitions went through without any hitches.

His marriage had gone south a long time ago. Whose hadn't? He wasn't willing to keep up the charade and didn't give a shit what anybody thought. His daughter hadn't spoken to him in years, even changed her last name just to piss him off. A divorce settlement had seen her through college. *His* money, not a dime from her mother. Never so much as a thank-you.

There were times he missed the emotional connection to his only child, someone to give a Christmas present to, give away at a wedding, crank out some grandkids. A fantasy. Deep down, he didn't want to be involved and have her poking her holier-than-thou nose in his business. Just as well. If his enemies knew of her existence they could use it against him.

Up to now Alex had kept the Mob out of Natchez, not that the city was high on their wish list. He took care of business hometown style, and so far the powers that be seemed to be content with the arrangement. That was one of the reasons he wanted Davey on his team, to keep a eye on him and his Jersey connections. Davey was competent and had been tactful when he brought Inez and her visitor to Alex's attention.

"That weird guy with the sunglasses, the one you wanted me to tail? He's been seeing someone you may know."

Alex had thanked Davey for the information and surprised him by getting proactive. Time to nip whatever this was in the bud.

Inez stared at the figure standing in her doorway. They had a tacit agreement to keep their distance, but this was no social call. She stepped outside, backing him off onto the porch, probably the only person on the planet he would allow to do this. His glance had swept the room behind her, taking in the paraphernalia on the table and getting a fleeting glimpse of the Mysterious Stranger. White, most likely from north of the Mason-Dixon.

"What's up, Alex? What do you want?" Inez asked.

"Just passing by. You're not going to invite me in?"

"No. You're not just passing by. Got your goon squad following me?"

It was easy to let her anger build. Inez didn't know what sort of shady deals he was involved with in his back rooms, but she wanted none of it. Looking at her, proud and defiant, the only one with balls enough to stand up to him, Alex felt a mixture of admiration and regret. The road not taken.

"Look," he said, "that fella in your living room shows up on my doorstep couple of weeks ago. You know him?"

"What do you mean, 'shows up at your doorstep?' What was he, selling raffle tickets?"

"You know this guy? He a friend of yours?"

"I really don't see why it's any of your business who I choose to speak to."

"He doesn't speak English, does he?"

"He speaks alright."

"What language?'

Inez unloaded her zinger just to see his reaction.

"Natchez. He speaks Natchez."

"Yeah, right," Alex snorted.

"Fluently."

"Bullshit."

"Suit yourself. I gave you a straight answer. You speak Natchez?"

"A little," not wanting to loose whatever edge he had.

"Know anyone in the family who does? Your uncle?" Inez asked.

"Let me hear him," Alex said.

"On one condition, no - two. Put me in contact with someone who knows the language."

"The second condition?"

"Stay away. You and your men in black. Keep away from me and my friends. If I need you, I know how to reach you."

"Very good," he said after a moment's pause.

"I mean it," she said. "You start nosing around and I'll get a restraining order. That'll go down real good at the next Kiwanis Club luncheon."

"I promise. Let me hear him speak."

"Wait a moment," Inez said, and went inside, closing the door behind her.

"It's my father," she said, fairly certain Skyfisher understood the word.

"He wants to meet you. He knows some Natchez. Will you speak to him? Say a few words and he'll go away."

Skyfisher sensed her nervousness and concern.

"I speak Natchez?"

"Yes."

He nodded in agreement.

"What am I, chopped liver?" Hilton asked.

"Pretty much," Inez said. She went to the door and beckoned The Man to enter.

"My father, Alex Samson. Hilton Gervain and - Mister Samuels."

Hilton stood.

"Gentlemen," Alex said, and proceeded to take off his sport jacket, remove a gold cufflink, initials *A.S.*, and roll up his sleeve. His muscled upper arm sported a tattoo. He turned to Skyfisher and spoke one of the few words he knew in Natchez.

"*Cenkololo,*" and pointing to the tattoo, he added "*Hanusu,*" a greeting and the word for warrior. The tattoo was typically worn by a guardian, someone who protected a chief.

"*Cenkololo,*" Skyfisher responded. Continuing in Natchez, he said it was an honor to meet a warrior and the father of his friend.

Alex listened. Sounded like the language he'd heard his relatives speak many years ago. Might be Kurdish for all he knew, which was why he had turned his smartphone recorder on while waiting on the porch.

"What's the word for this?" Alex asked, walking over to the table and picking up an ax-head.

"*Ohyaminoo,*" Skyfisher replied.

"O-ya-mee-new," Alex repeated and wrote it down on a scrap of paper.

"So Dad," Inez said, in a lame attempt to sound cheerful, "thanks for dropping by and showing us your ink. When you find that contact, send me an email." She jotted her email address on the same paper he had written on. Handing him his jacket and cufflink, she walked him to the door and said, "Remember your promises, both of them."

Before leaving, Alex turned towards Skyfisher and asked, "Where are you from?"

Inez began to protest, but Hilton spoke up.

"Here," he said, pointing to the ground, "right here."

"And you are –?" Alex asked.

"Hilton, like the hotel."

The Man filed this bit of intel, gave a benedictory nod and turned back to his daughter.

"I would -" he began.

"Don't," she said, closing the door behind him.

Back in the living room, both Hilton and Skyfisher waited for Inez to speak. When she said nothing, Hilton began, "Your father…"

"Some other time," Inez said. "I want hear what Salvo has to tell us."

He stood alongside the table looking at a pile of papers, maps, drawings, artifacts, books, Hilton's laptop and a globe. Skyfisher could tell that Inez was disturbed. He too, was uneasy. All the past week he'd thought about this moment and how inadequate he felt for the task at hand. If any of the elders were here, they could find a way without words. The Bald One would dance. Falling Star would enter their dreams. What could *he* do?

Skyfisher might describe something, but it would be meaningless without an experience they could relate to. Something they had seen, felt and touched.

Still, there were tools in Salvador Samuels's world, formidable tools that Skyfisher had never imagined. Perhaps they could help him reveal the secret that lay behind every color, every sound, taste and touch. Every breath.

"Hilton say true," he began, "I am from here."

Having spent the last week helping Skyfisher prepare his Powerpoint, Hilton smiled conspiratorially and displayed a picture on his laptop.

"It's one of the small mound sites, maybe five or six miles away," Hilton said. "We ought to pay it a visit soon, because I think Wonder Boy has a car," reaching into Salvo's sack and dangling a set of keys. "It may still be there."

Skyfisher brought his hand to his heart and inclined his head to them each, in turn.

"Inez, sister. Hilton, brother." Then he began to softly intone a few words in Natchez.

Breath of Sky
Breath of Sun
Through you
Even now

Skyfisher nodded to Hilton. The next image on the screen was a photo of the Milky Way.

"Sacred place," Skyfisher said and gave the signal for the next image, a time lapse animation of our solar system, each planet in its own egg-shaped orbit around the sun. Mercury, Venus, Earth and Mars circling fairly rapidly, the other planets barely moving, like snails. The succeeding image was a blue planet flecked with clouds - Earth.

"Sacred place," Skyfisher repeated. Next a copy of Inez's map of the network of mounds throughout the eastern United States, constellations of black dots.

"Sacred places."

He walked to a shelf where Inez had a few framed photos, a small eskimo soapstone sculpture and a Russian nesting doll. Picking up the figurine, a squat, hand painted babushka, he opened it, revealing another doll, from which he extracted yet another.

He pointed to the doll in his left hand and said "Skyfisher." Looking at the doll in his right hand, he said "Salvo." Then he opened the Skyfisher doll, put the Salvo doll inside it, and placed the doll on top of an artist's depiction of the Grand Village – the Temple Mound, in its hey day.

"Salvo there. Skyfisher here!" he said, pointing to his head. He looked at his two friends, Hilton fidgeting on the couch, Inez leaning on the arm of her chair, chewing the side of her finger.

Just to make sure they were all on the same page, Hilton added, "If you're buying this, Salvador Samuels is back in the 1600's. Skyfisher is here with us. They're sharing bodies, through time."

That hung in the air for a minute until Hilton made a football time-out signal.

"Coffee, anyone?"

He glanced at Inez. "There's more to come. Keep your disbelief in suspension just a little longer."

Inez didn't like where this presentation was coming from or where it seemed to be going. She had no faith in religion and little patience for spirituality. She'd never encountered anyone remotely like Salvo or Skyfisher, whichever he was. The notion of time travel insulted her intelligence, but she would hear him out. His knowledge of Natchez, still to be confirmed by someone she could trust, appeared to be genuine. He knew every word in the aural dictionary. How would you explain that? And there was her grandmother's song, that he had sung on the first day in the therapist's office.

Some kind of idiot savant? She'd seen him do some fairly amazing things, unerringly find his way blindfolded, for one. He was genuinely super-sensitive to light, had no apparent interest in money, having given Hilton the few hundred dollars in his wallet. Even in the midst of his preposterous story, there was no hint of artifice or subterfuge. He was completely in earnest, or else the best actor she'd ever encountered. To what purpose? Her father's involvement was cause for further angst, awakening an instinct to protect them all from Alex's machinations.

Inez poured her guest a cup of coffee, then pointing to the calendar, asked "My father; did you see him before today?"

"No," Skyfisher said, "I walk on road. *The* road. Big man in car. '*You, 'Bo!*'"

"Jean-Baptiste!" Inez exclaimed, smiling at his simulation of a Cajun accent.

"Big man, Skyfisher, bad place." Wary expression. "Other man talk Skyfisher."

Authoritative voice, "'Speak dog!'" A bark for good measure.

"Dog not speak."

"OK, I think I get it," Inez said. She pictured JB picking up the weird stranger on the road and taking him to her father's office. All this could be confirmed.

It was dusk and Inez turned on some lights in adjacent rooms and lit a few candles on the table. More coffee followed by shortbread cookies and Skyfisher resumed, pointing to a sheet of paper on the table. Two words were written on it, How and Why. Circling "How", he shook his head and crossed out the word. Then he circled Why and with a crayon, drew a yellow sun, underneath it a green plant.

Hilton drummed his fingers on the table.

"Finger painting is next," he muttered.

"Plant need sun," continued Skyfisher. "No sun, no plant. Plant breathe sun."

"Photosynthesis," Hilton added for the benefit of slow learners.

Pointing to the globe, Skyfisher said, "World."

"Earth," Hilton said.

"Earth needs sun. No sun, no earth." Then Skyfisher drew a crescent moon and said, "Moon needs earth. No earth, no moon." Then he looked at Inez and Hilton in turn and asked, "What sun need?"

When there was no response, he said "Sun *want* feed earth, like mother want feed baby. Sun need what?"

"You mean, what does the sun need to feed the earth?" Inez asked.

"Plants?" suggested Hilton.

"*You*," Skyfisher said. "Sun needs you. No people, sun not feed earth, earth not feed moon. No people? No earth, no moon." He regarded his hosts expectantly.

"What sun need from people?" Skyfisher asked.

"I give up," Inez said. "What?"

"That why Skyfisher is here," he said, content to let the matter rest for the moment.

"I don't know about the sun," said Hilton, "but no Chinese food, no me."

Later, over egg rolls and Almond Gai Ding, Skyfisher smiled benevolently at his two friends.

"I stay in Hilton."

"With,' Hilton corrected, "you stay with.."

"I work. Give Hilton greenbacks."

"He wants to get a job, pay his way", Hilton explained.

"OK," Inez said, leaning back in her chair. She pointed to a photo of the mounds at the Grand Village, "Where do the mounds fit in to all this? Help me, Hilton."

Pointing to the photo, Hilton asked, "Mound, why?"

Skyfisher, pointing at the following week on the calendar, said "You see."

149

Chapter Nineteen

Somehow, a Jew from New York, supposedly speaking fluent Natchez, had wormed his way into his daughter's life.

Even if it was Natchez, it didn't make any sense. Bottom line, if his livelihood or Inez's safety might be in jeopardy, all pledges were off. Saving your daughter's life from some psycho eclipsed any promise. Follow along for now, find someone in Oklahoma who could recognise the real thing when they heard it and get them to translate what he had recorded. He checked the paper for the phrase he'd written down, along with Inez's email address.

The Man walked down the block and crossed to the other side of the street where he'd left Davey, out of sight. They walked together for another block before Alex turned to him and said, "She made you, didn't she?"

Davey had learned long ago that it was always better to cop to a mistake. No excuses.

"Her friend saw me. Long black hair and glasses."

"Careless. I'm surprised," said Alex.

"It won't happen again."

"No it won't. It's a long way back to New Jersey. *Capiche?*"

"Yes, sir."

"Good. Here's what you're going to do."

Skyfisher knew Inez and Hilton were not convinced. How could they be?

He spent the following week wrestling with verbs. Late night sessions with English Level One, followed by tutorials from Hilton, complete with drawings, pictures and mime, searching for ways to express the inexpressible. Alignment, silence, tuning, antennas, listening, emanations, particles.

"The glossary for the 'Tao of Physics'", thought Hilton, who in spite of his skepticism, relished the challenge of coming up with a few inappropriate metaphors for alignment.

Skyfisher instinctively distrusted anything you had to turn on, an aversion tempered by an equal measure of fascination. He needed to know how the magic boxes with their buttons and switches worked. Hilton tried to give him the basics, but his physics chops were limited.

"What is electricity?" Skyfisher asked.

"Kind of like a current of water. Funny thing is, they don't really know what electricity is."

"Funny?"

"Never mind." He did the best he could, starting with Ben Franklin and the kite, and ending up with Thomas Edison and light bulbs. Skyfisher pointed to a lamp.

"Electricity makes light?"

"Yes."

"Lightning is electricity?"

"Yes. Electricity is dangerous. Touch an electric wire, it can kill you. Remember the boys we saw in the street last week carrying metal poles, golf clubs?" Hilton asked. "Guys playing golf, they get struck by lightning all the time. The metal club attracts lightning."

"Antenna?" Skyfisher asked.

"Yeah, like that."

Hilton brought home a copy of "How Things Work", and they pored over it. Skyfisher was particularly interested in transmitters and receivers. Media content was another matter, television being Bad Medicine incarnate. Computers, smart phones and the internet were peddling illusions, reflections of something finer.

When Tell Me A Story became her name, stories lived. She was a transmitter; you were a receiver. The story appeared between you, amplified. She breathed life into it and you became the expectant father, witnessing a rebirth. Television was a straw doll some dark shaman had reanimated.

There were stories about this. A ghost child coming in the night and substituting itself for a real child. The ghost stole a mother's love, but stayed cold and empty inside. In the end it would vanish like a thief.

Skyfisher wondered if he was the ghost child, living inside the body of another man. This was different. He was not here to steal.

For years, he'd been trained to be a finely tuned antenna, one of the most sensitive on earth. There were others, he hoped, and the time was approaching when he would have to find them. He needed to father a new story, one that could re-awaken this world. If only he knew what that story would be.

They drove Inez's Honda Civic to the mound site Sky-fisher had identified from a photo.

"Sacred Place," he said.

The Green Stamps had the keys to Salvador's car. Hilton had predicted it would be there, but the parking lot was empty. Skyfisher took them up the hill, through the scrub. The tent and the rest of Salvo's belongings were missing, too. The only hint of its presence was a bent metal stake left in the ground, a scrap of physical evidence in a story that needed proof.

"This Salvo's?" Hilton asked.

Skyfisher shrugged, sensing the disappointment in his friends. He led them to a clearing, positioned them seated on the ground facing each other in a triangle formation, and waited for them to get comfortable.

"We gonna start singing "Kum Ba Ya" now?" Hilton asked, with a low intensity eye roll.

"One of your songs?" asked Skyfisher.

"It means 'Come By Here,'" Inez said.

"Good name," Skyfisher said.

"Please, no, I'll vomit." Hilton said, explaining the new vocabulary word with a few graphic gestures.

"One day, I hear this song," Skyfisher replied. "Now close eyes." They did as instructed, Hilton wondering anew why he had gotten sucked into this whole scenario.

"Back straight. Your body, friend. Listen body. No think."

Hilton thought he heard a rattlesnake, but kept his eyes closed for the moment.

He was allergic to New Age crapola. Inez seemed to be hanging in there. He would suffer in silence, for the moment.

"Be antenna," Skyfisher said.

Hilton pictured a huge erector set tower trampled by Godzilla, showering sparks and mayhem.

"No, Hilton. Listen."

Mind games. A parlor trick.

Hilton remembered doing magic shows as a kid with his Gilbert chemistry set, turning water into wine with the help of phenolphthalein solution and sodium carbonate. Mixing the chemicals, his thoughts swirled like a brew in a witch's cauldron, his mind's eye caught in their vortex. After a while, the churning thought-mill started to run out of steam. It wasn't center stage anymore. It wasn't *him*.

Hilton heard a faint fluttering in the air, barely perceptible. Probably his imagination. His legs and back ached. He waited. No one else was quitting and he wasn't going to be the wuss. Not yet anyway. In the spirit of the former body-builder governor of California, he tried to make friends with the pain.

"Oh my gosh." It was Inez who said this, in a child's voice. Hilton opened his eyes to a mass of fluttering caramel, coalescing into a humanoid shape. Countless butterscotch wings bordered with black and white spots shimmering, quivering to stillness. An organic body suit of living butterflies, clusters of them circling the larger mass and landing on it.

Salvo had transformed into a butterfly man, sheathed in a fairytale membrane of insect life, overwhelming in their numbers.

It was an astonishing sight. Visions of homing trees in Mexico, migration patterns, pheromones, magnetism - a myriad thoughts and theories all dissolved in the pure magic of the miraculous. For once in his life, Hilton was speechless.

Chapter Twenty

The young warrior lay broken in the field, a meal for crows and coyotes. Buffalo turned away from him and advanced towards Tell Me A Story.

It was easy to appear desperate and scared, stumbling, catching her breath, looking around wildly, running through a thicket, letting its branches tangle and slow her down, all the while scanning for trees. One chance, one story, and it depended on the tree.

Buffalo came on, keening his song, leaning on his staff, favoring the leg where she had sliced him. It looked scorched and ugly, but searing the wound had apparently staunched the flow of blood. She gauged the distance, staying close enough to encourage his pursuit, far enough to give her time to find the right tree. Dropping her sack, Tell Me A Story feigned a collapse and while on the ground, felt for her cane knife, razor sharp, still wrapped in a cloth inside a pouch tied to her waist. She lurched to her feet, a bit too quickly. Her head was spinning and Buffalo was close. Too close.

The edge of a deeper stand of trees was not far off. With a prayer of thanks she staggered towards it, reaching for the trunk while looking at the lay of its branches, stumbling towards another, leaning on it for support. All the while surveying clusters of trees, searching for the right combination. Best to choose quickly. Sooner or later Buffalo would charge or simply wait for her to tire out. A group of trees fifty paces away caught her eye. They might do. The lowest branch of the center-most was high, but she would risk it. She dared not wait any longer; he was closing fast.

Tell Me A Story leaped for the branch and began to pull herself up, but her moccasins slipped on the smooth bark and she collapsed to the ground with a thud. Less than a tree length away, Buffalo picked up his pace and began singing with renewed vigor. Should she run for another stand of trees? If she went sprawling again here, it was over.

Pulling off her moccasins. Tell Me A Story leapt for the branch, missed, landed on her feet and jumped again, her hands sweaty and slippery. But the tough soles of her feet clung to the trunk and gave her the purchase she needed to pull to the first branch, her hind leg lifting just beyond Buffalo's grasp. She clambered to the second and third branch of the tree, and then risked one quick glance down.

He was standing directly below her, a glimmer of petulance in his eyes, a blend of Little Rock not getting what he wanted, mixed with Buffalo's stoic admiration of a woman giving him the slip. She wavered, looking wildly for the next foothold, as if caught in her own snare. Would he pursue?

Tell Me A Story begin to sing.
Master of Breath
Thank you for the tree
A warrior is here
Who's killed many men
Now he's chasing a woman
Such a brave man!

She heard the thud of his staff hitting the ground and the sound of him reaching into the branches. Climbing! She feigned being stuck. Then she climbed a bit higher and then one more branch up for good measure. Barely enough time to remove the knife from its pouch. She wanted him angry. Angry enough to act without thinking.

Using his immense strength, Buffalo pulled himself up limb by limb, impelling his large body through the branches until he reached a gap. Tell Me A Story could see the sweat on his forehead glistening as she threw her cane knife right at his face. He swatted it away, slicing his hand, leaving a thin red line.

Master of Breath
Thank you for the knife
The woman chaser
Is bleeding

Buffalo kept climbing. Every muscle in her body urged Tell Me A Story to move up out of his reach. She forced herself to stay, a whisker ahead of his grasp. Surveying the canopy around her - a bird's nest, a beetle crawling on a leaf, and the adjacent treetops swaying gently in the breeze. A sound in the branches above, a small chestnut brown bird landing in the nest, regarding Tell Me A Story with curiosity. In that instant of inattention, Buffalo reached up and grabbed her by the ankle. His hand was slippery with blood, and she jerked her foot out of its grasp and moved higher up the tree, her heart pounding wildly.

The branches were thinner at this height and they rocked with her weight as she leaned on them. It had to be now.

She pulled herself up as high as she could on the branch, leaned back and let it rock her forward, like a child playing squirrel. As it reached the end of its forward arc, Tell Me A Story let go of the branch and leaped. A breathless instant in the air, and she reached for topmost branch of another tree. It broke as she tried to grasp it with her right hand, but her left hand had hold of another branch. She wrapped her legs around the treetop, swinging away from Buffalo and then back towards him. Exultant, the squirrel reborn leaned her treetop away from his reach, and let it swing her towards a third tree. Tell Me A Story leaned and embraced the tree, transferring her weight to it easily.

> *Master of Breath*
> *Thank you for the trees*
> *The woman chaser*
> *Is in the branches*

Buffalo jumped for the nearby treetop as its upper branch whip-lashed back, slapping him squarely in the face. He grasped for a handhold, but the upper branches of the second tree could not support his weight, as Tell Me A Story had hoped. From her perch, she watched with professional interest as the big man became his name. Buffalos cannot fly, not in this story.

He fell, his great bulk breaking cross branches, his head slamming against the trunk of the tree, his left eye speared by an upright sucker branch. With a roar of pain he crashed to the ground and lay in a heap, moaning.

Tell Me A Story let a wave of relief wash over her and began her descent. Much to do. Skyfisher, with his broken ribs, might not have subdued High Eagle. Halfway down, a voice called out.

"Ho!"

She froze. Through the foliage of the tree, it was possible to make out the outline of a man carrying a pack, his bald head glistening in the first rays of the morning sun. He set his pack on the ground and began to sing quietly.

Grey Turtle!

Tell Me A Story climbed further down and jumped to the ground. Although glad for an ally, she was ashamed of being completely disheveled, covered with mud and leaf litter.

The Bald One, leaning on his walking staff, chewed tobacco leaf, the edges of his mouth stained brown with it. He was short, stocky and though slow and deliberate, he was no turtle. Tell Me A Story had seen him humble many a young warrior, armed with just a staff. Bald as an egg, with a face as round as a full moon, Grey Turtle surveyed the situation and smiled.

"Find what you were looking for up there?" he asked.

"He found me," she said.

"And the way down," observed the Bald One. *"He still breathes."*

"Skyfisher -" began Tell Me A Story.

"Alive."

"You saw him?

"Resting."

"High Eagle –"

"Bound securely."

Grey Turtle walked over to where Buffalo lay, a mass of bruises and broken limbs, his left eye dangling like a plucked fruit on a bloody stem.

"What will you do with this one?"

"Nothing," she replied. *"He's going to hunt buffalo in the spirit world."*

"Soon enough," the Bald One agreed. *"His life is in your hands, but he can be more useful alive than dead."*

"How?" asked Tell Me A Story, brushing some of the dried mud from her tunic.

Grey Turtle rubbed the back of his head and regarded Tell Me A Story with a keen eye.

"What will happen if you kill High Eagle and let Buffalo die?"

"They got into a fight with the traders –"

"– and they were killed? Buffalo and High Eagle are warriors ordered to search for you. Others will follow. They will find bodies, not yours. There is no doubt in this," the Bald One said, shaking his head.

"If we let them live –"

"They owe you their lives. You think they want the story told of how they were defeated by a woman and a blind song carrier? We trade their silence for ours."

"They have no honor," Tell Me A Story said.

"They have no choice."

"I don't trust High Eagle."

"What else can you do? You must not kill them."

Tell Me A Story stood in silence for a moment and finally said, *"I will agree on one condition."*

Skyfisher was covered with a blanket, sleeping on the ground next to the tree he had been tied to. Tell Me A Story kissed him softly on the forehead and turned to Grey Turtle. The Bald One was a healer and dancer, not that these were separate things. His dancing wove a patient's spirits into the fabric of the medicine.

"What Skyfisher needs now is rest," he said.

Grey Turtle had reluctantly consented to Tell Me A Story's condition and the two of them set out gathering herbs, moss for bandages, wood and scraps of cloth for splints. Working together, they washed the warriors' wounds, pulling the arrow through High Eagle's thigh and setting a broken arm and leg on Buffalo's battered body. His vacant eye socket was covered with a poultice. High Eagle was sullen. Buffalo, in great pain, had regressed to Little Rock. His one eye regarded Tell Me A Story with a grudging appreciation. Both men agreed to Grey Turtle's terms when told their healing came with a price.

"You met a Chickasaw trading party," Grey Turtle said. *"Though outnumbered, you fought bravely and defeated them, receiving serious injuries. You found no sign of Skyfisher, his wife, or myself. Your lives are given back to you on condition that you will not pursue or harm us. Never. You swear this promise with a blood-spirit oath."*

Grey Turtle approached Skyfisher, lying with his back against a tree.

"Name?" asked Grey Turtle, pointing to him.

"Lewis."

"Loo-is means?"

No response.

"You are 'Skyfisher' now. Skyfisher," he repeated, patting Lewis's chest. *"Me, Grey Turtle. Understand?"*

He laid his hands on Lewis' shoulders, much as Falling Star had done.

"You are full of questions. Later we will walk your path together." His face crinkled to a smile. Lewis intuited the goodwill behind his words, and for the moment that was enough.

He had not been able to thank Tell Me A Story for saving his life. She was the only good reason to be in this place, not that he had a choice. Why in heaven's name was he here, in a dream he could not awaken from, a dream with pain and death?

For a few days, the Bald One kept High Eagle bound. When his leg had begun to heal, they built a litter for Little Rock Buffalo. Tell Me A Story retrieved Lewis' sack from the tree where they had encountered the traders. The Bald One redistributed their loads and they broke camp, heading west towards the big river, avoiding the main trail. Grey Turtle and a brooding High Eagle pulled the litter, with Tell Me A Story helping when she could. Too painful for Lewis to pull anything.

Traveling off the beaten path, they encountered no scouting parties. The ache in his side notwithstanding, Lewis appreciated the resilience of a new, improved body. The soles of his feet were leather, his leg muscles sinewy, and when was the last time he had triple abs?

There had been plenty of nature walks with his father when he was a kid, but hiking in the woods had never been like this. The forest was lush, full of life. Wild turkeys, rabbits, red squirrels, deer, even a small herd of wild pigs, all a bit cartoonish in what passed for Lewis's field of vision. He saw what looked a mink or a stoat peeking at them through a bush and half expected it to start singing. In the afternoon when they paused for a rest, Grey Turtle hunted small game with his bow. When he wasn't helping to pull the litter, they hobbled High Eagle's legs, tying him securely at night and taking turns to keep a close watch on him.

"*We have your promise,*" said Grey Turtle, "*but this will bind it.*"

That night, Tell Me A Story gutted and skinned a rabbit, lighting a fire with flint and steel, using dry moss for tinder and twigs for kindling and charging Lewis with the task of gathering more wood. Tell Me A Story fashioned a spit, and as the rabbit cooked, she sang to Lewis, not caring whether he understood or not.

Spirit brother
Wrapped inside the flesh and blood of my husband
He cannot hear this song

Spirit brother
Take these words
Send them to him when you can

It took four days to reach the big river and another three to build a raft. Buffalo was in no condition to help, so the others cut, gathered, and bound the poles for the raft's platform. High Eagle grudgingly accepted the labor and security measures. Blood oath or no, he was still their prisoner. When the time came for the parting of their ways, he displayed no surprise as Tell Me A Story revealed the final condition for their release.

"In case either of you decide to break your word," she said.

She had Grey Turtle and Lewis hold High Eagle's hand securely on top of a log. With no preamble, she took her cane knife and began carving his left pinky finger as though she were slicing venison sausage, deftly working the blade into the slot above the knuckle. High Eagle gasped but did not cry aloud. Lewis promised himself that he would never on any account, piss this woman off. Tell Me A Story staunched the bleeding with sphagnum moss and then turned to one-eyed Buffalo, recovering from his wounds, but still weak and bound to the litter.

"I have this," she said, opening a medicine pouch and pulling out a putrefied shrunken eyeball wrapped in a piece of rabbit skin, *"but it will not keep."*

She gestured to his left hand and the big man began to sing. Tell Me A Story took her knife and commenced to slice into his small finger, and after a few passes the cane blade broke. Grey Turtle offered his hatchet, but it was not quite sharp enough to do the job cleanly. For lack of a better tool, they placed the finger on the log, positioned the hatchet blade on top of the joint and hammered a heavy rock on to the back end of the hatchet. It took two blows for the finger to pop, Buffalo singing all the while. After covering the stump with moss, Tell Me A Story collected her digital trophies.

"I will keep these," she said, *"and if you try to break your oath, I will display your fingers and tell their story. To everyone."*

They set the raft adrift on the big river with enough dried meat aboard to sustain two men for a few days. High Eagle did not look back, not once.

Chapter Twenty One

"We'll go to a place where you can heal," Grey Turtle said. *"A day's journey. Can you walk another day?"*

When the question was conveyed to Lewis via gesture-talk, he agreed. He was getting a bit better at sensing facial expressions, reading Grey Turtle's smile like a florescent map.

"Not a word of complaint from this man," the Bald One said.

"Wait till he learns our language," said Tell Me A Story.

They set off following the river, then veering away to the northeast. Grey Turtle gave Lewis a freshly cut walking staff and beckoned to Tell Me A Story.

"Give him new words."

Pausing for rest on the trail, Tell Me A Story sat next to Lewis on a log, the Bald One leaned against a tree, eavesdropping. With mime and a glossary of words, she recounted the tale a hunter who went searching for game along the river they had been following.

"Hot and tired, the hunter jumped into the river for a swim. A large snake swam up and wrapped itself around him." Tell Me A Story's tongue flickered and her arm slid around Lewis' waist.

"He pulled himself out of the water, only to be dragged along the ground by the snake." A tug on his elbow elicited a wince from Lewis.

"Cracking his ribs," she added.

"That big old snake wouldn't let go. Just kept dragging him along. Some say people blazed this trail, but it was the snake pulling that poor hunter. And he never complained. What a man!" she added, warming to the story.

"The snake took the hunter to a lake. Pulled him in. Deeper and deeper."

Her fingers walked on his shin.

"Up to his knees, his thighs, his private parts —"

"Aiee!" interjected Grey Turtle.

"— his belly, his chest. The hunter was really getting scared now, but still not a sound. Who could he complain to - the snake? What do you think happened?"

Lewis, who had been following the gist of the story with the help of some play-acting and a few word-assists, mimed someone being lassoed, then pointed to Tell Me A Story.

"A turtle saved him," suggested Grey Turtle.

"An alligator," Tell Me A Story straightened her arms out, palms together, nipping in provocative places.

"The snake had to choose: let go of the hunter or be eaten by the alligator. He let go, thinking the alligator would go for the hunter. But that old alligator was angry. He wanted the snake bad, with its tail waving all around." Minor pandemonium, simulated tail thrashing.

"So the alligator caught the snake and they fought and fought. The hunter, he was so hurt from getting dragged along the trail, he could barely pull himself out of the water. He found a walking stick, like this one, and he headed home."

Grey Turtle laughed.

"We go now. More stories on the trail," he said.

Shouldering their loads, they set off again. Tell Me A Story became her name, imagining Lewis as a spirit-brother trapped like a caterpillar inside the cocoon of her husband. Maybe he could be coaxed out with tales of the Great Flood and Lodge Boy.

"Corn Woman shook herself to gather beans and seeds. Lodge Boy ran from his pursuers, tearing his shirt on these brambles…"

The paths they traversed became stories, Lewis asking for help with words he didn't understand. He listened, smitten like a child at a puppet show. When he could absorb no more, they walked in silence listening to the calls of birds and insects, giving Lewis time to fathom the mare's nest he had tumbled into, waiting for the Slithy Toves to gyre and gimble.

It was real enough when he'd been hammered in the ribs and tied to the tree. A deep breath brought a jab of pain in his side. Despite the latent strength of a younger body, his muscles ached from the morning's walk. Though blind, he was living inside a four dimensional organic sonar thermal-imaging life force detector that was relentlessly sending him signals he could barely decipher. Like being hardwired into an ultra-sophisticated Star Trek device without a manual. Anyone trying to help him might as well be speaking Klingon. In the midst of a fairy tale forest thrumming with life, he was the idiot son who needed to be a contender. It seemed the only way to explain the mystery was to figure it out for himself. Braille this world with his ESP.

The woods were older, more primal than the forests he had walked in with his father on nature hikes. Lewis stopped to turn over a log, revealing an old cob web and a centipede, or rather the dye-transfer vibrational imprint of their forms. Rolling over a decaying branch rewarded him with a spotted salamander, glowing like a Huichol bead figurine. A thrill of discovery, as though the salamander had been waiting for him to be seen and validated. Grey Turtle came up behind him.

"Others wait for you," he said.

They journeyed at a leisurely pace, the forest growing more lush, the animals somehow less skittish. The path followed a meandering stream which broadened and roiled over an outcrop of rocks. A waterfall twice as tall as Lewis descended into a deep pool lined with ferns. The ground bordering the pool was covered with a carpet of moss.

"We stay here," Grey Turtle said.

They left Tell Me A Story to luxuriate in the pool while setting up camp nearby. Lewis had spent a week at a survival school in the Pine Barrens of New Jersey and remembered a few things - pine needle tea, carving a wooden bowl, making a lean-to. Still, feeling mostly clueless in this dream forest, he followed Grey Turtle's lead.

The Bald One gathered from the resources at hand as if he was pulling supplies off the shelf at a hardware store. They set up two primitive shelters from branches and boughs.

Lewis collected kindling and dead wood for a fire. With his knife, Grey Turtle scraped wood shavings and shredded bark fragments, laying them on a dry wood base. He found a straight, sturdy stem as long as his arm and carved a small hole in the wood platform, fitting the stem upright in the hole, and surrounding it with a small pile of wood-bark tinder. Kneeling, he began to rhythmically roll the stick between his hands, twirling back and forth in rapid oscillation as his hands moved up and down, the smooth stick turning one way then another, blurring. In the space of five minutes, a thin trail of smoke lifted from the notch.

On cue, Lewis blew gently at the notch, nudging the pile of tinder closer to the source of friction. A glowing ember coerced the tinder to ignite. A small miracle. A flame appeared and slowly spread through the tinder. Grey Turtle gently pushed the wood platform with its burning altar into a nest of kindling he had prepared. The flame licked and danced, and with a few more breaths of encouragement, the kindling complied and crackled. Lewis husbanded the fire with more wood, and turned to see Grey Turtle heading off, bow and arrow in hand.

That night, they feasted on roast rabbit. Lewis curled up next to Tell Me A Story, whispering in the best words he could muster, how grateful he was for her having saved him.

They awoke to the aroma of tea. Sunlight filtered through the canopy; the surface of the pool reflected a grey sky, the deeper greens of the forest coming to life. The steady white noise of the waterfall blended with the thrum of insects and amphibians, transitioning to plaintive coos of morning doves and the trill of wood thrushes. To Lewis, the forest ignited and came to light like a fire. Everything was alive and in motion, even the plants, trading light for breath.

"What do you see?" asked Grey Turtle, holding a steaming brew of tea in a bark cup.

Lewis had no words. Grey Turtle turned to Tell Me A Story.

"What did Falling Star tell you?"

"Inside of Skyfisher is a spirit from another time. Loo-is. Some-where else, my husband is a spirit inside of Loois. I ask, 'Why is this?' Falling Star says if he tells me, they feed him to the dogs."

"They are feeding him now." Grey Turtle said.

"What do you mean?" Tell Me A Story asked.

"Falling Star is no more."

"Who did this?"

"The Lesser Sun thinks anything hidden is a threat. If we were to return to Flour Village now, our lives would be forfeit."

Tell Me A Story turned to Lewis.

"Falling Star - dead," with an accompanying grisly gesture. She asked Grey Turtle, *"What is Skyfisher's mission?"*

"You won't believe me."

"Bald One, stick your head out of its shell and remember my name."

Grey Turtle shrugged. *"Skyfisher is trying to save our world. That is his story."*

All the events of the past weeks had been unbelievable. This was no different.

"We don't know if Skyfisher or any man can do this," Grey Turtle said. *"In time, Loo-is will return to his world and keep trying. Our work is keep Loo-is alive, teach him what he needs to know for when he returns. At the moment, we are safe here. We head towards White Apple Village soon, or risk being captured."*

Lewis wasn't able to follow the conversation, but he instinctively trusted Grey Turtle. There was a hint of humor and compassion in him, even while managing to be as deadly serious as an advance man for the Apocalypse. Perhaps he knew why Lewis was here. Falling Star had fallen, that much was clear. Lewis figured it was his arrival which had triggered Falling Star's death in some way.

A moment's respite was welcome. Lewis's body ached, his mind a whirlpool of unanswered questions and conjecture.

This couldn't be a dream, nor could it be real. Tell that to his busted ribs. He yearned to wake up in a proper bed and see the world the way he used to, without 4D mescalito avatars broadcasting from every entity in his field of vision. He longed for business as usual and the food of his people. A lean tongue sandwich with hot mustard on a Kaiser role would go down particularly well right about now. A half-sour pickle and a hot potato knish, the flakey round kind.

In this realm of thought, it was a short leap to the lower chakras. Lewis regarded Tell Me A Story with a blend of awe and ardor. He didn't know all the details of how she managed to mangle so formidable an opponent as Buffalo. The fact that she had was disconcerting, to say the least. Recalling their night of intimacy, he knew categorically there was nothing he could do to woo her, except perhaps to wait.

"Walk?" he asked. She consented.

They explored around the waterfall, the swimming hole, the shallower pools it fed, the trees which grew thickly around them.

"Eden must have been like this", Lewis thought. "All that's missing is —."

No sooner had this synapse fired when a coiled rope appeared on the path in front of them, as though willed into being. Lewis, still not quite familiar with the way his sensory system processed color, perceived the shape as non-descript until the top end of the coil opened its mouth.

Cottonmouth.

Tell Me A Story had seen it and spoke its name.

"Ula," miming bite and death. Lewis nodded, remembering the tale of the water snake. Divining his thoughts, Tell Me A Story said, *"There is another story about a boy who tried to shoot a snake. It nearly shot him! Understand?"*

Lewis shook his head, *"No."*

Giving the snake a wide berth, they walked on. With patience and gestures, Tell Me A Story told the story slowly and simply, making sure he absorbed the words.

"Now you tell it back to me."

Lewis stumbled through the narrative and was rewarded with a hand squeeze. Over the next two days, she attempted to translate what Grey Turtle had told them about Skyfisher and Lewis saving the world.

"How?" he asked.

"You will learn. We will help."

As he leaned to kiss her, she raised her hand and his lips touched her fingertips. They walked to the waterfall in silence, watching its spray rise and dissolve in the morning mist.

In spite of the pain in his cracked ribs, Lewis was able to spear a fish, to the delight of Grey Turtle.

"Just like Skyfisher!"

Lewis gathered a flat stone from the river bed to cook the fish on, but when he was about to place it in the fire pit, Grey Turtle stopped him.

"A river rock will explode!" Fist-knuckles rapping and fingers spread apart, with prolonged guttural bombs-away sound effects. Lewis, ashamed, remembered the warning from Survival 101. Rocks taken from a river held water trapped inside them. Put them in a fire and - bam! There were no written disclaimers here for things like booby-trapped rocks and poisonous mushrooms. In an oral tradition, if you forgot the warning, it cost you.

The three of them sat around the fire, the aroma of cooked trout inspiring appetites. Tell Me A Story watched the glow of the flame flicker on Grey Turtle's face.

"Falling Star told me the future looks bad for our people," she said.

"We see it coming," Grey Turtle responded. *"A dry stream bed in the winter will tell you which way the river will flow in the spring. The waterfall has to be there,"* he pointed. *"It can be no other place. Soon enough we fight the Fran-zay. There are more of them than we can count. They have guns. Our warriors will be shot, our women and children made slaves. Other tribes will ally themselves with the Fran-zay and - ,"* he slap-wiped his hands, *"we will*

lose our land, our villages, everything. Some will survive, like scattered kernels of corn. Few know how to tend the true Sacred Fire."
"Anyone can tend a fire," said Tell Me A Story.

"You of all people understand that the meaning of a story is hidden, like the water inside that rock," Grey Turtle said, pointing to the flat stone Lewis had taken from the river.

"In the wrong hands, the rock will explode. In the right hands, the rock serves its purpose."

"You speak in riddles," Tell Me A Story said.

"The rock needs to be with its brothers. The force of the river is too great for a single stone. Together, many stones shape the course of the river."

"Someone could build a dam," Tell Me A Story said.

"They could," Grey Turtle responded. *"That might be a good thing, for a while. It would make a larger swimming hole. You could catch more fish. But the fish would be trapped. They could not swim upstream to carry the life of the river. So a dam might not be such a good thing after all."*

The Bald One looked back at Tell Me A Story, mimicking her own suspicious expression so she couldn't help but laugh.

"One day you will understand what the stones and the river are telling us," Grey Turtle said. *"In the meantime, this fish is ready to eat."*

The next day they continued their journey, moving through the forest to more open ground, land that had been burned and cleared. They saw a few bison, deer, wild turkeys, rabbits aplenty. The pasture turned to scrub and then swamp. Grey Turtle had them coat their exposed skin with a mixture of mud and a pungent herb Tell Me A Story had found. It reminded Lewis of catnip.

At dusk, they were set upon by hordes of mosquitoes and Lewis was convinced the insects were avoiding the others, having sniffed out the first Jew in the Lost World. The ground was muddy and he had been faithfully following Grey Turtle's footsteps, which emitted a pale phosphorescent glow for his eyes only. Lewis stepped to the side to smell an orchid and his leg quickly sank up to the knee, stuck so fast he could not extract it.

"Don't move!" Tell Me A Story cried.

No shit, Lewis thought.

A few minutes later, Grey Turtle retraced his tracks and returned with a length of vine, tossing one end to Lewis, holding the other end high. Lewis pulled but his hands kept slipping. Wrapping the vine around his hand for a better grip, he let Grey Turtle attempt to pull him out. After several tries, they heard a pop as the suction seal of the mud broke.

"Moccasin!" Lewis cried.

"Leave it," Grey Turtle said, as a muddied Lewis crawled out of the muck. *"Later you can change your name to mine. For now, step where I step!"*

Lewis nodded ruefully. Walking with one moccasin wasn't so bad. The soles of Skyfisher's feet were callous hardened.

As the moon rose they kept moving to get past the swamp. Not so far away, what sounded like a large cat was killing something, breaking its bones and ripping it apart.

Dryer ground led to the banks of a stream, where they watered and washed themselves. In the distance the faint glow of a campfire flickered. They gave it a wide berth. It wasn't until late in the evening that they reached a spot Grey Turtle deemed safe to rest at.

Since their night of intimacy, Tell Me A Story and Lewis had shared virtually no physical contact. They spooned each other now, too weary for anything but sleep.

Lewis dreamed of getting stuck in the mud up to his chest, his arms outstretched to stop the overpowering suction, sinking deeper to his neck, breathing in short desperate bursts, the earth opening and swallowing him.

Grey Turtle shook him awake.

"Something didn't want to let you go."

It was still nighttime. They broke camp and walked in the moonlight, their path flecked with pale green sentinels. Glowworms. To Lewis, they appeared pretty much the way he perceived the rest of world, in muted neon.

Heading east now, towards the dawn. The trees thinned. On the horizon, the silhouette of a long hill appeared, its shape suggesting it had been honed by men, like a giant flint-knapped spearhead. As they approached, the scale of the earthwork became more apparent. Thirty feet high, Lewis figured. Maybe two football fields in length. They must be near the White Apple Village.

Drawing closer, there was something vaguely organic about the mound, as if a hive queen had stung the earth and this massive lump had spring from the ground to be carved and cultivated by a horde of workers. It seemed incomplete, a foundation waiting for a building, a petroglyph ready for the sun to slant in a particular direction on a specific day, revealing hidden scripture. The mound was a blank canvas, an empty stage beckoning for players to be more alive on it than they are in life. *Mount this hill if you are worthy of being here.*

Closer still, the shadowy outline turned brown-green in the half-light of morning. Lewis heard the faintest of rustles nearby. Two lines of men emerged from the woods on either side of the path. Grey Turtle stopped and raised his hands. A ring of warriors armed with bows, arrows and spears surrounded them.

Chapter Twenty Two

It took three days for the raft to reach an outpost near Flour Village. They drifted right past, no captives, no honor. High Eagle was in no mood to offer explanations, especially concerning the loss of their fingers.

He had spent his nights imagining the Story Woman naked and vulnerable. He would find her and the Blind One, bring them back to face the Lesser Sun. She will watch as her husband takes his last breath.

A moan interrupted his thoughts. Buffalo was drifting in and out of consciousness. He needed attention and a healer. They had run out of food and only one option remained, Yatanocha, Little Rock Buffalo's village, a bit further downstream. The big man had been respected there, mostly out of fear. Would they help him now that he was helpless?

Grey Turtle dropped to his knees, laid his weapons on the ground and beckoned for Lewis and Tell Me A Story to do the same. Their belongings were taken and they were herded towards the plateaued hill whose profile loomed in the moonlight. The Bald One spoke a few words to their captors and was ignored. At the foot of the plateau, there was a brief, heated exchange between two members of their escort. A short, stocky man gestured for Tell Me A Story to stay with him and another warrior. Lewis and Grey Turtle were escorted by six guards up a series of steps carved into the steep slope, some thirty feet to the top.

The sky was clear. The broad belt of the Milky Way swept overhead like a cosmic highway, festooned with countless jewels. A few torches blazed at the top of the mound where other guards awaited. White Apple seemed more of an armed encampment than a village.

At the top of the mound plateau, Lewis's radar vision surveyed the expanse, flat ground with three pyramid-shaped hills, each of which seemed to rise at least as high as the mound itself. They marched to the pyramid at the far end. At the top of it, there was a small hut with a fire flickering inside.

The guards gestured for Lewis and Grey Turtle to be seated on the ground outside the hut. One of the warriors entered and returned accompanied by a tall, thin elder. He moved with an aura of authority and gave Lewis a neon flavored look of distaste. Grey Turtle uttered a few words, but the older man cut him off. He barked a few questions and Lewis heard him mention Tell Me A Story's name. Undaunted, the Bald One spoke at length, gathering force as he did so. It evoked a sharp retort from the old man, met with an even-tempered rejoinder and a gesture towards Lewis.

A debating match, Lewis thought.

The elder paused, weighed Grey Turtle's words, took another look at Lewis and shook his head. He turned away and walked back into the hut.

They were kept waiting a long time. Lewis sat with his arms wrapped around his knees and eventually nodded off. He was awakened by one of the guards, who pulled him to his feet and ushered him to the edge of the pyramid. The Bald One was nowhere in sight. A full moon illuminated the top of the mound where a larger pyramid hill stood, roughly 100 yards away. Lewis and his guard mounted its steps to where another hut was situated at its summit. No fire within. The guard showed him a place on the floor where he could lie down and left without a word.

Lewis, shivering from the cold, curled into a ball and rested his head on his arm, wondering if the Red Queen would call for his head in the morning. Would any harm come to Tell Me A Story? This was the place where Falling Star had directed them, unless the Bald One was mistaken. His argument with the elder carried the tone of two men who'd known each other for a long time. Feeling as though he'd been weighed in the balance and found wanting, Lewis drifted into an uneasy sleep.

He awoke famished, roused by a guard who escorted him off the plateau to a place where he could relieve himself. A path through the woods led to a large hut which smelled of food. One main room and a smaller anteroom to one side. The larger room had two tables with log benches. A mess hall.

It was empty, except for someone seated in the corner on a stump, unmoving. With a gesture for Lewis to sit at the table, the guard left and returned with a bowl filled with some form of sustenance and a wooden spoon.

It was a warm, tasteless porridge, but Lewis was hungry enough to chew a shoe. Which reminded him of the lost moccasin. Easy to forget, with the bottoms of Skyfisher's feet as tough as leather. The dirt floor of this hut was slightly damp and hard from the passage of many feet. Few emanations here, a slight thermal pulse from the one who sat in the corner. The guard had not brought him any food. Lewis called out, but there was no response.

A sound of voices nearby brought Lewis to the doorway, only to be stopped by the guard who made it clear he was to stay inside. He did, attempting without success to communicate to his fellow inmate, a young man in his early twenties, with hair in the upside-down bowl-style, cut to above his ears like Skyfisher's, a cross between the Beatles and Benedictine monks. His readout was low on Lewis's Kirlian Richter scale, like someone you'd expect to see in a psyche ward. The eyes were open but they did not seem to focus or recognize anything. He wasn't home.

Me neither, thought Lewis. Nothing to do but wait, hoping Tell Me A Story was being treated better than this.

Around mid-day, a chorus of male voices shouted in the distance, then silence. A tall lean man barely out of his teens appeared in the doorway as a ghost silhouette, carrying a bowl of food. His hairstyle curved over his ears like the petals of a flower, as if cupping them to hear better. A pair of arched eyebrows and an aquiline nose added to an incandescent birdlike appearance. He glanced for the briefest instant at Lewis, then looked away and moved to a far corner of the room. Other men followed him in, each carrying a bowl. The bird-man was joined by his physical opposite, glowing like a firefly, a short, slightly over-weight youth, his hair tied in a knot, who swayed, almost waddled, into the room. A Samurai Baby Huey. A cluster of men followed, thirty or more. Two were twins, whose foreheads were flattened and elongated, with long loop rings hanging from their ears, giving them an iconic look, like the statues on Easter Island. They vibrated bluish colors, corresponding to their temperament. Too many others for Lewis to get a sense of as individuals.

The guard brought Lewis a bowl of vegetable stew, a slight improvement over the morning's porridge. Everyone sat at benches and ate in silence, studiously avoiding looking in Lewis's direction. At one point, an older man poked his head in the doorway, glanced around the room and left. The atmosphere lightened perceptibly after his appearance, but no one spoke.

Lewis, noticing that the catatonic guy in the corner still had no food, stood up and brought his half-finished bowl to share. The bird-man intercepted him mid-course, and ushered him back to his seat. Lewis wanted to say something to break the ice, but this was not the moment. The bird-man reminded him of an older Alfalfa from Our Gang, minus the antenna hair-spike. His facial tattoos gleamed like a watch dial in Sky-fisher's Geiger-vision.

Alfalfa commandeered a few portions of leftover stew from several donors and discreetly handed the fellow in the corner a bowlful. Then the guard came for Lewis and he was led, along with the entire group of men, to a lodge similar to the ceremonial meeting place in Tell Me A Story's Village, a large room with one entrance.

They entered; Lewis, nudged by the guard, last in line. Though it was midday, a fire burned in the middle of the room. A row of benches ringed the walls. The group circled the fire counter clock-wise and stood in front of the benches. A drum began to pound. Through the door a line of elders entered, eight in all. Several had circular breast plates hanging from the necks; all had feathers tied in their hair. One man beat a hand drum; another wore a face mask made of bark. Even with the mask, his body was unmistakable. Grey Turtle, the Bald One, carrying several long feathers, his feather earrings swaying, his upper torso bare, a loose garment draped around his waist. He moved gracefully, somewhere between a walk and a dance. Next came the austere tall elder who had argued with Grey Turtle, wearing a long robe, followed by someone smaller in stature but more regal in bearing, seeming to take in everyone in the room. He was one of the elder's in Lewis's dream, Marsh Fox. He recognized some of the others as well and oddly enough, recalled their names. Black Hawk, Wind on the Water, Rattle Spirit, Rough One, Twisted Foot. Last to enter was a reedy, weasel faced man, Lightning, who looked as though he was itching to pick a fight.

The elders formed a ring with their backs to the fire, facing the outer circle of younger men. The drum, which had been sounding all the while, stopped and everyone stood in silence, the only sound the crackling fire. Wind on the Water began to chant, the drum joining in again.

Grey Turtle started to move to the drumbeat. His gestures morphed effortlessly into a dance, as if the drum was animating his body. It reminded Lewis of someone doing sign language interpretation at a concert. Grey Turtle embodied the music, shivering with the drum pulses and embellishing them in ways the sound could not express. It wasn't flashy, like the fancy hoop dancers Lewis had once seen at a Pow-Wow. Simpler, with elegance and grace. The movements were spare, a flick of the wrist, a cock of the head, a gentle sway, which somehow combined to convey a suite of images.

His mask had a blank, vacant look. On Grey Turtle, it seemed to take on a multitude of faces, each gesture engendering an expression, a rainbow of emotions flickering by like picture cards in a shuffling deck or images in a kinetoscope. A shy child walking in the wake of an older brother, a coquettish young woman, an impatient suitor, an angry rival, a despairing mother, a proud father, a resolute elder, the transitions as seamless as a set of rippling waves.

As a tenant in Skyfisher's body, Lewis sensed his surroundings as a glowing impressionist tableau. Grey Turtle's dance emanated bursts of light like showers from firework sparklers, with the movements taking on an ephemeral life of their own, the formless taking form, and before you could name it, gone, replaced by another shape. A hint of recognition, then it was gone, too.

Lewis thought he saw the first stages of a human embryo, the flight of a hummingbird, the beating heart of a wildcat, the predatory dive of a hawk, the flick of a fish tail.

Then the scale of the dance seemed to shift as Grey Turtle's movements took on less recognizable forms. Everyone else in the room began to move – Lewis, too - beckoned by an invisible partner, impelled, shuffling around the fire.

The chant was repetitive and simple, as were the movements, a series of shuffling half-steps. Swept along by the current of the music, they moved in time with the drum beat. Grey Turtle wove his dance around and between the circle of elders and younger men, hovering, touching each of them with one of his feathers. When it brushed against Lewis, it was as though he'd stepped on a live wire. A surge of electricity whipped through his body, CAT-scanning every neuron. Lewis felt his material self become like carbonated water, zillions of bubbles bursting in effervescence, his thoughts dissolving as inexorably as an Alka Seltzer tablet, leaving him a dancing rhythmic being embraced and animated by a finer force, a planet orbiting with others around a sun-fire. Grey Turtle was a comet, a wild card, an angel whisking amidst the denser dancers like a neutrino incarnate, carrying a wordless message on behalf of the force impelling the dance.

Whatever it was, it seemed to be hungry. Not for power, animal sacrifices or good intentions, but for something which could be only experienced with every fiber, every synapse wholeheartedly engaged. If Horton was going to hear this Who, every cell in Lewis' body had to be on board, every bubble bursting with a quantum wave particle of love.

In the whirling logic of the dance, an indescribable feeling re-animated Lewis's body husk, resonating with the nameless signal. Everyone in the room was adding strength to it, brother planets revolving, listening, and suddenly silent and still. Grey Turtle removed his mask and joined the elders and younger men, sitting on the benches around the room, facing the fire. A long silence, punctuated by crackles and hisses from the fire pit.

Something had transpired, shifted, although Lewis couldn't say what. Words evaporated, like the memory of a dream. Everyone in the room had been shown a possibility that beckoned, reminding them what they were capable of.

They sat together for a while, then taking a cue from the elders, filed out of the lodge into the open air. Early evening. They had been inside for hours. The air was warm, moist and delicious. Lewis drank it in and followed the group to the mess hall, now set for a feast, cooked meat, fish, roasted vegetables, oysters. Before eating, every man offered a morsel of food to the four sides of the room, holding each piece and then placing it on the table in front of them. Four small mounds of food compassed every place setting.

One of the elders murmured a prayer. They all began to eat. It was the first serious food Lewis had in days and it was hard not to just wolf it down. There was a low murmur of conversation in the room. Lewis was seated next to Alfalfa, the bird-man, who identified himself as Haeden.

"You walk in Skyfisher's moccasins," Haeden said.

"One moccasin. The other is in a swamp."

"You didn't leave his wife behind."

"You know where she is?" Lewis asked.

"No," Haeden said. *"Skyfisher was a friend. You haven't said your name and it is impolite to ask."*

Lewis was about to state his name when it hit him that he was having a conversation with this man and understanding him perfectly. Every word. Snatches of conversation wafted in the periphery and he could understand them, too. Dumbfounded, he stammered, *"How –."*

A voice rang out from across the room.

"You see what is possible!"

It was the smaller elder Lewis had noted earlier, the one with the regal bearing. Marsh Fox.

"Here, we all speak the same language!" He pointed to Lewis and laughed.

"Like bees, one mind." Marsh Fox bowed slightly to Lewis and lightly placed his hand on his chest.

"You have met Haeden. Good."

"Is my – is Tell Me A Story alright?" Lewis asked.

"She is alright." Marsh Fox paused, glanced around the room and said, *"but we are in danger. The Great Sun, the Tattooed Serpent, the elders of our tribe, have heard whispers. We are outside their laws. Even though we are here for them, for all people, they do not know this. This is how it always has been. Everyone here came of their own will, except for you,"* looking at Lewis. *"There are those who prefer you were not here. I understand that."* Lewis glanced at the austere chief who had treated him so dismissively, but his face was as impassive as Grey Turtle's mask. Marsh Fox continued, *"They have killed Falling Star and if they find us here, all will be lost. We don't have much time. For now, we continue training."*

Without a word, the younger men arose and Haeden motioned for Lewis to follow.

"What about him?" Lewis asked Haeden, looking over at the catatonic young man who sat in the corner.

"Little Panther stays here," Haeden said.

Working as a team, the men cleared their bowls from the table and took them to a nearby stream to wash. The bowls were stored in an adjacent hut, where dried fish and fruit hung in string nets that draped across the ceiling.

Every man stripped to breech clothes and moccasins. Many went barefoot and Lewis followed suit, not wishing to be known as *One Shoe*. Haeden removed his earrings and other ornaments.

"Can you run?" he asked.

"We'll see," Lewis said. He still felt twinges of pain from his ribs, but he was not about to ask to see the nurse.

They took off in a jog, running in pairs, the twins leading, Lewis paired with the smaller, round-faced man, Spanky to Haeden's Alfalfa, a young Oliver Hardy at Boot Camp. They held a steady pace through the woods, Lewis letting Skyfisher's radar do the navigating. From his days running cross-country, Lewis figured it to be about a nine minute mile, but this was no golf course, with fallen limbs and boulders to dodge or hurdle, branches to duck under. Even with the extrasensory help, Lewis was on high alert, leaving little attention to free associate as he followed the trajectory of the pair in front of him, until they split around a sapling and Lewis's body bent its branches. Haeden shouted, *"Keep your eyes open, blind man!"*

They ran for about half an hour through forest and meadow, Lewis feeling a jolt of pain in his ribs every time his heels hit the ground heavily. Arriving at a lake, the leading pair of the group dove in and began to swim across. Lewis and Oliver Hardy were in the middle of the pack, and Lewis, sensing the large body of water ahead, rekindled his fear of being in water over his head far from any shore. He'd never swam across a lake. Pulled by the momentum of the group, he knew it would be extremely bad form to bail. Skyfisher's heart was beating faster and it wasn't only from the exertion of the run. A hint of panic, borrowed from Lewis like an emotional virus.

Skyfisher can swim this lake for breakfast. It's his body. All Lewis had to do was let him.

He dove in, a passenger in Skyfisher's boat, his arm movements morphing from a frantic windmill to a series of smoother strokes, his mind taking a back seat, refusing to dwell on the depth of water beneath him, trusting the strength of Skyfisher's arms. All systems go, until Oliver Hardy, who'd been swimming alongside him, dropped back and grabbed Lewis's leg. Reflexively, Lewis kicked him full in the face. Feeling the knee-jerk blow hit home, Lewis turned about in time to see the other man, arms flailing, go under. Haeden had seen it too, grabbed for the drowning man's hands and missed them. He dove and for a moment there was nothing but air bubbles on the surface. Lewis was trying to suppress the rising level of panic in him. He was the closest one and could not let this man drown on his account. Taking a deep breath, he dove and kicked to go deeper.

Truly blind underwater, no auroral displays here. Yet he could hear and sense the movement of the two men. He reached out and touched someone's arm - Haeden's, who guided his hand to Oliver's shoulder and together they attempted to haul him up. His body was dense and for whatever reason not prone to buoyancy. Lungs bursting, they managed to get him to the surface and hand Oliver's body to other swimmers who brought him ashore. Lewis, breathing hard, reached the shoreline a few moments later. Seeing the swimmer's body lying inert, he went into Red Cross mode, first turning Oliver face down and pressing on his back to force out water, then turning him back up, taking a deep breath and passing the breath on to the unconscious man.

"What are you doing?" Haeden barked.

Lewis ignored this, continued the mouth-to-mouth, followed by pressure on the chest. A few moments later, Oliver gagged, spitting up water and much of his lunch. He blinked and his eyes focused on Lewis.

"I feel like a fish," he said.

"Then you can't drown," Lewis said.

"You pulled me out?"

"That was Haeden. I'm the one who kicked you."

They brought him to his feet, a bit wobbly, but after a few minutes he shook off the shoulder support and walked unaided. The others ran on, Lewis and Haeden stayed behind with their bedraggled comrade attempting to re-establish some sense of dignity.

"I am Willet." He coughed, and added, *"They call me Moon Face."*

"They call me Skyfisher, but at home I am Lewis."

"Skyfisher was a good swimmer," Haeden said. *"You are not. But you breathed Willet Moon Face. You breathed him."*

"I can show you how," Lewis said.

"Ah," said Haeden, *"Then I will show you how to swim. Again."* Turning to Willet, he added, *"You as well."*

"Too much venison," Willet said. *"I sank like a stone."*

When they returned to the lodge, Grey Turtle, aka the Bald One, master dancer and spindle of the universe, was waiting for them, along with the rest of the group.

"Late," he said, and without further comment began to lead them in a series of exercises which involved using the arms, legs, and head in different sequences and rhythms. It started with a simple pattern but soon became quite complex, vaguely akin to tapping your head with the right hand while rubbing your belly with the left. However, this was on a whole other

level, as different as calculus is to simple addition. The others had had more practice, but Grey Turtle kept changing the pattern so that in short order they were all discomfited. Lewis felt like a total greenhorn, an object of scorn from his compatriots.

Monitoring the mood of the class, Grey Turtle spoke up.

"Yes, he did hold you back. What are you going to do about it? He's one of us."

The class was dismissed. Grey Turtle beckoned to Lewis to follow him to the elder's hut atop the mound. They entered the central space where a fire still burned, then went into an adjoining room. Inside, Marsh Fox, the weasel-faced man named Lightning, and the austere elder were waiting. Grey Turtle and Lewis stood before them, stirring thoughts of the Inquisition.

"What do you see when you look at me?" Marsh Fox asked.

"It's not really seeing," said Lewis.

"Describe."

"Your face is glowing. If you look a fire for a long time, or the sun, and then look away, the light still burns in your eyes. This is like that. With brighter colors, more detail. I see you nod your head, your face. I see your heart shine with what feels like good will. And," with a glance at the tall elder, *"I also can sense the opposite."*

"Anything else?" asked Marsh Fox.

"There are things I don't understand. I don't know the language of the things I see."

"Explain," Marsh Fox asked.

Lewis looked at the three elders for a moment and said, *"You are surrounded by sparks of light, like glowing embers from a fire, all of you. I see these sparks hovering around everything, even this table sparkles. The sparks are most active around living things, especially people. It's like you are surrounded by fireflies. It's –* Holy Smokes." These last words, spoken in English, came unbidden as Marsh Fox's fireflies coalesced into two shapes fanning out from his shoulders .

"*What do you see?*" Marsh Fox asked.

"*Wings,*" said Lewis, "*glowing wings.*"

"*And now?*"

"*Flapping like bird's wings. Not a bird. Moving very quickly now. An insect, an insect that's ..*"

"*Flying.*"

"*Yes.*

Marsh Fox looked at this fellow elders. The weasel faced man remained impassive, reminding Lewis of someone who kept his cards so close to his chest you wondered if he had any cards at all. The austere elder shrugged.

"*Well, he seems to have some of Skyfisher's abilities.*" He admitted.

"*I am Alakan,*" he said to Lewis. "*And yes, I disapprove. You bring wolves to our door.*"

"*He is our greatest hope,*" Marsh Fox added. "*Skyfisher caught him.*"

Marsh Fox placed his hands on Lewis's shoulders, as Falling Star had done. Again, a shiver of electricity down the spine.

"*You will plant a seed. You will return to your time to make sure it grows. Understand?*"

"*No,*" said Lewis.

"*Squash grows and thrives,*" Marsh Fox said. "*Does it know that someone planted, watered and cared for it? We are the caretakers. Clusters of us, scattered. Alone, we are unimportant. Together, we are what sustains life on this world.*"

"*All life?*" Lewis asked.

"*Yes.*"

"*What kind of seed are we planting?*"

"*You will learn that.*"

"Do I have a choice?"

"No," said Marsh Fox with the barest hint of a smile.

"And Tell Me A Story?"

"There is no place for her here," Alakan responded.

"She can't go back to her village. Where is she now?" Lewis asked.

"Not far," Marsh Fox said.

"She saved my life. I won't abandon her. Can't you find a place for her?"

Alakan began to speak, but Marsh Fox cut him off.

"We'll consider your request," he said.

"May I see her now?

"If you wish."

"I wish!"

Chapter Twenty Three

There was little conversation aboard the raft when the wounded warriors reached Yatanocha, Buffalo's village. He was in another world, neither awake nor asleep, mumbling snatches of song, becoming Little Rock, one-eyed and vulnerable. They floated past a fishing weir. High Eagle secured the raft and went in search of a healer, skirting a field where women were planting rows of *choupichoul* grain. No one greeted them. A few small boys clustered nearby when Little Rock was lifted onto a wooden sled and dragged to a medicine tent by some villagers. With that done, High Eagle went looking for Red Wolf. He was directed to a hut on the far side of the village, next to a rack of fish drying in the sun. Inside, he found Red Wolf sitting on a log, knapping a spear head.

"*Cenkololo,*" High Eagle said.

"*Cenkololo,*" Red Wolf responded. "*I see you are diminished*", Red Wolf responded, with a glance at High Eagle's left hand.

"*It was nothing,*" High Eagle said, hoping to sound unperturbed. Instead, it came out as indignant, which was in truth how he felt. He'd known Red Wolf most of his life, besting him in hand-to-hand combat. Over time, Red Wolf had achieved a certain reputation as a stalker. High Eagle needed his services if he was to ever retrieve his escaped prisoners and reputation.

"The same nothing that took Little Rock's finger?" Red Wolf asked. Word had travelled fast.

"A fight with traders. I will not blow smoke from my fire."

"Of course not," said Red Wolf, who had never heard this particular phrase before. It didn't matter. He enjoyed turning up the heat on High Eagle, who was famously arrogant. His story stank. Perhaps it was a good expression after all. Blowing smoke.

"In this fight you —."

"Our prisoners escaped. The Blind One and his wife."

"So you come to me."

"To help find them."

"Why don't you use a tracker from your own village?" Red Wolf asked.

"You are the best."

Red Wolf grunted.

"I had to bring Little Rock here," High Eagle continued, *"to be healed by his own people."*

"The village meant nothing to Little Rock. He was attached to it by this," Red Wolf wriggled his little finger and smiled. High Eagle was attempting to make an offer, after all.

"I will give you a rifle if you find them," High Eagle said.

"No one else can stalk this woman for you. Four nights."

"What?"

"Four nights," said Red Wolf. *"Four nights with the woman. And the rifle."* Though he had not seen Tell Me A Story since she was a child, he knew of her beauty.

"She is to be taken to the Lesser Sun," High Eagle protested.

"Where is the messenger from the Sun asking for her? Four nights."

"One night."

"Six then." Red Wolf said, returning his attention to the spear head.

High Eagle shook his head in resignation.

"Four nights," he said.

Tell Me A Story ran to Lewis and held him. They were alone in a small storage hut she had been sharing with bundles of vegetables.

"Are they treating you well?" he asked.

"You are Lewis, still?"

He nodded.

"You speak now," she said in surprise.

"I can't explain it," he stammered.

"They have said only a few words to me. You'd think they had never seen a woman."

"You are the only one here, I think," Lewis said.

Tell Me A Story snorted. *"They are behaving like old women."*

Lewis laughed and realized how much he had missed her.

"What is going to happen?" she asked.

"They are training me and a group of young men, for some kind of task - hallesh, they call it."

"Young men," Tell Me A Story mused. *"No wonder they want to keep me locked up."*

"They don't know what to do with you. I'm supposed to ask you about your moon."

"Such poetry. 'My moon!' I've heard when a warrior bleeds, he is also kept apart. You think that's true? Ask your teachers." She sighed and regarded bunches of wild onions, maize and a pile of acorns. *"My moon rides the half moon."*

"I'll tell them. If they want my help, they'll have to protect you as well."

"What do they want you to do?" she asked.

"Not much. Subdue a few warriors, hack their fingers off," he said, reaching for her shoulder.

Tell Me A Story gently took his hand and cradled it in hers.

"You speak from inside my husband. You are a crab that crawls inside a snail shell to find its home. The shell moves, but

it is the crab. I don't know who you are. I don't know where my heart is."

In the dim light of the hut, Lewis saw her the way someone appears through night vision goggles, emanating a pastel incandescence.

"Skyfisher will return and I will go back to my home," he said. *"That's what they told me."*

"I have no place to go back to now," she said, shaking her head. *"These men think they know something. They think whatever they're up to is worth doing."*

"They say we're going to save the world."

"You believe them?" she asked.

"I don't know what to believe," he said, wondering how a small group of well-intentioned people could help an entire planet. He imagined the earth swallowing the Shining Ones like a mouthful of homeopathic pellets.

"Skyfisher never told me," Tell Me A Story said.

"I better go," said Lewis. *"Is there anything you need?"*

"A bath."

"I'll see what can be done." He kissed her between the eyes and left the hut.

Lewis settled into the daily rhythm of training at the lodge. It was indeed run like a boot camp, pre-dawn awakenings, rigorous physical exercises, and a devilish series of positions and gestures taught by Grey Turtle. Every afternoon, one of the young *Shining Ones*, Slow Deer, took Lewis aside to practice the sequence. The name was an old joke; Slow Deer was by far their swiftest runner. Beyond showing the positions, he offered no advice. Lewis sensed a hint of resentment, figuring Slow Deer had drawn the short straw, giving lessons to the blind man.

Lewis had never been a particularly good dancer. He supposed mastering these steps would be like learning to type or drive with a stick shift. Sooner or later he'd figure it out, so he gamely persisted as an act of faith. Not a simple thing to trust a body that was not yours, even though it was stronger and more resilient than your own. In the beginning, it felt like Ironman piloting a robot from inside a virtual suit of armor. Walking, eating, even running had come relatively easily. This workout was something else again, movements precisely choreographed for the head, arms and feet, each to specific changing rhythms.

During one morning's session, attempting a complicated set of gestures while orbiting round a circle, Lewis collapsed, dizzy and frustrated.

"I can't do this!" he said, trolling for some compassion.

"Not with your head," Grey Turtle said. *"Stop trying! The positions are inside you now. The horse knows the way. Let it show you. Begin with the feet."* Grey Turtle tapped the rhythm on his drum. *"Good. Now move around the circle, slowly."*

Lewis stumbled; Grey Turtle kept drumming. The class watched, grateful for a breather and the spectacle of witnessing someone less adept.

"Help him!" Grey Turtle shouted. *"He's your brother. If he fails, we all do!"*

Shamed by Grey Turtle's words and wishing to please their teacher, the class sent Lewis a few beneficent vibrations, or so it seemed. Something inside shifted and for a moment, his mind relinquished control. A few false starts, and then the drum beat began to motivate his feet. He found himself circumnavigating without initiating his movements. As though he was being danced. One by one, the other members of the class joined him, circling Grey Turtle, who stood tapping his drum. After half an hour he stopped them. They stood, exhausted and exhilarated, their palms upraised, mid-gesture. Like Skyfisher, each of the Brothers had an image of an eye on the center of his right palm. Every eye was glowing and pulsing.

Over the coming weeks, Lewis began to regard Skyfisher's muscles and bones as allies. With every training session, he came closer to being on par with the rest of the group. However, as soon as the class seemed to be on the verge of mastering a gesture or sequence, Grey Turtle would change a detail, making Lewis feel like he was back in Kindergarten again.

"We call it the Demon Dance," Slow Deer confided to him one day during a break. Grey Turtle, the Demon personified, admonished them not to be complacent.

"Your bodies are horses, for some of you, donkeys. They learn something and that's it, they never change." He mimed a lame donkey loping up a hill, braying, *"Show me the oats!"*

Though chastened, the class couldn't help but laugh.

"Help the horse," he said. *"Don't fall asleep."*

Gradually, Lewis found himself more accepted by the group, although a few still regarded him with suspicion. Understandable, considering he was the ultimate covert observer.

He made inquiries about Tell Me A Story, but the elders had come to no firm decision. Confined to quarters, she was allowed to work in their garden and do kitchen chores in isolation. No baths.

In Flour Village, food preparation and other essential tasks had been mostly done by women. On the mound encampment, everyone chipped in with chores, including the elders. Lewis longed to try his hand at hunting, but he was assigned to harvest maize, which he did with a curved L-shaped tool, like a scythe, made of hardwood. Maize was a bit smaller than the ears of corn he was familiar with. It was partially cooked, then dried and ground with mortar and pestle. The flour was mixed with beans to make a kind of bread. They also used it to make porridge and sometimes smoked and cooked it with squash as a gruel which tasted like grits.

Unlike Flour Village, there were no caste distinctions here. Stinkard or highborn, it made no difference. They had no system of writing; everything that passed between the elders and younger brethren was learned by repetition. When Lewis asked about the Shining Ones' mission, he was told to wait for *ipli hallesh*, which translated to something like "The Listening." Certain things had to be experienced, not explained.

"But surely you can give me an example," Lewis asked Grey Turtle one afternoon. *"It would help me be better prepared."*

They were sitting together on the rim of the mound, waiting for the rest of the Shining Ones to join them for yet another round of the Demon Dance.

"What do you see when you watch the trees, the tall ones over there?" Grey Turtle pointed to a stand of birches, swaying in a breeze.

"Their colors are shimmering; they're healthy."

"What else?"

"They're moving."

"Ah. What moves them?"

"The wind."

"I suppose for you, the wind has colors. But the rest of us - you think we can see the wind?"

"No."

"Yet we see the trees move, a little bit. In a small breeze, we don't even feel the wind, but the leaves dance and shimmer. The ipli hallesh is like that. We're listening for something you can't see or even hear, but we know its there. Sometimes we can it sense it move us."

Lewis wanted to ask more, but at that moment, they heard shouts and excited voices as the members of the *kuash* clambered up the hill. Word was that Alakan, the elder who had disapproved of Lewis' presence, had been bitten by a snake.

High Eagle rounded up three members for his party - Red Wolf the stalker and two brothers, Otter and Broken Twig. The brothers had become their names, Otter a fine swimmer, his brother strong as an ox, with a deformed left arm. Untested in battle, they had come to bask in the fading glory of the infamous Buffalo.

After many weeks, his injuries began to heal. He would walk with a limp for the rest of his days. Gone were his pinky finger and sullen bravado. Buffalo appeared to be complacent or perhaps less self-absorbed, as if the brush with death had sobered him. With his one eye, he saw the life of the village anew, paying particular attention to the children who delighted in daring each other to see who could get closest to the big warrior before he barked at them. He seemed to have lost his bark, letting the bravest of the knee high warriors-to-be count coup by touching his leg and scampering away in triumph.

This disturbed High Eagle somewhat. He needed Little Rock to find his inner Buffalo. At High Eagle's insistence, the big man began to train, first swimming, then walking and finding other ways to re-establish his strength.

"How else will you get the Story Woman?" High Eagle asked. No plans were outlined. It was enough for Little Rock to know that Tell Me A Story was the destination. He worked for a few hours every day, chopping wood, digging post holes, whatever would exercise his muscles. His vigor and some of the old fire began to return.

One morning, in a moment of abandon, Broken Twig told a joke and clapped Little Rock on the shoulder at the punch line.

"Touch me again and your other twig will be broken," he said. High Eagle overheard and smiled.

No one had ever seen a snake on the mound before, yet a cottonmouth had been found in the corner of Alakan's hut, coiled behind a basket. The elder lay moaning on his cot, his body shaking. As the Society of Light's primary physician, Alakan was in no condition to heal himself, and his apprentices knew nothing of snake bite cures. The Bald One could dance till doomsday, a master herbalist was needed. Grey Turtle consulted with Marsh Fox and sent for Tell Me A Story. When she arrived, Alakan's foot was red and swollen and he was vomiting bile. She put her ear to his chest and listened to an erratic heartbeat.

"What do you need?" Grey Turtle asked.

"Hardwood charcoal from a fire pit. Make a poultice," she said. *"Can you do that?"* Grey Turtle nodded and she added, *"Make sure it stays moist and keep it on the place where he was bitten. Find me two men who know the area well."*

It was done. Tell Me A Story led Alakan's two apprentices into the woods, dispatching one to search for a particular plant she described in detail. She asked the other to lead her to the nearest stream. Along its banks, they dug in several locations until they found the kind of clay she was searching for. It was good to be outside again, doing something, even digging in the mud. They were in the midst of harvesting a basketful when the second apprentice approached, empty-handed. Tell Me A Story sent both apprentices back to the lodge with instructions to replace the coal poultice with one made from clay. After a few hours, the swelling on Alakan's foot went down. He slipped in and out of a coma.

Lewis wondered what modern medicine would do with a snake bite, or if homeopathy offered a cure. A micro-dose of arsenic? The scale of the snake that bit you?

In the late afternoon, Tell Me A Story returned, carrying several plants by their roots. She felt Alakan's forehead and pulse, took a clump of unused clay and left with one of the apprentices. They returned after an hour with a new poultice blended with clay and herbs, and a decoction of the same herbs for the patient to sip. He was too far gone to drink, but Tell Me A Story spooned the liquid into his mouth, gently stroking his throat until he swallowed.

Alakan sputtered, coughed, opened his eyes and croaked, *"What is she doing here?"*

"Saving your life, my friend," Grey Turtle responded.

As High Eagle's party was preparing to depart, a woman approached them.

"I wish to join you," she said.

None of them knew her. Slight of build, dressed in men's garb, she wore her hair warrior-style, shaved in front, cropped close in the back, with a long forelock to which a feather was attached, giving her a somewhat fearsome aspect. High Eagle was not impressed.

"Go home," he said, *"wherever that is."*

"I will," she said defiantly, *"once I am done. I can cook, hunt and fight. You could use my help."*

It was tempting, at least the cooking part.

"How will you help in a fight?" High Eagle asked.

"As well as any of these green ones," she said, regarding the brothers. High Eagle laughed.

"What's your name? he asked.

"Let me fight your young brave here and I will tell you."

High Eagle glanced at Broken Twig, but the woman stopped him.

"No honor in besting a man that is not whole. Let me face the other."

High Eagle didn't relish having to explain to the village elders why they had injured a woman. This one was not going to back down. He whispered to Otter, *"Teach her a lesson. Nothing too painful."*

"Very well," High Eagle said aloud. *"We have five witnesses who will swear you brought this on yourself."* He nodded to Otter, who was annoyed at the prospect of fighting a woman. Why go easy on her after she had insulted his brother? He took off his pack and fur robe, and faced her.

A spanking, then send her back where she belonged. Hopefully none of his friends would hear of this.

The woman crouched, slowly circling Otter.

Let her have her moment of playing warrior.

She darted towards him. It happened so quickly that no one, certainly not Otter, saw precisely how she did it. Sliding into him, legs first, bringing him down and having a knife at his throat with one hand, while her other hand pulled his head back by his hair.

"Touch me and I will slice you, deeply," she whispered to him.

"My name is Waya! Take me with you and I let this one go. I ask to fight alongside you! That is all I ask."

For a moment High Eagle thought he should call her bluff, but he would not risk losing a warrior for the sake of a crazy woman. If she could fight like that, she may well prove useful.

"Alright," he said,*" if you agree to follow my orders, starting with letting him go."* Waya did so. Otter arose, humiliated.

Chapter Twenty-Four

Alakan began to recover. It was generally accepted by everyone that Tell Me A Story's knowledge of plants and healing had saved him. Everyone except Alakan. She was soon housed in more comfortable quarters, and began instructing the two apprentices in herbal lore. How a cottonmouth had ended up where snakes had never been seen was the lingering question, but there was little time to dwell on this. About three dozen Shining Ones were training rigorously every day for *ipli hallesh*, slated for the longest day. Whenever the *The Listening* was mentioned, Lewis would invariably hear that Skyfisher had been a potent attractor, although no one would tell him precisely what that meant. After the tenth "you will see," he had taken to pointing to his sightless eyes. The clue came during an afternoon with one of the instructors, weasel-faced Lightning.

Lightning led a group of Shining Ones to a low-lying rock ridge not far from the mound, waiting for them to gather around two boulders lying next to the ridge in a shallow depression. Without any explanation, he slid down the depression, ducked behind the boulders and disappeared. Clambering into the ditch after him, the group discovered a crevasse behind the boulders, a small slit between the ditch bottom and the ridge.

Slow Deer, the first in line, shrugged and bent down to enter. The rest followed suit, most having to get on their hands and knees to crawl through the hole. Lewis was last in line.

With his claustrophobia coiled and ready to spring, Lewis reminded himself that he had survived the lake, swimming across it every day, buoyed by the mantra, *this is not my body.*

Crawling through a tunnel elicited groans from a few Shining Ones, hitting their head on the low ceiling before the passage opened into a larger space. A cave.

It reminded Lewis of the arrival lounge where he had awakened into this world. Miles away, or had he dreamt it?

Pitch black. To Lewis's 24/7 night-vision this made no difference. The rock walls thrummed a dull grey-brown. The Shining Ones shone as glowing green forms, huddled together, vibrating slightly. Their footsteps and breathing echoed, cueing the cave's dimensions. Some members of the group stretched their arms out, groping. They were blind here, the tables turned. Next to them stood Lightning, implacable.

"You who walk in Skyfisher's body," Lightning said, *"Help your brothers."*

"How?" Lewis asked.

"Try."

So he did, describing what he saw.

"Lots of green – ."

A travelogue for the vision-impaired, the stream-of-conscious commentary of a mescaline tripper.

"What else?" Lightning demanded.

"What else do I see?" Lewis asked.

"What must we do to see like you? Remember Grey Turtle's dance? We want to dance with you."

Lewis felt like a kid who had stolen the keys to his father's car. On a dare, he had to prove to his friends he could drive.

He took a few steps and heard the faint scrape of his foot on the ground.

"You hear that?"

He rubbed his foot on the ground with more force.

"This place is talking to us."

He stamped his foot and they felt the thump and heard its faint echo. *"The sounds paint a picture,"* he continued. *"A bigger cave sounds different. Your ears know this. Make some sounds and listen."* They tried, first tentatively, then escalating in an eruption of hoots, like first graders on a field trip.

"Stop!" Lightning shouted. *"This is what you know,"* he said to Lewis, sounding like a petulant teenager. *"What about Skyfisher?"*

"When he shows up, you can ask him." Lewis said, rising to the bait. Lightning's aura warmed to a dull red, then back to green.

"Yes, he is not here. But you see this cave like him, yes? Help your brothers see."

"I'll try. I'll try."

Thinking of Blind Man's Bluff, Lewis had the group form two lines, converging, with himself at the intersection of the lines. It felt like a bluff, but it was the only idea he had.

"Each of you, place your hands on the shoulders of the person in front of you."

The two men behind Lewis stood next to each other and touched Lewis's shoulders with their inner arms. V-flight formation, with him as lead goose.

"One step at a time."

Lewis led them slowly to the perimeter of the cave.

"There's a rock wall on the left. Smell it? Hear the water dripping. Feel the coolness. The wall is grey with a bit of yellow. Those on the left line, touch it with your left hand. It's pulsing slightly.

Grey with a hint of orange. If I can see it, you can, too. Everybody step left. Stop. Left line – reach out and touch the wall. Right line, without touching it, can you feel the wall, too?"

Lewis tried as best he could to send the image of what he sensed to the others. Nothing happened.

"Wait," said Lightning. *"The ones at the end of each line, find each other. Keep your hands on each other's shoulders. Turn towards the center."*

The V became a circle with each man facing inward. When Lightning joined the circle, Lewis felt a jolt as when Falling Star had first touched him. This time it was amplified by twenty others.

"Try again," Lightning said. Lewis took a breath and attempted to transmit the 3D image of the wall from his mind's eye to the others.

Nothing.

"The circle of men here, can you see us?" Lightning asked.

Lewis was experiencing the current of electricity passing through them intensifying, coursing through his body, as if he was holding a live wire.

"I can," he said, keeping the circle in his field of attention.

"Look at them," Lightning said. *"You know these men. Let every face burn into you. See every man and tell me when you're ready."*

Five minutes later Lewis said, *"Alright."*

"Name them," Lightning demanded.

"Slow Deer, Haeden, the Twins, Willet Moonface, Thistlehead..." Lewis described those whose names he did not know.

"Now," said Lightning, *"hold the sight of all of them, and see the wall, the whole wall, sharing its life with you. You see it?"*

"I do."

"Let the wall and the men see each other."

Lewis was about to say that he didn't understand, when he felt Haeden's image flicker inside his head, then Moonface and all the others. It was like having a conversation with someone who had been pre-occupied and then unexpectedly focused on you. In an instant he knew that everyone of them was sharing this experience.

"Do you see the wall?" He asked.

A chorus of *"Yes!"* with some voices spoken aloud and others as echoes inside Lewis's head. The force of their attention magnified the intensity of the wall, mingling with the delight of the Shining Ones in a virgin sensory experience, a genuine feedback loop.

Amazing, Lewis thought.

"Don't let the horse ride you," Lightning said. *"Show them something else."* For the next two hours, Lewis did just that, exploring the cave with the circle cohorts facing outward, hands on shoulders, walking through the cavern as if they were a multi-footed organism, a human colony.

At a certain point, Lightning had several members break the connection and Lewis saw the shared impression begin to falter.

"Try harder, everyone," said Lightning, *"especially you who shares Skyfisher's body. You have no name. You are nothing. Try harder."*

The networked sense-image flickered for a moment and then disappeared.

"Work at this every day, all of you, until smaller groups can accomplish it," Lightning said. *"Do what this man can do. What others cannot see and hear. Then you will be ready for ipli hallesh."* He approached Lewis.

"Take them to the entrance and come back to me here," Lightning said. Lewis did as he was asked, returning to find

Lightning glowing a dull yellowish green in the depths of the cavern. The cave was quiet, a few drips of condensation on its walls.

It felt ancient. Lewis couldn't explain why he knew that to be true; perhaps it was just another signal on the internal dashboard for which he had no instruction manual. Lightning stepped closer to him, a bit too close for comfort considering they were the only two people in the cavern. He smelled of tobacco, sweat, whatever he last had to eat, and something else. Not an odor per se, an emanation akin to a layer of perfume masking yet another emanation.

"You will work with smaller groups. Four or five. Different men each time, then report to me," Lightning said.

When Lewis agreed, Lightning fumbled with a pouch hanging from his neck and pulled out two irregularly shaped metallic rocks, each about the size of a thumbnail. He put them in the palm of his hand a few inches apart and then nudged one closer to the other until they snapped together.

"You know this?" Lightning asked.

"Yes."

"What do you call it?"

"Magnet," Lewis said.

"Explain."

So Lewis told him how some minerals attract metals, and how magnetism is connected to electricity.

"There's electricity in your name, in our heads and our bodies. When we were in a circle before, the force that passed between us? That was like electricity. It needs a circle to move, to flow. When electricity moves, it makes magnetism, just like these rocks."

"When rocks move, they make electricity?"

"I think so," said Lewis, on shaky ground.

"You believe all these things?" Lightning asked.

Lewis, who was living a dream as real as his fingernail, said yes, he did believe.

"The earth itself is a giant magnet."

Lightning chewed on this bit of intel as they walked back through the darkness to the opening of the cave.

When they reached daylight, Lightning pointed to the source of all light and asked, *"You think the sun is a 'magnet'?"*

"I don't know," said Lewis.

"Many things you don't know. 'Know-Nothing' is a good name. You like it?"

"I know I don't like it," Lewis said, eliciting a brittle laugh from Lightning.

"You say earth is magnet. Maybe you are a magnet. All people, magnets. We move, make electricity in the air. You breathe, sun breathes. You breathe the sun." Lightning started to pace back and forth.

"The first Great Sun came from the sun," Lightning said, reminding Lewis of a grade school teacher trying to pound a lesson into the head of the class dunce. *"He created kuash, the Society of Light. We'll never see anyone like him again. The Great Sun who rules now? He knows nothing, like you. The Shining Ones help the sun feed the earth. If we stop, no earth. Understand?"*

"How many of you are there?" Lewis asked.

"Enough," Lightning said.

"Why am I here?"

"Bad idea. You come, things get worse. Skyfisher goes to your time, maybe he keeps the world alive."

Lightning stamped his foot on the ground, just to make sure Know-Nothing knew which world he was talking about.

"You are here only because he is there. You're no help here, only trouble. Maybe you learn something for when you go back. You ready to go back?" Lightning paused for a few breaths and continued.

"There is one who sits in the lodge. He does not speak."

"Yes."

"Little Panther did what Skyfisher did, he travelled into the body of another man. A slave. He spoke from inside of Little Panther, like you speak to me. Said when slaves make trouble, white men with torches hang them from trees. Maybe that is what happened to him."

"So.." began Lewis.

"If Skyfisher dies, you become like Little Panther. Better you go home now. Kill slaves. Destroy your world. While I am alive in this world, I will not let that happen here."

"What if I die here, while I'm in Skyfisher's body?"

"Only one way to find out, Know-Nothing." Again, the brittle laugh. *"For now, teach the others how you see. Then we give you a different name."*

Lewis wasn't sure why the others needed to see like Skyfisher, but he was willing to try. At least it gave him something to do.

Every morning for the next week, he met with the Shining Ones in groups of three of four at a small clearing not far from the mound site. Their progress was uneven. By the end of the week, he shared their frustration. It was a cool morning; dew hung on a few cobwebs and leafier plants.

"Let's try it again." Lewis spoke to a small group - the Twins, Willet Moonface, Slow Deer and Thistlehead, sitting on logs at the perimeter of the clearing. One man would get up, walk out of sight and try to send an image to the others of what he saw. It was Slow Deer's turn, one of the younger members, tall, gangly, fast on his feet but awkward in his movements. As Slow Deer moved away from the group, Lewis noticed a few errant signals on Skyfisher's inner vibrometer; the Twins provoked each other with forced gaiety; Thistlehead

fidgeted uncomfortably; Willet sat uncharacteristically rigid. Something was up.

Slow Deer sent a thought-picture of him peeling a piece of bark off a birch tree. Lewis received the message and was fairly certain no one else had. He still had to ask.

"Anything?"

No one responded, nor did they look at him. Considering his blindness, nothing unusual in that. Willet still as a statue, was intentionally *not* looking at something. In fact, they all appeared to be looking in every direction but north. Slow Deer returned looking dejected. Then it was Lewis's turn. A quick scan of the clearing revealed nothing amiss.

"We'll try again." Lewis stood, nonchalantly pointing his radar north while he addressed them.

"Form a circle."

They complied, and as they came together, Lewis *saw* it. A straight line, stretched ankle high between two trees about twenty feet away, northwards. A trip line.

Tell Me A Story had, after some prodding, told him bits and pieces of how she had snared High Eagle and Buffalo. This was a page from the same book. Lewis paused to consider options, sampling a whiff of the emotional climate. All the earmarks of a fraternity prank. Which gave him an idea.

"Take off your breech cloths."

"What?" The Twins, taken aback, spoke in unison.

"You heard me. We're trying something different. Lightning's orders."

Reluctantly, they complied. Lewis had them tie the cloths over their heads, like hoods.

"This stinks!" Thistlehead said.

"Try washing yourself," responded Willet.

An incongruous sight - five naked, hooded men.

"Alright. Find each other, form a circle. Hands on shoulders. We're going to play Hide and Seek. Find me."

Lewis walked north, sending the group a picture of his route, skirting some brush and a few trees.

He paused, noting their progress, waiting for a sign that they were receiving his signal, a surge in his feedback loop.

They faced inward, hands on each other's shoulders, moving at a snail's pace, cautiously ducking out of the way of some low hanging branches.

"Faster!" Lewis shouted. Thistlehead, on the leading edge of the circle, attempted to lift the bottom of his hood for a peek.

"No cheating! I am your eyes!" Lewis shouted at them. *"See what I see! You can do this!"*

Thistlehead backed into a tree trunk. Lewis honed his uber-sight on the texture of the tree, reached out to Thistlehead to touch-see it with him. The grooves, the roughness of the bark. The life of the tree manifest in its shape, its branches and leaves overhead. Lewis felt the hint of a response from Thistlehead, like a tug on a string between them. Then a pushback and Lewis's image of the tree appeared slightly denser to him, as if there were more pixels on his inner screen. Resonance.

That's it! Now show the others.

The link between Lewis and Thistlehead strengthened. Then, in a kind of quantum jump, everyone was sharing the signal, walking around the tree. With Lewis as their seeing eye, they moved towards him, picking up speed as they mustered confidence.

What have we here?

Quietly, Lewis transmitted an image of a length of rawhide stretched taut about six inches off the ground. He invited the group towards him and felt a momentary flicker in the emotional content of their signal as they stepped over the line.

Never know what you'll find in the woods.

He missed Tell Me A Story, the memory of their intimacy, the odor of spice and herbs when she had leaned in to kiss him between the eyes, the defiance in her stance when she had taken High Eagle and Buffalo's fingers without regrets or apologies.

A warrior woman - and he was part of her story. As a clown, no doubt.

Between the daily training, the impossible exercises, the efforts to teach the others Skyfisher's way of seeing, Lewis had not had much opportunity to visit with her and he regretted it.

At the same time, he felt that his role in *ippli hallesh – The Listening,* was starting to come together, like a piece in a puzzle.

After the breakthrough with the group in the clearing, he was anxious to share the same experience with the others. Following Lightning's suggestion, Lewis continued to train groups of three or four at a time, trying different combinations of people. Sometimes it happened; sometimes it didn't. The signal wouldn't transmit, as if a wireless server was down.

When Lewis presented his report to Lightning, the elder asked whether he'd kept track of the groups.

"Who was there when it worked, and when it didn't?" Lighting asked.

Lewis tried to picture the different groups in his mind, the scenarios of success and disappointment. After a few moments, he remembered a common denominator.

Alfalfa. Whenever he was present, the feedback loop invariably collapsed.

"Haeden," he said.

Lightning paused and Lewis observed his color palette morphing from one side of the rainbow to the other.

"Watch Haeden, not so he knows." Lightning said. *"Include him in some of the practice circles so you won't arouse suspicion. The others need to learn Skyfisher's way of seeing on their own. I will send Haeden on an errand."*

That afternoon, Lewis met in the cave with his best pupils. Thistlehead, not exactly the brightest star in the sky, was a natural telepath. The others, Moonface, the Twins and Slow Deer, were learning fast. They formed a circle, one arm around each other's shoulders, like Greek dancers.

A rock wall inside the cave, the object of Lewis' scrutiny, began to reveal its detail and complexity, its nuances enhanced slowly, as though the wall were alive and shyly sharing its secrets. Lewis felt the revelation spreading through the group, first to Thistlehead, then the others, each man contributing to the vibrancy of the vision. There was an exuberance in the sharing, like going to the movies with your friends, except the film was in your mind's eye, and you all were in it.

"Now!" Lewis cried, and everyone in the circle lowered their arms, breaking physical contact. The intensity of the shared vision diminished perceptibly, then gradually began to return. The Shining Ones were still linked, a skeletal backbone without connective tissue.

Over the next few days, they were able to expand their virtual loop, first around the base of the mound, then in a circle roughly a half a mile in diameter, sharing the image of something that Skyfisher *saw,* a tree, a squirrel, a lodge building. It wasn't long before some were initiating the transmission of their own images with a bit of low-level commentary, like an open party line.

The next step was to break up the core group and let each member train the other brothers. Haeden had not yet returned from his errand and in his absence, things went well. Gradually, they all began to share their visions over short distances. Lewis reported their progress to Lightning, who said they were nearly ready for *ippli hallesh*.

"We will see what they can accomplish without you hovering over them like a mother hen," Lightning said.

Lewis was finally able to steal a moment to visit Tell Me A Story in her new quarters, a hut not far from the mound site. It had become an apothecary, with plants hanging by their roots from the ceiling, baskets full of herbs and bowls of powders and liquids. The confluence of smells was a bit overwhelming as Lewis entered. Tell Me A Story was in the midst of preparing a poultice.

"For Alakan," she said. *"A strange one. Would hurt his face too much if he tried to smile."*

"It's good to be with you again," Lewis said.

"Skyfisher didn't smile much, either," Tell Me A Story said. *"Maybe because he was blind. But he could still be happy."*

"I'm not him."

"No, you're not. You smile here," she said, touching his cheek lightly.

"I can't see like you do, but I know your face from the inside when you smile, how you feel. I just do," Lewis said.

"That was Skyfisher's way."

"He's been sharing some of his secrets with me."

"A good thing," Tell Me A Story said. *"I'm trying to share what I know with your "Shining Ones". Like walking in the mud. They still don't trust me. Alakan especially. He's stuck in his ways. I still try. Tell me what you do."*

Knowing how much she had resented her husband's keeping her in the dark, Lewis did what he could to share his experience. In any event, he valued her input. She was particularly interested in the snake incident, plying him for details.

"No accident," she said.

"They have someone guarding him now, day and night," Lewis said. *"You saved his life, whether he realizes it or not. This is no place for you. You deserve better."*

"I can't return to my village, not without you," she said.

"If I can speak to your leader – the Lesser Sun, as Skyfisher did, then maybe we can go back together. But Grey Turtle told me the reason I speak your language is because I'm here, with the others. Some kind of magic I don't understand. Not like I understand any of this."

"You stopped smiling," she said.

"As soon as The Listening is over, we could leave here, you and me. Grey Turtle too, if he wants. They didn't exactly welcome him with open arms. We'll find a place, if not the Flour village, somewhere else. I'll learn to hunt better."

Tell Me A Story stood and walked to the other side of the hut, smoothing her tunic as she went, glancing at the baskets and bowls as if searching for a remedy.

"You have your own story. It's about returning home, where you belong", she said.

"I'm beginning to feel at home here," Lewis said, *"like I have a purpose."*

"Carry that with you when you return my husband to me. And his child."

"His child?"

"Loo-is. I missed my moon and in the mornings I am unwell. You know what that means. I am going to have a baby, Skyfisher's baby."

"Oh." He paused, amidst a whirlwind of thoughts.

"That's... What can I say?"

"Nothing to say."

Lewis sounded her body for the traces of another life within, sensing only her heartbeat and traces of sadness. He wanted to comfort and hold her, but feeling sorry for himself and the loss of the best part of his dream, he didn't notice the salt tear coursing down her cheek.

"I will get you to someplace safe where you can have your baby."

"Find what you have to do. Good-bye, Loo-is." She reached for his hand and gently rubbed the image tattooed on Skyfisher's palm, wishing the eye could open and see her.

Chapter Twenty Five

Preparation for *ippli hallesh* proceeded at a blistering pace. Long periods of sitting in silence followed by intense repetitions of Grey Turtle's demon dance. In the middle of the dance, Willet Moonface collapsed from exhaustion. They pulled him aside, gave him something to drink and kept on training. After the class, Lewis approached Willet, who sat against the wall of the lodge, looking like a limp rag.

"Are you alright?" Lewis asked.

"No. None of this is alright." Willet glanced around the now empty lodge, the flames of the central fire pit burning low.

"Can I ask you something?"

"Ask," Willet responded.

"How long have you been here?"

"Six, seven moons."

"Did Skyfisher train you and the others?"

"Not like you," Willet said.

"How do you mean?"

"He kept it to himself. We saw when we were with him. The visions were strong, stronger than yours, but he had to be there."

"Without him, you couldn't see or hear each other from a distance."

"No."

Perhaps Skyfisher wouldn't want Lewis to be training the others. Too late now.

Two days before the Solstice, Marsh Fox met the Shining Ones as they assembled in their lodge in the morning.

"No food, only water until the Longest Day. Some are leaving. We will be of one breath in the ippli hallesh."

Marsh Fox, Grey Turtle and most of the other elders departed with twenty of the Shining Ones to various strategic locations. Alakan was still recovering. Lightning was in charge of the mound.

Before he left, Grey Turtle spoke in private with Lewis. *"Be on guard,"* he said. *"Something doesn't smell right."* What the smell might be, Grey Turtle wouldn't say.

At first the lack of food seemed to sharpen everyone's edge. Next morning they were peckish, sullen, and by evening as feisty as a flock of roosters. Even Thistlehead, one of the more reticent brothers, seemed to walk with a bit of swagger. No sign of Haeden. Looked like he was going to miss the party.

On the morning of the solstice, Lewis was awakened well before dawn. It seemed like any morning - a low-lying fog and some trilling toads in the distance. He struggled to remember what the position of the earth was on June 21st and why it was different from all other days. Something to do with the tilt of the planet on its axis and how much light the northern hemisphere received as it leaned towards the sun. The elders said the mounds' locations and the way they were situated were not random. Some were supposed to be aligned to sunrise, and the positions of the stars and planets. Like Stonehenge.

It made sense. If they really were a kind of organic receptor, you'd want to place your antennae in an optimal position.

Apparently they were part of web of receptors positioned in a network of sites, many of them earthworks.

Some of the Shining Ones, including Moonface, had been ordered by Lightning to stay at the Lodge with the caretakers. Others headed off in the pre-dawn to the mound, where twelve men were positioned, three at each corner of the lozenge shaped hill. They waited in silence. Hours of training to banish stray thoughts and it still seemed impossible for Lewis. Try as he may, enticing scenarios floated past, like aromas wafting in from a kitchen. One moment he was mindful of his backbone, the next he was riffing on snakes and what Tell Me A Story must look like to a person with a working pair of eyes. He surfed his associations, each one blossoming forth to another, spreading through his mind like invasive weeds. It didn't help having a never-ending light show inside his head, a perpetual vibrometer responding to his surroundings. Any attempt to stop the inner trialogue by dictatorial force conjured up a se-ries of plucky Resistance fighters, an underground cadre of unstoppable thoughts and dreams, defying the tyrant by sheer persistence and numbers.

Grey Turtle's approach had been a dance of vigilance. Marsh Fox had shown them the way of softness, loosening the muscle knots, spiralling down to the *cave inside us,* the whirl-pool's center, relaxed but not asleep. Lightning had helped them hone their telepathic skills, with Lewis as his point man. Despite all their preparation, the entire team felt the tension in the air. Something important was at stake. The fact that no one seemed to know precisely what the something was left them all uneasy. At the first hints of dawn, a few tentative bird calls trilled.

Lewis and the twins took their positions at the northeast corner of the lowest tier of the mound. They sat in a tight triangle, their backs to each other facing outwards, first establishing contact among themselves, and then expanding their mind network to the nine men, three groups of three, gathered at the other corners of the mound. He recognized the presence of Slow Deer and Thistlehead. No words, but they were used to the familiar flavor of each other's thought signals. *The brother vibe.*

That old chestnut from the sixties had become literal, each member of their group expressing a particular blend of tone-colors, a different instrument in a synaesthetic orchestra. When all twelve had established contact, they reached out to the other brothers at their distant locations, and came to a kind of multi-sensual harmonic stasis, their mind-notes overtones in a subtle chord.

A new voice came on the party line. Marsh Fox, clear as a crystal bell, his voice an admixture of warmth and seriousness of purpose.

"Kuash, there are others waiting to meet you."

A shot of adrenaline, a triple espresso buoyed by a mind-boggling panorama of colors, hues, textures, thought patterns interwoven with tones, emanating, pulsating, coming in tune with each other, finding their niche in a harmonic convergence whose scale taxed the limits of Lewis's imagination. Every movement, every vibration with its own integrity intimately linked to something vaster.

More than singing in a larger choir. The choir was singing inside of him, chords swelling and subsiding. His window of perception had been opened so wide that even with all the preparation, Lewis felt on the verge of losing his identity, becoming a particle adrift.

Marsh Fox's voice continued, *"We listen."*

Presences, rather than voices, came in from different directions. Lewis wondered if there were a vast web of *kuash* at sites throughout the world. The Guinness Book record for the Largest Telepathic Assemblage of a Collective Consciousness.

The vibrations descended to pianissimo, and Marsh Fox continued.

"Listen to the sun, the stars, the silence that is always with us. Listen on behalf of everything that lives and breathes in this world. Listen to the world itself. Open to what we receive together. Shining Ones, become your name."

In silence, they became a vast receptor, their minds antennae, their neural networks live-wire circuitry. Through their sinews, tissues and bones, electrochemically through their blood, coursed a signal.

It embraced Lewis's body like a long lost friend, passing through him as if by osmosis into the crust of the earth itself. The wordless experience, imbued with a sense of joy and wonder as he re-discovered what it means to be truly alive.

The sun rises every day, its song yearning for a critical mass of beings capable of attuning to it. Life on earth had evolved to create a species specially suited to fill this role. On the Longest Day, a group of humans responded to the call.

Others were in the loop now, coming online as the sun rose for them, wherever they were. Their location or affiliation did not matter. United in purpose, the signal pulsed through them all as conduits.

They were feeding the earth, and it in turn was nurturing something else. Lewis had become a link in a food chain of unfathomable scale. The current's in-flow fed him, calming the chaos of his thoughts and engendering a deep-seated feeling which seemed as old as the earth itself. When the chord diminished at noon, it was as though a few minutes had gone by instead of hours.

The Shining Ones arose from their respective corners of the mound and walked slowly back to the lodge as if emerging from a collective dream. The air tasted clean. A slight breeze gently brushed the foliage. Things which usually passed beneath one's notice took on a new significance. The trajectory of a bird, its chatter when landing, the ghost of a bulls-eye spider web, a lone parachute seed borne on a current of air. The simultaneous phenomena gave the moment a quality that begged to be savored. This unique instant, two blinks of an eye, would never be repeated.

Approaching the lodge, Lewis sensed a disturbance. The caretakers who had stayed behind were in turmoil, their voices rose and fell. Alakan was dead and the Story Woman had been found in his room, covered with blood.

Chapter Twenty Six

"Butterflies?"

"Coated with them," Davey said, "head to toe. Never seen anything like it."

They were in an air conditioned office, the Man sitting behind his glass table desk, reflexively running a hand through his pony tail, Davey in at-ease stance.

"What kind?" asked Alex, gesturing to his collection on the wall, a gift from a client in lieu of interest on a debt. Nice to look at. In fact, he had no deep knowledge of butterflies, which he wasn't about to reveal to Davey or anybody else.

"Monarchs," Davey said, pointing to a specimen on the wall." Alex glanced at the butterfly, then back at Davey, who clearly felt he was onto something.

"It's a distraction. A con," Alex said. "Guy's a trickster. He's smokin' you. Probably covered himself with honey or something."

"Maybe, but with respect, I wonder if you're seeing the big picture, sir."

"Don't tell me what I'm seeing or not seeing!" Alex snapped. "Big picture my ass. Guy doesn't add up. He's got his hooks in my daughter. I need to find out who the hell he is, who he's working for, not some bullshit about butterflies."

Davey took a deep breath and said, "You asked me to tail them discreetly and report back. That's what I saw. I'm not making it up." When Alex did not reply, Davey continued.

"Monarch butterflies.." he began, meriting a Level One eye-roll. "They navigate by magnetism and they cluster on trees. I've seen pictures of it. Never heard of them settling on a man like this."

"So maybe he was carrying a shitload of magnets. Where are you going with this?

"I saw no magnets on him, nothing electrical, no wires. Maybe he's found a way to, I don't know, harness magnetism in some way."

Like the guy in X-Men. Davey kept that one to himself, knowing it would bring a speedy end to the conversation.

"I get it," Alex said, leaning back in his chair. "Instead of putting a bank calendar and pictures of my dog on the refrigerator, I can stick 'em onto this guy's ass. Great suggestion. Thank you."

In for a pound, Davey continued.

"Everything electrical has a magnetic field. Computers, TV's, radios, phones, communication networks, your car. It's conceivable they could be disrupted, controlled by magnetism." Before Davey could drop the final penny, that controlling magnetism might just be the world's most powerful weapon, Alex slammed his hand down on the desktop.

"Basta! Stay focused on who he is, where he's from, who he's working for and what the fuck he wants with my daughter. That's it!"

The drifter's apparent knowledge of Natchez was something Alex would investigate himself.

"I don't give a flaming rat's ass about magnetic butterflies! Go talk to an enta – to an insect collector. I don't want to hear another word about it."

"Very well", said Davey.

First time he'd seen The Man miss an opportunity. Usually had a nose for such things. Perhaps someone else would.

"I've got good news and bad news," Hilton said, looking on as Skyfisher dropped an egg onto a hot frying pan.

"Bad first," Skyfisher said.

"There is no Salvo Samuels on the Internet."

"Is bad?" Skyfisher asked.

"Well, the good news is that I found out what your name means – Salvador," Hilton said. "It's from the Latin *Salvator*, which means savior."

Skyfisher savored the word as he placed four bits of egg on the circumference of his plate.

"Someone who saves," Hilton said.

"Almighty Greenbacks?" Skyfisher asked, chewing some egg white.

"People! A savior protects people in trouble. Like a fireman or a lifeguard. A savior could be someone you worship, a saint or God. Maybe even the Great Sun. A heavy name."

"Great Sun.." Skyfisher said, levering the yellow orange dome of egg yolk onto his fork. "He was savior once" popping the yolk intact into his mouth, "not now," he mused, remembering his *now* was a long time ago.

Skyfisher had tried to explain to Hilton and Inez how *kuash*, the Society of Light, had been formed at the behest of the first Great Sun. After his death, the Shining Ones had been compelled to go underground. The Great Sun's successors neither understood nor condoned *kuash*, seeing any such organization as a threat. The dire prediction of the end of the Natchez didn't help the Shining Ones' cause either. Officially they had disbanded. Unofficially, they moved their center of operations to an abandoned mound near White Apple Village, several days journey from the Temple Mound.

Skyfisher planned to take his friends there. Hilton had grown more interested since witnessing the butterfly feat, longing to see it go viral on YouTube. Skyfisher had cautioned them not to speak to anyone about what they had seen, unless that person was a serious candidate for the Mission. Hilton was still mystified by the trick.

"How did you do it? I mean, can you talk to butterflies?!"

"Not talk," Skyfisher said. "More like.." He took crayons and paper and drew an image of a man with lines emanating from him and at the end of each line he penciled in a tiny butterfly. "They find candle at night. This like that."

Tractor beams, Hilton thought. "So now what?"

"Ten men."

"What about women?" Hilton asked.

"Always men."

"Look where that got you." As the words tumbled out of his mouth, Hilton realized with a shock that he was sounding perilously like his mother, a Gloria Steinem devotee.

"These are different times, Salvo. Include women and I'll bet you could find ten people easy. If it's just men, we'd need a drum circle or something."

"Drum circle is good," Skyfisher said.

"No one would take it seriously. Why not give women a chance? What have you got to lose?"

Skyfisher knew better than anyone what he had to lose, but he kept this to himself. "Alright," he said. "You and Inez, One and Two."

"We'll make her an official Green Stamp. Then you can teach us how to call in the butterflies," Hilton said.

"We listen to sun, stars. And butterflies." Skyfisher left unsaid what they would really be doing because he had no words for it. No one did.

After knocking the idea around for a while, Hilton had an idea.

"We'll call it an experiment in telepathy. ESP. That'll get some college kids for sure. A great way to cheat on tests!" A brief explanation of extra-sensory perception followed, with a tangent into the Vulcan Mind Meld. Skyfisher agreed to Hilton's circulating a low-key flyer for an ESP experiment at a local campus.

That night, Hilton had to work late at a library event, a reading from a local author. He dropped Skyfisher off at Inez's house for dinner, the first time since meeting that they would be alone together.

"You OK with this?" Hilton whispered to Inez before leaving.

"Fine. If anything weird goes down, there's always pepper spray."

She had made pasta with pesto, enlisting Skyfisher's help chopping vegetables for a salad and setting the table.

As he was placing the silverware on the table, she asked him, "Did you use knives and forks?", feeling the absurdity of the question, as though she was an actor playing along with his delusion.

"No forks. Yes knives."

The same feeling that she had had all along with him. No guile or premeditation. On impulse, Inez reached for Salvo's right hand, turning it over to regard the tattoo and lightly tracing its outline on the palm.

"What does this mean?"

Inez's gentle touch was a surprise. Until now, Skyfisher had regarded her as a friend, her actions those of a concerned sister. He had to be careful, not knowing the customs here well enough. He slowly lifted his hand to face Inez, gesturing her to do the same. Their palms touched. Three breaths. Skyfisher lifted his right palm and with his left hand traced a line from his heart across his chest and shoulder down the right arm to the palm eye. Then he reached across to Inez's palm and traced his finger down her wrist, arm, shoulder, across her chest, skirting her left breast to rest on her heart. Three breaths.

As unexpected as it was, the gesture seemed oddly familiar to Inez, as though she was reliving a memory from the past. At the same time, years of dealing with men raised a few yellow flags.

"Let's have dinner. Afterwards, maybe you could sing me another song."

He sang a lullaby, Inez listening closely to the words. A candle flickered on the dining room table, its light reflecting off the water glasses.

"I think my grandmother sang that to me, too" Inez said. "The melody is the same." She hummed it back to him. "The words are not how I remember them. They're different."

Skyfisher nodded and smiled. "Mother sings song at me. She change words because I listen no! Song say, 'sleep'. Mother sing, 'wake' because I do when she say, 'No *do*.' She know me."

"Now I know you a little. Maybe." Inez laughed, then sounding a bit like an anthropologist, asked, "Did your mother tell stories? "Can you tell me a story, one of the stories of your people?"

This woman speaks my wife's name like it is hers to become.

"Words not good. I say story my language."

"Wait a moment." Inez left the room and came back with her recorder and a blank tape. "Is OK?"

"Is OK." Skyfisher closed his eyes. She and Hilton were his only hope at the moment. A fragile thread, but songs had managed to connect her with his past. Without that connection, he was truly in exile, far away from anything familiar, a slave imprisoned in another man's body.

The stories were not meant for this place. Animals communed with men and shared their secrets. People killed without remorse. Men's wives stolen from them.

In the Natchez language, Skyfisher told the tale of seven villagers who sought a vision. They fasted, first for seven days, then seven months. Over time, the seven grew fearful and more distant from their people, until one day they decided to hide away by turning themselves into pine trees.

They looked into the future and saw that marauders would come and cut them down with axes. They turned themselves into rocks instead of trees. The invaders hungered for the rocks as well. There was no escape except to turn themselves into stars. A constellation.

"End story," he said.

Inez switched off the recorder. "Sad, I think," she said.

"Yes," Skyfisher agreed, remembering what Hilton had told him about what had happened to the Natchez. Lightning had been right about the invaders. It was a miracle any of his people survived the wars with the French and their allies. Years later, the few remaining Natchez were with the Cherokee, Chickasaw, Choctaw and other tribes, all taken from their homelands and force-marched to Oklahoma. Over 60,000 Indians died on the Trail of Tears. Some of his people still remained. He would find them.

Chapter Twenty Seven

In a few days, the Grand Village of the Natchez would be hosting its annual Pow-Wow. Members of the Natchez tribe were traveling from Oklahoma to attend.

"Pow-Wow's aren't exactly my cup of tea," Inez informed Hilton, "but I'll tag along to keep the Green Stamps out of trouble." Probably as good an opportunity as she would get to see if *Nasootka Shudef* was the real thing.

The day before the event, a fleet of RV's and trailers invaded the field adjacent to the Grand Village. A tent village sprang up, with generators humming - traders, craftsmen, dancers, drummers and the Native American wannabes who followed the Pow-Wow circuit throughout the summer. Most Pow-Wows were held on athletic fields and county fairgrounds. This was one of the few that took place on ancestral ceremonial land. The Natchez had been living on or near the mounds when DeSoto's expedition encountered them in the 1500's. Now they were the centerpiece of the Grand Village, which also had a small museum with artifacts, dioramas, a gift shop and a reproduction of a Natchez hut. The annual Pow-Wow was timed to coincide with Natchez's Spring Pilgrimage, when tourists came en masse to tour the city's antebellum mansions. Some of the overflow visited the Grand Village as well, so the attendees were a conglomerate of vacationers and camp followers. The remnants of the Natchez tribe made their own pilgrimage from Oklahoma to make sure the mounds, their sacred ground, survived the Pow-Wow. They discretely participated in a few of the celebratory processions and openly indulged in their passion for stick ball, Indian-style.

Arriving in a convoy of SUVs and mini buses bursting like seedpods with kids, parents, uncles and other kin, the Natchez established eminent domain near the playing field by sheer force of exuberance, much of it channeled into preparation for the upcoming match with the Choctaws.

A pile of sticks materialized out of the car trunk collective. Each was a few feet long with a curved oblong loop on one end circling a leather thong net roughly the size of a child's hand. Shorter than a lacrosse stick, the flat net gave it the appearance of a burly flyswatter or a mini tennis racket. Each player carried two sticks. The ball, roughly the size of a golfball, was caught clapper-style, the player sandwiching it between the two stick-nets, and tossing it with a flick of the wrist, while pulling the front stick down at the last instant.

The rules of the game were straightforward. Two teams had to get the ball between their opponent's goal posts. You were not allowed to touch the ball with your hands. No other restrictions. None. Stick-ball was played as a wilding blend of tackle football, rugby, lacrosse and a World Wrestling Federation melee.

The Natchez fielded a ragtag medley of players, from lanky elders to a sumo-sized goalie, with a host of wiry high schoolers and bandy-legged pre-teens in the mix. They procured their sticks and began to practice in loose-knit groups. An hour later, a caravan of Choctaws arrived.

Inez and the Green Stamps watched on the sidelines. Sky-fisher was pacing backing and forth, looking intently at each member of the Natchez team, searching for a vision of his past.

To Hilton's eye, the Choctaws seemed the more serious bunch, with lean and hungry-looking nascent line-backers wielding their sticks like weapons.

"Those guys are gonna eat the Natchez for breakfast," Hilton said, "like Natchos."

A brief dissertation followed on the concept of junk food, of which there were examples aplenty at the Pow-Wow, including Hilton's personal favorite, fried dough.

Wisdom and experience guided the choosing of sides for the stick-ball game, with each team sporting a mix of young, old, fit, fat and most importantly, different tribal affiliations.

A simple, elegant solution, Inez thought. "We could achieve world peace this way."

"It's the All-Star game," Hilton said.

They scrimmaged a bit. A Natchez grandfather passed the ball to a young macho Choctaw, orbited by a youngster who very nearly intercepted the pass. The players circled their respective goal posts, chanting, whooping, knocking their sticks together in rhythm. Then the sides squared off, the ball was tossed and mayhem ensued, with elders getting body-slammed by their nephews, and leprechaun-sized forwards weaving around rotund goalies, scoring with triumph as though they were counting coup.

Skyfisher was enthralled, and during a brief pause in the action he asked one of the players on the sidelines if he could play, too. They escorted him over to meet the ref, Thurman Goode, headman of the group. Bald, slightly overweight, yet with a powerful demeanor, he sported a circular tattoo on the nape of his neck, the symbol of a Great Sun. Goode regarded Salvo's fiftyish body with empathy.

"I'd like to play, too," he said, "but they'd kill me. You know what you're getting yourself into? No insurance forms. You play at your own risk. We used to have an ambulance standing by. Couldn't afford it this year."

After a brief translation consultation with Inez and Hilton, Skyfisher nodded in thanks. Not the moment to start spouting the home dialect. This man could be a descendant! Skyfisher wondered if Goode had any inkling at all of who he was inside.

"You sure about this?" Inez asked, and Skyfisher smiled.

"Lose the shades," Goode said, "they'll break, for sure. You can play on Jobie's team," pointing to a lanky pony-tailed elder. "They could use another man. Good luck. You'll need it!"

He laughed, hoping this idiot wouldn't sue when he got toasted. Hilton took the sunglasses and made a rather lame attempt to talk Salvo-Skyfisher out of his folly. But with visions of *Rocky* meets *Dances With Wolves*, he wanted to see what his friend could do.

They found a mismatched pair of sticks for him and a white T-shirt. One of the kids tossed the ball his way, to give him a little practice. He missed it. On the sidelines, Inez and Hilton watched with a growing sense of dread.

"Snagging that little ball is like trying to tweezer a fly with a pair of chopsticks," Hilton said.

Skyfisher fumbled again and committed the unpardonable gaffe of picking the ball up with his hands, an automatic penalty that gave the other team possession. Henceforward, his team considered him a liability and behaved accordingly. A high lob from the other team sailed in Skyfisher's direction and sidestepping past a team mate, he jumped and commandeered the ball. Not having mastered the overhand throw, he tossed an underhand lob to a member of the other team, having forgotten that his side wore white T-shirts. Still, the catch restored his confidence and it wasn't long before a teammate tossed him a pass. As Skyfisher sprang towards it, a searing pain ripped through his left calf. Salvo's body rolled on the ground and the other players swept past him, the game not stopping for minor injuries. Hilton shouldered him off the field, limping.

"You pulled a muscle," Hilton said, reminding Skyfisher he was borrowing the shell of an older man's body.

"Looked good out there for a little while," Inez said to cheer him up.

A few of the women in the crowd regarded him with sympathy. In short order, a knee-high girl had been dispatched to the vendor area. Returning with some ice wrapped in a towel, she shyly offered it to Skyfisher. He thanked her in Natchez and watched as the dark T-shirts scored another goal. The girl whispered something to her mother. The woman glanced over at Skyfisher holding the ice to his leg, flanked on either side by his friends, then summoned one of the boys on the sidelines, who came over to Skyfisher.

"*Cenkololo.*"

"*Weda Sokonon,*" Skyfisher responded with a smile, wishing him good day and asking his new friend how he was doing.

"*Ketanesoo. Tua shuxu nin?*"

The young man stammered a reply and returned to his mother. Shortly after, one of the older men, a second string goalie, approached and squatted in front of Skyfisher. Inez listened with interest.

"How's the leg?" he asked.

"OK."

"My son tells me you speak our language."

"*Nahtchi ihiwe 'ltagik,*" Skyfisher responded. "*Sokone ha.*"

A good game.

The man nodded gravely and after a moment left with a polite nod. The match ended in an eight goal tie, and both sides gathered in the center of the field, knocking their sticks together, chanting and congratulating each other. Not long after, a small delegation came by, ostensibly to ask about Skyfisher's injury.

"You played well –," said Thurman Goode.

"I was bad!" Skyfisher laughed.

"– for a non-Indian," Goode added. "You speak some Natchez?"

"Long story," Skyfisher said, and he began to tell it in the language of his people. After a minute, Goode politely gestured for Skyfisher to pause.

"Maybe you and you friends would like a soft drink?"

The little girl who had brought the ice had been dispatched again, returning with an egg cart tray of cups filled with soda.

Goode conferred with a few of the older women and men around him, then turned to Skyfisher.

"Did you know Archie Sam?"

Skyfisher shook his head no.

"Some of us knew him," Goode said. "The last fluent speaker. Archie searched for years for anyone who spoke the language. He didn't find anyone, but he left some tapes and a basic English - Natchez dictionary. We try to teach the next generation what we remember from our elders and the tape." Goode paused and lowered his voice. "None of us could follow you, completely. Sounds genuine to me. If you're making it up, we'll have to scalp you," he added with a smile. "Tell me in English how you came to speak our language."

Skyfisher's knowledge of English seemed to be more or less on par with the Natchez's grasp of their own language. Consulting with Hilton and Inez to make sure he understood the request, he began to speak, drawing from both languages.

He was *Nasootka Shudef,* Skyfisher, inhabiting the body of Salvador Samuels.

"A sacred duty is given to our people. If we do not follow *piha-o schi-shis* - this duty, bad things happen to this world. There will be a —"

"Catastrophe," Hilton said hopefully.

"I am here for help."

Looking at the faces of his audience reminded Skyfisher of Inez's expression when she listened to a pair of Jehovah's Witnesses making an unannounced visit at their doorstep. He might as well have handed out copies of *The Watchtower.*

Thurman Goode thanked him and said they would take his message to a council that decided all tribal business on consensus.

"Come visit us in Oklahoma and we'll record some vocabulary for our archive."

"Here, take this," Inez said, handing over the cassette she had recorded of Skyfisher's story. "It has him speaking the language. Maybe it could be a help." Goode took the cassette and thanked her. Skyfisher's ice bag was replenished and the group dispersed.

"Let me give you a hand," Hilton said, and they headed towards a fried dough stand for Hilton to get his fix. As they left the stand, Jobie, one of the elders, approached them. He gestured Skyfisher towards a log nearby. There was only room for two, and Inez sensed the older man wanted privacy.

"We'll be back," she said, steering Hilton towards the museum.

"Please stay," Jobie said. "Sorry there's no place else to sit here, except for seniors and injured athletes. This is going to be brief."

Jobie and Skyfisher sat in silence for a full five minutes. While Hilton fidgeted, groups of tourists passed by, families with strollers, kids getting their hands and faces sticky with cotton candy, dancers in full regalia of feathers, bells and bright colors. Jobie discretely pointed to the tattoo on Skyfisher's palm.

"Saw that when you were talking before. My grandpa told me about it," Jobie said. "Not much. Something his granddad told him. My Natchez is rusty, so I'm gonna say this in English, OK?" He looked at Inez. "Maybe you can fill in the blanks, explain it to him later."

"We'll try," Inez said.

"We still remember the songs and the ceremonies," Jobie said. "The Natchez were the ones that kept the spirit flame burning on the Trail of Tears. That's what grandpa told me, anyway. There are some things no one can take from you. Very few know about that," Jobie said, glancing at Skyfisher's palm. "I heard it in pieces, mostly around a campfire." Jobie looked intently at Skyfisher.

"They didn't hear you. You could be the reincarnation of Hiawatha bringing back the sacred corn and no one would listen. Except maybe an old fart like me. You don't pass the sniff test."

Hilton spent a few minutes with Skyfisher attempting to navigate around *reincarnation* and *old fart.*

"What is *sniff test?*" Skyfisher asked.

"You're not an Indian!" Jobie said. "Speaking the language is one thing, a powerful thing. Blood is another." Jobie scratched behind his ear. "It would be like Jesus coming back, except he's Chinese or something. Look, can you blame us? It's been, what, three hundred years of broken treaties, stolen lands and broken promises. Even stealing our identities. Look around you! He nodded towards a non-indian dressed in full regalia - a beautiful headdress draped with eagle feathers, buckskin pants and moccasins. He paused, took a sip of some bottled water. "Remember Iron Eyes Cody?"

"Who?" asked Hilton.

"Iron Eyes Cody, the famous Crying Indian, except he wasn't an Indian and even the tear wasn't real. Look it up." He closed his eyes and sighed deeply.

"Bottom line," Jobie said. "What do you need?"

A few words with Hilton and Skyfisher responded.

"Ten men."

"I'll get you two," Jobie said. "My nephews, Trevor and, uh –" his eyes went skyward, "Simon! I'll talk to 'em. This is just between us, unofficial. No council."

Skyfisher smiled, and although it emanated from another man's face, it was indeed *his* smile, as if the muscles in

Salvo's face had reconciled to it. He turned away from Jobie, conducting his own version of the sniff test. One of the unexpected "gifts" of Skyfisher's sensory awareness had been a way of *seeing* each person's unique set of gestures, postures, rhythms, appreciating these vibrations the way a wine connoisseur would savor a fine Pinot. Picking up the scent of someone familiar, Skyfisher suggested that Hilton discretely slip away and get a better look at one of the customers at a nearby souvenir stand.

Chapter Twenty Eight

Davey liked the South. They understood hierarchy, respect and minded their own business. The women talked too much, but they possessed a sense of grace. And smelled good.

Be that as it may, it was time to move on. Somehow, he'd been smoked again.

He was being as cryptic as a fucking leaf mold and there was that goddam pilgrim guy looking him right in the eye with a shit-eating grin. So much for discretion. He was through here.

Davey wasn't sure of the protocol, but there seemed to be no choice except to resign and head north. The Man would be mightily pissed. The only possible good news was he had another card to play. A picture card, for sure.

Skyfisher had the loan of Jobie's nephews, Trevor and Simon, for a week. They were wiry, freckled and sandy haired, sporting buzz cuts and loose fitting clothes.

Rubber bands with arms and legs, Hilton thought.

Trevor, the eldest, was navigating the currents of puberty, with a wisp of a moustache and a voice that cracked every now and then, along with a slight case of acne joining his freckles. Simon the Younger, as dubbed by Hilton, chewed gum incessantly, and was the more outgoing of the two. He had a natural curiosity and an adventurous spirit, which on a few occasions got him called onto the carpet, like when he climbed a tree and started shooting sparrows with a potato spud gun.

They camped out in a tent in Inez's back yard for a few days and when it rained they crashed in Hilton's apartment. Inez was preparing to attend a conference. She delegated logistics to Hilton, strongly suggesting that Salvo get temporary work to help defray household expenses, which now included feeding two extra mouths.

With a few phone calls, a personal reference from Inez and a brief interview, Salvo landed a job as a dishwasher at Mammy's Cupboard, a breakfast hut-cum-roadside attraction that stood underneath a huge plaster statue of an Aunt Jemima-esque figure holding a tray of food. The roof of the hive shaped building was Mammy's capacious dress. In the North, it would be a poster child for political incorrectness. In Natchez, Mammy's had been grandfathered into local culture.

The cover story was that Salvo, an old friend of Inez's, was recovering from a stroke which had affected his speech.

"It's not like dishwashers need varsity communication skills," Hilton remarked. In fact, Salvo's quietude was a selling point. He worked the breakfast shift, and gave Extra Sensory Perception 101 lessons to the nephews and Hilton in the afternoon. Inez joined them for a few sessions before heading off to her conference.

"You're in charge, Hilton. I expect to see this house in one piece when I get back. The boys seem well enough behaved, but they are *boys*, so keep a lid on 'em."

"Right you are, boss," Hilton said, saluting her. "Just to show you my heart's in the right place, I won't even make any snarky remarks about how now we can keep the toilet seat up."

On this reassuring note, Inez departed and Team Testosterone had the place to themselves. Their training began in earnest.

Skyfisher had Hilton and the boys sit in a line facing away from him with their eyes closed.

"Raise hand when I look at *you.*"

Hilton demurred, but the boys each raised their hands when they felt a prickle on their neck.

"Good," Skyfisher said. "We try more." They were reluctant and shy, but that changed on the third day.

Sitting all together in a tight circle, Skyfisher had them lean in and reach their arms out for each other's shoulders. A few giggles ensued, along with a whispered rebuke from Simon the Younger about the overuse of underarm deodorant.

When things had settled down, Skyfisher said, "No move. Speak when you feel it." He sent a low level current coursing through the circle.

Simon spoke up immediately. "A tingle!"

"Liar," Trevor said.

"No, I do!"

"Where?" asked Skyfisher.

"In my arms," Simon said.

"And now?"

"Ooh, it's in my legs."

"Good," Skyfisher said. "Hilton, you feel?"

"Yeah, I got something."

"Trevor - listen, feel. I send something for you."

"Ah!" Trevor shouted as he jumped off his chair, breaking contact with the others.

"What happened, Trev, you OK?" Hilton asked.

"Something stung me. A bee or something!"

"Where?" asked Skyfisher.

"My back," Trevor said, pulling off his shirt. Skyfisher patted him on the back.

"I send something strong because you tough nut, like Hilton say. You feel?"

"Damn, that's scary!" Trevor said.

"Send it to me, too. I ain't scared!" Simon said, wide-eyed. The rest of the afternoon was spent modulating the sting to a low-level electrical charge that all of them could feel.

"I got goose bumps," Trevor confessed, and the boys spent the next hour jazzed and eager to zap each other with virtual bee stings.

"Ice cream!" Hilton declaimed. "You guys deserve it." A raid on the freezer produced an eclectic assortment of experimental flavors, mostly due to Skyfisher's affinity for peanut butter with everything. His latest creation was a blend of Hagen Dasz vanilla, jalapeño peppers, pine nuts, chocolate syrup, crushed graham crackers, a dash of cumin and peanut butter. Simon and Trevor settled for vanilla, straight up.

Despite the initial thrill of their newly acquired super powers, inspiring "A mask and a cape, yes!" from Simon the Younger, the boys were soon distracted by the lure of the city and the freedom of being away from home. Practice sessions were interrupted with field trips to downtown Natchez to get *normal* ice cream at the Malt Shop. And they were getting homesick. The *goose bump thing* soon became less of a novelty, a Mister Science parlor trick. Trevor asked Skyfisher how he did it.

"I no do," he said, "forces do." Graced with Trevor's "*Duh*" look, Skyfisher asked, "Radio has little people inside?"

He might as well have told them he'd heard a voice from a burning bush. Hilton had regaled Skyfisher with the story of Moses, just to give equal time to both sides of the Judeo-Christian equation. Skyfisher didn't have 40 years to wander in the desert. He needed to homestead an organic receiving apparatus, something that had taken him years to learn, and it had to happen soon. If human beings were not doing what they had been created for, then a bevy of bad things was going to happen, as inevitably as fall follows summer. He had explained this dispassionately to Hilton and Inez, sounding like a frontman for a Hollywood style dystopian epic – fireballs in the sky, famine, drought, disease and other delights, recalling the plagues visited upon Egypt.

"At least there's no zombies," Hilton said.

The Shining Ones' tea leaves had predicted a catalytic event that would tip the scales towards the destruction of the entire planet. When pressed, Skyfisher didn't know when it might happen.

"Soon," was the best he could offer.

At the end of a week, Skyfisher was despondent. No one had responded to the ESP experiment flyer. Hilton had not come up with any other ideas that might attract more help. Nothing else to do but keep on working with his little group. Of them all, Inez had shown the most promise. When she returned from her conference and rejoined their practice sessions, the water level seemed to rise for everybody, surprising Skyfisher. He'd never entrusted a woman with the secrets of his practice, not even his wife.

One evening he had tried to send Inez a mental projection of Tell Me A Story as he knew her, from the inside out, a stream of vibrations coalescing into an image.

"She looks like me!" Inez said. Abashed, Skyfisher suggested, "See under skin."

Inez attempted this, glimpsing through the surface vision of Skyfisher's memory-visage to tap a wellspring of emotion.

"She loves you," Inez said. "There's fire."

Skyfisher nodded in agreement.

On a hunch, Hilton had done a bit of surveillance at JB's auto body shop. An old Chevy Nova with New York state plates was parked in the back lot.

"The time has come for a covert operation," he said, attempting to sound like an MI5 agent and coming off more like a cartoon version of Doctor Who. He presented the bones of his plan and Jobie's nephews leapt at it, thrilled at the prospect of a noble, illicit enterprise, a fitting coda to their visit, not to mention a chance to see if they could use their newfound super powers, with or without capes and masks.

Inez said, "I'll stay here to answer the phone, for when they allow you one call from jail." She did, however, lend them her car.

"Making me an accessory," she admitted.

Hilton and the boys scavenged the basement and garage for supplies and tossed a duffel bag of tools in the trunk. At midnight, Team Testosterone set off, high on adrenaline, coffee and honey-dipped donuts.

Natchez has no shortage of auto body shops. Jean Baptiste's was tucked away behind an abandoned machine parts outlet. With the aesthetic appeal of a concrete bunker, it stood in a yard surrounded by heaps of junk metal, bordered by a chain link fence topped by two rows of razor wire. Two bare light bulbs illuminated the yard.

On the other side of the fence, the Nova sat in the back of the yard, its hood raised.

The boys found two quilted movers' blankets, climbed the chain link fence and draped the blankets over the razor wire.

A lean Doberman Pincer emerged from the shadows, baring its teeth, emitting a deep growl, and making it clear there was nothing on earth it would rather see than their climbing over the fence. Loud barking ensued.

Skyfisher knelt and went into receptivity mode, but the dog was oblivious. Something was blocking his efforts.

"If we don't silence Fido soon, we're going to have company," Hilton said.

Skyfisher tried again to attune to the dog without success.

"I get close to dog, speak to him," and Skyfisher began to climb the chain link.

"Whoa!" Hilton cried.

Skyfisher reached the blankets and as he lifted his leg over the barbed wire, Hilton saw something he had not noticed before, an electric collar on the Doberman.

"Wait!" he cried. Too late. Skyfisher dropped to the ground.

The dog was suddenly wary. No one had ever climbed over the fence before. This man did not carry a stick that stings. Baring its fangs and drooling copious amounts of saliva, it made ready to spring.

Chapter Twenty Nine

A cold morning. The sun's rays had not yet touched the lodge at the top of the mound, where Tell Me A Story was being kept as patient and prisoner. On the morning of *ippli hallesh*, she'd been found unconscious on the floor of Alakan's room. He lay in his cot blue-faced, strangled or suffocated, his life breath stolen.

Lewis was now at Tell Me A Story's bedside, refusing to leave. She'd been hit over the head; that much was clear. Ridiculous to assume she had killed Alakan. Lewis was surprised others saw things differently. The apprentices remembered Alakan's dislike of her and conveniently forgot she had saved him from the snake bite. The fruits of envy.

Lewis cleaned her wound, made sure she had a cold compress on her forehead. Beyond that, he didn't know quite what to do. If he left, who ever harmed her would return.

Lightning came by with the apprentices and instructed them to do their duty, even if their patient was a murderer. Lewis was about to protest, but Lightning silenced him with a gesture. After dismissing the apprentices to gather herbs for a healing tonic, Lightning turned his attention to Tell Me A Story.

"Breathing well. Her heart is strong. She is in a kind of sleep. This happens when you receive a strong blow to the head," Lightning said.

"I know," said Lewis, *"but why – "*

"Better the killer thinks he is safe. We don't know who it is."

"Haeden?" Lewis asked.

"He wasn't here," Lightning said.

"Maybe he came back while we were at the alignment."

"I will question the guards," Lightning said. *"There could be others."*

"Why would anyone want to kill Alakan?"

Lightning rubbed his thin nose as if sharpening it to a finer point.

"Some see the Society of Light as a threat."

"Who?"

"Allies of the Great Sun or one of the Lesser Suns."

"What now?" Lewis asked.

"As soon as this woman is better, you both leave."

The apprentices returned, edgy and uncomfortable under Lightning's baleful scrutiny. When one was about to administer some medicinal tea, Lewis stopped him.

"You sip first."

After the apprentice had sipped, Lewis commandeered the cup, propping his step-wife's head on a pillow. He moistened her lips with a few drops, watching her breath, wondering if she was dreaming.

"Leave us, please," Lewis said to the others. To his second sight, the wound did not appear serious, though it left a good size lump on the back of her head. She was indeed in some kind of kind of coma. He leaned close, whispering.

"There is a story about a beautiful woman who saved the other women of her village by telling stories to a chief, a different story every night."

He stroked her cheek.

"You could do that."

It was true. She was a dream woman, a worthy sister of Scheherazade. He could not help but love her, even knowing she was married to another man, one he shared flesh and bones with. Lewis was beginning to be more familiar with his host's uncanny way of seeing into things. If he stayed, would he transform into Skyfisher, *become his name*? Somewhere in the future, was Skyfisher becoming him?

He imagined Tell Me A Story loving him, not because he wore the skin of her husband, but because of who he was inside. Lewis had promised Grey Turtle and the other elders that he would not speak in his own tongue, but needing a lifeline to himself, he began to sing.

Go to sleep my weary hobo
Let the clouds drift slowly by
Can't you hear the steel wheels humming?
That's the hobo's lullaby.

The lullaby did its job. Lewis nodded off, dreamless for once. He awoke with a start. An apprentice was in the room. Tell Me A Story's eyes were open. She was smiling.

"You were snoring," she said.

"You're back! How are you?"

"My head hurts. Some water would help."

Lewis gave her cold tea to sip and Tell Me A Story asked the apprentice to prepare a tonic using a specific herb. The apprentice nodded and left them.

Lightning returned shortly thereafter. He leaned near Tell Me A Story, his mouth stretching into a thin line, the hint of a smile.

"I'm going to need your husband for a day," Lightning said. *"A guard will be posted here."*

"Who will protect me from the guard?" she asked.

"I need to know who Alakan's killer was," whispered Lightning.

"I didn't see him," Tell Me A Story said. *"It was dark. I was resting. Someone entered the room. I called out to him. When he did not respond, I stood up and went towards him. He grabbed me. We fought. He hit me with something and I went down."*

"A big man?" Lightning asked.

"Short."

"Can this wait?" Lewis asked. *"She's still weak. I want to stay by her."*

"It cannot wait," Lightning said. *"With Marsh Fox gone, you answer to me, as does the guard. You must trust me in this."*

"You can have my husband for a day," Tell Me A Story said. *"Bring him back."*

"Will you give us a moment alone?" Lewis asked. With a grunt, Lightning departed.

"Keep this hidden," Lewis said, handing her his knife. *"Just in case. You know how to use it."*

"I'll be alright," she said, tucking the knife beneath her. *"Go well."*

Lightning instructed Lewis to take neither dinner nor breakfast. They set out at first light, Skyfisher's stomach grumbling, Lewis's mind vainly trying not to listen to it. In the forest canopy, a wood thrush trilled, their footsteps muffled by the forest growth. Every now and then a twig snap would startle a resting bird. Lewis did not recognize the path. After a few hours they reached the edge of a marsh that reminded him of the one he, Grey Turtle and Tell Me A Story had passed through on their journey.

"Where is Grey Turtle?" Lewis asked, breaking the morning's silence.

"Later," Lighting said. *"Now, you try. With your bones, with the blood that beats in your heart, with the breath that connects*

you to the world above. Let the Sun Breath in, penetrate you, every part. Walk." Lightning let Lewis take the lead as they moved further into the swamp.

"What do you see here?" Lightning asked.

"Water, plants..."

"Underwater - fish, frogs?"

"I cannot see underwater."

"You see inside cave. Why not water?"

"I don't know," Lewis said. In moments like this, he was still a rookie, an intruder trying to work the console of Skyfisher's senses.

"Try harder," Lighting said. *"Sun Breath needs you. You think too much. See into the water. It will open to you, if you listen. Keep walking. I will wait here."*

Lewis moved further into the marsh. He felt the pressure of the elder's senses attempting to open a back door into Sky-fisher's way of seeing, just as he had tried in the cave.

Lewis felt uneasy, slightly nauseous. He paused, poised between the impulse to obey and the feeling that something was wrong with this picture. He walked on, the water up to his ankles, his pace slowing as the ground became much softer. When he realized what was happening, it was too late. He was in the swamp, knee-deep in water, as if in a trance. His feet had settled deep into the mud, royally stuck to a subterranean tar baby.

No need to turn around. Lightning was gone.

Lewis was settling in the muck, visions of jungle B-movies in his head, where there was always a handy vine nearby. He surveyed the marsh around him. Nothing within reach to grab hold of.

Some kind of test?

Were he not sinking deeper into the mud, he would've enjoyed the morning. Dayglo blue skies, no mosquitos. Doubtless they would come later. He flashed back to Lake Seymour, Vermont, his first experience at a country lake. Must've been six or seven years old. A girl named Diana showed him how to lie face down in the water without sinking. Kids were shouting, "Di does the Deadman's Float! Di does the Deadman's Float!" How weird to recall a past still to come in the future. Di would do the Deadman's Float five hundred years from now. Maybe.

The water level was rising above his waist as he slowly descended.

Something unexpected. An echo of an impulse that his body, not his ears, had somehow heard. A compulsion to stay, go deeper, merge with the water and what lay beneath. An overwhelming desire to obey, join with the soundless sound.

Chapter Thirty

Trevor had seen adults do some pretty lame things, but this stunt topped them all. He began scavenging for rocks. The dog was snarling, trigger-hair poised to attack.

"Distract him!" Trevor shouted to his brother. Simon scaled the fence, drew a Snickers bar from his pocket and threw it, hitting the Doberman on the rump. The dog wheeled around, sniffed at the candy bar and wolfed it down, wrapper and all. Cradling a few projectiles in one hand, Trevor climbed the fence, yelling at Salvo.

"Get your ass out of there!"

Salvo held his ground.

Leaning on the fence-top blanket, Trevor picked out the most promising rock, figuring he'd get one shot before the dog attacked.

"His collar – it's electric!" Hilton shouted.

The dog, momentarily diverted by the brothers, circled and hesitated, not quite ready to strike someone who displayed no fear, waiting for whatever weapon the man might have, some clandestine juju that would turn this piece of meat into an alpha dog.

Skyfisher didn't understand the word "collar", but he was starting to get the picture. The dog's senses were bathed in static. The communication lines were down. He slowly stood up, putting him right in the path of Trevor's throw. The dog lunged and chomped on Skyfisher's dungarees, ripping off a piece of denim from the pant leg and shaking it furiously.

Balanced on the top of the fence, Trevor drew his arm back and channeled his best fastball, like when he was hunting squirrels back home. The dog paused between shakes and readied itself for something more nourishing than Levis. The throw, a startled whelp and the dog was down. Right between the eyes. Still breathing. Simon scaled over the fence, duct tape in hand, and quickly hogtied the Doberman's muzzle and legs.

The brothers low-fived. Hilton carefully climbed over the fence and went to Skyfisher.

"Salvo," he said. "You are one crazy fucker. Figure out how to say *that* in Natchez. Let's get your car!"

Bolt cutters liberated the lock on the fence. The keys fit the ignition, but the Chevy would not turn over. A jump-start from Inez's car didn't do the trick either. Asking his brother to hold the flashlight, Trevor stripped some wires under the dashboard, reconnected them, and with a spark, the engine coughed. He tried again, and the car started.

"Bravo," said Hilton, who made sure they left nothing but footprints, a broken lock and the aforementioned duct tape.

"Trevor, you know how to drive?"

"Yes, but –"

"But what?"

"No license."

"No problemo. Follow me, go slow. Salvo, you ride with him. Simon the Younger, with me. It's a test drive. I'll do the talking if you get stopped."

Thankfully, they didn't. Pulling into Inez's driveway, the boys jumped out of the cars with a few war whoops and visions of Teenage Ninja Natchez dancing in their heads.

"I'd like to see JB's face when he comes to work tomorrow," Hilton said.

"It's going to smart when they pull the tape off the doggie." Simon said.

"True," said Hilton. "That's what happens when you play with the big boys. Well, he was breathing through his nose. He'll be alright. Just doing his job."

Homecoming was replete with instant replays.

"Inez! Oh my god, you're not going to believe this!" Trevor was jumping up down, windmilling his arms.

Inez put her hands on his shoulders, letting the jumping subside. "I want to hear all about it in the morning. A full debriefing. Right now, it's the tent for you both. Sleeping bags and flashlights." A gentle shove, and they were off.

"A woman's touch," Hilton said, nodding in approval. Inez, arms crossed, regarded the Green Stamps. "I'm beat. Those guys are going to be bouncing off the walls in the morning. I'll need your help with damage control. You want to crash here for the night? Hilton gets the couch. Salvo prefers the floor, right? One question. You didn't do anything stupid, did you? Better to know now."

"We rocked," Hilton said.

In the morning, Team Testosterone recounted its exploits to rounds of whistles and applause. At a lull in the conversation, Skyfisher spoke up.

"Boys brave. Trevor, new name. 'Dead-eye!'"

"What about me?" Simon asked.

"You?" Hilton sounded surprised, but when he saw Simon's sad face, he relented. "Yeah, we got one for you, too. 'Big Dog'. You like it?

"Dead-eye is cooler," Simon said.

"I think Big Dog is very cool," Inez said.

"Next week, Longest Day," Skyfisher interjected. "You remember?"

"We remember," Trevor said. "I gotta ask you something, Salvo."

"Ask," Skyfisher said.

Trevor took a deep breath.

"All this stuff we did. It was kinda weird and I know we're not supposed to tell anybody –"

"Except Jobie!" Simon piped in.

"Except my uncle. All this stuff. Is it real? I mean, are you like really from way back? From like - before?"

"You understand him?" Hilton asked.

Skyfisher patted his chest, "This Salvo." Pointing to his head, he added, Skyfisher here. Yes?"

"I guess," said Trevor, wishing he hadn't asked.

"Dead-eye brave. Goose-bump real. Skyfisher real. My time - long ago. True. OK?"

"OK," Trevor said.

"Something for you both on the way back to Oklahoma," Inez said, presenting Simon with a tin of chocolate chip cookies.

"Bus reading," said Hilton, handing a Sandman graphic novel to Trevor, and some old-school Spiderman comics for Simon.

Skyfisher gave them their last minute instructions for the solstice, just over a week away. As his parting gift, Trevor rewired the car so it could be started with a key.

"What time does the bus leave?" Inez asked.

"One-thirty," Hilton said.

"Better get going before the sheriff sends a posse out looking for Dead-eye and Big Dog," Inez said.

The next day, using a hand lens, Skyfisher started a fire from the sun, a technique he'd learned from Hilton. The elders would have approved.

That evening, Hilton drove Salvo's Nova to the Emerald Mound, Inez riding shotgun, Skyfisher in the back seat, cradling a metal bucket that held glowing embers from the sun-fire in a bed of ashes.

The Emerald Mound was seldom visited by tourists, even though it was only a dozen or so miles from Natchez. Rising about twenty feet off the ground, a little over two football fields in length. Its top was flat turf at one end of which stood a smaller pyramid-shaped mound.

A sign near the parking lot showed an illustration of what archaeologists thought the site had originally looked like, a ghost image of Skyfisher's past. He pointed to where the temple and Marsh Fox's lodge had been. Both long gone, along with the pyramid earthwork on which the temple had stood. Inez wondered whether an archaeologist would believe Skyfisher any more than the Oklahoma Natchez had.

Hilton helped carry some dead wood and kindling up to the top of the pyramid and together they coaxed a flame with the embers.

It was good to sit by a fire. A slight breeze cooled the air. Inez had been quiet for most of the trip, caught up in her own doubts and uncertainties, half-listening as Hilton recounted the saga of the car liberation for the third time. Finding Salvo had brought Alex Samson back into her life, reminding Inez of all the reasons she didn't want to see her father.

Skyfisher's thoughts were colored with remorse, having failed to train ten men in time for the solstice. It was on this mound that he had been inducted into the Society of Light and met his teachers. He began to sing, hoping to open a portal to a mystery he did not fathom.

The wind is whispering
The earth is moving
The world is chanting
Can you hear it?

The sun is breathing
The moon is waxing
The world is listening
Can you feel it?

Skyfisher let the song spiral, marvelling that Salvo's voice could take the journey, riding the melody like an old friend.

Inez wondered that something as simple as a song could change your life so profoundly. The thing was, she didn't want her life changed. If she had to do it over again, Salvo would be in a sanatorium sharing a cell with somebody who thought they were the Prince of Wales. Still, the simple re-petitive chant re-awakened memories of her grandmother, singing just like this. *She* would have known what to do with this man.

The song ended and all three sat in silence.

Hilton finally spoke up with the latest news. Salvo's key opened the Nova's glove compartment. Inside, they found a registration made out to Salvador Samuels with a Kingston, New York address. Which mollified Inez somewhat. She'd been against their cutting-out expedition, fearing they'd be caught, not relishing having to explain the situation to Natchez's Finest, let alone her father. Skyfisher had no need of the car. He was just glad they'd be able to return Salvo's property to him when *he* returned. But something puzzled him.

"All dogs, my brothers. This one, no."

"He had an electric collar," Hilton said, explaining the concept.

"In this world, electricity - god," Skyfisher said.

Hilton laughed. Inez thought of the Nacirema, the tribe Anthro 101 classes are introduced to mid-semester via a dry monograph. With all the trappings and buzzwords of classic anthropology, it tells of the daily practices and culture of a seemingly exotic society, which becomes vaguely familiar as the text unfolds. When the monograph details the worship of animated images on a flat grey monolith, that usually brings a shock of recognition. Sooner or later, someone in the class would spell Nacirema backwards for the final clue. Inez wondered whether the writers had updated the original version of the monograph to include smart phones, which have evolved in the Nacirema's daily life from worship to addiction.

"In your world, no electricity?" she asked.

"No," Skyfisher said.

Despite the fact that Salvo could apparently speak something akin to fluent Natchez, not to mention his ability to rally butterflies at will, Inez didn't necessarily subscribe to everything he had told them.

"You think electricity is bad for your mission?"

Skyfisher shrugged and asked them to return with him to the Emerald Mound on the longest day to answer this question. To his great relief, they both agreed.

When the fire began to die, they stamped out the ashes, buried them and headed down the side of the mound towards the parking lot. A black sedan was parked near Salvo's car.

Skyfisher headed to the far side of the parking lot to relieve himself. As soon as he had finished, the sedan suddenly revved its engine and pulled next to him. Two figures jumped out, hustled him inside and sped off. It happened so quickly that both Hilton and Inez were in a shocked silence before they reacted.

"Quick, into the car!" Hilton shouted.

He cranked the engine, headed in pursuit down the dirt road, with visions of putting the pedal to the metal as soon as they hit the highway. After a few moments he brought the car to a halt and jumped out.

"What's the matter?" Inez called out.

"Flat tire," he said.

Skyfisher sat in the back seat of the sedan next to one his abductors. Driving the vehicle was the man he had encountered in the cold room on his first day here, the same one he had sniffed out at the Pow-Wow.

"Time we had a little talk," Davey said.

Chapter Thirty One

A yearning to submerge, return to the Mother of all things. Nothing to do. Just wait and let it happen. The earth is beckoning. *Come home, where you belong.*

A wave of relaxation and submission swept through Lewis. Gratitude for the act of returning as the water rose above his navel, cool and inviting.

A voice in his mind's ear. Lightning's, calm and slow.

Stay at peace. All you have to do is let go. Give this up…

A swarm of thoughts, images and sounds blossomed in the dome of Lewis's mind, as if it were the roof of a planetarium. Flashcard snapshots of a kid on a bicycle with an Ace of Spades clothes-pinned to the rear tire rim, the Camel sign in Times Square puffing smoke, a news headline - John Lennon Shot, spinning tea cups at Disneyland, a dwarf playing a giant harmonica on the Ed Sullivan show, the sugary taste of a cluster of white pills under his tongue, his father with a pair of binoculars hanging from his neck, walking alongside his mistress, Carl Yastrzemski hitting a homer at Fenway Park, rubber-necking on the Thruway as the Jaws of Life pulled someone from a crushed SUV, a halo of fireworks around the Statue of Liberty, the voice of Fiorello LaGuardia reading the funny papers, flecks of pale green lichen on an ancient boulder,

Betty Boop dancing with a skeleton … an unending cornucopia of ephemera, spiralling.

All of this, Lighting's voice intoned. *You don't need it anymore. Waste. Be rid of it. Give it up and no one will ever bother you again.*

Reasonable request. A blessing. Lewis took a deep breath, ready to exhale all of the effluence he'd been carrying, and wipe the slate clean.

A sudden pain in the palm of his right hand, as if he'd been stung. Another voice, one he didn't recognize.

It's an ambush. Hold on.

The signal became scrambled. He didn't want to hold on. Things had been, well, comfy. But the pain in his hand intensified, like someone was poking a sharp stick in the tattooed eye. A moment of disorientation as the side door of his mind opened to the gravity of his situation. And gravity ceased to be a friend.

The mind fog lifted, revealing the wizard behind the curtain, twisted and mendacious, Lightning's specious offer tossed into the waste basket of memory like the trailer of an old movie.

Lewis was waist deep in water, stuck fast in a murky swamp, his heart beating faster, a sense of dread and panic welling. At least his hand was no longer stinging.

He thought of Tell Me A Story, alone and vulnerable, no one to help her. Trying to pull his foot out of the mire, he remembered vaguely what he had read about quicksand. Small movements, wriggles. A bit at a time.

A pocket of space popped under his right foot, a trickle of water seeping into it, allowing a bit of movement. That could be the way. Hold down the panic. A bout of dizziness sent his body backwards into the water, loosening his heels. Holding his breath, he crouched forward submerging into the water, and reached down pulling on his legs as he twisted his feet.

Lewis beamed a telepathic APB to his would-be rescuer, to the Shining Ones. His right foot was loosening from the mud's grip. He bent down into the water again, leaning on his right knee, wrenching his left ankle free of the muck, crawling backwards on all fours as if through a vat of molasses, lifting his head above water to breathe and continuing to inch backwards into the shallows, like a mud puppy.

How long could he stay like this?

A wordless suggestion came to keep moving.

Maintaining the crawl-pace, slithering through the shallows, covered with thick mud, he gradually reached firmer ground, grabbing handfuls of grass and wrestling free from the mire.

Exhausted, he did not dare rest.

Lewis staggered to his feet, a swamp monster lurching for the woods, thorn bushes scraping his battered body. By the time he reached a stream and found a pool he could fall into, it felt as though he'd been dropped into a Waring blender. His clothes were ripped to shreds, his body covered with cuts. The water stung, the cold mercifully numbing him. A *thank you* to whoever had sent the rescue beacon brought no reply.

No time for a long soak. He managed to stand up without losing his balance, and shambled through the woods in what he hoped was the right direction, following the stream until he reached a trail, a shortcut that Skyfisher's senses recognized, the right combination of pathway, understory and smell.

The outline of the mound loomed ahead and Lewis circled to a spot where he could enter unchallenged. Filthy and disheveled, he would risk no time explaining himself to a guard. He labored up to the lodge where Tell Me A Story was being held.

No one was posted outside. He stepped into the antechamber, the space between the two larger rooms that comprised the lodge. A guard stepped out of the shadows, Willet Moonface, with long scratches raking the moon.

"You don't look very good," Willet said.

"Neither do you," Lewis replied. *"I need to see my wife."*

"She's not really your – " Willet began.

"Right away." Lewis brushed past a stammering Willet into the room where Tell Me A Story lay.

Her eyes were closed. Asleep. Lewis thanked whatever passed for God here. He shook her gently. She awoke, gave him a smile which turned to shock as she saw his face more clearly.

"What happened?!"

"Lightning tried to feed me to the swamp. Can you move? We've got to leave."

"It hurts if I move my head," Tell Me A Story said.

"It will hurt more if we stay," said Lewis.

"You go," she said. *"They're not going to kill a woman."*

"They'll make it look like an accident. The one who attacked you is standing outside the door!" Lewis said.

"What about Marsh Fox?"

"Gone. I'm not leaving without you." He scanned the room and noticed a glow emanating from a number of small pouches piled in a basket. *"Are those your medicines?"*

"Herbs and remedies. One is for sleep; one is for pain," she said. There was a pot filled with water near her bed. Lewis poured some into a cup and asked if she could take the pain medicine with it.

"It's meant to be brewed as a tea," she said.

"Try chewing the leaves and drinking some water. It might work," Lewis said.

"It might. What about you? You look terrible," Tell Me A Story said.

"Your husband's body is strong. I can support you if you stand up," Lewis said. A bald faced lie, but there was no other way to convince her to leave.

"You're bleeding," she said.

"Scratches. Listen. If we stay here, we're both dead. I'll be all right. You'll take care of me." He managed a smile.

"Grey Turtle?" Tell Me A Story asked.

"We have to take our chances without him. Will you try?"

Tell Me A Story nodded, and he whispered his plan.

A few minutes later, Lewis slowly opened the door to the antechamber.

A radar sense image showed an uneasy Willet, his sweaty hands holding a spear, a leather thong around his neck, the pulse of the artery beneath it quickening.

Lewis masked his own intentions with a swath of anger, ostensibly at the contents of the bowl he was carrying, powdered dry herbs.

"Willet, Tell Me A Story is in great pain. These are the herbs the apprentices gathered. I can't give them to her."

"What's wrong with them?" Willet asked suspiciously.

"Look, you'll see." Lewis said, and Willet took a step back.

"I'm not carrying a weapon, Willet."

Lewis held the bowl in one hand and showed him there was nothing hidden in the other. He took a step closer.

"They're moldy. They won't do. You see?" Leaning on his spear, Willet leaned over.

"I don't –" he began. With a flick of the wrist, Lewis tossed the bowl of pepper and stinging nettles into Willet's face.

Coughing and sneezing, he made a blind lunge with his spear. Lewis side-stepped and pinioned Willet's arm

behind him, forcing him to drop the spear. He tied Moonface, wheezing and crying, with rawhide thongs from the bed,
gagged him with some cloth and took his loincloth and knife.

Tell Me A Story gathered what medicine bags she could
and placed them in a sack which she slung over her neck. With
a grunt of pain, Lewis lifted Tell Me A Story and carried her
piggyback towards the outer door.

Broad daylight. No one was posted in front of the lodge.
About a hundred feet away a guard stood on the lip of the
mound. Lewis stepped back in the doorway, shaking his head.

"Look!" Tell Me A Story whispered, peering over his
shoulder. The guard had just been summoned, and for a moment the coast was clear. Carrying Tell Me A Story, Lewis
headed out the door, around the lodge and down the back of
the mound.

This side of the earthwork was steep and slippery. He set
Tell Me A Story on the ground.

"Slide, it's the only way."

There was no path. Lewis headed first down the slope. Tell
Me A Story sat on her haunches and slid down behind him
until the strap of her sack became entangled in a bush.

"I'm stuck!"

Lewis scrambled back up beside her, tugged at the sack,
pulled it free.

"Ho!"

A guard on the mound plateau noticed them. Lewis ignored him, and pushed Tell Me A Story down the rest of the
incline. Without looking back, he lifted her onto his back
again, heading across the strip of cleared land that surrounded
the mound. As they reached the woods, the guard's voice rang
out again. He was moving towards them, spear in hand.

Lewis had Willet's knife. All the same, his host's body was weakened from exhaustion. He could not run with Tell Me A Story on his back. He set her down next to a large oak, knife at the ready, hoping he would not have to fight this man.

As if in answer, a voice came from about twenty yards deeper into the forest.

"Put your blade down." It was Haeden, the one who had been jamming the Shining Ones' signals. Lewis gripped the knife. Now would be as good a time as any to wake up.

Chapter Thirty Two

Black Lexus, tinted windows, Jersey plates.

"The thing you did with the butterflies. I saw it." Davey pointed at the man sitting next to Skyfisher in the back seat. He reminded Skyfisher of a pufferfish, fat cheeks, a bloated body reeking of an unidentifiable scent.

"My friend wants to see your trick, too."

"My English -" Skyfisher began.

"He wants to help you, make you rich."

"Rich?"

"Money, lots of it," Davey added with a sly smile.

"Almighty dollars?"

"You got it, pal. More almighty dollars than you've ever seen in one place. All you got to do is call in those butterflies, like I saw you do. You know, 'butterflies'?" Davey steered the car with his forearms as he pressed his thumbs together and waved his hands.

"Insects," Skyfisher said.

"Yes!" Davey, making progress, glanced in his rear view mirror at the sumo-sized passenger. Dark glasses, bull neck, flattop haircut. No reaction.

"Why?" Skyfisher asked.

"We like butterflies," Davey said.

"Where are friends - my friends?"

"Show us your trick, we'll take to back to your friends. I promise," Davey said.

"What means *trick*?"

Davey rolled his eyes. Must be one of those idiot say-vants.

"We want to see you bring in the butterflies. That's all." Davey said, doing his best to sound like a nice guy.

Skyfisher had been the village go-to whenever the Lesser Sun needed to parse the truth. What this man said was clouded.

"You give greenbacks, I show butterflies *trick*."

"That's it," Davey said in triumph.

They spent the night in a motel, Skyfisher sharing a room with Davey. Under his grey suit, he wore a holster with what Skyfisher recognized as a gun. Davey placed it under his pillow. Next to Skyfisher's bed was a box that had the image of two hands under the words *Magic Fingers*.

"What this is?" Skyfisher asked.

"You don't know?" Davey asked. "No, of course you don't. Used to be everywhere," he continued. "This is the last place I know that has 'em. Check it out. My treat," he said magnanimously. "Lie down."

Skyfisher complied. Taking two coins from his pants pocket, Davey deposited them in the slot atop the metal box. The surface of the bed began to vibrate. Skyfisher leapt off the mattress as if it were a bed of hot coals.

Davey laughed, shaking his head, "You are a piece of work." Skyfisher took the sheets and blankets off the bed and slept on the floor.

In the morning, they were joined by Davey's partner. In an attempt to blend with the locals, he wore a sport shirt with an animal stitched on near the lapel.

"Alligator," Skyfisher acknowledged. The big man, who had still not said a single word, merely nodded. They drove to

Mammy's for breakfast. Davey figured they probably should have headed further out of town, but it was hard to resist the best home fries in greater Natchez. Where else could you eat under a woman's skirt?

Before entering, Davey quickly surveyed the parking lot and clientele for familiar faces. All clear.

Their waitress, Natasha, recognized Mammy's second string dishwasher and approached their table gushing.

"Saal-vo, you 'gone introduce me to your friends?" In a whisper to his companions, she added "His English ain't so good."

"Friends," Skyfisher said. "They like insects."

"Insects?" Natasha repeated.

"Butterflies," Skyfisher said.

"Oh, I *looove* butterflies," Natasha, with a significant look at Davey. "Are you with the college?" she asked.

"Nah," Davey said dismissively, "we're amateurs."

Natasha took the order, having nothing else to say on the subject of butterflies. They breakfasted on eggs, grits and hash browns and left without further incident.

Back in the car, Davey turned to Skyfisher and said, "That was good, the way you handled it. Smart guy." He was going to tell his partner about the Magic Fingers, but thought better of it.

"OK, Mr. Samuels," Davey said. "You gonna do your trick for us?"

"Give greenbacks, I do trick."

Davey, who liked to negotiate, said, "You do trick, we give greenbacks."

"No," Skyfisher said, sensing he had his catch on the line. "First, almighty dollars."

Davey's partner sighed, reached into his jacket pocket and pulled out a slim, black pistol.

"Wrong pocket," he said. Returning the pistol, he retrieved a thick envelope from the other side of his jacket. Opening it up, he selected one of the crisp, new bills, snapped it and handed it to Davey for inspection. Davey whistled, "Grover Cleveland. You don't see him often."

The man with the crew cut removed half the contents of the envelope and handed it to Skyfisher.

"Half now, rest on delivery," he said.

"You understand?" Davey asked, the good cop again. "Show us your trick, we give you the rest."

Skyfisher nodded, took the envelope, riffled the Grovers with appreciation and gave Davey a smile.

Davey pressed a button on the console, and "Walk Like a Man" blasted on. Skyfisher listened, gazed out the window and marvelled at their speed.

"Singer is man?" he asked.

"The Four Seasons," Davey said, "You don't know these guys? Of course you don't. All guys. The one with the high voice is Frankie Valli."

"Good," Skyfisher said, and he meant it. The singer's falsetto reminded him of the chanting of his people, where men's voices often hit the higher registers.

Skyfisher directed them away from the city, while attempting to send thought messages to his friends.

When they reached a location near where he had taken Inez and Hilton to show them the butterflies, he shouted, "Stop!"

Davey pulled over to the side of the road. The three of them exited the car. No trails. Bushwhacking was the order of the day. Leading his companions into the scrub, Skyfisher took them away from the road. He sensed the annoyance of the crew cut man, whose shoes were meant for sidewalks. His pants were collecting sticky Burdock seeds.

They came to a clearing and climbed a small hill which gave them a view of a meadow and a few houses far in the distance. Except for the buildings, this could have been how it was 500 years ago.

He situated Davey and his companion on the trunk of a fallen tree and told them to be still.

"Eyes close. Listen." he said.

"How the hell can we –" Davey began.

"Eyes close now. Listen."

Skyfisher relaxed, let go of the disruptive presence of the two men, and surveyed the life forces around him. There were butterflies, to be sure. No traces of another signal he was listening for.

Too bad.

He tried another approach, like tuning in a station on a radio. That was how he had explained it to Hilton. The difference was you were the radio. You needed to find the vibration in yourself that corresponded to the signal you were listening for. Resonance, Hilton called it.

He sensed a particular note, a subtle tingle. He nodded.

That would do.

Butterflies came first, Swallowtails. They settled on him and the log.

"No move, no talk. Open eyes."

Several butterflies landed on Davey's arm. "What I tell –"

"No talk!" Skyfisher whispered. He had to do this slowly. The timing had to be exactly right.

"Close eyes."

Grasshoppers and katydids began to trill, building slowly to a hum, masking the sound that Skyfisher did not want these men to hear. They sat on the log, incongruous in their attire, waiting expectantly, more like little boys than city warriors. He almost felt sorry for them.

A gentle buzz in the distance began to mass and coalesce. On the ground, a silent hoard was approaching in increasing numbers. More butterflies came, mixing with other flying insects. Nothing overtly threatening.

"Open eyes." A swirl of fluttering wings, butterflies of all sizes, shades of brown, beige and purple – beetles, locusts, dragonflies, stinkbugs, June Bugs, alive and aloft, swirling in whirlpool patterns around them.

Skyfisher walked over to the man with the crew cut, gently removed his sunglasses and handed them back to him.

"Greenbacks," Skyfisher said, sensing the man's uncertainty. Crew cut reached into his pocket and handed Skyfisher a wad of bills.

"Close eyes," Skyfisher said.

He pocketed the Grovers, stepped away and invited the full complement of guests to join the party. Bees alas, were in short supply. But there were others coming who would keep things interesting. Skyfisher walked away from them briskly, and had not gone twenty paces when the angry shouts began, quickly turning into high-pitched screams.

Sounded a bit like Frankie Valley.

On impulse, Inez and Hilton drove to Mammy's to ponder their options over breakfast. Although crowded, they managed to secure a table. Hilton began fingering his napkin, tearing bits off the end and rolling them into tiny spindles. Inez scanned the room for anyone carrying a coffee pot.

"If we go to the police, it's going to create more problems for him and for me," she said. "That must sound pretty selfish."

"Sure," Hilton said, "feed him to the sharks. Inez, we should've called the cops last night. He's been kidnapped for crissake!"

"Keep your voice down. We don't know what's going on. He's not – there's no ransom demand or anything. We don't really know who Salvo Samuels is, not to mention Skyfisher. You want to tell the police somebody from another time has been abducted by Men in Black?"

"That about sums it up."

"We have his car, which you stole," Inez said.

"Liberated," corrected Hilton.

"The police could trace the car, but what good would that do?" Inez said.

"You think your father is behind this?"

"I wouldn't put it past him," she said. "The last thing I want is to be tangled up with him and the law together. God knows he wouldn't want that either. Sure you didn't make out any details of the car? You were closer."

"Dark sedan. Couldn't see the plates," Hilton said.

Their waitress appeared, holding a Pyrex pitcher of coffee.

"Natasha!" Hilton said, adding with a Russian accent, "Keel moose and squirrel."

Ignoring this witty riposte, Natasha poured them both coffee. "I'm thinking poached on toast, burn the fries for the dude. OJ and oatmeal for the missus," she said.

"You are good," Hilton admitted.

"Just missed my favorite dishwasher," Natasha added absently, followed by a startled look when both their heads shot up to attention. "About an hour ago with two other guys. Glad to see he's makin' friends."

Hilton started to speak, but Inez interrupted him. "Locals?"

"One was, least I've seen him here before. Buff."

"They happen to say where they were going?" Hilton asked,

"No," said Natasha. She pulled a yellow pencil resting on her ear and bit the eraser. "Wait a minute. Salvo said something. What was it? Ah jeez. I was humming *Ina-Gadda-Davida*."

"Iron Butterfly," Hilton said.

"That's it!" Natasha said, reeling in the thought. "Salvo was talking and it got me goin' Retro, sixties rock. Inner juke box, you know? You don't hear about Iron Butterfly any more, 'cept on Oldies stations. Maybe they'll do like a revival."

"Remember what Salvo said?" Inez asked.

Natasha paused, stared into the upper reaches of Mammy's dress and said, "Butterflies! They were gonna study butterflies."

Inez stood up, paid for the coffee, told Natasha they'd be back for breakfast later and left, drafting Hilton in her wake.

As they drove out of town Hilton asked, "You're thinking they went to the same place he took us?"

"Got a better idea?" Inez asked.

"Not really. It means that same guy must've tailed us, otherwise how would he have known about the butterflies?"

"This has my father's smell all over it. You remember the turn off?"

"Vaguely. I think it's – Hey, look who's here!"

Salvo was walking nonchalantly on the other side of highway, heading towards the city. Inez pulled on to the shoulder and rolled down her window.

"Hop in, stranger."

He did, sensing the relief in his friends. They headed back to Mammy's, commandeering a table for a meal-cum-debriefing, and a second breakfast for Salvo, who after all, was eating for two. Natasha had finished her shift and left the premises.

A good thing, Inez figured.

They plied him with questions and Skyfisher told them about the two men, their dark car and Frankie Valley, warrior singer. When he described Davey, Inez slapped the table and muttered, "I knew he wouldn't stay away."

Hilton jumped in.

"So Spook One wants to show the Butterfly Thing to Spook Two, someone higher up in the food chain. Inez's father?"

With a bit of translation, Skyfisher told them he had not seen the other man before.

"Go on," Hilton said in a conspiratorial whisper, "what happened?"

Skyfisher described the scary vibrating bed in detail, with the barest account of what happened in the meadow.

"They want butterflies. I show butterflies."

"That's it?" Hilton asked.

"Yes."

Unsatisfied, Inez asked, "Salvo, what else did you show them besides butterflies?"

"Insects."

"What kind of insects?"

Requisitioning a pencil and paper from the cashier, Skyfisher drew stick figures of a wasp, an ant and a spider.

"Uh-huh," nodded Inez. "How many?"

"Many," Skyfisher said.

Inez took a teaspoon of sugar from the dispenser and poured it onto a napkin. "More than that?"

"Yes," Skyfisher said with a modest smile.

"I'm beginning to get the picture. These yellowjackets, or whatever they are," she said, pointing at the drawing, "did they –?"

Skyfisher made a jabbing motion with his finger and nodded.

"You left those guys there?" asked Hilton.

"They run," Skyfisher said.

"You are the man," Hilton said.

Breakfast arrived and they ate in silence, Inez digesting the news.

"When you see Natasha, the waitress, if she asks, say you showed the men the butterflies and you left. That's all. Understand?"

"Oh," Skyfisher said, "I have something for house. Greenbacks."

Inez waved him off.

"Keep your salary. Put it in the cookie jar for you and Hilton."

They headed back to Inez's for a barbecue and prep, the Solstice being less than a week away. Skyfisher promised he would reveal his mission in all its grandeur on the Longest Day. The Green Stamps worked on English into the afternoon, Hilton delving more deeply into verbs and idioms.

"'How's it going', is like, 'how are you.'" Hilton said.

"Why not, '*Where* is it going?'" Skyfisher asked.

"More like, "How're you doing?'" Hilton responded.

"Why not, '*What* you doing?'"

Inez was in the kitchen, confronting a pile of sliced onions and peppers, when her cell phone rang. Frowning, she muttered "I better take this," to no one in particular, and went into her bedroom. Her voice, raised in anger, carried throughout the house.

"Do you expect me to –?" and the rest was muffled. Five minutes later, she emerged, shaken, and walked over to her friends.

"My father, calling from the hospital. The guy who worked for him, the one who was spying on us? Well, my father said he quit. He went - roaning?"

"Ronin," Hilton corrected, "masterless samurai."

"Whatever. He's in the hospital in a coma. The other guy is dead. Anaphylactic shock. Stung hundreds of times, both of 'em. Doctors had never seen anything like it." She looked at Skyfisher.

"There's more," Inez continued. "The cops were called in to check on the dead guy. Turns out he had a phoney ID and they suspect he was connected with organized crime. My father is doing damage control, trying to distance himself and figure out what the dead goon was doing with *his* goon, or former goon. The guy in the coma."

"Your father is telling you this because–?" Hilton asked.

"He knows Salvo was involved. His man, Davey is his name, went to see my father after he'd spied on us in the valley. He'd seen the butterflies and he was trying to sell my father on magnetism, or something like that. Whatever it was, my father figured it was all nonsense and dismissed him, or claims to have, anyway. He thinks Davey wanted to show Salvo off to the Mob. It was gonna be his 'entry ticket'".

"Magnetism", Hilton mused.

"So now," Inez continued, "we've got a dead foot soldier and some Capo in New Jersey wants to know what my father is going to do about it. The deceased was carrying a pile of money." She turned to Skyfisher.

"Salvo, what did those men want from you?"

"They want to see butterflies."

"Did they give you anything?" she asked.

"Greenbacks."

He retrieved the envelope from his coat pocket and put in on the table. Hilton peered inside.

"Holy smokes. Thousand dollar bills!"

Inez laid them out on the counter.

"Forty-five thousand".

"Almighty dollars," Skyfisher observed.

"You can say that again," Hilton said.

"Christ," Inez said. "Now we've got the Mafia, or whoever the hell that guy worked for, to contend with. My father is probably the only one –." She ran her fingers through her hair. "I don't see any other way around it. The police would make a total bollocks of this." Inez bit her lip. "We have to get the money back to them, for starters."

"Back? Who to?"

"Who do you think? The Mob!"

"Seriously?" Hilton asked. Visions of Costa Rica and tanned women evaporating before they'd even had a chance to congeal.

"This kind of money, blood money, belongs in my father's world, not mine. I know one thing. You don't want these guys after you. You really don't."

"Bad men," Skyfisher said.

Inez looked at him as if for the first time. He had fina-gled his way into her life with a story so outlandish no one could possibly have made it up. Old wounds were being ripped opened. She and Hilton, her best friend, were exposed to real danger, all for some dubious mission.

"One of those men is dead, the other dying," she said. "Dead, Salvo. You killed him."

"Not quite," Hilton interjected. "Self-defense. They kid-napped him."

"Right. They tortured him with massage beds and gave him a pile of money," Inez said, closing her eyes. "Look, I know these were bad guys. The world is probably a better place without them. The thing is, they didn't hurt him and they didn't deserve – this."

"Think about it," Hilton said. "If we take Salvo – Skyfisher, at what he claims to be, as weird as that is, well, he comes from a whole other, ah - value system. This is probably standard oper-ating procedure for threatened members of the Shining People."

"Sure. Take out the bad guys with hornets. You sound like his attorney," Inez said. "I'm not going to argue the morality of it or judge Salvo. We're just going to have to deal with this situation before it gets worse."

"What do you suggest" Hilton asked.

"Let me think for a minute," she said.

Skyfisher didn't need a translator to tell him he had violated a taboo. "Five days is longest day."

"Is that all you can think about?" Hilton asked. "Yeah, I guess it is."

"Emerald Mound, longest day," said Skyfisher. "Then I go away."

"Maybe that's for the best," Inez said. "Let him finish his mission and he leaves." She was sorely tempted to show him the door now, but it would be dangerous to cut Salvo loose. He was unpredictable and the last thing they needed was another dead body. Probably his, if the Mob was involved.

"Well, you can still stay at my place," said Hilton.

"No," Inez interjected, "not safe anymore. I doubt I'm safe here." She thought a moment and then peeled a thousand dollar bill out of the envelope, "Take this. Let's hope they won't miss one. Be careful where you get change for it."

It came back to her in a flood, like a bad dream. Everything that had led to her parent's divorce, the shady dealings, the latent violence simmering beneath the surface of her father's tight demeanor, the bribes, the goon squad he used as bodyguard-enforcers, the obsequious officials, the late-night meetings, the metal briefcases, the smell of large quantities of money, the way it twisted men's souls. A life she had distanced herself from, and now it was sucking her back in. Like Pacino in the Godfather.

"Take Salvo's car," Inez said. "Go home. Get some clothes and whatever else you need. Stay in motels, a different one every night. I'll join you at the Emerald Mound on the solstice." She was going to see this through.

"What are you going to do?" asked Hilton.

"Go to my father. Believe me, I don't want to."

The last thing Alex Sampson wanted was a confrontation with New Jersey. Fifty G's was tempting, but he wasn't going to dick around with them. He'd settle this clean. Neutral ground, definitely not Natchez. If they want to play games, he'd be ready.

Wouldn't hurt the boys to do a little muscle flexing. The lesson from Davey was a good example for them all. Improvisation is one thing, disobeying an order was another. If he died in the hospital it'd be better for everybody. Except Davey.

Key thing was to keep his daughter out of it. If he had to, he'd feed them the schmuck who started the whole thing, Samuels. Alex just hoped the Jersey boys wouldn't ask too many questions about how their soldier had died. At the moment, he didn't know himself. That bothered him. The question which kept nagging at him was whether Davey had been right about this drifter who had latched on to his daughter. Maybe he really had something up his sleeve that was bankable.

A visit to the hospital proved useless. Davey was in a coma, his face entirely covered with bandages, a tube in his throat supplying oxygen, another tube dripping some clear fluid into his arm. The doctors and nurses wouldn't speak to Alex about a prognosis, since he wasn't family. To the untrained eye, Davey's future did not appear to be rosy.

Best case scenario.

The Green Stamps were preparing to depart on their adventure, gathering clothes, camping gear, books, whatever Hilton's packrat mindset deemed useful. It had proved harder to break the large bill than he had figured. In the end, a storefront

"We Cash Checks" outlet did it, no questions asked, for a fifty dollar service charge. Cash in hand, they hit the road. First stop, the Red Carpet Inn on the outskirts of town. They ordered Chinese and settle in to watch cable TV, channel surfing until they settled on a Technicolor western. Skyfisher watched in fascination at a scene showing Indians trading fur pelts for beads and blankets.

"That's you," Hilton said, "the friendly Indian."

"I speak like this one?"

"Well, yes."

"Bad," Skyfisher said.

A discussion on verbs followed, with Skyfisher vowing to master *to be* so he wouldn't sound like the Indian on the ghost screen.

"I should take you to the Pageant sometime," Hilton said.

"Pageant?"

"Yeah. A tourist thing. A show like a movie, but live, with people, actors, kids mostly. Tells the story of Natchez, the city. You're in it! I mean, an actor that plays one of your people is in it, for about three seconds. The rest is stories about the glory days of Natchez before the Civil War, leaving out a few minor details. Like slavery."

Skyfisher's people had been taken into slavery by other tribes, and they, in turn, kept captives as slaves. When Hilton related the story of how Native Americans and Africans had fared over the past 300 years, Skyfisher shook his head.

"I *am* not slave of Great Sun," he said, verifying with Hilton that the troublesome verb was behaving correctly.

"I am slave of *kuash*. We *are* slaves of Master of Breath. No," he corrected himself, "not slaves. We Brothers. We —", a bit of consultation for the right word.

"We *serve* Master of Breath."

Hilton, with a bit more political correctness than his usual comfort level, suggested that Salvo not forget the Sisters, especially since Inez had been grandmothered into the fraternity.

Skyfisher got to his feet, turned off the television, the AC, and the lights. He unplugged the coffee maker, the clock and every electrical device in the room, and began to welcome his friend, the unlikeliest of candidates, into *kuash,* the Shining Ones, the Society of Light, the Brotherhood of Breath.

To Hilton, it seemed at first to be a pastiche of meditation, yoga, and every fruity New Age workshop he had ever encountered. He was deeply allergic to all of it. Despite this, he liked Salvo. Even though his story strayed stupendously far beyond the bounds of credibility, he trusted him. Lord knows, Hilton had never crossed trails with anyone remotely like the bastard son of Buster Keaton, who had performed feats that defied explanation. For the moment he was willing to make a stab at "starting from the empty place." Thoughts, doubts - out the window.

Nothing. I can do that.

It wasn't so simple. Hilton found it impossible to maintain *nothing* for more that a few seconds before a stray thought balloon popped up. With Salvo's gentle insistence, he persevered, and once, briefly, something shifted. For a few seconds he and Salvo came into synch, with an invisible third listener joining them. The weird part was the third listener was neither and both of them at the same time. Put that in your pipe.

They spent the next three nights at different locations, choosing from Greater Natchez's dwindling selection of low-end motor hotels, Hilton rejecting one after reading online rumors of bedbugs. During the day, Skyfisher offered training in Radar 101, Hilton retaliating with grammar lessons. *To be* or not *to be,* laced with useful tips on when to use *if, should* and *maybe,* all in the spirit of keeping Skyfisher from sounding like Tonto.

Chapter Thirty Three

The eve of the Solstice found the Green Stamps camping on the Emerald Mound. No sign of Inez, no critical mass of brothers-in-training. Skyfisher would try as he had before, hoping the others would follow.

Despite all odds, he was here, laying the groundwork for when the rightful occupant of his body returned.

As they looked up at the night sky, Skyfisher asked, "Hilton, are you spirit man?"

"You mean like a medicine man?"

"Spirit man."

"I'm a Sunday School dropout. I never bought into religion."

"What religion say?"

Resisting the impulse to deflect Salvo's weighty poser with another lesson in grammar, Hilton chewed on his lip.

"Religions say we have a soul inside. If we're good, this soul goes to heaven when we die. Most of 'em say something like that."

After clarifying a few points, Skyfisher reflected on this.

"Hilton. No soul inside."

"There's a cheery thought."

"Little butterfly worm inside. You feed it. Feed little worm."

"Caterpillar," Hilton said.

"Tomorrow, you feed caterpillar to soul of world."

Skyfisher watched the stars. Hilton had explained that this was looking into the past, maybe even Skyfisher's own time. Tell Me A Story's sky. Hard to believe she was long dead and buried. No, she would wait for him, like some sleeping cicada that rises from the ground in the spring.

Sleep brought a dream of the *kuash* under siege, lodges burning, men dying. Skyfisher ran to warn others, but they could not see or hear him. Out of the smoke came Little Panther, the one who always sat staring in the corner of the lodge. He pointed to the sky where flaming arrows transformed into long ribbons of fire, as if the stars themselves were falling to earth. Golden molten fireballs struck the earth with cataclysmic explosions. The dreamscape morphed to present day Natchez, with buildings bursting into flame, people screaming in the streets, running towards the Mississippi.

Skyfisher awoke on the cold ground shaking, having glimpsed the fate of a world that had forgotten to feed its soul. Someone was stroking his forehead.

"You were dreaming," Inez said, cradling a corrugated cardboard tray with three cups of coffee. She set it down on the grass. The stars were still in place. Inez looked rumpled, tired, somewhere between scared and sad.

Five a.m., time to awaken Green Stamp number two. Still groggy, Hilton asked Inez whether she had contacted her father.

"I gave him the envelope. The good news is he's going to make up any missing funds and return the money. The bad news is they want a body."

"They?" Hilton asked, emerging from his sleeping bag.

"Jersey Mob."

"Why can't your father just ship up the dead guy to New Jersey? Bet they do this all the time. Probably have an account with UPS."

"They don't want –" Inez began. "Jeez, I can't think straight. Been up all night." She took of sip of coffee. "They're not buying it was an accident. They want an eye for an eye."

"Last I heard, Davey wasn't exactly in tip-top shape."

"More bad news. Davey's gone, disappeared. No one knows where."

"Shit. What does your dad say?"

"'Sit tight'. Davey was messed up. He's got to surface sooner or later. My father's got his *boys* searching for him."

It was cold. Hilton hugged himself, stomped a circle. On one of the signs posted at the base of the mound, he'd read that tons of dirt had been brought to the site in baskets, on top of an existing hill.

"Salvo, is it true? They carted all this dirt here by baskets?" Hilton said.

"Mounds from long ago, before my time," Skyfisher said. "We bring – ground?" pointing down.

"Soil."

"Bring soil every year. In baskets. Many things I don't know. How I am in Salvo's body? I don't know. Elders teach. I try. I catch Salvo. Hard to catch someone."

"You're like a fakir," Inez said.

"What is fakir?"

"Someone taught to do something, but doesn't know why," Inez said. "They sleep on nails or hold their breath for an hour, things like that."

"I know why I *am* here. Men make signs here, what they name?"

"Archaeologists," Inez said.

"They know why mounds are here? Hilton say books tell mounds are star pictures."

"Some of those books are a little flakey," Inez said, "but yes, some people believe the mounds are made to be like constellations, star-pictures. They align with the stars."

"That's a word we spent hours trying to find," Hilton said. "*Alignment*! Salvo says it's one of the secrets of the Solstice."

"Stars speak every day." Skyfisher said. "Solstice Day we listen. *Ippli hallesh*. We align. "

Carrying their sleeping bags, the three of them walked down the middle of the main plateau of the mound towards the pyramid earthwork situated at one end, the same spot where they had lit a fire.

At the top of the pyramid, roughly a twenty foot square, they laid their sleeping bags on the ground.

"Wait for sunrise," Skyfisher said.

A falling star streaked across the sky. Skyfisher shivered, recalling his dream. With failure looming, he pictured the glowing presence of the one elder he did not trust, Lightning. Yet when Skyfisher had informed Marsh Fox, he'd been told to keep it to himself. To his credit, Lightning had warned them about the invaders, the Anglay and the Fran-zay. He'd foreseen their coming just as Skyfisher had envisioned the fireballs.

Nothing he could do about that now. Time to clear his mind and wait with his friends for the eastern horizon to turn from pale grey to a pastel pink.

Inez unfolded a sleeping bag and rested on it. Skyfisher put his arm around Hilton's shoulder and walked with him towards the lip of the pyramid mound.

"Temple lodge here," Skyfisher said, "sacred place." He paused and said, "Hilton – you most best person friend." He tapped Hilton's head with his knuckles. "This week, you crack your –"

"Skull?"

"Egg –"

"Shell!"

Skyfisher dangled a finger at Hilton's forehead.

"Shell open. A little."

He tapped Hilton lightly on the chest.

"Big heart."

Hilton was about to dismiss all this, but Skyfisher put his finger to his lips. They circled back towards where Inez sat, watching the pinkish color spread on the horizon. When the glow of sunrise became imminent, Skyfisher had them sit on the ground in a triangle. At its apex, Skyfisher faced the dawn directly, and positioned Inez and Hilton where he could see their faces.

"On longest day" Skyfisher said, "people come all places on Inez map."

"The map of the mounds?" Inez asked.

"Mounds sacred places, like stars." Skyfisher pointed to the sky. "No see stars. Stars there. No see Dead-eye, Big Dog. They there, and others. We listen for sun, stars, others."

The corona of the sun appeared on the horizon, then a flare of light. They closed their eyes, Hilton squirming for a more comfortable position, feeling the hard ground underneath the sleeping bag. Skyfisher sensed Inez's tightness like an acorn, hard and impenetrable, her thoughts clouded with visions of her father and the consequences of their predicament. They waited together. The sun slowly rose on schedule. Nothing happened. Hilton grew restless.

"Hilton, you have mother?" Skyfisher asked.

"What do you think? Ridiculous question."

"She alive?"

"Yes."

"You love?"

"Well yeah, sure."

"Mother alive now. She breathe with us. Sun warm mother now. Sun love her. You send love, *to be*, her now."

How could you send something as ephemeral as love? Nevertheless, Hilton dutifully thought of her, the better to defend himself with Salvo when he had to fill out the evaluation form later on. He pictured his mom at Halloween years ago in a costume as Maid Marion. She had dressed him as Prince Charming. Her auburn hair, the shape of her back curved with scoliosis. The sadness in her eyes, knowing she was losing the affection of her husband along with her beauty. He saw in the midst of all that, the unquenchable candle of love in her eyes. Unconditional love.

Like Cupid's arrow, Skyfisher's words had found their mark. It hit him so deeply he began to weep. Hilton could not help but love her back. The flood gates opened and a wave of emotion flowed through him that was palpable to both Inez and Skyfisher.

"Hilton," Skyfisher said. "Ride horse. Horse not ride you."

"What?" Hilton asked.

"Listen," Skyfisher said.

Hilton's opening touched Inez as well, which was what Skyfisher had hoped for. Like tuning in to signals from distant, ethereal radio stations, they found themselves in contact with others, not through sight, audible sound, touch or smell. More like intuiting the edge of another dimension. A line perceiving it was part of a plane, a plane conjuring the impression of a three dimensional solid. Suddenly countless other points of contact appeared, linked together like neurons, nodes of energy across the surface of the earth. A massive nexus, spinning in space, morphing into curves and spirals, riding the Sun Breath.

Inez envisioned monasteries surrounded by Himalayan peaks, shamanic yurts in Siberia, stone cairns on the Iberian peninsula, caves in the Middle East, pyramids in Central America, earthen mounds in Australia, Europe and Asia. Embracing it all, a prodigious solar emanation.

Hilton was a floating bubble, a particle, a grain of pollen, a dust mote among a cluster of particles dissolving into a larger mass, too many to count. They were calling to him.

The Sun Breath was flowing through every inch of Skyfisher's body. There were others all over this world who had not forgotten. Perhaps it was not too late and earth would not end in a rain of flaming stars.

They were breathed.

The Sun Breath played Skyfisher, Hilton, Inez and the hive mind-body conclave of the world like musical instruments. They became their name in the spirit of the mighty verb. Human *be*-ings.

A vast chord, a silent *I am,* thrummed as subtle as a sigh, resounding without sound, moving them into a deeper silence. A current, a flow of pure quantum energy, neither particle nor wave, passed through them like an exhalation.

They had become collective alveoli, part of a membrane of sentient life essential for all life, each obliged to palpably connect with the very bones and fiber of their bodies, every cell, just as they were being contacted by an immense, invisible body that they were cells in. Somewhere in their DNA was the re-affirmation that being a human *being* meant intimately inhabiting the space between two worlds - the ethereal cosmos above and the granular microcosmos below.

We are here. We remember. Even now.

A long moment passed, celebrated in silence, the strands of interconnectivity weaving a protective web, a membrane of pure energy. Without it, the mounds would be piles of earth. Now they had come alive, pulsing.

In the midst of witnessing this miracle, Skyfisher's world exploded in a thunder crack of pain, dissolving into blackness.

Inez and Hilton opened their eyes as if awakening from an otherworldly vision. Salvo's body lay slumped on the ground.

Chapter Thirty Four

"Put down the knife," Haeden said.

"Why?"

"Trust me."

Lewis couldn't believe he was having this B-movie conversation. Next it'll be, 'Give me the girl!'

"I should have let you sink into the swamp," Haeden said.

"That was you?" Lewis asked.

"It wasn't Lightning!"

The guard reached the edge of the platform mound. Haeden called up to him.

"War parties coming. Red poles not far." Haeden said, pointing in the direction of the stream. *"Tell the others. I have these two."* When the guard hesitated, Haeden added, *"By the Sun Breath, the poles are there. See for yourself."*

Without waiting for a reply, Haeden turned and walked into the woods. Lewis followed with Tell Me A Story on his back. After a few minutes they paused. The guard was not pursuing. Haeden regarded Skyfisher's body staggering under the weight he was carrying.

"Give me the girl."

"What?!"

"Let me carry her."

"Yes," Tell Me A Story said, stifling a protest from Lewis.

She rode piggyback on Haeden, who set a slow, steady pace, Lewis following. When they had gone about half a mile, Tell Me A Story whispered to Haeden.

"We need to rest. He's going to drop."

Lewis dropped at the base of a large oak. Tell Me A Story slid from Haeden's back and sat next to her husband, reminding herself for the hundredth time of the other man within. Haeden took a sip of water from a leather flagon and offered it to them.

"Lightning told me you were blocking our thought messages," Lewis said.

"He was right," Haeden replied.

Lewis stiffened.

"Hear me," Haeden said. He turned to Tell Me A Story. *"Have you met the Great Sun?"*

"He came to a ceremony at my village, before I was born. They say he was carried in a litter so his feet didn't touch the ground."

"Most people only know stories like that," Haeden said. *"A close circle know his worth. They also know he has enemies, so they protect him, maybe too much. The Great Sun is no fool. He knows of the Shining Ones, but not their purpose."* Haeden paused and asked Lewis, *"Do you?"*

When there was no response, Haeden continued.

"The Great Sun knows the kuash have power. He suspects they will use it to overthrow him. Two winters gone, he dispatched someone to find the Shining Ones, gain their trust, learn if anyone was plotting sorcery against him. He sent me." Haeden paused, making sure he was still being understood. *"The rumors were true."* He let these words sink in.

"Right now, we must move. They will send guards in pursuit. If they catch us, it's not a story you would want to tell." Haeden

placed his hand on Lewis's shoulder, *"If you have half of Sky-fisher's brain, you'll know I speak the truth."*

"If Skyfisher was so good," Lewis's asked, *"how come he trusted you?'*

"I never said he did."

As High Eagle and his party were preparing to leave Buffalo's village, a runner came with a request from the Tattooed Serpent, war chief and brother of the Great Sun. Twenty warriors needed for a scouting party. High Eagle asked to lead them, but the village chief turned him down. His group could walk in the warriors' shadows to a camp not far from the abandoned mound site, tending their own fires.

Waya kept her distance from them all, hunting for herself, sleeping in the woods and showing up when they broke camp in the morning. The brothers, Otter and Broken Twig, walked side by side, Otter still brooding from his ignominious defeat at the hands of a woman. The tracker, Red Wolf, would have been a member of the warrior contingent, perhaps even its leader, had he not pledged allegiance to High Eagle. Little Rock Buffalo was recovering his strength, day by day. On a few occasions one of the warriors from the larger group would drop back, try to engage him in a conversation. He rebuffed them all. In the end, they left him alone.

High Eagle became his name, aloof and alone. He would find the blind-man-who-sees and his woman, bring them back, restore his reputation. A pity that Tell Me A Story would have to spend four nights with Red Wolf. He'd given his word, and with a man like Red Wolf there'd be no backing down. In the end the Story Woman would be his. Waya he found intimidating. The one time he tried to learn her story, she told him to mind his own affairs. Still, she might prove useful. If not, a hatchet could stop her as easily as any man.

They smelled White Apple Village before they saw it, campfires and cooked meat mixed with the odors of domesticated animals. Women were preparing food around dozens of fire pits, dogs underfoot, scavenging for a scrap of something tasty. Most of the men appeared to be members of a large war party, laughing, haranguing each other, preparing to bivouac for the night.

High Eagle had discretely wrapped his injured hand in some cloth bandages. He need not have bothered, for no one paid them any heed. Typically, a clan member would have greeted him or sought the company of Buffalo, a warrior with considerable reputation. Maybe it was better this way, no explanations.

High Eagle accosted a young warrior carrying a small log on his shoulder, destined for a fire pit. He was in a hurry and slowed his pace only slightly to hear what was on this stranger's mind.

"Ho! Where can someone find the Tattooed Serpent?"

The young man sized him up.

"He's not seeing anyone." Then he turned away.

High Eagle's party rested near where the warriors from Buffalo's village had encamped. Red Wolf was dispatched to see if they could gain an audience. He returned empty-handed.

"It's as the young buck said. The Tattooed Serpent keeps his own counsel. Seven days gone, runners were dispatched to the surrounding villages. Many came. They're being sent to an old mound site. Some secret society encamped there."

The war party had orders to attack the mound and capture its leaders. Their followers would swear loyalty to the Great Sun or be slaughtered.

"What do you make of it?" High Eagle asked and Red Wolf shrugged.

"No glory in subduing a bunch of fanatics," he said.

High Eagle was inclined to agree. Unless the Blind One was involved with this group. That would explain Skyfisher's strange behavior and his vow of silence. He had been close to Falling Star, who was executed for treason. Might well be a connection. High Eagle was surprised he'd not seen it before.

No feast was given the night before the war party was set to depart. They were served with vats of a steaming, acrid liquid, ladled into bowls and cups. The Black Drink.

It tasted like bat piss, bringing visions, making men battle-crazy. High Eagle cautioned his team to stay away from the foul smelling brew. However, in the evening there were two vacant places around the campfire, Otter and Broken Twig. He'd deal with them in the morning, if they returned. They did not.

Haeden continued to carry Tell Me A Story on his back, but several times she asked him to put her down to gather some moss and the leafs of certain plants. She used these to treat her wound, binding wads of plant material around her head with a vine.

"I must look like a wood spirit," she said.

Haeden led them away from the mound site past the swamp, giving it a wide berth.

"You know this place," he said to Lewis with a dark smile. As they traveled, Haeden began to tell his story.

"When the Great Sun learned of the kuash, he had to find out whether they were planning any mischief."

The further they journeyed, the less Lewis understood. It was as if Haeden's speech was morphing. Lewis asked him if this was some kind of a trick.

"No trick. Same tongue."

Tell Me A Story assured him that Haeden was still speaking the language of their people. It brought to mind what Grey Turtle had said. Lewis's understanding of their speech was one of the benefits of being at the compound with the Shining Ones. The effect lessened as he moved away.

"Speak now, while I can still follow," Lewis said.

"Alright," Haeden said. *"Rest here."* He found a log, beckoning Tell Me A Story and Lewis to sit on it, while he squatted before them.

Haeden had joined the Shining Ones several years ago. Though not a member of the inner circle, he had a glimpse of their purpose, coupled with the certainty that none of the elders had a taste for politics.

"Except Lightning."

Lightning had taken Haeden and Willet Moonface under his wing, dropping hints of bigger things to come.

"He says there is a special group. Hidden. Asks me and Moonface to join."

Haeden played along, but swore no oath of allegiance. He learned from Moonface that Lightning was plotting to turn the Society of Light against its current leaders and use their combined abilities to overthrow the Great Sun.

"Skyfisher could smell lies. He warned the elders about Lightning, but for some reason, they didn't act. Lightning knew Skyfisher was his enemy and he never fully trusted me. When you came along, he saw an opportunity."

"To get rid of both us," Lewis said.

"Yes," Haeden said. *"First he squeezes Skyfisher's secrets from you. Like he did with Little Panther. Took what was left of him*

to get more power. In the swamp, he tried to take your mind. I've seen what he can do. With Marsh Fox and the other elders gone, Lightening had Alakan killed." Looking at Tell Me A Story, he added, *"letting the blame fall on you."*

Growing up, Lewis's first impressions of Native Americans had come courtesy of Walt Disney. Davey Crockett battled warrior-redskins, while noble chiefs smoked peace pipes in teepees and dispensed wisdom in pithy epithets. His latest insight was that Indians could teach anyone lessons in treachery.

"Lightning told me you were a spy," he said.

"True! I spy on him, not kuash. Why do you think Lightning went away when he was busy sucking your brains out in the swamp?"

"You stopped him."

"No. He's too strong. I distracted him, praying you come to your senses. He turns on me. I stay out of reach!

"Why?" Lewis asked.

"We find Marsh Fox and Grey Turtle now. They will believe you, not the one spying on them. They stop Lightning. Hand him over to the Great Sun. We smoke the Calumet of Peace. No killing. The Shining Ones - safe. The Great Sun - lives. Maybe he helps kuash."

"You really think the Great Sun would help you?" Tell Me A Story looked incredulous.

"Yes." Haeden said. *"Problem is, he is surrounded by warrior-chiefs. If anything happens to him, they pay with their lives. They say kuash is a threat. With Lightning as leader, they are right. We find Marsh Fox, save the Society of Light."*

"You care about the kuash?" Lewis asked.

"The Shining Ones are friends. Willet makes mistake. Bad choice."

"You said warriors are coming for us. True?" Tell Me A Story asked.

Haeden nodded. *"High Eagle and Buffalo, with a tracker. High Eagle, angry man. Maybe you take something from him?"*

Ignoring the remark, Tell Me A Story asked, *"You speak like you know the Great Sun."*

"I am his son," Haeden said. *"He does not speak to me."* With that, he stood and beckoned for the others to follow. Tell Me A Story tried to walk, but she was still shaky on her feet. Haeden leaned down and swung her onto his back.

"We go faster now," he said.

They walked a good ways though the pine forest, a bed of needles dampening the sounds of their passage. No bird or insect calls greeted them. The quiet filled Lewis with a sense of foreboding. He tried to ask if Haeden knew where Marsh Fox and Grey Turtle were, but couldn't. Like trying to remember a forgotten name, the words wouldn't come. He stammered the word for *place*.

"Try this way." Haeden's voice was inside his head, an uninvited guest.

"No," Lewis said aloud, unwilling to let Haeden's mind in his. Strange that he understood Haeden's thoughts, but not his spoken words. No stranger than waking up in the seventeenth century.

Haeden said something, pointing northwards. Tell Me A Story nodded. To Lewis, it was as though their speech was being encrypted. They moved inland to dryer terrain, Lewis admiring that Haeden could find his way without any obvious landmarks. At lunchtime, they were all famished. Haeden shared what dried meat he had. Exhausted and frail, they were grateful for the brief respite.

Haeden said a few words to Tell Me A Story, and then Lewis sensed his voice inside his head.

"I need your help."

299

Tell Me A Story touched Lewis gently on the face and shrugged, as if to say, 'what have we got to lose?' When Lewis nodded his assent, Haeden continued, his voice gently insinuating itself into Lewis's mind, like a whispered gesture.

"*Find Marsh Fox and Grey Turtle. We both try, maybe they hear, point us in the right direction.*" Lewis agreed.

Haeden continued, "*As we did at the lodge. See Grey Turtle in your mind - and Marsh Fox, their faces close up, every detail. You make contact, say we come. We are here. Where are they?*"

Lewis tried, but it was no use. He could picture Grey Turtle, nothing more. They attempted to both focus on Marsh Fox. Again, nothing. Lewis's wounded ribs throbbed, his body clamored for rest.

"*One more try,*" Haeden mind-spoke. "*Stay with Grey Turtle. Send his face to me. I do same to you.*" They tried again and Lewis sensed their images become one, both visual memories coalescing. It had a different quality than a memory, flickering to life and gesturing like a sentient hologram. Haeden's eyes snapped open.

"*That way*", he pointed.

As they rose to depart, Lewis' radar picked up the presence of others nearby. He tried to speak, but Haeden raised his hand to silence him.

Too late.

Haeden saw the figure of Red Wolf emerging from the woods. Behind him, High Eagle, with no hint of stealth in his stride. Then the lumbering form of Buffalo. Next to him, a woman Haeden did not recognize, a look of simmering exultation on her face, a wildcat poised to strike.

Chapter Thirty Five

A moment ago Inez had been suffused with the miraculous, conducting a vibration so fine it brought tears to her eyes. In an eye-blink, she was gaping at Salvo, the man who had guided her and Hilton into the stratosphere, lying on the ground, unconscious. The perpetrator stood over them, silhouetted by the rising sun. He wore camouflage fatigues, a ski mask, and his gloved hands clutched a baseball bat, shaking uncontrollably.

"My God," Inez said, "you —"

"Shut up," he wheezed. "Lift him, both of you. Do it!"

He waved the bat at them. Inez and Hilton rose to their feet, their legs asleep and cramped. They struggled with Salvo's limp body, his head lolling from side to side like a rag doll.

"Get him down to the car."

Each took an arm and shouldered him down the mound.

"Keys, cell phones!" the man barked. Inez handed him the keys to her car.

"Yours, too!" he said to Hilton, who complied reluctantly.

"This way." He led them to his black sedan and opened the rear door.

"Put him in."

With difficulty, they dragged an unconscious Salvo into the back seat. The masked man was shivering.

"Get in front," he said to Inez and turned to Hilton.

"Keep your mouth shut and you'll get her back."

He lurched into the car and drove away, leaving Hilton in the parking lot, again. The sedan's rear plates were covered by cardboard and duct tape.

Davey could barely hold on to the steering wheel, his hands were trembling violently, his breathing labored.

"Let me drive," Inez offered.

"No." And that was that.

After ten minutes, he pulled off to the shoulder of the road, took out an inhaler, managed with both hands to depress the button of the canister and aim it into his mouth. Slowly, his breathing became more regular.

The cortisone they'd given him at the hospital was wearing off and the cream he'd applied wasn't doing anything. His world was a massive suite of pain and itch, the sort of itch you want to scratch down to the bone.

Stung by every goddam bee in the state of Mississippi. If he never saw another fucking insect in this life, he'd be happy. As good as dead if he didn't get the clown in the back seat back to Jersey. They could have him for nothing.

Just give me back my life.

He had two choices, let the girl drive, or take off the ski mask. Not exactly what you want to be wearing if a trooper glanced in your direction.

Under the mask, he was the Invisible Man, all bandages and what used to be his face. Wasn't worth the risk, especially with out of state plates.

"If I let you drive and you try to do anything stupid, I will kill your friend. Without hesitation. He gets delivered dead or alive, your choice. Understand?"

"Let me check on how he's doing," Inez said.

"I'll take care of him. You drive." Davey stepped out of the car, removed the cardboard from the license plate, opened the rear door. Salvo lay on his side, unmoving. Davey leaned in to have a better look.

"He's breathing. Step into the driver's seat. You know how to get to the Trace?" Inez nodded. "We head north towards Jackson. Not a mile above the speed limit. Anything funny and he's dead meat. Got it?"

The Natchez Trace ran all the way to Nashville, the most direct route northeast and a slow go. On the up side, there were no towns, not much traffic and few, if any, cops. Might take a little longer, but they had better odds of not being hassled. He carefully removed his face mask and pulled the bill of his ball cap down low.

"Drive," he said.

Inez drove for an hour and pulled off the highway for gas and a rest stop. Davey did not let her go to the bathroom at the station. Instead, he had her pump the gas while he headed to the station's convenience store with his cap lowered, bought toilet paper, pretzels and bottled water. After a few more miles on the Trace, he pulled over and let Inez relieve herself in the woods while he did the same. Back in the car at a steady fifty, passing through the nondescript pinewoods of Mississippi. After about twenty minutes, Skyfisher moaned.

"He's coming around," Inez said. I'm going to stop the car and give him some water."

"Keep driving." Davey leaned over the back seat, moistening Salvo's lips with a few drops. Inez readjusted the rear view mirror.

"Salvo, you alright? It's Inez. Can you hear me?"

Skyfisher opened his eyes to see a ghost man holding a bottle of water.

He opened his mouth for more. The man's hands shook as he poured, splashing the water, some of which Skyfisher managed to swallow. He coughed.

"Sleeping Beauty wakes."

Under his bandages, the ghost man's mouth twisted into something like a smile.

The mound loomed next to the parking lot, turning from shades of grey to a dull green. It wasn't emerald, for sure.

Hilton walked over to Salvo's Nova, the one they'd reclaimed from JB's junkyard. The creep had taken the keys, but the doors were unlocked. Hilton looked under the dash, saw the wires the twins had cut and crossed, now covered with electrical tape. He vaguely recalled what they had done to jump it, and after fifteen minutes and one electrical shock, the engine stirred. Leaning on the accelerator pedal with his elbow, he gave it some gas, touched the wires again and the car started.

"We have lift-off," Hilton said, imagining what actor might play him when they filmed the movie. John Turturro with straight hair. The bad guy from "No Country for Old Men." Someone edgy. He could write the script, play himself. Total control. Jennifer Lopez would be Inez.

Hilton, fresh from receiving his nomination for Best Supporting Actor, was having brunch with Jack Nicholson at the Beverley Hills Hotel, when he realized he had to make a choice. Go to the cops, find Inez's father or follow the dark sedan, which already had a quarter of an hour's lead. They could be headed anywhere. What would Pancho do? He'd go over after Cisco.

Davey wasn't quite sure what to do with his injured captive. Fucking guy tried to kill him. He searched Samuel's pockets and found a wallet with about a thousand dollars in cash.

"That's a start. Where's the rest, asshole?"

Skyfisher tried to speak, no sounds came.

"I gave the rest of the money to my father," Inez said. All of it."

"Keep your eyes on the road, OK? Know what your father did with it?"

"He gave it to whoever sent you and - your partner."

"Good. That's good. OK, I gotta think for a minute. Just keep driving and looking at the pine trees."

If she was telling the truth, that would take some of the pressure off. He'd deliver the weirdo and still walk out of this. They could have him, free of charge. Fucking guy would sic every cockroach in New Jersey on them. Let him.

Still a few loose ends. He took Inez's phone and the display showed a few bars. He had her pull over.

"Call your father."

"I don't have his number."

"You're lucky day. I do." He gave her the number and said, "Call him and say exactly what I tell you, nothing more, not a syllable."

"Alright."

"Tell him you're OK. He just has to cool his heels until I've done what I gotta do. Then you go home. You are my insurance policy. That's it."

Inez called the number and heard the recorded voice of her father.

"This is Alex Sams; leave a message." A female voice asked if she wanted more options. Inez wondered if anyone ever asked for more options.

"It's his voice mail," she said, "should I?"

Davey nodded. At the beep, Inez began, "Dad, it's me.."

There was a click and her father came on line.

"Keep talking," he said softly.

"Uh, what I'm supposed to tell you is that I - um, I'm alright. With the guy who used to work for you. And everything's OK." She glanced at Davey who nodded for her to continue.

Alex interjected quickly.

"Cough if you're on the Trace."

Inez coughed.

"You – he said to say that you have to back off. Then I get to come home. I'm insurance. I guess that's it."

"Hang up now," Davey said, and she did.

Inez glanced in the rear view mirror. Salvo appeared to be drifting in and out of consciousness. The back of his head was a mass of clotted blood. Davey didn't look much better. For a moment, his body was still, then a wave of convulsions would pass through him, twitching and trembling.

Inez attempted to speak to him, but he would have none of it. She set the cruise control, trying to put her mind at ease. Little traffic and zero scenic wonders along the Natchez Trace. Seen one pine tree, you've seen them all, whipping by in a peripheral pale green-blue blur. For some reason, Davey didn't want the radio on. Inez found herself hungering for anything to break the monotony, even a Burma Shave sign, long extinct.

In the mirror, she noticed a vehicle a good ways back. Orange. After twenty minutes of the car maintaining this distance, Inez realized it might be Salvo's Nova. She tried to be discreet, checking the side mirror when she rounded a curve, catching a glimpse of the driver's silhouette. Hilton.

The idiot had jumped the car.

Something in her body language triggered Davey's curiosity, because he turned around and looked out the rear window.

"Faster," he said to Inez. "There's no cops around. Faster!"

Inez depressed the accelerator, her heart beating faster, too.

"Pull off the road when I tell you. Wait for it." They descended a long slope which gradually curved to the right, then more acutely to the left.

"Now," said Davey, "quick!" Inez hit the brakes and with a swirl of gravel and dirt, went on to the shoulder, bringing the sedan to a stop.

"Keep the engine running."

Twenty seconds later, the orange car drove by, Hilton at the wheel.

"Schmuck couldn't stay away. Get into passenger's seat," Davey said to Inez, "I'm gonna drive." He was shaking violently, but he managed to get his hand on the shift lever. With a shudder, the car lurched forward onto the highway. One handing the wheel, Davey reached into his chamo jacket and fumbled for something.

"Please don't – ", Inez began.

"Shut up!" Davey barked.

There were no cars in sight. Davey accelerated. The turquoise blur of the pine forest gave Inez the sense they were traveling at light speed. The cop that's never there when you need them wasn't there. She strapped her seatbelt on.

Hilton, what have you done?

If they got out of this, she would kill him. A set of headlights approached in the opposite lane, heading south. Davey slowed down, then resumed his speed when the other vehicle passed. In a few minutes he caught up with the orange car. Davey flashed his brights. When Hilton didn't slow down, Davey passed and nudge-creased the Nova onto the shoulder.

Just like the movies, Inez thought.

The cars came to halt in a cloud of dust. Davey pulled the sedan in front.

"Stay here," he said to Inez, striding quickly over to the Nova, pulling out his pistol.

"Open the door or I'll put a bullet through it. Right now!"

Hilton did as instructed.

"What the fuck were you trying to prove? All you had to do was stay put, but no! So what am I supposed to do with you now, you putz? One thing. Did you tell anybody?"

"Did I tell —"

"You heard me."

"No. Yes!"

"Shitty liar," Davey said. He fumbled with the pistol, trying to pull the safety with his shaking hand.

"Wait!" Hilton cried. A car was approaching from the other side of the road, heading south towards Natchez. Davey lowered his pistol.

"You got five more breaths. Enjoy them."

Davey assumed what he thought was a casual stance, putting his left hand on the roof of the car, as if he was giving instructions, the right hand low, holding the gun pointed at Hilton. The oncoming car flipped its bright lights on. Davey flinched and instinctively glanced up to have a look-see. In that instant, the car accelerated and swerved into their lane, heading right for them.

Davey dove into the Nova just as the oncoming vehicle slammed the open door with a thundering crash of metal and glass. He fell screaming onto Hilton's lap.

"My leg!"

Hilton pulled away from Davey in shock. Several figures jumped out of the car that had just hit them. Someone was shouting orders.

"Nelson, Jimmy, contain him. Malone, with me."

The Man and his posse. Alex ran to the sedan, checked inside, said a few words to his daughter, went to have a look at the Nova. His men were in the process of pulling the Davey from the car, still raving. The bottom of his leg was spouting blood, a severed foot lay on the ground. Alex shouted orders, drill sergeant style.

"Keep him horizontal. Elevate the leg. No belt on him? Malone, use yours, make a tourniquet. Bag the foot. Some ice, pronto. Both the leg and the foot. Call Myers, the vet. See what he can do. Tell him this stays under the radar. Get this asshole some pain killer, sew him up, keep him alive and get him the fuck out of here fast. He's got a date with his friends in New Jersey."

Malone was going to say something clever about Davey getting his foot in the door with the Mob. One look at Alex's face and he thought better of it.

Hilton clambered out of the car, looking like he had caught a case of Davey's shakes. Alex strode over to him.

"You alright?"

"I – I.." Hilton stammered.

"Yes or no will do."

"I think I'm shot," Hilton said.

"No shit! Where?"

"Shoulder."

"Lemme see. Yeah, he nicked you. Malone, you got his gun? Good. This guy's coming with us, too. Here's what we're gonna do."

The procedure was familiar to Alex from his days as a Cleaner, although there was always a certain level of improvisation.

The Nova's engine was still running. The driver's side door was smashed and there were little cubes of broken glass scattered on the grass and gravel. Inez watched as her father's men towelled up the blood with the efficiency of a team of janitors cleaning up a kitchen spill.

"Don't make it too pretty," Alex said. "There was an accident here and the driver got hurt."

He went back to the sedan where Inez still sat in the passenger's seat.

"Can you drive?" he asked her.

"Yes," Inez said, doing her best not to cry.

"You're gonna be OK. Him, too," glancing at Salvo in the back seat. "We have to do this quickly. You're going to drive your buddy here to the hospital. He was the driver. He stopped on the Trace to take a leak, look at a map, whatever. He pulls over on the shoulder, maybe not as far off the road as he should. Anyway, he's just opening his door when some asshole coming the other way, weaving down the highway, probably drunk or high, crosses the lane and clips the door. Your friend wasn't wearing a seatbelt. His head got hurt from the broken glass. You got that?"

Inez nodded.

"OK, I'm going to scratch your friend's face here with some glass and make him bleed a little more. It's got to look like he was in an accident. It'll hurt for a second. Look worse than it is. Scratches. Hospital will take care of him. He speaks English, right?"

Inez let her father take control. She felt like the wind had been knocked out of her and now she was caught in the undertow of her father's world, which inevitably led to pain and suffering. At least he knew what to do. She asked about Hilton, and Alex responded, rapid fire.

"He's winged. A scratch. Can't send him to the hospital with a gunshot wound. We'll clean him up, get him back to you in one piece." He had two of his men walk Skyfisher to the Nova. The driver's side door was inoperable, so they slid Inez into the driver's seat from the passenger side, Skyfisher next to her into what Driver's Ed instructors like to call the Death Seat. Alex took a handful of broken window glass and showed it to Salvo.

"Gotta make this look real. Close your eyes." He rubbed the broken glass hard and deep onto Salvo's forehead, cheeks and scalp. Inez cried out in dismay.

Hilton, still in a state of shock, came over to speak to Inez.

"I'm so – ", he began. Inez shushed him, leaning out of the broken window to press her fingertips to his lips.

Alex handed Hilton over to his men, then turned back to his daughter.

"I'll be back in touch, once things have settled down. If they bring the cops in, tell 'em you didn't see the car that hit you. All you know is it was heading towards the city - towards Natchez. Got that?"

"Yes," she said. My cell phone -."

"Later," Alex said. "There's a hospital in Jackson, next exit. Get going."

His men did one last sweep, leaving only broken glass.

With Salvo seat-belted in the passenger seat beside her, Inez drove the Nova towards Jackson, the wind blowing through the broken window. It had all happened so quickly, there was no time to think. Blood was seeping from the cuts on Salvo's face. She handed him a handkerchief.

"My god," she said, "what a day. Are you all right? Can you speak?"

"All right. Hilton?"

"Shaken up, but he's going to be OK."

"Ghost Man?"

"Gone."

They drove on in silence for a while, the night air whistling. Inez turned on the car heater for some warmth and then flicked the radio on, desperately wanting to expunge the image of Davey's foot and the accident from her thoughts. The radio was dead.

"This morning on the hill," she said, "I've never had an experience like that before. Not anywhere. All those other people with us somehow. So beautiful. Then this. I just don't understand. Why?" She waited for a response. When none came, she continued.

"Where you come from, is there much violence, killing?"

"We hunt, fight other tribes. Warriors take hair."

"Scalps." Inez interjected, her helpfulness on autopilot. "Do all your people do what we did this morning, on the mound?"

"No. Only *kuash,* the Shining Ones. I come here for this. You and Hilton, you tell others."

Inez reflexively reached for her cell phone. Why did she let Alex keep it?

No point in beating herself up. Who can think clearly in moments like this? She glanced at Salvo, a sorry sight, rivulets of blood scrolling down his face.

"Are you – does Skyfisher have wife?" Christ, she was starting to sound like him.

"My wife is *Tell Me A Story.*"

"Will you go back to her?"

"I go back."

"When? How?"

"Salvo and me, we —" He made a rubbing gesture with his hands, somewhere between washing and praying.

Inez regarded him, wondering what would Salvo be like when he reclaimed his body.

She almost laughed aloud at the incongruity of the thought and this impossible situation, which she had actually come to believe.

"I will miss you," she said, and reached for his hand.

St. Dominic's Hospital was just down the road from the Mississippi Museum of Natural Science in Jackson, engendering memories of elementary school field trips and fossil skeletons of a sabre tooth tiger and other extinct species. Salvador Samuels, extinct human reanimated, was taken to the emergency room, having been instructed by Inez to say as little as possible. She gave the admissions clerk the scenario her father had outlined. The clerk took Salvo's information and insurance card from his wallet.

Later as she sat in the waiting room reading *Field and Stream*, Inez was called back into the admissions office. In a tiny cubicle lined with pictures of a golden retriever, a perky young woman in a pink striped smock peeked over a computer screen.

"The police want to talk to you, since it was a hit-and-run. Would you mind heading over to the station? We need to do some tests on your friend anyway."

Inez kicked herself for saying too much. The receptionist hadn't even asked about the accident. Well, it probably would have come out sooner or later.

She drove a short distance to the station, told her story to a bored looking desk cop who took some notes. There wasn't much they could do about a hit-and-run, given she hadn't a good look at other car. The officer examined the Nova, searching for signs of paint on the driver's side door.

"Looks like it was a dark blue car. That ring a bell?" The officer was middle aged, slightly overweight, with wavy grey hair. Reminded Inez of a character actor playing a cop on television. These days, it felt like everyone was playing a role or wearing some kind of mask. It was what lay behind the masks that scared her.

"You said they was heading south?" The cop asked. "We'll notify the police in Natchez to keep an eye up for a blue car with orange paint dings on its – front left fender, right? I mean left," he said, chuckling.

"Driver's OK? Didn't see what hit him?" He humpfed, "Lucky man. He didn't get slammed. Must've been some kids, drinking. Off from school."

He took Inez's phone number, told her they'd call if anything turned up. In the meantime, she'd have a record of making the report for her insurance company.

Inez thanked the cop and left the station feeling famished. Wolfed down a BLT at CS's diner, several notches above hospital food.

Just walking around the block cleared her head a bit. If only it was possible to trash some of the stuff in our memory banks, like swiping an etch-a-sketch pad. Doubted she'd ever lose the image of Davey's foot lying on the side of the road.

A parade of random store windows. Brent's Drugs, Butterfly Yoga, Sneaky Beans Coffeehouse, with posters for the world renowned Budweiser Clydesdales coming to Tupelo in the Fall, the Millsap College basketball schedule and an

Elvis festival. All the rituals of the Nacirema. Eating turkey at Thanksgiving, giving presents at Christmas, getting hung over on New Year's. What would they make of Skyfisher and his high-minded mission?

Back at the hospital they let Inez into the inner sanctum of the Emergency Room. Salvo lay on a cot in a curtained enclosure just large enough to accommodate a bed and an IV stand dispensing clear liquid into his arm. He was sleeping soundly, bandages on his face and the back of his head. Inez sat on a chair in the cubicle, listening.

A chorus of triage from the surrounding patients. An elderly gentleman with a finger sliced by an overhead fan. Woman with chest pains who sounded like a regular ER customer. Kid with a broken arm and an anxious mother.

A nurse entered the room and asked Inez to step outside. One of the doctors wanted to speak to her, a physician's assistant wearing blue scrubs, probably Indian or Pakistani. His left eye twitched when he spoke, looking more at a clipboard than Inez.

"You're a relative?"

"A friend."

"Hmm. Doctor wants to keep him for observation. Nasty bump on the back of his head. You were in the car, too?" giving Inez a professional glance punctuated by several rapid eye twitches.

"Back seat, wearing a seat belt. He wasn't."

"Ah. When will people learn?", waggling his head slightly from side to side. "Well, he's going to be with us a little while longer."

"How long?"

"Overnight. Need to run some tests. You local?"

"Natchez. Got to get back home. I'll call. They have my number in the office." The assistant nodded, made a note on his clipboard, gave a parting twitch, and went on with his rounds.

Inez pulled aside the curtain to Salvo's enclosure and stepped back inside. He was snoring gently.

Which world was he dreaming of? Hers had been turned upside down by this shamanic figure who could commune with butterflies, send telepathic messages and be the master of ceremonies at an experience there was no index card for on her inner Rolodex. Unless it was under I, for *Impossible.*

She leaned over, kissed him lightly on his bandaged cheek and left.

Chapter Thirty Six

No one moved, then Haeden bolted like a rabbit.

So much for trust, Lewis thought.

Red Wolf started off after Haeden, but High Eagle stopped him.

"Let him go. These are the ones we want." He was mighty glad to have found them, although they were a sorry sight. *"They're in no condition to run away."*

Red Wolf spoke up, *"A few bruises, No matter. She still has spark. I would lie with her tonight."*

"Yes," said Buffalo, *"you will lie tonight."* He turned towards Red Wolf, who quickly drew a knife.

"Little Rock, this is between High Eagle and me." Red Wolf stood knife in hand, ready for combat or negotiation.

"You will not have her," Buffalo said. In one swift motion, he reached to the ground, grabbed a handful of dirt and threw it at Red Wolf's face. The tracker, seeing it coming, turned his head away. In that instant, Buffalo grabbed his arm and wrested the knife from the tracker's grasp. He tossed the weapon to High Eagle. Red Wolf struck at him with his free arm and legs, but it was like kicking a tree stump. Still holding the tracker's arm, Buffalo ducked into his midsection and lifted him onto his shoulder like a sack of grain. He tossed Red Wolf to the

ground, giving his arm a twist at the same time. There was a popping sound. The tracker roared in agony. Buffalo let go of the arm and it dangled askew from the shoulder.

Red Wolf tried to speak. No words came. Buffalo grabbed him by his belt with one hand and reached for his neck with the other. With four fingers it wasn't so easy to get a good grip. No matter, the fight had gone out of his opponent. Buffalo straight-armed the tracker high above his head, as if offering up a sacrifice to the Sun. Knowing what was coming, Tell Me A Story looked away, just as Buffalo dropped to one knee and brought the body down on it. A sickening crack, and Red Wolf crumpled to the ground.

No one moved. In the distance, a crow cawed. Tell Me A Story shook her head and mouthed a silent prayer. Knife in hand, High Eagle walked over to the body and brought the blade to Red Wolf's forehead, holding a fist full of the tracker's hair with his other hand.

"No honor in that," Buffalo said.

"Strategy," High Eagle said. Pulling back the hair, he sliced his knife into Red Wolf's scalp and peeled it off his head, as though skinning a rabbit. He pointed to the body.

"The Tattooed Serpent's scouting parties will see this, get their blood up, looking for their enemy. We head south," High Eagle said, tying the scalp to his waist belt.

Waya, seemingly unfazed by the killing, approached Lewis and spat in his face proclaiming, *"I bind this one!"* As she tied his wrists, Waya raised her voice so all could hear.

"Two moons ago, the Blind-One-Who-Sees killed my brother."

"Your death will be slower," she whispered to Lewis.

The loathing in her voice needed no translation for Lewis, nor did the horror of sense-seeing someone snapped in two and scalped. He watched as the colors of Red Wolf's life force faded. Buffalo draped Tell Me A Story over his shoulder. She offered no resistance.

They headed south. Lewis, his hands tied securely behind his back, followed them. Every few minutes High Eagle would prod him to walk faster. Waya scouted ahead, returning to make sure her prize was still there.

Lewis moved like a donkey, whacked with a stick every time he paused. He read his surroundings with the Blind-One-Who-See's sensory array, sharing his host's weariness, hunger, and the pain of his injuries. Nothing to do but retreat from his damaged outer shell, search for the place deep inside that Falling Star and Grey Turtle had introduced him to. The strange thing was, even with the pain, he was becoming accustomed to being encased inside a foreign body. Trusting his legs to find their own steady pace, Lewis's attention journeyed down to the pit of Skyfisher's stomach, rallying his stray thoughts.

Here is where I am.

From this place of refuge, the core of Skyfisher's planet, it was possible to follow the rhythm of his breathing, the movement of his legs. Skyfisher's spine became an antenna, trolling the sky, listening. As he walked and waited in this empty space, a signal came, a current - a sense of warmth. He recognized the flavor of it from the *ippli hallesh*, like welcoming an old friend. He could sense there were others tuning in, riding the current. A rap between his shoulder blades brought him up from the depths to a sparsely wooded area not far from a stream. High Eagle called out that they would make camp here.

"No fire," he said.

Lewis had been rejuvenated by the re-connection with the Shining Ones and the Sun Breath, if that indeed was what it was. He sat against a tree and before long, fell asleep.

High Eagle reminded Buffalo to keep a careful watch on Tell Me A Story.

"She must not have any contact with the Blind One."

Night was coming on, a chill in the air.

Waya approached Tell Me A Story, but Buffalo stopped her.

"Women's business," Waya said.

"Give me your knife," Buffalo said.

She eyed him warily and agreed, provided that he would return the knife when her conversation was over. The women moved apart from the others, watched by Buffalo from a discreet distance. Tell Me A Story, beckoning Waya to sit beside her, became her name.

"Speak your mind," she said.

"Blood for blood. The Blind One is your husband?"

"My husband is Skyfisher. This one wears his skin. He means nothing to me."

"My brother, Yellow Hatchet, you saw this one kill him?"

Ah, the story unfolds, the memory of the young warrior racing towards Buffalo. If only he had thrown his hatchet.

"Your brother's back was snapped like a twig. You think this one has the strength to do that? What do your eyes tell you?"

Waya took three breaths, stood up and shouted.

"Your husband is dog shit!" She stalked over to Buffalo and demanded her knife.

"One day you cut him. First, this one must see the Lesser Sun," Buffalo reminded her.

"I will wait," Waya pocketed her knife and departed to her own bivouac.

Buffalo placed a blanket over Tell Me A Story as if she were a child. He took the first watch while High Eagle slept next to Lewis. They were taking no chances this time.

Lewis dreamt he was at home in bed, in the grip of a violent nightmare of blindness and despair. All he had to do was to emerge from the depths and climb out into fresh air. Then it became dark. A cave, by the sound and smell of it. He'd been here before, and with a dread certainty he knew that if he was going to emerge from the dream it would be through this dark place. Nearby, he heard a scraping sound, coming closer. Something moving, calling to him.

He awoke on hard ground, his back sore, hands bound, head aching. Skyfisher's radar detected two sleeping bodies, High Eagle and Buffalo glowing, dimly pulsing, breathing.

A movement in the bushes, as if something had crawled out of Lewis's dream. The outline of a human form creeping along the ground like a stalking cat. Waya, knife in hand, slinking towards Tell Me A Story.

Lewis was about to call out a warning, but Waya abruptly turned toward Buffalo's massive form as he lay on his back, snoring to the stars.

Crouching next to Buffalo, she whispered, *"For my brother!"* and sliced her knife across Buffalo's throat. He awoke choking blood, grabbing hold of his attacker. She stabbed at him wildly. Buffalo grabbed Waya's hand, shaking away the blade, then closed both his hands around her throat. She tried to claw at his one eye, but he lifted her up away from his face. The sounds were muffled. High Eagle sleeping through it all. Lewis bound and helpless.

Let them slaughter each other.

Tell Me A Story was on her feet, Waya's knife in hand. She brought it down on Buffalo's chest, the tip of the blade breaking against his rib cage. Buffalo was standing now, blood gushing from his throat, still grasping Waya around the neck. Tell Me Story reached for his arm and pulled down on it with all her weight and strength. Buffalo kept one hand tight around Waya's neck and reached for Tell Me A Story with the other. She bit down hard on it. He released his grip on Waya, attempting to swat Tell Me A Story, who jumped back, avoiding the blow. Waya tumbled to the ground. Tell Me A Story ducked, grabbed Waya by the foot and pulled her out of reach. Buffalo's hand moved to his throat, feeling the warm blood pulsing, his one eye a beacon of anguish. Tell Me A Story, wielding the broken blade, faced the big man in defiance. Lewis, the only witness to the struggle, marvelled at her courage. Ulysses squaring off against the Cyclops.

Little Rock Buffalo staggered, nodded at Tell Me A Story, hung there for a moment, and folded to the ground.

Waya gave a rasping cry as she took in a breath. High Eagle awoke, shaking the sleep from his head. He lurched towards them cursing. Tell Me A Story brandished the broken knife, one jagged edge that could still do some damage. High Eagle backed away, quickly scanning the ground, snatched up a blanket and tossed it at Tell Me A Story, draping her knife hand. The next instant, he slapped her hard and took possession of her weapon.

"I will have you, by the Great Sun!" High Eagle shouted. *"You will spread your legs for me and your husband will watch. I'll roast you both over a fire. I will do this. I swear by my blood."*

Stunned by the slap, Tell Me A Story knelt by Waya, who tried to speak but could only make a croaking sound. Lewis struggled to free himself from his bonds, but they held tight.

Gesturing at Buffalo, High Eagle barked a few words Lewis could not understand. There would be no scalping this time. Buffalo was as bald as an egg. Lewis wondered if a Native American would find that even remotely amusing. Not High Eagle, whose plans were unraveling. It would be a bad business leaving Buffalo to feed the wolves, but there was nothing to be done. He still had his two captives.

How had the Story Woman gotten hold of a knife? High Eagle checked Waya's body for other weapons, feeling her breasts as he did so.

Small. Her flesh lean and hard, a warrior's body.

If she could not fend for herself, Waya could stay here and keep Buffalo company in the afterlife.

"She walks or dies," he told Tell Me A Story, who could barely walk herself.

Tell Me A Story leaned close and whispered in Waya's ear, *"Can you speak?"* A negative shake of the head.

"Try and sit up."

Leaning on Tell Me A Story, Waya arose, hand to her throat, still struggling for breath. Tell Me A Story held her, swaying and stumbling to keep balance.

"Lean against me," Tell Me A Story Said. Waya touched Tell Me A Story's forehead lightly with two fingers, and brought the fingers to her own chest. They stood together wobbling for a moment. Tell Me A Story put her arm around Waya's shoulder; they took a few tentative steps.

High Eagle pointed southwest and his motley crew began to trudge in that direction, the sun rising behind them.

Small satisfaction in prodding the Blind One. For now, no danger of the Story Woman's straying. Several times High Eagle stopped, listening, sure he heard shouts in the distance. Must be nearing the mound site.

Once again, Lewis assumed the conn of Skyfisher's inner GPS. The lay of the land seemed familiar. Waya seemed to be recovering a bit, walking without any assistance, her breathing belabored. She found a sturdy stick on the ground, gave it to Tell Me A Story as a walking staff. Lewis wondered what could had passed between these women to bring about such a turn of events.

It was Waya who saw the first incised club, sticking out of the ground like a mini totem. Carved into the top of the club was an image of the sun.

"War parties," High Eagle muttered. *"That way!"* he motioned to Lewis. *"Go!"*

Lewis set off. High Eagle hoisted Tell Me A Story on to his shoulder and came after Lewis, Waya following. No other war sticks. Perhaps they were outside the range of scouting parties. High Eagle had no desire to encounter apprentice bucks crazed on Black Drink, out to make a name for themselves.

It was a hell ride for Tell Me A Story, balanced on High Eagle's shoulder, his hands grasping her buttocks and thighs.

She put her thoughts inside the story of Lodge Boy, from the time when people and animals could speak to each other. He lived in the woods on bugs and berries. As a child, Tell Me A Story believed *she* was the wild boy, who could fly. It was a complicated tale with cannibals, magic and death. Like so many of her people's stories, there were countless details, seemingly irrelevant, and an ending that did not bode well for its central characters. Her life task was to carry the stories - all of them, in all their gory, scatological, scary, transcendent weirdness.

Bouncing on High Eagle's shoulder, the tale unravelled in her mind. She became Lodge Boy again, escaping from his father through the smoke hole of their lodge. As the father reached up through the hole to grab the wild boy, his hands became High Eagle's, sliding her from his shoulder to the ground.

High Eagle stopped and listened. In the distance, the soft sound of rattling shells. He turned. The sounds were coming from behind them as well.

About a dozen warriors, faces painted red, wearing nothing but belts dangling with shells that chinked rhythmically as they ran. Each of them carried a war club. Some of the clubs were covered with red dye or blood; several of the younger men had fresh scalps tucked into their belts.

They raised a cry that was enough to raise the hackles on Lewis's neck. One of them was the most magnificent looking man he had ever seen, let alone sense-brailed, walking with regal authority. It was as if the statue of David had come alive, carrying a cudgel.

High Eagle recognized the warrior as Ten Kills, a name which might grow larger today from the look of things. A mischievous gleam in his eye. The war drink. Fountain of invincibility.

"*Ho, Ten Kills,*" High Eagle raised his hand.

Ten Kills did not return the greeting, but turned to one of his scouts.

"*High Eagle is giving horse rides to women. I thought we're supposed to be riding them!*"

Not much of a jest, but one of the scouts convulsed with laughter, mucous spouting out of his nose. He wiped it with a bloody hand.

"*These are prisoners for the Lesser Sun,*" High Eagle said. "*We were in a fight.*"

"*Yes*", Ten Kills responded, appraising High Eagle's hand, sans pinky. "*Looks like you gave them a little present.*"

More snorts, suppressed laughter from the younger scout. He stood a head shorter than Ten Kills and resembled him. High Eagle considered challenging the young buck, thought better of it as the other scouts converged.

"*Where is your companion, Big Little Rock the Buffalo, or whatever he calls himself these days.*"

"*Dead.*" No sense in denying it. They'd find his body sooner or later.

"Dead? That's something. How?"

"A fight."

"Ah. Who had the honor?"

High Eagle almost turned to Waya, but checked himself. *"Night attack."*

"This one sees in the dark," Ten Kills pointed to Skyfisher. *"Maybe he saw. His pretty wife a prisoner, too. She'll tell us the story. Who is this one, walking like a wounded cat?"*

"She cannot speak," High Eagle said.

"Hah! We have a mute, a blind man, a famous warrior — minus a finger, carrying a delicious woman. Good story."

High Eagle opened his mouth to respond, but Ten Kills cut him off, his eyes glinting like steel.

"Come with us. We'll keep you safe from those night attacks."

Tell Me A Story had heard of Ten Kills. This was a rescue of sorts, but these men were caught in their own stories of war and blood. She rose to her feet unsteadily, walked over to him and bowed her head submissively.

"Ten Kills, great warrior. Protect us. My husband is injured, blind, cannot hurt anyone. Please remove his bonds, if not for me, for my family. Your kindness will be rewarded."

"My kindness?" Ten Kills laughed. *"You must face the Lesser Sun. That is the law. I will release him, blind or not. We have you. He will not run."*

High Eagle wasn't happy about this turn of events, but he was powerless to protest. So long as he got them to the Flour Village, he supposed it didn't matter if the Blind One was bound or not. Once High Eagle told his story, the Lesser Sun would pass judgment and the woman would be his.

Circulation returned to the hands and arms of Skyfisher's body. Lewis collapsed to the ground, completely exhausted, curving into himself, oblivious to Tell Me A Story's gently stroking his head. Inside, Lewis dreamed of the cave near the mound, as if it were a pore in the earth-skin, breathing him in.

The buck who looked like Ten Kills younger brother pulled Tell Me A Story to her feet. High Eagle was poised to intervene, content to let this play out for the moment. A little fear would tenderize her. Ten Kills was nowhere in sight and Skyfisher was out cold.

"Let's have a look at you," the warrior said, grabbing at her buckskin shirt. *"Take that off. I want to see the whole story."* He laughed, beckoning the other scouts to come closer.

Tell Me A Story hugged herself, shaking her head, too weak to struggle, to fly away like Lodge Boy. She was slapped and then caressed by the hand that slapped her.

"Take that off or I will," he said. A knife was at her neck now, the blade under the buckskin draping her shoulder, slicing it. The garment fell away, exposing her breasts.

The young warrior gloated, letting his knife dangle in his hand.

Waya had been creeping along the ground, unseen like a cougar. Now she pounced. Before he had a chance to react, she snatched the warrior's knife, whirled, had one hand on his manhood, the other holding the knife edge against it. The scouts moved to intervene and Waya began to slice, gesturing for the others to keep away.

"Back off!" the buck shouted.

Waya glared at them while Tell Me A Story covered herself with her buckskin.

Ten Kills appeared then, coming from out of the woods, assessing the situation with a glance. He began to convulse with laughter, the other scouts joining in. He folded his arms across his chest.

"This is a very good story. A short one, I think!" Again he laughed, holding his sides as if they hurt.

"I'm taking a piss. I've got my pecker in my hand and I come to find you with a woman's hand around yours. Ha! Go ahead, piss. I dare you to, if you can! Do it, Squirrel! High Eagle lost his pinky finger. Squirrel's going to lose his tail, I think. Do it!"

Squirrel, red faced and flummoxed, pissed. Waya directed the flow at the nearest warrior, who sprang away to the amusement of all.

Lewis awoke, taken aback by the spectacle. He had not witnessed this level of mirth in his entire sojourn. All it took was a guy getting circumcised.

"Have you learned your lesson, brother?" Ten Kills asked. *"I think not. Make his tail grow,"* he said to Waya. She complied with one hand, still holding the knife close in the other.

"Do you think it'll be longer than the knife blade?" Ten Kills asked the others. *"Nothing doing. Alright, stop before he falls in love with you! Let him go in one piece. I want him to father some nephews when he grows up. All of you. Heed this. You too, High Eagle. They are under my protection. Touch the Story Woman and —"* pointing to Waya, *"this one will slice you. I will not stop her next time!"*

With reluctance, Waya released the abashed Squirrel.

Ten Kills addressed his men, *"We will join the attack on the mound. Prepare yourselves. Do not shame us."*

Each warrior busied himself smearing his face with colors, mostly reds and browns, some blue-green. A few draped garments over their shoulders which Lewis thought looked like togas. Others wore something akin to an apron or skirt around their waist. All of them had necklaces and shells hanging from their waist belts, which rattled as they walked. So much for a surprise attack.

Led by Ten Kills, the dozen men set off at sunrise, excited at the prospect of battle, yet marching in orderly files.

Behind walked Tell Me A Story and Lewis, with High Eagle and Squirrel bringing up the rear, keeping a wary eye on Waya, who circled the procession at a distance.

They arrived at an encampment that Lewis guessed was about an eighth of a mile from the mound. Being closer to the Shining Ones, he found himself able to glean more of what was being spoken. Mostly speculation and bravado about the coming confrontation.

Two trees, festooned with feathers, arrows and war clubs, formed a makeshift gateway, their leaves and branches splashed with red dye. At least a hundred warriors were already in the camp, passing in review in front of a grandly dressed chief. Tell Me A Story watched from a distance. Turning to Lewis she made a discrete gesture imitating the movement of a snake. This was the Tattooed Serpent, war chief and brother of the Great Sun. He wore a feather headdress and his body was completely covered with inked symbols. Each warrior stepped in front of the war chief, bowed his head slightly and declaimed in a loud voice. A few were fervent and lengthy, testifying their willingness to die for their people with honor. Most were brief and pro forma. Case in point was High Eagle, not a happy camper at the moment.

The Tattooed Serpent raised his hand and several vats of steaming hot liquid were brought out. Each warrior drank two ladles of it, downing the scalding brew as quickly as possible. In due course men began to stagger towards the bushes, vomiting violently.

When the mass retching had subsided, scout chiefs reported to the Tattooed Serpent and discussed a plan of attack. According to the scouts, the men stationed on the mound site had set up blockades of wood and brambles at locations vulnerable to attack. The high ground of the mound was easy to defend, but most of its perimeter was unfenced. The prevailing guess was the defenders were outnumbered three to one. Ten Kills' men had captured a small party of defenders, but they had not talked, even under torture. The Tattooed Serpent sent word to Ten Kills asking if he had any further information which might help the attack.

That evening, a huge bonfire was lit in a clearing, and the men danced around it with rattles and drums. A leader chanted a phrase and the group responded, punctuating their singing with piercing wails, sounding to Lewis's ears like a turkey gobble on steroids.

They circled the fire counter-clockwise, first facing towards the flame, then turning their bodies away from it. When the dance was finished, some of the more experienced warriors began declaiming their exploits. Half-spoken, half-sung praises of the men they had faced in battle. How many kills, how the earth shook with the force of their blows. Each warrior sang his death song in turn. If the end came on the field of battle, they were ready.

Waya and Tell Me A Story heard the spectacle from afar. The Tattooed Serpent tolerated their presence so long as they stayed out of sight. After listening to a few of the death songs, Tell Me A Story said, *"Any more of this and I'm going to start vomiting, too."*

Later that evening, Lewis found the women sipping cups of bark tea by a campfire.

"Join us," Tell Me A Story said, offering him some tea.

Lewis regarded Waya, pointed to his throat then back at her with an inquiring expression. She waved her hand in what seemed to be a dismissive gesture.

"This one saves me," she whispered, with a nod to Tell Me A Story.

"Understand now?" Tell Me A Story asked Lewis.

"Yes." His comprehension was returning, like water seeping into dry ground.

"These men see spirits everywhere," she said. *"Look for signs. Bad sign - afraid!"*

Lewis wondered if the troops had any idea what they were getting themselves into. An empowered Lighting was a bad sign indeed. He wasn't exactly chomping at the bit to confront his former teacher. Then again, if he died maybe he'd wake up in his own world. Not that he was ready to test that theory. Tomorrow he would march alongside the warriors. He had no death song, wondering what the reaction would be if he belted out a few verses of It's All Over Now, Baby Blue. Nor could he imagine returning home. This place had become his reality, Skyfisher's wounds his to bear. The smell of the campfire, the warmth of its flames against the cool of the night was real enough. Even Skyfisher's dayglo palette, which was painting the outline of an approaching figure.

"Ho!" Ten Kills greeted them. *"I sit with you?"* he asked.

"Some tea," Tell Me A Story said.

Ten Kills sat, sipped his tea and spoke in a kindly voice with no trace of swagger. Earlier in the day, High Eagle had informed him that the Blind One was likely involved with the mound folk in some way.

Tell Me A Story began to excuse her husband's loss of speech, but Lewis stopped her. He was grasping the gist of what was being said. Words were popping into his head like thought balloons in a comic strip.

"Hit head," he said to Ten Kills. *"Not talk so good."*

Ten Kills asked about the mound and its defenders.

"Forty," Tell Me A Story guessed. *"Maybe more. Chief is Lightning. You know him?"* Ten Kills did not.

"Dangerous," Lewis said.

"Let him strike," Ten Kills said.

Lewis did not have the words to describe Lightning's power, nor was he inclined to inform on the Shining Ones. When Ten Kills suggested Lewis accompany him on the raid, it was more of a command than a request. In the timeless tradition of generals in combat, the Tattooed Serpent would be staying behind with a few retainers. High Eagle was sitting this one out as well, waiting for an audience with the Tattooed Serpent.

The warriors embarked the next morning in two files, one hundred strong, singing like boy scouts on the way to a jamboree. Lewis felt buoyed by their enthusiasm, as though he'd been morphed into a James Fenimore Cooper tale, marching with the Indians. Except it was hard to tell who the good guys were.

What if all the Shining Ones were under Lightning's power? If Haeden was right, Lightning meant to use the collective oomph of the *kuash* to overthrow the Great Sun. Hence this expedition, a chance for the Great Sun to see how the Society of Light would stand against a hundred seasoned fighters.

They were an impressive sight, at least two dozen rows of four files, with the more experienced warriors in the front lines, each man carrying a club or an axe. Feathers and shells hung from pendants on their ears and on their belts. Their faces were awash with color, mostly vermillion, tattoos aplenty on their faces and bodies. Some of the men had sloped, flattened foreheads, like the twins, which gave them a particularly fierce look, as if they were living icons of battle.

Ten Kills walked alongside his men, near the front ranks. Lewis marched with them, reflecting on whether the war party would make an example of Lightning while sparing the others, as Haeden had hoped. Haeden's disappearance was another tangled thread. Was he really the son of the Great Sun and his spy?

With every step he took towards the mound, Lewis felt closer to the hive mind of the *kuash*. Snatches of conversation from nearby scouts were comprehensible, a blend of bluster, hearsay, women and food. Not so different from soldiers marching to Thermopylae, Verdun or the Valley of Death.

On that note, a large flock of birds appeared, circling overhead, capturing the attention of many of the marching warriors.

"A good omen!" one shouted. When the flock dove and attacked the front lines, that notion quickly turned.

An attack by a massive flock of birds was an off the charts bad sign. In an instant, the front rows broke for cover, and the orderly march transformed into a rout, with panicked warriors pursued by mobs of birds, squawking and swooping. Lewis was in no mood to do battle with birds, however he sensed they weren't inflicting much damage. The sight of the entire flock descending and harassing was quite enough.

Chaos reigned and in the end, only Ten Kills' scouts and a dozen others held their ground, swatting at smaller clusters of birds with their war clubs and spears, while most of the flock pursued the retreating war party. Ten Kills dropped back to Lewis.

"Lighting is behind this?"

"Yes," Lewis affirmed.

"Can you find him?" Ten Kills asked.

"I will try."

He'd been hearing the ghost voices of the Shining Ones in his head, realizing with a shock they must be hearing him as well. Lewis tried to convey this to Ten Kills.

"They know I'm here. Maybe this is a trap."

Ten Kills considered.

"We'll split up," he said. *"Draw them off. We'll circle behind. Squirrel, go with the Blind One."*

Ten Kill's brother, anxious to redeem himself, agreed without hesitation. A few birds still mobbed them, but the brunt of the attack had abated. Ten Kills and his men, tensed for action, went clockwise around the mound, expecting arrows, stones, or warriors wielding tomahawks.

Too easy, Ten Kills thought.

As his scouts began to climb the slope of the mound, a warrior named Tall Breeches shoved his friend Three Scalps from behind. It looked as though he was being playful. Then Tall Breeches grabbed Three Scalp's leg, and as he slid down the mound, Tall Breeches pulled a knife and slit his throat. Ten Kills ran uphill towards them, but was hit with a war club from behind, grazing the side of his head and slamming into his shoulder. He stumbled and whirled around in fury to face ManBoy, who he had known all his life.

"What are you —" he began, as Man-Boy came at him again, swinging his club. Ten Kills dodged the blow and brought his own club behind Man-Boy's knees, sending him sprawling down the slope. He turned to see the rest of his men fighting each other with weapons drawn. A voice in his head assured him that his scouts had all betrayed him, gone over to the other side.

Strike them down and save yourself.

Ten Kills fought the impulse and shouted to his scouts, *"Leave this! Come away!"* A few stopped in confusion, only to be cut down by others who came after Ten Kills, clubs raised. For the first time in his life, Ten Kills ran from his own men.

Lewis and Squirrel circled counter-clockwise around the mound, Squirrel making a great show of being ready for anything. Lewis stopped in his tracks, sensing hostile tentacles of intention reaching out for Ten Kills' party.

"Something's wrong," he said. *"We head back."* He concentrated on Ten Kills, trying to buffer the thought-weapons converging upon him.

"He said to go this way," Squirrel said, determined to follow his brother's orders to the letter.

"We are a —" Lewis did not know the word for *decoy,* so he tried *duck,* a lame one at that. *"Ten Kills is under attack."*

"How do you know this?" Squirrel asked, incredulous.

"No time to argue."

There wasn't. Two dozen *kuash* armed with spears appeared, among them, Willet Moonface.

"The one who walks in Skyfisher's moccasins!" Lightning shouted to his men.

Lewis sensed a blast of thoughts overwhelming Squirrel, who twisted his head around, as if stretching his neck. He came at Lewis in attack mode, raising his club and bringing it down in a stroke that would have easily cracked a skull. Lewis side-stepped just in time, circling away from Squirrel, concentrating on the wave of thoughts assaulting the young warrior. It was like trying to pull an octopus off a clam.

"You see what this one can do," Lightning commented to the others. *"Keep them apart."*

Squirrel allowed himself to be disarmed without a fight. He looked dazed and deflated, as if awakening from a sleepwalk. They led him away.

Lewis felt the taste of rough camaraderie amongst the *kuash,* like a rugby team after a close match, the same ones who had been touched and united by *The Listening,* Thistle Head and Slow Deer among them. With Marsh Fox, they'd been in the service of the Sun Breath. Now they were under

Lightning's sway, sucked into his vortex of power and greed. Lightning called to Willet.

"If the Blind One tries anything, cut him down." Willet, his moon face still crated from the encounter with Tell Me A Story, escorted Lewis, avoiding his gaze.

Lewis tried from a distance to marshal a defense for Ten Kills, apparently under attack by his own men.

At that moment, a searing flash overwhelmed the arcade of his sensory array. Lewis had a glimpse of Skyfisher, more of an emanation than an image, pleading to meet him at the cave. Then everything around him seemed to dissolve.

He was alive, breathing in a cold, dark place, lying on hard ground. No X-Ray Vision, no emanations or color, only a formless grey void. Something else was breathing, too. Coming towards him. Heavy steps. Animal breath. He tried to stand up. His substance became diffused, scrambled and vaporous, coalescing into a body lying on a bed in a metallic tunnel, overwhelmed by a loud, clanging noise.

Chapter Thirty Seven

"Weirdest thing I've ever seen," the nurse technician said. She had been monitoring the brain scan and ordered the patient removed from the MRI. Most likely a computer glitch, but she wasn't taking any chances.

"Mr. Samuels, you OK?"

He had been running from something, the after-burn of a bad dream, tinged with claustrophobia. At the moment, he was lying face up on a narrow cot, in front of a metal coffin-size tunnel that had just spit him out, a giant donut saying *Aaah*. He blinked his eyes. He could see. Why was this surprising?

Several people were looking at him with concern, wanting him to engage so they would not be held responsible. A woman in a white lab coat was speaking English.

"Lost you there for a few seconds. You alright?"

"I guess." He was speaking English, too.

"Can you count for me, backwards from seven?"

"Yeah. Who are you?"

"I'm a nurse technician."

"What place?"

"Saint Dominic's."

"Where?"

"Jackson, Mississippi."

"Seven, six, five, four.. How long have I been –?"

"You were admitted yesterday. Who's the –"

"Obama."

"– president. What's your –"

"Samuels. You just said."

He did not remember his first name, but he knew that a blond candy striper was about to enter the room and turn on the television. A nurse's aide was going to bring him a sleeping pill. They were going to keep him under observation.

Memories of microscopes. A stocky, bald man taking photographs of microorganisms. *My father.*

He asked the aide to see his belongings. Keys and a wallet. A familiar face, apparently his, on the driver's license. An address in Kingston, NY. He was in Mississippi, far from what must be home. He certainly wasn't speaking with a southern accent.

How the hell did he land in a hospital? Nurse mentioned something about a car accident.

An odd feeling he was playing a role along with all the orderlies and nurses. So long as he kept to the script, everything was OK.

But if they knew that he knew…

These well intentioned folks would stick him back in that humming oven like a Pop Tart, scramble his brains good and shuffle him off to some Sanatorium. He knew the scenario as surely as he knew a black orderly was about to take his blood pressure. The wallet contained $1000 cash and credit cards, which should more than suffice to get him above the Mason Dixon line. He had to bail.

After what passed for breakfast *sans* the sedative in the Dixie cup, it was a surprisingly simple matter to get dressed and walk right out of the hospital. All a matter of timing, moving when no one was posted at the nurses station, which he foresaw as clearly as if he were watching previews for a movie. He tucked his plastic wristband under the sleeve of his hoodie, walked to the elevators, rode to the first floor, down the main hallway. A heavyset woman with a clipboard asked if he would like to fill out a survey evaluating his hospital experience. He declined, headed out the revolving door into a waiting taxi.

"Bus station."

"Greyhound?"

"That'll do."

At the station ticket counter, a balding man with a moustache sporting a white shirt and bow tie took his plastic and regarded his bandaged face with empathy.

"If I was you, I'd pick up a sandwich or two for the road. You're going to be spending 24 hours on buses - three of them, to Kingston. Atlanta and New York are fine, but in between, you best stock up."

He thanked the man and said he'd pick up a sandwich right away.

The waiting room in the Jackson bus station had a TV monitor running a CNN story about a country singer. As Salvador Samuels watched, his left hand curled.

The position for a C chord on a guitar.

He felt his left hand's fingertips, slightly calloused. No ring or other evidence of a marriage. Scraps of memories began to appear, as if he was rummaging for artifacts in a crate full of sawdust. The waiting room television triggered a string of recollections.

Watching a black and white television screen in a living room of an apartment in Forest Hills, New York, Casper the Friendly Ghost emerging from a garbage pail, Pinky Lee wearing a checkered hat, Princess Summer Fall Winter Spring, Little Ricky playing his drum set, Alice Cramden going to the moon, Bill Haley's doughy face and cowlick, Spanky, Darla, Alfalfa, Amos, Andy, Kingfish.

His mind wandered, skipping over images and grooves of thought like a phonograph needle on a damaged LP. A sister, her eyebrows arched high like the queen in Snow White, making an egg cream with Fox's U-Bet, a brother with a flat-top crew cut making drawings with a Rapidograph pen in a black note-book, a father driving a steel blue Studebaker, turning around and slapping him in the face, hard.

His way or the highway.

Try as he might, Salvador could not get a clear picture of his mother, other than a grey figure who hovered in the shadow of the man in the driver's seat. Jigsaw pieces of memory, clues to unraveling his past, like teasing the story of a Norman Rockwell painting from its details. All he had to do was sift and wait, avoiding the dark woods and the white-cloaked men with clip boards.

Another name, one he had given himself.

Lewis.

Tip of an iceberg. Sooner or later he would recall the rest and remember himself. Like peeling an onion.

Unless there was nothing truly his in the middle of the onion except for layers of debris all the way down. Oddly enough, the more he recalled the past, the less he seemed to foresee of the future. The precognitive glimpses that had helped him leave the hospital so easily came less frequently, until they disappeared altogether. He wondered if they had occurred at all.

More blasts from the past. Deeper down were things he didn't care to dig up. Memory fragments swirled around a darker center, a black hole he wasn't about to re-enter, no more than he could willingly make himself vomit.

A straitjacket. The culminating attire of a bad trip, circa the sixties. His girlfriend had transformed into a witch, the devil was at his back, the landscape morphing into something akin to Purgatory. Dr. Jekyll resurfaced from being Mister Hyde in Scaryland.

The thought reignited a particular nuance of paranoia, close to the bone.

Keep it buried. Never let on that you know it's as as real as Dark Matter. Ever. Better to dwell in Fantasyland, where Ozzie loved Harriet and Father Knew Best.

On the waiting room monitor, the Discovery Channel was running promos for Disaster Week, celebrating the many ways we are heading for Doomsday on a biblical scale. Earthquakes, volcanoes, tsunamis, tornadoes. Grist for the grizzly mill, replete with live footage and slo-mo animation of nature wreaking havoc. The dark side of science.

Asteroids loomed large. Lots of them out there, lest we forget what happened to the dinosaurs. A smiling Japanese scientist, touting his latest book, cheerfully explained that we are entering into the height of an eleven year cycle of solar activity, yielding sunspots and mega explosions on the surface of the nearest star. Our sun will soon be hurling solar flares, massive gouts of energy, into the cosmos. Were our planet to be hit dead-on, the result would be catastrophic, frying our communications infrastructure and electricity grids, making the solar flare event of March 13, 1989, when a quarter of Canada was plunged into darkness, seem like a trip to the Epcot Center.

No one in the bus station seemed particularly perturbed. Their hides have been thickened.

The reports and relentless imagery ruffled Salvador Samuels somewhat. No matter. He was heading home, poised to re-invent whoever he was.

Chapter Thirty Eight

Ten Kills had never tasted defeat. Small consolation that he and a handful of his warriors had survived.

"No one hears of this until I speak with the Tattooed Serpent," he told his scouts.

They marched back to their camp, somber and furtive. Other remnants of the war party had already returned with their tails between their legs, spouting stories of birds and sorcery.

Tell Me A Story approached Ten Kills as the ragged group entered the camp.

"Skyfisher. Is he alive?"

"Missing."

On receiving word of their return, the Tattooed Serpent invited Ten Kills to sit with him by a fire, away from his retainers. High Eagle, sensing an opportunity, asked to accompany him.

The war chief was bivouacked outside his lodge, sitting on a log next to a roaring fire, smoking his pipe. He gestured to his two visitors to sit by him. Tell Kills greeted the Serpent and said, *"This one is High Eagle. He was not with us."*

"Tell me about it," the Serpent said. *"Leave nothing out."*

Ten Kills began. When it came to the avian attack, he gave a straightforward account of how he and others turned back when flocks of birds descended on them.

"I have never seen such a thing," he said.

"Nor me," agreed the Tattooed Serpent. *"Too bad this one wasn't there. You could have used an eagle. Now you see why the Great Sun wants them stopped."* High Eagle figured it was now or never.

"The Lesser Sun ordered me to bring the Story Woman to him," he stammered. *"I found her. With your word, I take her back."*

"We need every warrior," the Tattooed Serpent said, *"but this is no place for a woman."*

Ten Kills barely suppressed a laugh, however High Eagle did not rise to the bait. Battling tricksters was not his kind of fight. If any one wanted to call him out, let them try.

The Tattooed Serpent motioned for Ten Kills to continue the account. When it came to the warriors turning on one another, the Serpent shook his head in wonder.

"How did you escape this?" he asked.

"I don't know," Ten Kills said, *"perhaps the Blind One helped in some way. I felt his hand in this."*

"He was killed?" asked the Serpent.

"Taken, along with my brother," Ten Kills said.

The Tattooed Serpent considered this for a moment and turned to High Eagle.

"Bring the Story Woman back to the Lesser Sun with this message: We need more warriors and a medicine man."

Ten Kills walked with High Eagle back through the encampment. It was late; fires smouldered, dogs roamed, searching for scraps of food. Men sat smoking, talking softly.

From time to time, High Eagle reflexively tugged at the bandage on his hand but kept his own counsel. They reached the fire pit where several of Ten Kills' scouts had been posted to keep watch over the two women, who sat wrapped in cloaks, sitting by their fire.

Tell Me A Story stood, waiting for Ten Kills to speak. He pointed to High Eagle.

"This one will take you to the Lesser Sun for his judgment. I can spare no scouts. The cat woman will be your shadow on the way home, yes?"

To High Eagle, he added, *"She is under my protection. Remember that."*

"And Skyfisher?" Tell Me A Story asked.

"I will find and tell him where to find you."

Lightning figured Skyfisher was blocking any mind probes, hiding in his inner stockade. Teams of *kuash* attempted forays into the Blind One's consciousness, looking for cracks in the veneer. But there was no mind to probe, only shades of grey, a plasmid mist. No doubt he shared Little Panther's fate, the death of his other half in the future time, leaving this half a vegetable.

A shame, thought Lightning, who had come close to harvesting the secret of Skyfisher's talent. He was moved into Little Panther's billet, the pair of them staring like owls into space. In the morning, they were taken outside to relieve themselves. In the afternoon, one of the guards spooned them some soup.

Someone asked Lightning, *"Why do we keep them?"*

Lightning sucked in his cheeks for a moment, feeding on a thought.

"Little Panther we will not keep long. Skyfisher is bait for a Fox and a Turtle."

Half a day's march from the *kuash* main encampment, Marsh Fox, Grey Turtle, and two other elders sat with Haeden around a fire, smoking a calumet. Two dozen Shining Ones had set up camp here, making it as comfortable as possible for the elders. They'd erected temporary shelters - circular log and branch huts covered with thatched roofs. Deer, rabbits and wild turkeys were in abundance. The previous morning, several of their hunters had smoked out a bear from her den, and they had feasted on her legs.

The mood was somber as Haeden told how Lightning had orchestrated Alakan's death, assumed control of the *kuash*, and attempted to dispatch Skyfisher and Tell Me A Story. Now that Lightning had shown his true colors, the question became what to do next. Taking a few puffs on the pipe, Haeden spoke of Skyfisher and Tell Me A Story's escape from the mound.

"I was bringing them to you when we were attacked by a war party," Haeden said. *I ran and they did not pursue. But they have the Blind One and the Story Woman."*

"We tried to mind-speak with our brothers in the Lodge," said Marsh Fox. *"It was as though someone had put up a wall. Our scouts tell of a large host of warriors sent by the Great Sun to secure the mound."*

Marsh Fox took a long pull on the calumet and exhaled, watching the blue smoke rise. Not far from them, a pack of coyotes yipped in celebration of a kill. One of the Shining Ones draped a skin over Marsh Fox's shoulders to keep him warm.

"Now is the time to stop Lightning," Marsh Fox continued, *"and save the others if we can. Those who followed Lightning may have to be sacrificed, to save the rest."*

The four elders, Haeden and the twenty-four *kuash* encamped here were enough to carry on.

"The Great Sun must be convinced the Society of Light is dead," Marsh Fox said. *"Otherwise we'll be hunted down without*

mercy. *This is our chance to get rid of the traitor and remove ourselves from the reach of the Great Sun in one stroke."*

They were running out of time. There would be an attack on the mound soon, most likely led by the Tattooed Serpent, war chief and brother to the Great Sun. Such an attack would be the ideal moment to launch a rearguard mind-assault against Lightning and his followers. A critical mass of Shining Ones would be needed to accomplish this aim.

"If we can reach Skyfisher's visitor," Grey Turtle said, *"he must return to his own time. We need the real Blind One when the attack comes. But he has been lost to us. Perhaps he died in the visitor's body."*

"You would let the Great Sun's warriors kill our Brothers?" Haeden asked.

"If need be," Marsh Fox answered without hesitation. *"The Great Sun must think we are completely destroyed. Only then can we continue our work in peace. Their warriors must not know of our existence. We'll have to stay out of sight. It will not be easy. If they see us, they'll assume we are the enemy, too."*

"There is a way," Haeden said, and he told them.

When he mentioned he had been sent as his father's spy, Haeden had expected outrage or surprise, but the elders had simply nodded as if he was telling them what he had eaten for his morning meal. It felt better to lay bare his secrets. Otherwise how could he explain getting an audience with his father's brother, the Tattooed Serpent?

Haeden approached his uncle's encampment carrying a white calumet of peace. Although his official title was war chief, the Serpent was known as someone who would negotiate before ordering an attack. He was both brother to the Great Sun and, by the laws of their people, father of the Great Sun's successor. That would be Short Foot, Haeden's cousin.

They had played together as children. Although hampered by a slight limp, Short Foot had grown up to be a fine horseback rider and hunter, usually beating Haeden in athletic competition. They were still friends, although Haeden hadn't seen his cousin since joining the *kuash*.

The Tattooed Serpent's lodge smelled of sweetgrass and smoke. There was a fire burning in a central pit, a bed and several benches covered with animal skins. Pouches, nets and weapons hung on the walls. Haeden knelt, turning the ceremonial pipe stem towards his uncle.

The intricately drawn symbols and images which covered the war chief head-to-toe, didn't mask the smile of affection on his face. Since birth, Haeden had been closer to the Serpent than he was to his exalted father.

"Nephew, surely you don't need a pipe to remind me of your good intentions?"

"Uncle, it is a good thing to be with you. Short Foot?"

"Is well. You are here on other matters. Speak freely."

"I carry the pipe for those on the mound," Haeden said. *"Good men. Their leader is not."*

"You speak of Lightning?"

"I do."

"What do you know of him?"

Haeden described Lightning and his powers, confirming the reports from Ten Kills.

"I will help you capture him, if you promise to spare his followers," Haeden said.

"If they swear allegiance to the Great Sun, they may go free," the Tattooed Serpent said. *"How will you accomplish this? Lightning is a powerful medicine man."*

Haeden paused. This was the key moment. If the Serpent expected treachery, Haeden would end up as a hostage, nephew or not. The idea was to give Marsh Fox and the Shining Ones who stood with him, a chance to do their part without the knowledge of an attack force. It had to be presented in a way that the Serpent would understand and accept.

"I was a member of the kuash, the ones you are attacking."

"What does this mean?"

"I was sent to join the Shining Ones by my father."

"He never mentioned it to me."

"Or anyone else," Haeden said. *"I have been his eyes and ears among those men. I'm the one who told him about Lightning."*

"Which is why we are here," the Serpent said. *"What do you propose?"*

"Your men will fast tonight," Haeden said. *"After they take the War Drink, I give them a song, a power song they must chant. It will protect them."*

That much was true. The chant would help keep the warriors' minds occupied and less susceptible. It would not be enough to shield them from a full assault from Lightning's mind troops. That job would fall to Marsh Fox, Grey Turtle and their men, working from a distance.

"The song. Who does it belong to?" the Serpent asked.

"It was taught to me by one of the elders of the kuash."

"So Lighting spins a story and sends you?"

"You surprise me, Uncle."

"I speak to you as war chief. How do I know the song is not some trick and this sorcerer has not twisted your loyalty?"

"Lightning is your enemy, not me. If he wanted to, he would have destroyed your war party."

"Why didn't he?"

"I'm not certain," Haeden said. *"I think he was testing what he can do. He's never attempted anything like this before."*

"*No one has.*"

"*If we don't stop him, I think next time he will bring down your warriors.*"

"*He's that powerful?*"

"*Yes.*"

The Tattooed Serpent took the calumet from Haeden and reached for a pouch of tobacco hanging from the wall of the lodge. He lit a twig from the fire, brought it to the pipe's bowl and offered it to his nephew.

"*Say by the pipe.*"

"*Be that I swear unto this pipe, the calumet of peace,*" Haeden said.

"*And if it not be true?*"

"*Let me be cast off.*"

"*You will be a man without a home, unrecognized by me, your parents, your cousins, everyone you know.*"

"*I swear this by the pipe.*" Haeden sucked the stem, making the tobacco glow red. He passed the calumet to the Serpent who closed his eyes and breathed in the sacred smoke.

"*We will sing your song. You will be under the care of Ten Kills, a warrior who survived his first brush with Lightning. I will tell him what to do if there is any hint of treachery. Go and return. Become yourself.*"

Flour Village was a two day journey. Waya and Tell Me A Story walked side by side, keeping their distance from High Eagle. The sounds of the forest swelled to a full dawn chorus. They stopped to rest in a field of flowers, each a miniature sun, a spray of yellow petals circling a brown center. The children called them *kato-uwa tchisistiktinu*, little sunrise. They had no practical use except to make things beautiful. Tell Me A Story's mother used to lace them into her hair, entwining her daughter's name with the stories of their people. In the field of little suns, Waya's story unfolded.

"My brother arrives in the world same time as me. In the beginning, we do everything together. Play, hunt, wrestle. Two spirits, one heart. A day comes when our parents say he must be a warrior. I am to farm, weave, do things girls do. We fight this. My brother weaves, I train as warrior! My father thinks this funny at first. When we don't stop, he separates us. My brother is sent to another village, becomes Yellow Hatchet. I run away."

Both women took turns keeping watch at night. High Eagle let them alone, content for the moment to bide his time. When they reached Flour Village, he delivered his captive to the Lesser Sun, awaiting the decision that would seal the Story Woman's fate. The Serpent's request for more manpower was sent on to the Great Sun himself and approved.

Skyfisher awoke in the middle of the night and left the hut, as if to relieve himself. Little Panther lay with his eyes closed, oblivious. There were no guards. Skyfisher's body moved like a sleepwalker out of the hut and down the mound's sloping side. He tripped over a branch, picked himself up again, navigating towards whatever it was that was drawing him like a magnet, passing though brush and thistles towards a hill. At its bottom, hidden behind a boulder was a small opening. He went down on all fours and crawled inside.

Chapter Thirty Nine

Bits of Lewis Salvador Samuels' past had begun to appear, like a paper watermark held up to the light. Childhood in Forest Hills, NY. Fire escapes, a courtyard, kids playing Ring-a-Leveo.

Moving with his parents to a house a stone's throw from the ocean on Long Island's south shore. A deep fear of swimming. Several careers, never quite finding himself. A divorce. No children. He liked Chinese food, had a collection of old chemistry sets, was in reasonably good health. He had no explanation for the three month loss of memory or the tattoo of an eye on his right palm. His old Nova had been a candidate for the junkyard and probably had been totalled in the car accident. In any case, he had zero desire to return to Mississippi to find it.

He found the address on his driver's license, opened the front door with the key he'd been carrying. A musty smell, a pile of mail, mostly flyers and bills. No electricity. It took a few weeks, but he managed to sort things out, with the help of a bank account that thankfully had enough of a balance to handle outstanding debts and put a deposit on a used car.

A tick bite brought him to a local homeopath as an alternative to antibiotics. Wasn't just a matter of letting those little white pills dissolve under his tongue, though. The healer had been intent on delving into the missing mystery months, insisting they held the clue to his cure. Lewis left his office with a sense of foreboding, headed home, turned on the radio, when a report of a boat accident on the Hudson River drew his attention. As if watching a movie, he saw himself caught up in a series of actions that culminated in being on board a pleasure boat on the Hudson in rough weather, taking off his shoes and diving into the river towards an upended raft, swimming to a drowning, hysterical woman. The raft right itself, falling on top of him, his greatest fear descending like a bad dream.

Chapter Forty

Trusting no medicine man, the Great Sun deigned to send Dainwai, a legendary fighter, accompanied by 250 warriors, all painted and wearing ear pendants and belts from which hung shells and bones. They gathered alongside rows of tables joining in a feast, preparing for combat.

A dog had been roasted and set at the foot of the ceremonial calumet, flanked by a fire and vats of boiled deer meat and a roasted deer.

Before the meal began, Dainwai rose to speak.

"I have taken many scalps. Now I step aside and let you have your turn at glory. The Great Sun honors you with a mighty foe. Strong hearts! Walk on your toes. Keep your eyes clear. The scout has taught you a power song against the magic of the enemy. Sing it! Show them we are men and true warriors."

Dainwai filled the calumet with tobacco, lit it with a taper from the ceremonial fire and passed it to the Tattooed Serpent, then on to the other warriors in order of rank.

After every warrior had smoked from the sacred pipe, it was handed back to Dainwai for the last smoke. He took a small bite of dog meat, followed by the Tattooed Serpent and the warriors in rank order. They ate on their feet, walking restlessly, never stopping, making a show of their readiness for battle.

A loud scream arose from a nearby thicket, and the entire assembly ran towards it, clubs in hand. A young man, resplendent in war paint, emerged from the thicket shouting his death cry, every warrior responding in kind, with loud, searing wails. This was repeated several times during the meal. At its finish, they downed the war drink, partaking of its promise of invincibility.

Near the sacred fire, a post had been carved in the shape of a man, its head painted red. Each warrior ran at the post, wailing a death cry and striking the post with all his might, along with a stream of insults for the enemy and proclamations of his own deeds in battle. The last syllable of each oration was sustained, followed by a loud *Hou*! from the host that set the entire camp vibrating. They cleared away the vats and danced around the ceremonial fire, heads rolling, bodies shaking, eyes lit with war fever.

Well before sunrise, the warriors set off towards the mound in columns of five, each man chanting the talisman song. The plan was simple, a frontal assault as a diversion, with a separate band to capture Lightning. That task fell to Ten Kills, Haeden, and High Eagle, recruited whether he liked it or not. As the main force came within sight of the mound, the three splintered off, with Haeden leading.

A quiet night in Flour Village. Tell Me A Story and Waya were resting, recovering from their ordeal. They had not had much conversation, but a bond had grown, each needing an ally. They sat together by a campfire, listening to the web of sounds wove by frogs and crickets.

"*Explain something to this one.*" Waya said. "*First you say the Blind One means nothing. Then you tell the strong one the Blind One is husband.*"

Tell Me A Story sighed and considered what story would serve, the truth being somewhat unbelievable.

"My husband is carrying a spirit of another man. One day the spirit will leave and Skyfisher will return."

Waya grinned and pursed her lips to make a soft purring sound.

"Ooh. So you lie with with man who looks like your husband but is not."

Her smile widened and both women burst out laughing. In a few days, they would stand before the Lesser Sun and receive his judgment. Tell Me A Story expected nothing would be decided until Skyfisher's fate was known. That night, she dreamed he was singing to her.

The Sacred Breath descends

Drawing me closer

Awakened by the a hooting of an owl, she walked outside her hut to gaze at the stars. On impulse, Tell Me A Story walked to the Sacred Place and climbed its slope.

If Skyfisher can spend the night here, why not me?

Chapter Forty One

Two human forms floated, becoming themselves, circling their respective stories, facing an unknown other.

Lewis had been under a raft in the Hudson River a moment ago. Now a metamorphosis, a reformatting of his internal hard drive with the memory of who he was and where he had been in all its magisterial weirdness, waking in the skin of a blind man, falling under the spell of a warrior woman, joining a secret brotherhood whose mission was to save the world. Or perhaps he had drowned.

He had coalesced into the cave of a dark dream, first swimming, then crawling out of the water like a salamander on to a shelf of rock and pebbles. The sounds of dripping water inside the cave blended with the echoes of his own movements. Another sound. Something emerging from the water behind him, coming towards him, breath-snorting. He dragged himself away, scraping his knees, not daring to look back.

Get thee behind me.

Scrambling to his feet. Lewis began to walk away, dreading to run in the dark. The other sound stayed close, its footfalls echoing.

Chapter Forty Two

A bitter cold morning, a thin layer of fog hugging the treetops. Ten Kills and High Eagle carried war clubs. Haeden had no desire to wield a weapon but Ten Kills had insisted. His hands were sweating and the axe handle was slippery in his grasp. Perhaps there was still a chance to push Lightning away from his folly. Surround the mound and starve out the brotherhood. The kuash would end up as prisoners. Lightning could swear allegiance or die. Cornered, he was a formidable foe. What good would an axe do against someone who could twist your mind?

With Haeden leading, they circled the mound, listening to the *chink, chink* of the marching warriors fading behind them. On the backside of the mound all was silent. The sky was grey and threatening. No guards in sight. In the distance, the air was pierced by cries and the shouts of warriors.

"Now, quickly!" Ten Kills shouted, scrambling up the slope. They reached the lip of the mound near the chief's lodge. A wind was rising, bowing treetops, shaking countless leaves. Ten Kills sent High Eagle to scout behind the lodge. Haeden paused, panting, trying to focus his thoughts on where Lightning might be.

"*Close!*" Spoken aloud, as Lightning and Willet Moonface stepped out of the lodge. Squirrel, Ten Kills' brother, followed behind them, staring blankly at the horizon.

"*Thank you for bringing such a famous warrior to me, Haeden,*" Lightning said. He stood, arms crossed, his face impassive.

Haeden tensed, but did not move. Moonface and Squirrel circled behind them. No sign of High Eagle.

"*Why do you attack us?*" Lightning asked.

Haeden began to speak, but Ten Kills silenced him.

"*You are Lightning?*" Ten Kills asked, earning a tight smile. "*You and your men will come back with us, by order of the Great Sun.*"

"*I swore no oath to the Great Sun and I will not come crawling to him now,*" Lightning said. "*You've seen what we can do, yet you return. Continue your attack and you will lose your warriors, every one of them. Join us. We will return our people to their rightful place and defeat every enemy. Even the whites, who come to destroy us all. We can stop them. Without us you are nothing.*"

"*And the Great Sun?*" Haeden asked.

"*There will be a new, brighter Sun.*"

"*You?*"

"*Why not?*"

"*We are pledged to the Great Sun,*" Ten Kills said. "*Come with us to the Tattooed Serpent. He will decide.*"

"*I am honored to be worthy of the Warrior Chief's attention.*"

As Lightening spoke, Squirrel quietly stepped behind Ten Kills, raising a war club to strike. Haeden threw his axe. Ten Kills turned as his brother fell.

"*What game are you playing?!*" Ten Kills shouted to Haeden.

Squirrel fell to his knees, moaning, reaching for the axe embedded in his left shoulder. Haeden backed away from Moonface and Ten Kills. In the distance war cries turned to screams. Ten Kills crouched, not knowing who to strike first, watching his club transform into a tree branch.

Impossible.

"*No,*" said Lightning. "*Real. Your men will be slaughtered. You have one more chance. Swear an oath of loyalty to me and your men will be spared. Decide now.*"

"*I swear no oath. Fight me like a man.*"

Haeden turned to Moonface

He's going to destroy us, Willet. Help me.

Lightning's voice, too, spoke inside Willet's head.

Finish him, now!

Lightning pulled the axe out of Squirrel's shoulder and turned to face Ten Kills.

Chapter Forty Three

Something was behind Lewis, closing fast, along with every memory he had tried to suppress. The boogie-man was coming to take it all away, snuff him out like a candle, remind him of the deep taste of primal fear. It could be any one of his demons. Evil clowns, witches, an audience of white trash kids laughing mercilessly as they waited for Froggy to pluck his magic twanger, every schoolyard bully he'd ever cowered from, his father breakfasting on anger, and last but not least, the Prince of Darkness himself, waiting for the moment when Lewis would awaken to the true terror of his situation. His legs were moving, yet he did not sense the ground underneath his feet. Anything could happen here and this was the moment of truth, the turning point.

Marsh Fox's counsel came through as if on a whisper. No need to run. He could ride the Sun Breath, letting it course through him. The fear did not have to rule him. Behind him, the footsteps were closer now. He felt their cloven heaviness, heard the breath snorts. No. After a lifetime of running away, he would turn and face this. And he did.

A human form, an Indian, his body limping.

Lewis Salvador Samuels, having been drowned, dissolved and reconstituted with the memories of inhabiting another body, stared at the body in question.

"I was you."

"Yes," Skyfisher said.

"I thought you were a beast."

"Imagination."

"I was drowning."

"You're body is still in the water. The rest of you is here." Sky-fisher gestured to the cave's walls, where droplets of water were condensing and forming rivulets. *"You are a ghost. Your people know about ghosts. Hilton told me stories."*

"Hilton?" Lewis asked.

"You know Hilton? Inez?"

"No."

"You remember when you were in my body?" Skyfisher asked.

"Yes, I do."

"I know what I did when I was in your world," Skyfisher said, *"but not what happened when you were in me. Falling Star, Grey Turtle, did you meet them? Did they train you?"*

"Falling Star is gone," Lewis said. *"Grey Turtle and Marsh Fox taught me. And Lightning."* At the mention of Lightning's name, Skyfisher's head jerked to attention.

"You must speak to Inez and Hilton. Your body is in the Mississippi?"

"The Hudson River. New York."

"Far from Natchez?"

"Yes."

"Return to Natchez. Find Hilton and Inez. The mission —"

"The mission!" Lewis shouted. *"Your precious mission hijacked my life! I don't know whether to —"*

Skyfisher raised his hand, stopping Lewis mid-rant.

"Is there a better purpose to your life than saving the world? Did you learn nothing?"

"I learned," Lewis said testily. *"Your wife taught me."*

"My wife?"

"She saved me, several times. You have to save her. She is going to have your baby."

Four heartbeats.

"I will find her," Skyfisher said. "You know what you must do. Your people have forgotten why they are here. Why the mounds are here. Remind them."

"I will try."

"Others in your time remember. Find them! What is more important than this?"

Lewis had no answer.

Skyfisher described the house and street in Natchez where Inez lived and advised Lewis to stay away from cocoon metal beds in hospitals and electricity in general.

"There is nothing I can do to save my people," Skyfisher said, "but you can save yours. Flaming stars. Ast —"

"Asteroids?"

"Hilton say, 'Coming soon to world near you.' True friend, Hilton. Inez, true friend. Brave."

"How can we stop an asteroid?"

"One bee cannot turn a buffalo. Many bees can," Skyfisher said.

Lewis laughed. "Grey Turtle said the same thing. Hard to believe."

"Tell me of Lightning," Skyfisher said.

"He killed Alakan, took over of the mound, the big one near White Apple Village."

"It is 'Emerald Mound' in your time," Skyfisher said. "Alakan and Falling Star gone! Others remain?"

"Grey Turtle and Marsh Fox left the mound," Lewis said, "with more elders and twenty-four kuash. Once they were gone, Lightning gained control of the Shining Ones. He wants to overthrow the Great Sun and take his place. The Great Sun sent warriors to capture Lightning and wipe out the Society of Light."

Skyfisher nodded. "It's time to go," he said.

"One thing –," Lewis said. Of all the questions he could ask his time twin, he wasn't sure why this was the one he chose.

"No one, not Falling Star, Marsh Fox or Grey Turtle, no one ever mentioned love."

"In your world, everyone speaks love," Skyfisher said. "Love this, love that. They sell love on television. Every song - love. Empty words. Tell me, you listened on the longest day?"

"Yes."

"Feel something?"

"Very much."

"Real love. My brother, when I went fishing I did not know who I would catch. I'm glad it was you. Go and save your world!"

They reached out, holding their hands facing up towards each other, two eyes shining on their facing palms. Lewis shuddered and he was gone. Skyfisher straightened up, took a long breath and walked out of the cave, his body aching, his sensory array intact.

Chapter Forty Four

Grey blue storm clouds loomed in the distance, rumbling with thunder. A moist wind washed over the mound.

Haeden could hear the screams of war cries from the other side of the earthwork. He was hopelessly outmatched. Lightning's defences were tighter than a drum skin. Where were Marsh Fox and the rest of the *kuash?* He tried to connect with whatever vestige of conscience remained in Willet Moonface. Together, the two of them might at least distract Lightning long enough to give Ten Kills a fighting chance to subdue him.

Squirrel lay on the ground, moaning in agony. Willet stared at Haeden coldly, impervious. A few yards away, Lightning, wielding Haeden's axe, faced Ten Kills, readying to strike. Haeden reached out to Willet with mind-beams of good will and reconciliation. Hands outstretched, he closed his eyes to concentrate.

A swish.

Haeden stepped away from it intuitively, not quick enough to avoid the sweep of Lightning's axe. A searing pain in his left hand and the tip of this forefinger lay on the ground.

"Never close eyes in battle!" Lightning said. *"Moonface, kill him. Now!"*

Ten Kills' club seemed to be back to its original size and heft. Seeing an opening, he swung it with a blow that would have levelled any man. Lightning moved aside in a flowing motion, like a dancer. Ten Kills staggered and Lightning whirled around, swinging the axe and slicing Ten Kills' buttocks.

"A new name for you! 'Two Holes'!" Lightning made a high pitched keening sound. In the distance, the din of screaming arose.

"Your men are getting cut — like you!"

Howling with rage, Ten Kills moved again to raise the club to strike this sorcerer, but it was like trying to lift a fallen tree. In desperation he scanned the area for a weapon, an ally, anything. Blood was spurting from Haeden's finger and his brother's shoulder. Willet was moving towards him. The wind had picked up; the sound of thunder looming closer.

As if in answer to a prayer, High Eagle appeared from behind the corner of the lodge, striding rapidly towards Lightning.

Ten Kills' moment of relief turned sour as High Eagle brushed passed Lightning and turned towards him, war club raised.

"Strike him!" Lightning urged.

With all his strength, Ten Kills could not budge his war club or even his hands, which had joined with the weapon as if part of the same tree. Wailing his death cry, High Eagle brought his club down, but at the last instant, Ten Kills leaned forward. The blow glanced off the back of his head and he fell to his knees. Haeden stared in dismay at the tableau of agony. Willet smiled, hefted his spear, reached back to throw and froze. Someone else had joined them on the mound top.

Skyfisher approached them armed only with his mind. He saw inside Willet's glowing presence - Moonface, curled up in a fetal position.

"Wake up!"

Willet took another step forward, then seemed to sag into himself, his shoulders drooping. He looked around in disbelief and appeared to be on the verge of weeping. Sky-fisher focused on High Eagle, ripping open the coating of his mind-heart, not caring if he inflicted any damage. High Eagle dropped his war club and gazed at his hands as if they belonged to someone else.

Haeden and Skyfisher turned towards Lightning, warily.

"We can stop him," Skyfisher said, though he doubted they could.

"Skyfisher returns for a last lesson!" Lightning shouted, jubilant. He seemed to grow in stature, eyes sparkling. There was a faint odor, familiar to Skyfisher from his sojourn in the future.

The air around them crackled. Lightning was glowing. Even Haeden could see the atmosphere around him pulsing, an evanescent green aura. Wielding the axe, both arms raised to the sky, Lightning's form throbbed. His head went back and he howled like a rabid coyote.

There was something else riding the rising wind, a mind-posse joining the fray. Grey Turtle, Marsh Fox and a host of *kuash*.

If Lightning felt their presence, he did not show it. His look was exultant, revelling in triumph, feeding on the energy of the coming storm. The sky was black with roiling clouds. A sudden drop in the wind and a strong smell of ozone triggered an image in Skyfisher's mind's eye. Ben Franklin wielding a metal golf club, a blast from the future-past.

"Everyone down!" Skyfisher shouted.

A blinding yellow bolt and an ear-splitting thunderclap seared down from the heavens, striking Lightning's axe and playing over it with blue fingers. A red-yellow streak of raw electricity flashed from the axe down Lightning's arm, combusting his body in a explosion of orange-grey smoke.

An acrid smell wafted from the cinders. Skyfisher sniffed it. *Wood ash.*

He surveyed his surroundings. Five figures lay sprawled around a smouldering pile of cinders, stunned and singed. With the help of a healer, Ten Kills, Haeden and Squirrel would survive. He saw Moonface, dejected and disillusioned, muttering to himself. The sounds of battle in the distance seemed to be diminishing. Skyfisher gathered up Willet's spear, the axe and two war clubs and threw them off the edge of the mound. His inner vision perceived High Eagle wearing the colors of a man emerging from a bad dream. Skyfisher approached him.

"I will go with you to the Lesser Sun, not as your prisoner. He would like to know about the way you struck down Ten Kills. I only regret I was too late to stop you."

Haeden had been listening and joined them.

"I will stand with Skyfisher when you meet the Lesser Sun," Haeden said. *"But there is a way out. The Story Woman belongs to her husband. You vouch for them. You tell the Tattooed Serpent his enemy is destroyed, which is true. Lightning's followers will swear allegiance to the Great Sun. I will make sure of that. Maybe you can explain this to the Lesser Sun so you sound like a warrior, soaring high. Otherwise we will tell your story, all of it - including the finger. Understand?"*

High Eagle nodded, his thoughts a whirlpool of contradictions. Who could tell if this promise would be kept? What Skyfisher did hear was a familiar voice, mind-speaking.

"You come just as I was starting to like your visitor," the voice said.

"I have missed you, Grey Turtle." Skyfisher responded.

It had taken more than he alone to let Lightning become his name. Still, there was something not right about that wood ash smell. He wondered if they'd really seen the last of Lightning.

Skyfisher could not alter the future or know how many of the Shining Ones could be saved. Nor what would occur when he returned to his village, having helped defeat the enemy. Whatever happened, he swore he would hear his wife's voice again and that she would live to tell their story to their baby.

Chapter Forty Five

Underneath the raft in the cold grey water of the Hudson River, grateful to be back in his own body, along with some missing pieces of his memory. Oddly enough, Lewis felt calm. It was just water, not so different from the lake near the mound. If he could swim there, he could do it here. There was time enough to pull hand-over-hand across the bottom of the raft, reach the surface and give the life vest to a frightened woman. Time enough to reclaim his life in the service of something truly useful. Salvador Samuels rose to the surface, welcomed the Sun Breath and became his name.

Epilogue

With Skyfisher's directions and a little help from Google Earth, Lewis located Inez's house and found himself walking up to her front door, not quite knowing what to expect. It was Saturday, a car was in the driveway and the lights were on inside the house.

A young man with long straight hair and a pale complexion opened the door.

"Are you Hilton?" Lewis asked.

"Guilty as charged."

They clasped hands, Hilton keeping possession as he regarded his friend closely.

"The prodigal son! Holy Smokes. Never thought I'd see *you* again. You look all healed up. No scars. I got one from where that crazy dude shot me." Hilton released his grasp and continued. "Gotta ask you this. Is it you or the other guy? 'White man disguised as Indian?' Should I check for horseshoe prints?"

"I'm myself again. If that makes any sense."

"None of it does."

"Inez. Is she here?"

"Yes, but there's something you need to know —."

At that moment, an olive skinned woman appeared behind Hilton, reminding Lewis of the actress Irene Pappas, her long hair braided, a quizzical expression on her face. She stood staring at Lewis.

"A few days ago, we camped out at the mound," Hilton said. "Been like this ever since."

"*Cenkololo,*' she said, and continued for a minute in fluent Natchez. Then she slapped Lewis gently on the face, pried open his mouth and tapped his front teeth, saying *"Entv! Entv!"*

Afterword

This is a work of fiction. The true history of the Natchez people is no less remarkable. There really was a Great Sun and a Tattooed Serpent. *Chung-key*, stinkards and many other aspects of Natchez culture described in the narrative, were witnessed and reported by French missionaries who kept detailed accounts of their contact with the Natchez during the seventeenth and eighteenth centuries.

The author is grateful to Hutke Fields, Mark Six and other members of the Natchez, for their kind and generous introduction to Natchez culture and traditions, and to Jim Barnett, former director of the Grand Village Historical Site and the Mississippi Department of Archives and History. They made it clear to me that much of what the French missionaries imparted to history was colored by their own cultural bias.

The current plight of the Natchez is very real. Despite their cultural and historical importance, they are not recognized as an official tribe by the Bureau of Indian Affairs, and must depend upon other tribes such as the Cherokee, for financial assistance. Those interested in supporting the tribe are encouraged to send contributions to:

http://www.natcheznation.com/index.html

Jim Metzner

Glossary

Characters in the Story

In the Present:

Salvador Lewis Samuels

Jean Baptiste

Inez Delos

Alex Samson

Davey

Hilton Gervain

Thurman Goode

Jobie

Trevor and Simon, Jobie's nephews

Natasha, a waitress

In the Past:

Skyfisher – the Blind One Who Sees, *Nasootka Shudef*

Tell Me A Story

High Eagle

Deep Thunder

Little Walnut

Little Rock, Buffalo
Red Wolf
Otter
Broken Twig
Ten Kills
Squirrel
Waya
The Tattooed Serpent

The Shining Ones, the *kuash*:
Falling Star
Grey Turtle, the Bald One
Marsh Fox
Lightning
Alakan
Haeden
Willet Moonface
 Little Panther
 Slow Deer
Thistlehead
The Twins

Place Names:
Flour Village – Tell Me A Story's home
White Apple Village - near Emerald mound
Acorn Village, where the Great Sun resides
Yatanocha, Buffalo's village

Some Natchez Words:

cenkololo	hello
entv	teeth
hakshoo	tobacco
hallesh	task (act of doing something)
ispeshe	palm
Ipli Hallesh	The Listening
kuash	The Shining Ones, the Society of Light
mitche mitche kupe, puant	lower rank caste member, "stinkard"
tchung-key	game played with disc and spear

Jim Metzner with Hutke Fields

About the Author

Jim Metzner studied acting at Yale Drama School and enjoyed a brief career working as a singer-songwriter in London. He has been producing sound-rich audio programs since 1977, including Pulse of the Planet, which has been on the air since 1988 and is now heard widely as a podcast. For many years, Jim produced features and commentaries for All Things Considered, Marketplace, Weekend Edition and other public radio programs. He has recorded all over the world and received major grants from the National Science Foundation, NASA, the National Endowment for the Humanities and the Grammy Foundation. Stories about his work have appeared in Audio Magazine (cover story), the New York Times, Wall Street Journal, Christian Science Monitor, National Geographic, the Today Show and the CBS Evening News. His forty-year archive of sounds is now reposited in the Library of Congress in Washington, DC.

A bee-keeper and avid fly-fisherman, Jim resides in New York's Hudson River Valley with his wife Eileen.

For more information visit jimmetznerproductions.com and sacredmoundsnovel.com

CPSIA information can be obtained
at www.ICGtesting.com
Printed in the USA
LVHW010158270720
661579LV00005B/659

9 781952 570681